BILLY

ALSO BY WHITLEY STRIEBER

FICTION

Majestic
Catmagic
Wolf of Shadows
The Night Church
Black Magic
The Hunger
The Wolfen

WITH JAMES KUNETKA

Warday
Nature's End

NONFICTION

Communion
Transformation

BILLY

Whitley Strieber

G. P. PUTNAM'S SONS NEW YORK

G. P. Putnam's Sons
Publishers Since 1838
200 Madison Avenue
New York, NY 10016

The author gratefully acknowledges permission
to reprint from the following:

"You Always Hurt the One You Love" and
"Into Each Life Some Rain Must Fall,"
copyright © Alan Roberts Music and Doris Fisher Music.
All rights reserved.

"I Get Along Without You Very Well,"
copyright © 1938 and 1939 by Famous Music Corporation,
copyright © renewed 1965 and 1966 and assigned to Famous Music
Corporation.

"Do I Worry," copyright © renewed 1968 Leonard-Worth Songs.
Used by permission of Bobby Worth.

Printed in the United States of America

Quality Printing and Binding by:
ARCATA GRAPHICS/KINGSPORT
Press and Roller Streets
Kingsport, TN 37662   U.S.A.

FOR THOSE CHILDREN

Contents

Part One

BY REASON
OF DARKNESS

1.

Suddenly he was there, remarkable and perfect. The next instant he had disappeared into the crowd. Barton gazed after him, but not for long. People noticed you watching children. He walked on.

As soon as he felt it was safe he turned around and overtook the boy from behind.

He had no intention of being carried away yet again by his natural enthusiasm. Another mistake would be too much to bear.

On this particular day he was searching Crossland Mall for the fourth time. He'd been in Stevensville for a disappointing week; he'd been thinking of giving up on Iowa altogether.

He stopped at the mall bookstore and retraced his steps. Now he could safely get a good look at the boy from the front. And what a remarkable face he saw. There was fire in the eyes, along with a boy's natural softness. The face was the sort you could look at for hours; such beauty was a kind of food. His fair cheeks were pinked by the sun, his features at once gentle and sharp, and yet full of dignity. His nose was graceful, but there was also a sweet bluntness to it. His lips were as red as if they had been blushed. The boy's hair was strawberry blond, his skin like cream. His brown eyes were touched like the hair by subtle flame. The expression was affable, with an edge of mischief around the eyes—and yet there was also something else, almost a sense of command. That was so interesting.

The child held his head proudly. The tip of a smile played across his lips as he encountered another boy, obviously a friend. By comparison this other child was a shadow.

13

Barton watched carefully as they went into a video arcade. His target established himself in front of one of the machines. This was a bit of a disappointment. Perhaps this child was not the extraordinary creature that he seemed. But his looks! God. Barton had to be extremely careful with this one.

He could do wonders for the right boy, of that he remained convinced. The last time was so awful that he'd made the decision to change his ways. He'd sealed that decision by mixing his own blood with an innocent's.

For hours a given relationship could be so good. His heart opened, the boy's heart opened and they were truly father and son. In those times he would have given his life for his boy.

But inevitably the relationship changed. The boy sneered, he cursed or even spat. Then the truth came out: the vicious punk had despised him all along.

Ending a life properly was a craftsman's work. You had to do it with the dedication of a lover, the care of a professional, the considered pace of a libertine.

You didn't necessarily *want* to. But once the relationship had collapsed . . .

Obviously the boy in question couldn't be set free.

These thoughts, brief as they were, led him to other, darker ideas, tempting notions from a diabolic corner of his soul.

He found himself imagining that lovely face wet with tears, the eyes pleading, the voice shrill, and his own hands moving as if under the control of the terrible instrument that they held.

The image was so vivid and horrific, it made him shake his head and gasp. The floor rocked. He put a hand to his mouth to force back the sickness.

Barton had secret knowledge: when skin burns it smokes; a pierced lung sucks.

He had to will himself to calm down, let the bad thoughts fade away.

'OK, take it easy,' he told himself. 'All that's wrong with you is that you're very excited by this child. He's a treasure and nothing bad will happen. No, with the right boy, there will be no bad part.'

Barton was stable.

This time he would do everything exactly right.

In the past he'd picked them up off the street. "Your mother told me to come get you and take you home." "I'm with the police, son." "There's been an accident, we have to take you home now." It depended on how young they were and how neglected they looked. "Want to take a ride, go to McDonald's, get some candy?" And to the saddest, shabbiest of them: "Want to be my friend?"

Timmy had gone for that one. Jack had fallen for the police gambit. For that ruse Barton had worn a blue jacket and some insignia he'd bought at an army surplus store.

The current problem was going to be much more challenging. This child was happy and bright and might not fall for a simple lure, which meant that one could not be risked. If he wanted a specific boy, he only had the one chance. He'd tried forty kids before he got Timmy—who had been flawed, of course. When he'd trusted to chance, he always had problems. He had finally accepted the fact that he could not get a perfect child unless it was by careful choice.

To be certain that the child was right he was going to have to make a closer approach, risk some brief interaction with him.

There were benches for parents in front of the arcade. He sat down, pretending to tie his shoe, and looked the place over as he did so. It was very ordinary: a deep room with fifty or so games and a lot of noise. There were maybe ten kids listlessly pumping the machines.

Only one child looked as if he was standing in a shaft of light.

Barton ached to try a street ploy, but that was not the prudent course. Instead he would proceed slowly and carefully. First he would go outside and sit in his van for ten or fifteen minutes, then reenter the mall in dark glasses and wearing a different shirt. If he was lucky, he could have a brief conversation with the child. Tone of voice, vocabulary, expression— they would reveal volumes.

He did not want a coarse child, a bitter child, a delinquent child. This one must not be bruised. He must be intelligent, well adjusted, good of heart.

Then it would work.

He returned to his Aerostar which he'd parked not far from the mall's main entrance. To fill the time he enjoyed one of his secret pleasures: he wrote about the boy on a yellow pad. Usually he just wrote a description, which gave him the enjoyment of calling the child's image vividly to mind. Other times he might write a letter, or simply repeat the name again and again, such as "Timothy Weathers" written until it seemed a kind of sweet penance. But he didn't yet know this boy's name.

"Dearest Child, I would like to ask you if I can be your new father. I know it sounds crazy and you love your dad, but just please listen to me for a second. I don't have a boy and I can't, and I'd give you *every single thing* you could ever want. I won't ever punish you. You make all the decisions. I work, I'll earn the money for us."

He stopped writing.

It would be so beautiful!

"There is something so marvelous about you. Thinking of you now I can smell the grass in the backyard, see that wonderful old elm that was almost my second home in the summer. You make me feel so good, so deeply happy.

"I know you are a magnificent human being. I can help you fulfill your great potential. I can take you out of this wretched cultural desert and help you to flourish and become the great soul that God meant you to be.

"Let me love you, serve you, become you."

He stared at the last two words. That wasn't what he meant at all. "Become you"—what was that supposed to mean? Barton wasn't crazy. He crossed them out. In their place he wrote: "enter your life." Now that was precisely correct.

"Oh, my God," he said, "he's so incredibly special."

Obviously he had already fallen in love with this child. Oh, he would be *such* a good father! He could do it, he would be just wonderful.

Barton tore the paper into tiny bits. These he put into a plastic bag which he would eventually pour into some dumpster somewhere behind a gas station. Although he had no evidence that anybody was investigating him, the possibility was always there.

That was why he'd quit making his acquisitions in California, and partly why he was working rural areas. Small towns were so open, and their police departments usually had very limited resources. Also, his experience was that small-town America produced better-looking, sweeter, smarter children.

Another important consideration was location. He was always careful to choose towns close to the interstate. This wasn't only because of the need to leave quickly, but also because the citizens of such towns were used to seeing strangers passing through. One more wouldn't arouse anyone's suspicions.

His watch told him it was time to go back. The capture itself was always nerve-wracking, but these new preliminaries made the whole process much worse.

Barton said to himself, "You don't have to do it."

He groaned so loudly that a man walking past his van glanced his way. 'OK, you're losing it again. So take a deep breath, imagine every muscle in your body is melting. That's better.'

The thought of losing this boy was just unbearable.

Barton told himself he had to be strong. He must stick to his plan. What if the boy was rotten inside, foul-mouthed or dirty-minded? He certainly didn't want any of that, not anymore. This child had to be right.

The next step was to get back in that mall and make the final decision. If it was in the affirmative he would then locate the boy's home, find out his name and get some idea of his family situation. To some extent poorer was better, and it helped if the family was new in town. It was easier to get kids who had unhappy homes, but that had been his mistake in the past. They might look fresh and beautiful, but too many of them were grim and sullen and rotten with greed, the *vicious little bastards!*

Looking first to be sure nobody was near the van, he pulled off his tan knit shirt. Then he took the blue button-down out of his small suitcase and put on the dark glasses.

His clothes changed, he got out of the van and moved quickly toward the mall entrance.

Noon was approaching and waves of heat rose from the cars in the lot. Barton was sensitive to heat. The other kids had called him "Leaky," he sweated so much. That and "Fat Royal."

17

That was a long time ago—longer than it felt. But mentally Barton was never far from his own childhood. He kept going over things. People who remembered childhood fondly were lucky; they were the ones who had put the pain to rest.

Crossing the pavement he bowed his head against the sun and was grateful to push through the doors into the air conditioning.

In the old days department stores had smelled like malls did now. It was the perfume of merchandise. The smell always took him back to the days when his gang—well, not really *his,* but the gang he was in—used to ride bikes down to Woolworth's on Main and Mariposa where they had a comic book rack and cap guns and toy soldiers and a lunch counter where you could get a hamburger and large Cherry Coke for seventy-five cents. He wasn't really in the gang, of course, but he rode with them. Or rather, he took the same route. The guys would all sit at the counter; he would be in a booth nearby.

Remembering those days, he smiled a little. Mom had given him one thorough strapping that time he got caught shoplifting those Uncle Scrooge comics. If he'd only managed to pull it off and gotten one for every member of the gang, maybe then they would have taken him in.

Mom had laid it on right in the middle of the living room. Then they watched *Have Gun Will Travel,* and he lay there on the floor where she had left him.

He passed Midplains Savings and Wilton's Jewelers, its main window literally jammed with ceramic brooches illustrating flowers and little hats and ladybugs. In another window there must have been a couple of miles of gold chain.

The mall was moderately crowded. When he was in crowds Barton was compulsive about looking into faces. He was also sensitive to the aesthetics of skin. Smooth, pale skin inspired him. He loved to brush a soft arm or beautiful hand. To taste its salt sweetness, to inhale its miraculous variety of scents—of such things he dared only dream.

Another pass by the video arcade and he saw the boy again, still at his moronic game. Barton took a deep breath, stopped walking and closed his eyes for a moment.

Now came the frightening part: he went into the arcade.

18

There was a skeeball game in the front, and beside it a locked display case full of cheap trinkets and candy. Each item was marked with some ridiculous number—fifty skeeball coupons to get a miniature Whitman's Sampler, a thousand for some cheap sunglasses.

The electronic games all depicted murder and mayhem, brawls and violent death. They promoted machismo and reinforced unconscious racism. Little thought was required. Rather, they demanded what the streets demanded: dexterity and feral cunning.

Barton moved closer to the boy. His heart began to pound and his underarms to grow damp despite his powerful antiperspirant. He could see the boy's back moving as he breathed. The boy wasn't a fantasy anymore; he was a human being in a black-and-white-striped T-shirt and black shorts.

The vulnerability of children could be extraordinarily intimidating. Barton wasn't a predator, he was a romantic and did not like to see himself as an exploiter. Getting close to kids also meant seeing their imperfections, which could ruin everything . . . or it could be delicious.

On the side of this boy's perfectly white left hand there was a small brown mole. Farther up his arm there was another. These were not fatal imperfections, like Jack's relentlessly foul mouth or the black birthmark on Timmy's thigh. Rather, they enhanced the child's beauty in an almost poignant manner.

Watching this sensitive child play Space Harrier was like watching an angel hitting on a bottle of booze.

Barton moved closer. The boy's skin shone in the arcade's lurid fluorescence. It was all Barton could do not to touch the warm smoothness of his hand, to let his finger brush across the mole.

As the boy's Space Harrier game ended Barton put a quarter into the RPM machine beside it. This was a two-person game. In a quavering tone, he asked, "Want to race?"

"Sure."

Wonderful voice! Soft, yet richly melodious. And a real surprise: this voice was kind!

The boy came over and dropped a quarter into his side of the machine. He barely reached Barton's shoulder.

Even though Barton tried his hardest, he was bested three times in a row, which he found lovely. Nothing was said until the end, when the boy looked up at him and with a sparkle in his eye said, "Want to play for money?"

Barton smiled. "This is already costing me."

The boy laughed and went over to his dark-headed friend. A moment later the friend's brittle, sneering voice drifted back: "Just some queer."

The boy glanced quickly at Barton. There was apology in his soft eyes.

The boy's friend had, in addition to his pimples and his coal-black hair, the extended face of a horse.

Suddenly it hit Barton: *I'm being seen by a potential witness!* He had to get out of here, even if it meant losing the boy.

That was a monstrous thought! In his few minutes on RPM he'd fallen far: he could hardly bear the thought of letting the child out of his sight. But prudence demanded that he leave at once.

The van was stifling. He started the engine and turned the air conditioning on high.

The locals were all talking about how hot and dry a summer it had been. The corn was stunted, and the farmers wanted rain. Barton had learned to talk about it, too. Every morning he read the Stevensville *Iowan*, and when the waitress served his breakfast he might say a few words about the weather.

This way if she was ever questioned she would review the past few days and say, "No, officer, I don't remember anybody unusual at all." She would *not* say, "Gee, yeah, now that you mention it there was this guy that ate here a few times. Real quiet. Never said a word. Kept his head down."

Never mind waitresses, though; here was a strong, direct witness: "Yes, officer, there was this guy in the mall who played RPM with him." And then would follow the description, the IdentiKit portrait, the poster.

Thank God for dark glasses.

He pulled out of his spot and sped to the nearest exit. Once on Lincoln Avenue he headed for the Burger King. Eating would pass the time.

He entered the order line behind a blue Camaro. Three girls

were in it, ages sixteen to eighteen. He wished that he could say something to them about their smoking, offer them some help with their addiction. They were all so young!

He watched them order Whoppers, fries, shakes, desserts. Their blond heads bobbed as they talked, the driver's skin gleamed in the sun as she worked the microphone button.

If he got to a child in time, he was convinced that he could transform anyone of sufficient intelligence into a cultured human being. With the right care, the soul would bloom.

"A Whaler and a small dinner salad with blue cheese dressing," he said when his turn came at the order window. "And a glass of iced tea." Not "icetea," like they all said. "Iced. Tea." In the English language it was two words.

As the Camaro left the takeout window he drove up and got his things.

With his food on the seat beside him he accelerated into traffic. He fought the desire to go back to the mall earlier than was safe.

Please don't leave, son. Dad had called him that, and he enjoyed pretending to be Dad. Power was the greatest aphrodisiac.

He made himself go out on the interstate to kill a little more time before he attempted to relocate the child and follow him home.

Grueling hours of search might be necessary this time around. He just didn't know. This was all new to him. And as far as getting the boy—his idea was more a fantasy than a plan. Would it work? He had no idea.

Driving along, nibbling nervously at the Whaler, his thoughts returned to the boy. Wasn't that a wonderful voice? Just exceptional. And that extraordinary face. The word "handsome" did not suffice, and "pretty" was demeaning. This boy had a quality of the miraculous about him.

Even to glimpse such beauty was a privilege.

Barton himself was not beautiful and never had been, but he had made himself into a worthy soul.

The rich white clouds reminded him of the past. He had looked for shapes in the clouds, and had seen the Flying Dutchman there, and his mother had said, "There's a gallows and an old man hanging, and the wind is tearing off his head."

21

High summer: heat waves coming up off the fields, mirages on the roads, girls in clingy cotton dresses. His friends would ride out into the hard land, and he behind them, Fat Royal pounding his old Huffy to keep up.

In the heat of the day they would take comic books and Cokes down by Salado Creek and read and sip their cold drinks and talk of the matters of those days.

The van hummed on the highway. The Whaler tasted of plastic, as if the heat of the day had melted some of the container into the bun.

A summer had come when he was the only child who hadn't moved away or gone to camp or gotten too old to spend time down at Salado Creek. Eventually he'd had to face a hard fact: childhood was not eternal.

When the flowers had blown from the trellis in the backyard that autumn, he had become possessed by a soft, cloying anguish that had never since left him. He did not pine for his childhood because it had been beautiful. It hadn't been. What he wanted was to somehow escape the pain.

Alone by the Salado, he had first experienced the sort of fantasy that could still make his stomach churn with revulsion even as it stirred his desire.

In the fantasy he was carried naked to the creekside by the other boys. They laid him face up on the bank, with his head dangling over the water. He could see the sky above and the gently swaying cypress trees, and then they would push his head backward until it went under. Desperate, fighting the water that was forcing its way up his nose, he would be dimly aware that somebody was handling him where they shouldn't be.

The fantasy was wrong, it was a sin. So intense were his efforts to suppress it, more than once he imagined jamming a red hot soldering iron into his brain.

What he wanted now was a pure relationship with a child to prove the goodness that was in him. He could be a good father and a very special sort of a friend. He had to show that to himself. By giving joy to a child, he could heal the wounds of his own childhood. That was his great quest.

So on and on he went, searching for the perfect relationship with the perfect child. He dreamed of looking back one day and saying of that child: *I made him happy.* Then all would be well.

The closer the boy was to perfection, the more he brought back memories from Barton's own past: the blowing trees, the voices, the easy laughter of the old days—and Fat Royal and Let's Fuck Leaky and oh God, if only he could repair the past! The saddest memories are those that just miss being wonderful.

To get closer to kids he became clever in their ways. He learned to form friendships with them using a combination of kindness and firmness. He learned about their fads and fashions. He was aware of the importance of Nintendo, and of the differences between Super Mario Brothers Two and Super Mario Brothers Three. He knew all about Teenage Mutant Ninja Turtles.

When it was good with Timmy, the child had kissed him as he might have his own father.

Dad had died as quietly as a moth rising into the sky. "I love you, Dad!"

Barton had stood over his father's still body, and spoken those exact words.

At the graveside he had read one of his own poems, and Mother had said, "What a lovely thought."

Each Sunday since the death she put a single sprig of lilac on the grave. Her grief had been so intense for so long that it had come to seem like a sort of grim pastime.

Again and again Barton tried to puzzle out why he did what he did. Was it Dad's fault, or Mother's? Was it his? Had something terrible happened that he had forgotten, or was it an accumulation of little disappointments that had done it? The other children had been awfully damn hard on him. Every time he thought about it, he got *so fucking mad!*

But he wasn't dangerous.

He prayed for the new little boy. "God, let him survive."

If only the black room didn't exist, if only he never took them there, if only—

A child needed him.

2.

Because he had other things on his mind, Billy wasn't really working at Space Harrier. The American Legion was sponsoring a short story writing contest with an Iowa theme, and he intended to win it. His main inspiration was that first prize was the amazing sum of five hundred dollars.

He also had an idea. It was stimulated by a summer reading assignment recommended by Jim McLean, his English teacher. The inspiration was Kafka's *The Metamorphosis,* and the idea was that your typical Iowa farmer would wake up one morning and discover that not only had he turned into a giant bug during the night, so had all the other farmers. And they were hungry for corn.

Billy was excited about his story, so excited that he'd failed to better last night's crop of teenage records in Space Harrier.

As far as digital games were concerned, he much preferred Dungeonmaster on his Amiga computer. He was already deep in level ten and the way he computed the probabilities he had a fair chance of surviving until the game ended.

He wondered what would happen when it did. When you beat Super Mario Brothers all Mario did was lie there and sleep. Not a very big deal considering the magnitude of the achievement.

He worked alone; deep Dungeonmaster levels were too hard to crack with a bunch of kids arguing about every spell you cast, and then getting pissed off when they weren't allowed to take a turn.

Jerry Edwards was already sulking over Billy's performance

24

on Space Harrier. Acing games for the brain-dead like that was boring to Billy, but to Jerry it was the equivalent of climbing Mt. Amanda herself in the backseat of her parents' Vulva station wagon.

Being an undumb kid in a place like Stevensville was even more inconvenient than it had been in the last town, Iowa City. Iowa was not a state of genius, his dad said, but it made up for it with a big heart. Whee.

At least it was better than New Jersey had been, where drug dealers were always after you, sometimes even chasing kids down and forcing them to do crack.

Dad had been fired from the school in Jersey before he was fired from the one in Iowa City. That was how Billy ordered his past: from firing to firing. Dad had a mind of his own, and was therefore canned on a routine basis.

Dad could yell and wave his arms with excitement about LaFollette and Gus Hall and the House Un-American Activities Committee. He was capable of scoffing openly at everything from the CIA Charter to the Gulf of Tonkin Resolution, a Vietnam-era travesty only he had not yet forgotten. It was all pretty embarrassing, but the way he loved the hell out of you made up for it.

"Stevensville is a very tolerant, very midwestern place," Dad said. "I hope to last at least two full semesters."

Billy had disgusted Jerry by abandoning Space Harrier in midgame. Three minutes after Jerry grabbed the controls the GAME OVER sign came floating into the foreground.

Billy whipped through level after level in Afterburner while putting his short story together in his mind. Waves of planes came at him. He jinked and jigged, dove and climbed, and thought how great it would be to be really weird like Kafka. I mean, Gregor Samsa just plain turned into a giant bug. His mother hurled an apple at him and it got embedded in his back. He was even crunchy like a bug, but too huge to step on. His family was very embarrassed.

That was such a good story. When his own family went down to Des Moines in July Billy had taken a super-sharp Xerox of Kafka's picture to have a KAFKA LIVES T-shirt made at the Shirtworks.

His story was going to just totally turn everybody's stomach which would be incredibly fun. It would be the best-written submission, he was confident of that. But would it win? Only if the judges had the courage to recognize the best. It would certainly go into the fall issue of Stevensville Junior High's literary quarterly, the *Biblion*. Gum-popping goddesses would read it and say, "That was really, well, sort of unfiltered." They would also say, "That Billy Neary is so outa tune."

Suddenly Billy crashed. He stared at the screen, watching the smoke rise as his jet plowed into a town. That was what you got for plotting a short story while playing a game whose moves were measured in hundredths of a second.

To cover his embarrassment he instantly turned away from the screen. He had a reputation to protect.

"You screwed up, Neary. I saw you!"

"And you're gonna tell the world."

"Naturally!"

"I'll do you a favor sometime."

"You blew level ten. I can't believe it." Jerry grabbed Billy's head, rapped hard on the top of it. "Yep. I thought so." He rapped again. "Hear that? Sounds like there's wood in there."

The headlock was pretty painful, but Billy knew to give no sign. "Implying that I'm a woodenhead. I'm crazed with laughter."

"No, man, that sound means you have a brain tumor."

"My middle name is Melanoma. If you break my neck I'll vomit all over the warts on your chest."

Jerry dug his knuckles deeper into Billy's head.

"I will seriously retaliate."

Jer ought to know that Billy's threats were on the level.

"Remember the toilet caper, boy." Billy had flushed a Baby Giant down the toilet at Cinemas Three and gotten Jerry blamed for the explosion.

"I damn well do remember it, you smug son of a bitch."

"Now, now, children don't talk like that."

"The fuck they don't."

"Let me go or I put a time bomb in Lacy's mailbox and you'll take the heat."

"Lacy's in bed with my dad."

"So are most of the other men in town. You know you can't afford heat from Lacy."

Jerry released him—not because of the threats, but because something else had interested him. "There's that queer you pussywhipped on RPM."

"That's no queer, that's Lacy's twin sister."

"Don't speak that way about our police chief. It's unpatriotic."

The stocky man's eyes slyly turned. Billy felt himself being scrutinized.

"You could probably make a couple of bucks off that guy, you let him suck you off."

"Thank you, Jerry, but I can do without your kind of money."

"Your problem is, you got no head for business."

"Give no head for business, you mean."

"Is that funny, or just dumb?"

"Brilliantly hilarious."

"Dorked out."

It was lunchtime, and Billy was hungry. His finances were so low that lunches at Burger King or McDonald's had come to seem lavish, so he decided to head home for peanut butter and jelly or—if his mother was in her gourmet mode—a grilled cheese sandwich.

Billy left the mall, unlocked his spectacularly ancient Schwinn from the rack and went pedaling off. He loved this bicycle, especially the fact that it was old and rather low-tech. Reverse chic appealed, especially in a town packed with glittered Hard Rocks ridden by kids in glittered British Knights and Nike Airs. Also, riding a plain old bike and wearing plain old clothes pleased his plain old dad.

He took the usual route home, swerving briefly into the Burger King parking lot to spy out the society, even though he was fairly sure that Amanda and the other observables hadn't heaved their butts out of bed yet, knowing their established summertime routine. Most of them would be embarrassed to do their Egg Beaters before two-thirty at the earliest.

Despite the certainty of physical abuse, he intended to declare his love to Amanda at the next opportunity. He would

27

then accept the beating from Jerry. Amanda had already made an observation about the enormous Jerome that was probably fatal to Billy's hopes: "He has hair growing on both sides of his chest."

"William, my little twelve-year-old super-dork," Jer had said, "give up. She'll never buy into your girlish looks."

"I'm sure she'll love your wit, your brilliance."

"She'll love the fact that I'm thirteen and a half and I can get a hard-on that works."

"Gee, does it work a lot?"

"Only when I make scuzzbags like you chew it. Look Billy, if you talk her up somehow or other, I'll eradicate your face."

"Why so worried? Feeling insecure?"

"I like to kill guys like you, Billy. I really do. The last thing Iowa needs is more brains."

"Brains mean money, dear child." Except, of course, in a case like Dad's . . .

"I don't have brains. I come from a dumb family. My dad can hardly even run an automatic elevator. That's why we live in a little town, because there aren't any around here. But he owns a piece of this mall and a piece of the Sears mall and about six thousand acres of corn. And never forget, schoolteacher's son, that he is on the Board of Ed."

"Which explains why the Board of Ed has nothing to do with brains."

"Why should it? Clearly, school isn't about learning. It's about winning basketball games."

"Will I have a sense of humor too, when my hard-ons start working?"

"They never will, junior. They never will."

So it went. The day would probably come when Amanda would forsake Jerry, but not for baby-faced Billy Neary with his old bike, old car, old clothes and cheap Walkman.

He would never admit this to Jer or any other living soul, but he was beginning to wonder what it was *like* to reach puberty. He knew all about it of course, thanks to his father's stentorian and incredibly embarrassing sex education "conversations." But what was it *really* like?

It was just noon when Billy wheeled into his driveway.

A single place was laid at the red Formica table that dominated the kitchen. Mother had indeed produced a grilled cheese sandwich, but it was for his older sister. He slid half of it into his mouth while an unsuspecting Sally was rummaging in the fridge for some Hi-C.

"You thieving creep!"

"Slip of the tongue." He laid open his cheese-filled mouth. "Excellent cheddar," he said.

She took a swipe at him with the ice-cream scoop, which had been lying in the sink. Then she stared at it, her eyes widening with horror. "My Heathbar Crunch!" she gasped and ripped open the freezer. "Dad," she yelled, "you've been eating my Heathbar Crunch that I bought with my own money!" Throwing the ice-cream scoop over her shoulder she flounced out. "I hate men!"

Dad had not stirred from watching the Orioles slowly if ineptly defeat New York. "One to nothing and it's the top of the ninth," he commented as Billy passed through the den. He was working on a huge bowl of Heathbar Crunch.

"I ate her lunch. You've got her dessert. Retaliation is possible."

"She's scared of me, I'm much too large and awful. She'll take it all out on you."

"I'm going down to the basement to work on my short story."

"Have a plot yet?"

"Iowa farmers turn into giant bugs."

"Didn't I read that headline on the *Weekly World News* down at the A&P?"

"Dad, it's based on Kafka."

"Throw Kafka at the American Legion. They're sure to give you five hundred bucks for that."

"Well, it would be fun to write."

"What about doing something topical? Flag burning, for example?"

"I'm scared of matches."

"My God, a player has hit the ball. Oops, it's a foul. Kind of an interesting half-second there, though."

Billy was careful to lock the basement door against a raid from his sister.

Sitting down before his beloved computer, Billy decided that

his day was going pretty well. I⁺ was afternoon and the base
ment was cool and there was a large Butterfinger hidden behind his computer bench. There was also a beer there, but that
was part of another scenario. Bring Amanda down, impress her
with his ultra-boss computer, sip a little brewski, then, well,
connect faces. Billy Neary and his Flying Fantasies. He sighed,
then flipped on the computer and loaded ProWrite from the
hard disk. The white screen stared at him. "It was a dark and
stormy night," he wrote. Nah, not clichéd enough to satisfy the
American Legion.

"When Bob Hughes woke up one morning from dreaming
about his corn, he found himself changed in his bed into a huge
corn borer. All that was left of that farmer was his toupee."

'Oh, man, this would be an awful lot of fun, but Dad was right
that it wouldn't win the American Legion contest.' He hit ERASE
and sat staring at the blank screen.

"Young Freddy Krueger had a deep love of his country, and
especially its beautiful flag."

A yuckish story idea, yes, but Dad had closed the loan window in July and Billy was down to smelling other people's
breath after they ate their hamburgers. His last ever candy bar
was two feet away from his trembling fingers. He had to write
a winner.

"He would defend his flag with his life. To a true patriot like
Freddy, it meant everything. And everything else, too."

Maybe he'd better change the Freddy Krueger. They probably wouldn't make the connection to the Nightmare on Elm
Street movies, but why take the risk? He'd call his character
Martin Bormann. They'd never in a million years pick up on
the fact that he was one of Hitler's dearest, sweetest thugs.

While he stared at the screen, Billy's hand moved toward the
Butterfinger.

The thing was, he wanted to have fun. A story about the flag
was not fun; it was a chore. He killed ProWrite and played
around for a while with the birdsong he had recorded the night
before. All summer he'd been trying to get that bird to reply
to him. Whenever there was enough moonlight to keep it
awake, it sang on the wire behind the house. Billy sang back,
but so far the bird had never responded. He had been record-

ing its song in hopes of better imitating it. Now he was comparing the digital image of the birdsong to his own efforts. Slowly but surely he was getting closer to the bird's notes. It would be so extreme to have a conversation with a bird. Of course, it would just be sounds. He didn't know any vocabulary. He could imagine it translated:

Bird: "The moonlight-t-t-t is so sw-e-e-et!"

Billy: "I have a t-t-tortilla in my e-e-ear!"

Bird: "What an asshole is he-e-e-re!"

He became absorbed, and when he became absorbed the world around him just plain ended. Hours passed. His sister took down the bucket of water she had carefully positioned above the basement door and spent the rest of the afternoon making pecan divinity for the specific purpose of hiding it from both of the damn men.

Slowly, carefully, Billy was crafting his reply to the bird. He was producing deep music, amazing sonorities that were at once beautiful and weird.

Shadows came out from behind the furnace, from out of the disused coal cellar, down the steps that led to the storm door with its rusted hinges and loose lock.

Since it was a summer Saturday night, dinner was free icebox, no call and no formal table. At six he sucked up the Butterfinger, counting on it to sugar-high him through until about nine, when Jer would show up and they would hit B-King. Jer had promised to treat him to a small fries.

Finally there was no light in the basement but the pale glow of his monitor. It was past eight when Billy leaned back from his work and rubbed his eyes. He noticed with mild interest that there was a pair of legs visible beyond one of the basement windows.

Somebody was standing there. Dad? Jerry, inexplicably wearing gray slacks?

Never mind, it didn't matter.

But it did.

3.

Barton had felt sick when he saw the sea of kids in the video arcade. In only thirty minutes the place had filled up. Kids must have been pouring in steadily almost from the time he left.

He should have stayed; he'd never catch sight of his boy in this crowd. But he'd been seen, he'd had no choice.

Even now it was perfectly obvious that he was looking for somebody. He went down to the bookstore. Absently, he paged through a new novel, *Fire.* God, what an upsetting title. People did not know how much fire could hurt unless they had seen somebody being burned. If a person is burned extensively enough they start feeling cold. After a really thorough session they shiver like they were in a freezer—not that Barton had any knowledge of that.

There was such a thing as a wild scream. When a person knew that their agony would only be ended by death, that is how they shrieked. The black room had the most expensive ceiling tiles you could buy, and the cinder-block walls were double-thick. It swallowed screams.

If there is one place on earth where you can do absolutely anything you want, you are free.

A steam iron.

Barton's stomach churned. He put the book down. Again he made a run past the arcade. He rolled along casually, watching out of the corner of his eye.

And there he was, the angel being manhandled by the bigger boy who'd been with him earlier. Barton was livid. Had the situation been different he might have intervened. Then the muscle-boy saw him. As he moved off, he just glimpsed himself

32

being pointed out to the angel. Damn, that wasn't supposed to happen even once, let alone twice!

Uneasy about lingering in the mall, he had returned to his van yet again. He gripped the steering wheel, staring into the void of the parking lot. Stevensville might be a small town, but Crossland Mall was huge, designed to serve this whole part of the state. What was he going to do?

He'd definitely been noticed again.

Then a miracle had occurred. God must love him: he saw his boy coming out of the mall by himself. Barton was so excited he couldn't get his engine going. As he sat furiously grinding the starter the child moved toward the bike rack.

Barton's thoughts had flashed back to the first time he had seen Jack, on an October afternoon. Yellow leaves had been running in the streets and skywriters scrolling an enormous Pepsi ad across the blue of heaven. That had been at the Mill Run Mall in Tappan, California.

The engine ground to life, and for the first time Barton thought he might get this child.

The boy finished unlocking his aged bike and started for the exit. Despite the risk of losing him, Barton waited a full thirty seconds before following. He had to submit himself to the discipline of the quest. You had to know how to breathe, how to move, how to empty your mind and concentrate with total attention. Finally he started off, moving with the gliding slowness that most drivers adopt in mall parking lots. He wanted to jam the gas pedal to the floor.

By the time he caught sight of the boy again he was already turning onto crowded Lincoln Avenue. Accelerating smoothly as he slipped into traffic, Barton cruised past the child. He kept him in sight with the special wide-angle rearview mirror he'd bought for just this sort of maneuver.

He'd bought it when he was following Timmy. The technique was to get ahead and let the child catch up.

Poor Timmy. He had been—

'Not now, Barton.' He was on the hunt. It wasn't time for memories. He coached himself: breathe in, breathe out. "Control your breath and you control your soul," said those who were spiritually aware.

The boy rode into the Burger King parking area. Quickly

maneuvering the van, Barton cut into the far end of the lot. As he wheeled around he expected to see the bike cross right in front of him, but there wasn't a sign of the boy or his bike.

Barton looked out toward the street just in time to see the Schwinn disappear beyond some parked cars. As fast as he dared he left the lot. The boy was far down the street, pedaling hard. What did this mean? Surely the child hadn't seen him. Of course not. Boys changed their minds in an instant. Very well. He would keep his eyes on the bike. It was at least a quarter of a mile away—and just then it had turned a corner. To keep the boy in sight Barton had to gun his motor. So much for caution. He covered the distance to the side street in a few seconds.

Hicks Street. He looked down its tree-lined expanse. No bike. Damn. The boy must live in one of these houses. Unless— it was also possible that he had made the next corner and turned again. Barton moved to the end of the block. There he was, just disappearing up a driveway. In a moment Barton was cruising past 630 Oak. He had him. The boy walked his bike into the garage and dropped it onto an equally aged girl's bike. The child knew this place well. Barton was virtually certain that the boy lived here.

Next Barton checked the property for signs of a dog. What he glimpsed of the backyard revealed that it wasn't enclosed. There was no doghouse. He spotted no telltale heaps of dog feces, no spots of dead grass indicating that a dog had urinated there.

At the end of Oak, Barton turned onto Maple, then went up Elm to Hicks. Then he drove down the six hundred block of Oak a second time.

While the condition of the yard suggested that there was no large dog present, a smaller pet might still lurk within the house. When he penetrated he would bring a hammer, raw meat and a plastic garbage bag for the animal's body.

If people like him got caught it was because they were care-less. He could assume nothing, trust nobody.

He had never met another person like himself, but he had studied their failures in newspapers and magazines. He'd even done volunteer work for Missing America, a large support group for parents of missing children. He needed to get inside the mind of the parent and the police detective as well as the child.

He knew the law. He knew exactly what would trigger FBI involvement. He also knew police, and what telltale signs would make them suspect a runaway. If they thought a boy had left home on his own they would quietly downgrade the case.

Abduction by strangers was rare. In most places it was a sensational crime, not forgotten for years and years by the community. Etan Patz, abducted from SoHo in New York in 1976, was still being hunted.

Because Jack was listed as a runaway everybody had forgotten about him. But Timmy was on those damnable posters all over the country.

Barton had mixed reactions to that. The prospect of being investigated made him wake up sweating in the night—and yet the idea also caused a deep, illicit tingling.

Most guys like him took their kids right off the street. Barton had done that in the past, but his new method was far more subtle and extraordinary than simply luring a kid into the back of a van.

He drove slowly past the target house. Suddenly he became aware that his pants were soiled. There was a stain on his thigh. How long had he been wearing these pants? He couldn't remember. It could have been since last week, since Timmy. Revolted, Barton tried to pull the cloth away from his skin. He inadvertently turned the wheel. The van swerved badly.

There—another moment of inattention. Somebody might have noticed the white van that swerved the day before Johnny So-and-So disappeared. And under hypnosis the witness might remember the license number of that van.

It was so easy to fail.

He headed back out to the interstate, driving quietly for a time, to calm himself. He would have to live with the stain. It was probably just grease anyway.

He took an exit ramp about ten miles from Stevensville and drove down under a bridge where he had already scouted a good place to park the van.

He thought over what he had seen. The family lived in a

lovely old neighborhood, but their house was visibly shabby. In addition both of the kids' bikes were old, and the station wagon in the garage had seen better days. These were good signs. A poor child was easier to dazzle.

So he was part of a family of four or more. Unless the target had a brother whose bike Barton hadn't seen, it was likely that he would have a bedroom of his own in that big old Victorian house.

Barton looked at his watch. One-forty. He would not return to Oak Street until after dark, sometime between eight and eight-thirty. It would be his first chance to check out the house on foot. If they had their name on the mailbox, that would be when he would learn it.

Since it was likely that he could act tonight, he would have to check out of his motel now. Following his plan, he would start driving west immediately after making the hit. He'd sleep in Colorado and Utah, living in the van until he reached L.A., which would be on the fourth day.

It was a hard drive but he'd done it before in that time, without ever once exceeding the speed limit. The idea of getting stopped for speeding with a kid in the van was too horrible to contemplate.

Maybe he was pushing too hard.

He probably should have taken the week on Maui before coming out here. As it was, he was going to have a hard time convincing Gina that his extended absence was in any way legitimate, let alone forgivable. She had to give in, though. It would be suicide to fire such a popular employee. In his own very small way, he was a star.

He *needed* another boy, and it couldn't wait even *one fucking minute.*

4.

A hand dropped down on Billy's shoulder.

"Dad!"

"Would you believe it's eleven o'clock?"

"No. I thought Jerry was coming by at nine."

His father laughed. "He came. You told him to leave you alone."

"I've gotta just put this one sequence together, Dad. I've got all the tracks laid, it's just a question of linking—"

"It's the end of the day, Birdman."

"I'm not tired."

"You're never tired."

"So let me finish this. I want to talk to that bird."

"Formula for long life, says Chinese sage: bed, sleep and sweet dreams."

Hand in hand they went upstairs.

Barton was lying in the yard under a twisted old tree. The moonlit shadows of its limbs made crooked fingers in the grass. When the basement light finally went out he sat up. But there were still lights on upstairs. Didn't these people ever sleep?

It was a beautiful night, and every so often he would raise his eyes to watch the moon through the branches of the tree.

"I see the moon and the moon sees me, high up in the old oak tree . . ." On his nights of boyhood the breeze would come fifty miles from the sea, bringing with it the magical scents of the ocean mixed with night-blooming flowers.

Barton would dream of evil green waves and the ocean giant

37

the Bible called Leviathan. Whisper-quiet, Leviathan would come up from the depths of his dreams . . .

The last of the lights finally went out.

Earlier he'd watched the boy playing with his computer. There had been terribly complex images on the screen, and music, such music, wild and beautiful. He had watched that lovely face concentrating, seen the graceful curve of his neck, the softness of his boy's hands and the laughing, gentle eyes. He was the most perfect boy Barton had ever seen. Just absolutely perfect.

He wondered how this boy was punished. Probably just talked to, the lucky little *bastard!*

Barton would be laid in his mother's lap. The purpose of the ritual was to correct and teach. There was love in every blow, Barton knew that. Dad would never help him. Dad would never tell her to stop, tell her it hurt too much.

Dad had been so weak at the end, Barton had just laid his hand over his nose and mouth. He'd had to do this to see if his father was still alive.

Barton had called to his mother, who was in the shower. "Mother, Dad has died."

Dad had never come to his bed in the night.

And he hadn't smothered Dad.

He stood up, took three deep, hungry breaths and moved toward the house. His feet whispered in the dewy grass.

Billy dropped his clothes into the hamper. As always, there were a number of issues connected with the shower. First, how long. Second, how hot. Naturally the most desirable situation was very long and very hot. But Billy knew the risk of depriving his mother of her hot water. She also showered at night, and could become dangerous if this happened. "Since you wanted such a long shower, take mine, too."

"But it's cold, Momma."

"I know."

He wanted her to have her small pleasures. She saw to so many of everybody's needs. Given Dad's profound lack of technological skills, it was she who assembled the toys of Christmas, she who had connected up the Amiga and taught him the rudiments of it. Basics like food and clothing came from her, and she also was the one who understood that his mind was on a major growth curve. She had introduced him to *The Catcher in the Rye* when Dad was still promoting *Tom Swift and His Amazing Underwater Toaster Oven.*

Billy lathered himself efficiently with Ivory. He took special care with his underarms, for he had noticed again today a musky odor lingering around him during the noontime heat. As he washed, he touched his privates.

Amanda.

He almost collapsed. The merest flickering thought of her made his penis leap to life. It stood before him in the spattering water, and he checked to make sure the door was locked. What would his sister do if she saw this? Call the police, probably. What—would—Amanda—do?

You would end up wearing a bicycle around your neck, young man. Boy, if this thing wasn't working yet, it sure was about to start.

Amanda . . . to walk with her, hand in hand, to the gazebo in the center of MacIntyre Park, dear Lord, and there to place my lips against her lips and perform extremely pleasing acts . . .

Awash with desire he faced in the privacy of his shower the fact that there was no hope. Amanda Bartlett would never pay him the least attention.

"*Ach du lieber Augustine—*" And what was the rest? Two months out of school and he was already brain-dead in German. "*Du lieber Amanda . . .*"

You did not impress a girl like Amanda by being recording secretary of the German Club. Let's face it, Jerry had elaborate muscles and could prance the gridiron before her admiring gaze.

When baby-faced William Neary came up to her and said, "*Ich bin lieben—*or *lieber—*uh . . ." he could expect the proverbial wet *Spaetzle.*

As the shower turned tepid his erection collapsed and he stepped out. He dried himself and pulled on his yellow cotton pajamas.

Bedroom, bed. To sleep, perchance . . .

* * *

Because there were basement windows secluded at the back of the house Barton could take his time entering. He examined a window frame with his penlight, taking inventory of its various weaknesses. He did not want there to be any sign of entry or exit.

He'd learned from his work with the missing children group that policemen felt ill-equipped to fathom the secrets of families and read the hearts of children; the most beloved child could decide to leave home, and for unknown reasons. A flower of youth might end by turning tricks on Sunset Boulevard or Lexington Avenue in the Fifties and nobody would ever know why.

Barton intended to create the appearance that this particular kid had packed up and moved out. But before he did that, he had to face the tricky part; indeed, it was the best ruse he had ever contemplated.

In his pockets he carried wire in various grades, a group of plastic cards of different thicknesses and even some old-fashioned skeleton keys he'd bought at a yard sale. Small-town locks were sometimes old enough to give up their secrets to these keys. Finding that the window was secure, he tried the storm door. He was pleased to discover that entering here could not be simpler: there was a padlock, but that had been locked onto the broken hook. The tongue of the hasp hung open. He took out his 3-In-1 Oil and oiled the hinges—very, very lightly. Then he wrapped some felt around the loose parts of the lock. He checked his other equipment: the cloth packs, the ether, the duct tape, the hammer, the bags.

He was going to be a wonderful father to this boy. They would have a fabulous life together.

Billy listened to the quiet. Everybody's light was out. Only Billy was still awake—as usual. He simply did not sleep as much as other people, at least not as much as the members of his own family did.

He threw off his sheet and stepped into the faded shaft of moonlight that shone on his rug. He went to the window. The breeze was scented with the perfume of corn tassels. He loved the night, and was all too aware that this night fell at the end of his last childhood summer. In October he would be thirteen. He'd heard his father and mother talking one night, and his mother had said, "He's disappearing. Right before our eyes, he's just disappearing."

The moon was high, and the bird sang into the silence. He could see it sitting on its telephone wire. To his ear there was no sound in the world quite so pure as the voice of a bird. Carefully he directed the microphone of his tape recorder out the window. He drew in breath, rolled his tongue into the back of his mouth and let out three notes. The bird went on singing to itself, all alone on the wire.

The world swimming in moonlight, the whispering breeze, the bird's clear, sharp song—nobody could re-create such beauty. But he could try. This time he closed his eyes. He let his ears become his only senses. He filled his lungs and pretended he was a bird also, soft and quick and smitten by the moonlight.

He sang.

The bird sang back.

Again he sang.

And the bird sang back.

He replied.

The bird fell silent.

Billy opened his eyes. Goose bumps covered his skin and his blood rushed with wonder. His first impulse was to wake Mom and Dad up and tell them, but that might be a mistake. He would almost certainly get a strict order to slide back between the sheets.

There was no time for sleep now. He had to go down to the basement and play this recording into the computer, examine the exact nature of the notes that had gained response.

Had he actually duplicated the bird's voice, or simply deceived the creature?

As he slipped along the hall he heard the bird again. At the top of the stairs, he paused. Aside from the bird, the only sound was the ticking of the big clock in the living room.

Quietly he went downstairs.

5.

Barton lifted the storm door, went halfway down the steps and pulled it closed behind him. Admirably soundless.

He stood in careful silence, not even breathing. When he took a breath it was to test the odors in the room for what information they might impart. The air smelled of cool concrete, with a faint undertone of mildew. Ordinary basement smells, nothing to worry about.

He was surprised at the intensity of his feelings. This was a luscious moment. It was also extraordinarily scary. Sometimes he thought he could best understand himself as a dark element of God sent to haunt the world.

He padded into the center of the basement. He was hunting for the stairs with his penlight when he heard a distinct footfall above his head. It was faint, but very definitely there. He listened, but the sound did not repeat itself.

An instant later he was appalled to find himself standing in a flood of light.

Billy turned on the basement light from the pantry. He went down, his eyes on the Amiga. The quiet made the basement mildly creepy. It was a familiar sensation, and he would have ignored it except that it caused him to remember those legs he had seen earlier outside the window.

Dad had been wearing khakis. None of Billy's friends wore gray slacks in the middle of summer vacation. Had it been an extremely subtle trick played by his sister, to get back at him for eating her sandwich? No, she wasn't that subtle, at least not usually. There was, of course, the time last February she had taped the matchbox full of fruit flies from the bio lab inside his guitar. He'd noticed the change in tone, torn out the box and inadvertently released the tiny flies. He hadn't even noticed the bugs . . . until ten days later when their reproduction rate had caused his room to suddenly become a jungle hell. Given that he was owned by parents who did not believe in insecticide, getting rid of the flies had been a pretty major pain in the ass.

Well, there certainly wasn't anybody out there at this hour, unless it was some kid. By ten-thirty you could hear the lights changing from one end of Lincoln to the other. Kids at slumber parties would sneak out in the nude at midnight and nobody would see them. Once, according to Jerry, he and Dick-the-Prick Davis and Fo-Fo Garr had met up with Cynthia Stales, Rebecca McClure and Sue Wolf on Endower Lane, and both groups were nude.

Lying bastard.

He sat down at his computer and flipped the switch. The opening screen came up, followed by his hard disk icons. He went into his birdsong files. He plugged his earphones into the small amplifier he used with the computer, and unhooked the speakers. Instantly he was lost in the wistful, perfect music of the bird.

Barton breathed carefully, with infinite softness. He lay under the boy's workbench, his elbows grinding into the hard concrete floor. The child's bare feet were not eighteen inches away from his face. It would have been so easy to just reach out and grab one of those sleek ankles. But the boy would scream the house down.

Initially Barton had been so stunned by the light that his mind had gone blank. Fortunately instinct had prevailed and he'd dived under the table just in time. Gradually, he recovered his composure. His breath came more gently, the sweat dried on his face. He forced himself to think calmly and clearly. Things were by no means out of control. There were still lots of options.

If he could figure some way to get out from under this damned table and work his way around behind the boy, he

43

could put him to sleep in a few moments. Barton was a powerful man; the child had no chance of getting away before the ether overcame him.

Billy labored happily, but not for very long. He had to admit that he was a little tired, and digitizing a tape was a complicated process. Working with sound on a computer was slow, exacting and technical if you were interested in doing it right.

He killed the program and sat staring at the blue opening screen for a short time. When he thought about it, he wasn't so tired that he couldn't play Dungeonmaster for a while. And why not? Life wasn't supposed to be all work.

He loaded his Dungeonmaster disks and pressed the red RESUME button beside the great black door that appeared on the screen. In a moment he was deep in level ten.

Barton edged his way out from under the end of the workbench farthest from where the child was sitting. In the shadows ahead stood a fat old converted coal furnace with an evil grate.

He slid along inching like a great worm, until at last the furnace was between him and the boy. He pulled himself to his feet and peered out from amid the tentacles of ducts.

The boy was still playing with the computer. If this was going to work Barton would have to move like lightning. He opened the ether and crouched down.

Tensing his muscles, bracing, he prepared to leap.

The last thing he did was to soak his felt in the chemical. Its medicinal stench filled his nose, its coldness made his hand ache.

What was that smell? It was raw and fresh. Billy had been tapping his feet, tipping the chair back as he played. Had he somehow crushed a dropped tube of glue? He checked under the workbench. There was considerable debris down there, including that missing Amiga User utilities diskette. He retrieved it and put it into his diskette box.

There was no glue, and yet the whole basement reeked of the stuff. There was also another smell, a human smell. Billy sniffed his own underarms. It wasn't him. Could it be Dad, or his sister? No, neither of them stank. And the glue smell—it just didn't make sense.

Upstairs was suddenly very far away.

He decided that he'd had enough for one night. He turned off the computer, slid back his chair and left the basement. Although it wasn't a usual thing for him to do, he locked the basement door behind him. He also left the light burning. Burglars, he thought, don't like light.

But what would a burglar be doing fooling around with glue?

Too late Barton had realized his mistake. The boy had sniffed, looked around. Obviously he had smelled the ether. And then fear had entered his face. He'd hurried off, locking the basement door behind him.

After the door had closed there was no further sound from upstairs. Barton was left alone in the light.

That might just mean that the boy was waiting and listening. Barton contemplated violating a cardinal rule and leaving a trace of his presence: he considered locating and cutting the telephone wires.

As he looked for the telephone company's incoming service he glimpsed his own reflection in one of the basement windows. It startled him and he jumped back.

Beyond those black windows he couldn't see a thing. A coldness spread through him as he realized that the boy could be going outside to examine the room from a position of safety.

Never mind the phone wires, he had to get out of here.

At first Billy had tunneled into his sheets, hidden in his familiar bed with his beloved stuffed Garfie snuggled close to his chest. But that didn't work. Not being able to see out increased his feeling of vulnerability. He threw the sheets off and looked around him. The room was as always. He sniffed. No unusual odors here. He listened. No strange noises.

He knew what he'd smelled in the basement, though. He was almost sure that another human being had been in there with him, somebody who was sweating and—for whatever weird reason—using glue. Whoever it was hadn't made a sound.

Billy decided he might have been having a nightmare while

45

he was awake. Could that happen? He wasn't sure, but he thought maybe it could.

He decided to check out the rest of the family. Maybe he'd find the explanation in one of the other bedrooms.

Barton had withdrawn from the house very, very carefully. It had taken him a good five minutes to convince himself that the boy had indeed stayed inside.

Except for the basement, which blazed with light, the place was dark. He looked at his watch: one-fifteen. At least he had plenty of time left. He decided to return to his spot under the tree and wait.

The bird's song had drawn Billy to his window again, and from there he'd seen a bulky black shadow moving across the lawn. He could hardly believe it. When he understood that this was completely real, that he was wide awake, a cold shock flashed through him. Somebody really had been watching him while he was in the basement. That person must have been the source of the smells. And earlier—had he been the one in the gray slacks?

The thought of the weird guy who'd played RPM with him in the video arcade flashed through his mind, but that was too crazy even for Billy Neary. The guy would have had to have followed him home, for God's sake.

The prowler had moved with a sort of rolling scuttle, almost crablike, quickly disappearing beneath the twisty limbs of the oak. Billy waited for him to come out the other side and go off down the sidewalk, but he did not come out.

This was serious and he had to tell Dad. He went into his parents' room. They were so tangled up together in their four-poster bed that they seemed like one body with two dark heads.

"Dad?"

No response. He looked down at them. How would it feel to sleep bundled so close to a woman? He wasn't sure he was ready to spend the night without Garfie.

"Dad."

"Mmm? Hah—"

"There's a man in the yard."

46

"What?"

"I was looking out my window and I saw a man go under the oak."

"You're sure?"

"Yes."

Dad and Mother came untwined from one another and sat up. Dad looked angry. He swung out of bed and went to the window. "Where?"

"You can't see him now. He's under the oak."

"Maybe you should call the police, Mark."

"Let me take a look." He went over to their dresser and got the flashlight out of the bottom drawer.

Feeling a lot safer, Billy followed his father down the stairs.

Barton saw a glimmer of light touch the stained glass above the front door. It was only the slightest flicker, but it caused him to stand up and step back into the shadows. Then the door opened and the light jabbed like a needle into the dark yard.

With a single quick step Barton put the tree between himself and the flashlight. Obviously the boy had waked up his father and now they were searching for him.

As soon as he could get out of here he was going back to the van. He should never have tried this breaking and entering routine, it was just too risky.

But he had to have this boy!

He stood absolutely still, holding his breath, hardly daring to watch them lest they feel his stare. As if his thoughts could in some way control their actions, he willed them to stay on the porch.

Their voices drifted across the silent lawn. "There's nobody out there now, Billy."

Billy, his name was Billy.

"I saw him, Dad. He was right over there." He pointed straight at the tree. "He was fat."

"I don't see a soul."

"It was very scary, Dad."

So Billy had not only noticed his presence in the basement but also seen him as he moved across the lawn. He'd never

47

dreamed he'd been under observation then. This little boy was sharp. He was also kind, and intelligent and beautiful. No matter the dangers, Barton could not abandon him.

Billy.

6.

Barton's watch started beeping at exactly three-forty-five. Real sleep hadn't come, only a light nap. He opened his eyes into the warm blackness of the van. It was stuffy and the windows were fogged. He crawled up into the driver's seat, put the key in the starter and turned on the battery. When he lowered the windows the cool, rich night air brought him to full wakefulness.

The question was, should he go back? He already knew that Billy's father hadn't called the police; he would have picked up the dispatch on his scanner. There hadn't been anything, except when the one patrolman on duty made a routine check with the dispatcher.

The father must have decided that whatever his son had seen was innocuous. Even so, there was still great danger in going back tonight. But Barton couldn't risk waiting another day. There were too many imponderables.

While he'd been lying in the dark van, Barton had decided that he had been searching for Billy for all of his adult life. He just hadn't known it until now.

Barton Royal would give that child just a wonderful, wonderful life. There was so much love in him, so much giving, so much caring. Maybe Billy wouldn't believe it at first, but in the end he would love his new father so much the past would be completely forgotten.

He gripped the steering wheel as if it was the edge of a cliff. He told himself to breathe deeply and evenly. He was calm, alert.

Again he inventoried his supplies: ether, felt, duct tape, plastic cards, wire. The hammer, meat and plastic bag he could leave behind. Had there been a dog, it would have come out onto the porch with its master.

Billy, the little master.

You will be my soul's guide, Billy. I give you myself. I pray to you: dear Billy, open my eyes, guide me to the light.

He started the van. Ten minutes later he was passing the Burger King. Then he was on Hicks, then on Oak.

And there was the house. Thankfully, the basement light had been turned out. Dear old Dad must have noticed.

Barton imagined the conversation between father and son. Dad: "I know what happened to you. You got the heebie-jeebies down there in the dark."

Billy: "I saw a man, Dad."

Oh, Billy, I pray you deliver me. Be the one who is stronger!

He cut his lights and engine and rolled into the driveway. The tires hardly crunched on the concrete driveway.

Then he stopped the van. A glance at his watch: four-oh-six. He would take no more than ten minutes in the house. He went back in through the storm door, working quickly and efficiently. This time the basement stayed dark.

As he passed the workbench and its litter of computer disks and equipment, he noticed a Butterfinger wrapper. So Billy liked Butterfingers. Duly noted.

The door at the top of the stairs was locked with only a knob button, but nevertheless it slowed him down. He fumbled with the plastic cards that you were supposed to work into the crack between the door and the jamb.

There was quite a scraping noise, so he stopped. Closing his eyes, he leaned against the door. Carefully, he probed more delicately with the edge of the card. Finally he found the tongue of the lock. He twisted the card from side to side.

Quite suddenly the door swung open.

Every movement, every breath counted now. He could imagine the father lying still and silent, could imagine his eyes opening, glittering in the dark. Every creak and drip in the house echoed with hidden significance. He heard the clocks ticking, the breeze moving the kitchen curtains, the scuttling of a roach on the floor.

He took his ether from the knapsack and put it with the felt into his side pocket. The silent house before him was deeply disturbing. He smelled a fragrance of apples and, very faintly, the hint of Pine Sol. There was a faint scent of pecan divinity.

That odor carried him to his depths. In his neighborhood the older sisters used to make pecan divinity. They would gather into a muttering, unapproachable tribe and eat it in somebody's backyard. If Barton drew near, they'd scream "Fat Royal" and throw a rock or two.

When he stepped from the pantry into the kitchen proper he smelled bread. Now there was one of the best odors in the world. When they'd been baking at the Wonder Bread plant you could smell it up and down Mariposa.

A large white appliance stood in the middle of the kitchen table. Barton recognized the thing as an automatic bread baker. He'd wanted one, but he wasn't sure it would work.

Now he'd go ahead and make the purchase.

This was such a nice kitchen. It smelled wonderful, its curtains were fluffy and pretty, it was clean except for that one roach. Family life was such ordinary magic, but he was *not allowed!*

He ran his finger along the warm top of the bread maker, careful as always not to leave prints. Then he took out his rubber gloves and put them on. They were the kind with reinforced fingertips. He had read that new techniques could read a print left through a surgical glove.

Even though he was on a tight schedule, he did a quick inventory of the pantry and refrigerator. It was important to know what Billy liked. He'd already found that Butterfinger wrapper and a Bud Dry behind the workbench in the basement. From now on there would be plenty of Butterfingers in Billy's life. As for beer, Barton would introduce him to Anchor Steam and Dixie and Cold Spring Export.

There was Carnation Instant Breakfast in the pantry, and Tang. There were LaChoy Chinese dinners and Chef Boyardee spaghetti with meatballs. It was surprising how many kids enjoyed that stuff.

Adults starve quietly; children scream and pace and plead.

In the freezer he found Old El Paso enchilada dinners and MicroMagic cheeseburgers and shakes, and Aunt Jemima microwave pancakes. There were Dove Bars, vanilla with milk chocolate coating, Tabatchnick vegetable soup, Birds Eye frozen orange juice. (He'd stun Billy with fresh-squeezed.) In the fridge he found Coke Classic and Dr Pepper, Hi-C Fruit Punch, a package of Oscar Mayer hot dogs, sweet relish and French's mustard. He ignored the potatoes and lettuce and fresh squash in the crisper. The boy would consider them penitential foods. There was Pepperidge Farm toasting white in the breadbox, and he noted Double Stuf Oreos in the cookie jar. The peanut butter was Jif Super Chunky, and there were Smucker's peach and raspberry preserves in the fridge. As small a thing as the right kind of peanut butter sandwich could be an important ice-breaker.

Leaving the door to the basement open, he went through the dining room into the front hall of the old house, and began to mount the stairs. To reduce the chance of a creak, he took them three at a time, testing each step by slowly rolling his weight forward. Then he was in the upstairs hall. He didn't know who was in which bedroom. He had to guess, which was nerve-wracking.

Two of the bedroom doors were closed, one open. It made sense to look first in the open door, simply because that was the least risky.

He peered into the room. Against the far wall there was a window glowing with the thin last light of the moon. A bird's clear, lonely song pealed through the night. Under the window there was a bed, and on the bed a figure. His heart almost stopped at the sight of Billy sprawled in sleep.

Moving as carefully as a rat he crossed the floor, thinking of it as a dance. He was a good dancer. Mel Powell's Dance Studio, fox trot, rumba, swing, jitterbug, 1955.

He approached the bed. Swiftly he opened his ether, soaked the felt, laid it on the boy's face. The child was still for a moment, then he tried to turn his head. Barton was ready and bore down hard. A rush of movement went through the little body. There came a stifled sound, a cry of surprise. Billy's mouth opened, he tried to bite the cloth. He shook, his arms came out and flailed. His hands grasped and slapped. He made stifled gobbling sounds.

"Good, good," Barton whispered.

The boy shook and drummed his feet. The bed thuttered with a perverse echo of passion's tattoo. Only very gradually did his breathing become heavier, his movements slower.

Barton sang to him, sang in his sweet ear, "Where are you going, Billy boy, Billy boy, where are you going, charming Billy . . ."

Finally the child became unconscious.

Barton resoaked the felt and put it into a plastic sandwich bag, ready for instant use if needed. Then he scoured the room for precious belongings. He found a guitar, but it was too big to bring. The stuffed toy that the child slept with he left behind. Weaning Billy away from that would be hard, but necessary if he was ever to put his prese..t life behind him.

He took clothes, of course. The boy's wardrobe was not stocked with fashionable things like Gotcha and Ocean Pacific and Mexx. His clothes ran to plain jeans, shorts and T-shirts.

If this child was going to live in the Hollywood Hills with Barton Royal he would have to dress more fashionably. Once he was tamed a trip to some of the Melrose boutiques would be in order. But in the meantime, his old clothes would have to do. Barton stuffed the knapsack, then gave Billy another dose of ether and drew down his sheet.

How superb.

Barton pressed his face close to Billy's neck and smelled the natural sweetness of his skin. Why ever did boys turn into men? What a terrible curse! He lifted Billy in his arms and carried him out to the hall.

"Goodbye," he whispered on Billy's behalf, "goodbye to my dear old home." As he went downstairs, stepping because of his burden even more carefully than before, he felt almost like he had the moment Dad died, sad and yet joyous, his soul shot with sorrow even as it leapt free.

He was fully and completely aware that this was the most evil most hurtful crime he could commit. But what about him? He needed somebody, too.

He swept through the basement, a great black bird dragging prey, a fat man in the lost middle of his life, sweating under the weight of his stolen burden. He carried Billy across the front yard to the van. He had left the side door open, and he put Billy inside on the bunk. Then he strapped his wrists and ankles to the frame. Last, he sealed his mouth with gray duct tape.

One final time, he left the van. Returning to the house, he raised the garage door as quietly as he could. It rattled like hell but there was nothing he could do about it except pray.

Quickly he wheeled the boy's bike out and stowed it in the van. He already knew that he would ditch it in the Platte River outside of Lincoln. It was too old to keep and took up too much room in the van. Obviously, he didn't want Billy to have a bike, but its disappearance would make the police think this was a runaway.

He returned to the driver's seat, paused and thought. He inventoried everything. Penlight, felt, plastic cards—he'd left nothing behind.

He pulled off his rubber gloves and put them in the map case between the seats. For a long moment he looked at Billy, who lay very still on the cot behind him. Suddenly nervous, he leaned close to the boy. It was all right; he was breathing fine.

His fingers hesitated over the key. Then he grasped it, turned. The crystal silence of early morning was fractured by the starting of the van.

He drove off down the dark street.

Part Two

CHARMING BILLY

7.

In the silence that followed the alarm clock, Mark Neary became aware that the house was filled with a wonderful aroma.

"My God, it worked."

Mary sat up. "I believe you're right."

They had invested in a two-hundred-dollar automatic bread baker, which promised to deliver a fresh loaf when you got up. Sally and Billy had argued over the cryptic instructions, but apparently they had figured them out.

Sally stuck her head in their door. "The most recent reincarnation of Torquemada is not in his room."

As he shaved, Mark assumed that Billy had gone down early to supervise the bread maker. Mary rubbed her long legs with Jergen's lotion. It made a soft sound that he loved.

All the clocks in the house ticked on, passing through eight-oh-eight, eight-oh-nine, then eight-ten. Deep in Billy's computer a microchip silently marked the seconds, and in the living room the reproduction Regulator slowly retightened its spring after sounding eight chimes.

Eight-fifteen. In Billy's bedroom his digital watch beeped. His sister heard it and entered the room. She picked it up from the floor beside the bed and put it on his table. His ridiculous Garfie, which was in the middle of the floor, she threw onto the unmade bed.

A breeze blew through his open window, billowing the curtains.

Dressed in robe and slippers, Mark Neary hurried downstairs. "Smells like bread heaven," he called as he entered the kitchen. He raised the top of the machine and beheld a magnificent loaf. In a moment it was on the kitchen counter, steaming hot and wonderful. He pulled open the basement door and called Billy. "Come on up and get some absolutely fresh, absolutely hot oatmeal whole-wheat bread, complete with toasty crust."

He cut himself a big piece and spread it with strawberry jam. "It's heaven," he shouted.

Mary came in, her face glowing with the light of morning. Objectively Mark knew that his wife was no special beauty, but his heart did not know that, and it beat harder on behalf of the brightness of her skin, and his sex raised itself a little when she came up and kissed him. "You taste like strawberries," she said. He felt the laughter in her, and realized that he had dreamed again about her. They had gone to New Zealand in his dream. They had sailed a sunny bay. He remembered the water slapping the sides of the boat, the green hull, the white sails. Her dream body had been smooth and cool and her skin had tasted of the sea.

Mary turned away from him, absently tossing her hair, her eyes sparkling. On this day, he thought, we will be happy. "The bread's dynamite," he said as he cut her a slice.

"Let me do that. Those are defined as hunks, not slices."

"We need a bread knife."

"It's all in the wrist."

"Fresh bread! William! Appear!"

"You ought to set more limits, Mark. He's become part of his computer."

"You don't limit bright kids unless you absolutely must."

"Everybody needs boundaries." She went to the basement door. "William Neary, the computing window is now closed. You have thirty seconds to get up here."

When no young voice replied, "Hold on!" she looked down the stairs. "Billy?" She descended a few steps. It was dark. She was confused, perhaps even a trifle concerned. "Billy?" She went quickly down, turning on the basement light as she descended.

Sunday breakfast together was a rule. His father was just too lenient. Billy had to learn that rules defined a family and made it work. They were the foundation of relationships, and so of love.

She stood in the middle of the basement, struck suddenly by the way its present silence clashed with her usual impression. It was full of boys' things—an abandoned model airplane, the whole elaborate, painfully costly computer system, tape recorders, a Casio keyboard, the splayed open remains of a number of old appliances, things he'd found in people's trash, Mets and Lions Club caps from New Jersey days, toy cars. She picked up one of the cars, a Rolls-Royce with a missing door. So recently it had been a prize, so quickly abandoned for better things. Abandoned, lost, like boyhood itself. Such was the poetry of the matter: this twelfth was the last summer of her son's childhood. From now on there would be that touch of autumn.

In all its simplicity and perfection, the quiet moment among her son's beloved junk captured her heart. 'How rich I am,' she thought.

Then her thoughts went to Mark, her dear failure of a high school history teacher. They'd shared grand ambitions: he was going to be the next Walter Lippmann, a fine author of the left, full of literate fire. Except his sentences were generally too long, his thoughts too complicated, his words too dry.

He was a little heavy about the middle now, and he'd been fired a lot for his flaming love of the social ideal, but many sparks of his youth were yet unquenched.

She loved his body on hers, loved it when he shook with passion, adored the tickle of his lips upon her breasts, adored sweating with him in the night.

"I simply cannot cut it thin enough for the toaster," he shouted. "Help me!" The "help" was long and full of mourning.

Laughing, she returned to the kitchen. The table was only half set and now Sally had disappeared. This just was not a morning for a formal breakfast. The Sunday paper lay on the counter, "Blondie" and "Prince Valiant" huge and colorful on the first page of the comics section. Billy loved the comics.

"The kids are getting through the strainer," Mary said.

"Help me cut this darn bread. It's great but it's got its gluish side."

" 'Gluish' can't be a word."

"Don't Funk & Wagnall me, *help* me!"

"I'll just plain Funk you if you don't watch out," she whispered.

"Bad girl." He popped her on the bottom.

Sally came in the garage door. "His bike's gone."

"That's odd, Mark."

"Did you do something to him, Sally? Something that made him decide to escape your wrath?"

"Mother, he's twelve years old. He doesn't run away from me anymore. He fights back as best he can with his thin little arms and tiny fists."

They continued making their breakfast, as a ship might sail on even after its belly is sundered. Mary got the bread into the toaster and the water into the ancient percolator. Sally finished laying the table. Mark stood overseeing the bacon, Sunday comics in hand.

Mary did not tell him to be careful. If he wanted to set the newspaper on fire with his cooking, that was his business. She had decided this ten years ago. This time the bacon cooked and the newspaper did not.

They sat around the kitchen table eating bacon and toast and eggs, drinking frozen orange juice because they could not afford the kind that came in cartons. A pot of coffee steamed in the center of the table, beside the pile of Sunday paper.

Wrinkles appeared in the yolks of Billy's eggs. Eventually his sister stole his bacon and his mother put the eggs in the oven with some foil over the plate. Little was said during breakfast; the radio played a series of forgettable tunes, cars passed, one or the other parent looked up whenever a child shouted in the street.

"It isn't like him," his mother said. She was looking out the kitchen window into a yard flooded with sunlight.

They finally decided to make calls to the parents of his friends. One after another, the same answer came back. By ten there was a definite quiver in their voices, but the reason remained unsaid. At eleven the family drove over to the mall, but it was closed. There were a couple of people at Burger King, but no kids.

Knowing that his bike was gone, they drove the streets of

Stevensville. It was all useless, and at noon the family returned home.

Sally, deeply upset, withdrew to her room. Outside the grasshoppers sang, lawn mowers clattered, sprinklers whirred. The strains of piano practice floated over from the Harpers' house, and an engine endlessly revved and died as young John O'Hara tried to bring life to the fifty-dollar car he'd bought from a junk dealer.

Mark went to his daughter. She lay on her side reading and listening to the radio. Mark knew nothing about rock and roll, having lost interest when he realized at the age of fourteen that no girl would ever consider him a hep cat, never mind his pink shirt, black pants and Wildroot-soaked fenders. Mozart, Telemann, Bach: this was his music, the music of what the kids called "geese" in his day and time. His friends were boys with crooked horn-rims and sour-smelling white shirts, and pallid, bepimpled girls in harlequins and too few petticoats, who professed themselves to be "sent" by Beethoven's Sixth, "so passionate, Markie!"

Now when Sally's blooming classmates got crushes on their history teacher, he thought, 'You're about thirty years too late,' and laughed within at the irony of time.

It was remarkably poignant to watch a girl become a woman. He sat down on the bed beside her.

"Was he angry?" Mark asked her. "Was there a fight?"

"No, Dad. No way. He was fine."

"He didn't say anything to you—talk about taking a ride, going somewhere—" Mark stopped. He realized that he'd already asked her at least five versions of this same question. He fell silent.

Sally said it: "I'm scared, Daddy."

Mary came in. "Was there anything he wanted? A new computer program? Something he might have decided to go into Des Moines on his own to get?"

"Billy'd never go to Des Moines by himself without telling. And the computer stores're probably closed Sunday."

Mary bowed her head in acknowledgment. Her son wasn't *that* indifferent to limits.

Mark realized there was something he had to say. Let Sally

hear her father's fear, let Mary hear that he could be victim to his feelings. He had to get this out, and he had to do it now. "Last night, he woke me up." He took a deep breath. "He said he'd seen a man in the front yard. I looked, but there wasn't anybody there. I'm sorry to say, I just—"

It came then, the pain, welling up in him like a ball of red fire, bursting in the center of his heart.

"Oh, Christ—obviously, I—" It wasn't pride that stopped him this time, or the reticence of an inward man, it was the sheer horror of his mistake. "He must have been watching all the time—waiting for his chance."

Mary was absolutely silent and completely still. When she spoke her voice was very soft. "If it happened—and that's a very big 'if'—it certainly isn't our fault. We can't think that way." She looked at her husband. "We can't, Mark."

"We have to call the police."

"I agree," Mary said. At once what had been a slow decision became a desperate emergency. Both parents went for the phone in their bedroom, followed by their daughter.

There was a short delay while Mary fumbled through the phone book looking for the number. This was a small town; the police could not be reached by jabbing 911.

Outside the lawn mowers had stopped, and lunch was being eaten in the other houses on the block. Soon baseball would hit the airwaves and the men would disappear into their air-conditioned living rooms and dens.

Mary spoke the numerals. Her voice was loud in the noon hush, the digits enunciated with excessive care.

As Mark punched in the numbers a boy's voice sang out high and gay, and for an instant he thought—but no, it was some other child. A clawing, frantic urgency came over him as the phone rang, and when a voice said "Stevensville Police" he could barely manage to reply.

"My name is Mark Neary. I'm calling to report that my son, William, appears to be missing."

His call had been answered by Patrolman Charles Napier, who was on dispatch this Sunday until four. The call didn't surprise him. They got three or four of these a month. If the children were young the cases were always solved within a couple of hours. Older children might be runaways, and runaways sometimes took longer. But they all came home in the end, all of them. Kids got killed, even kidnapped, but not in this sleepy little town. The parents, of course, were always terrified, and Charlie was always gentle with them. "When did you discover William was missing?"

"When we got up this morning. During the night he woke me up. He said he'd seen a man in the front yard. I investigated, but there was nothing wrong. Then this morning he wasn't here anymore."

Charlie Napier had pulled out a missing persons form. He took the bare details of age and description. There would have to be an immediate investigation of this case, because a minor was involved. In adult missing person cases the department waited twenty-four hours before starting a search. "An officer will be out to see you in about ten minutes."

Mark hung up the phone. "They're coming right over," he said. His voice sounded to him like an echo. He had become his own audience, observing the tragedy even as it spun itself around him.

Distantly, "The Star Spangled Banner" rose from a neighbor's TV. The baseball game was starting, and everybody else was safe, and nobody else's child was threatened.

Mary's hand came into his. "Do you really think that the man—"

"I don't know."

She wanted to lean her head against him, but restrained herself. They needed to be strong for one another, not to display weakness. She squeezed his hand. "He'll be found."

"I guess it's the step we just took. It makes you face how damn scared you really are."

Mary herself felt light-headed. She asked Sally to go downstairs and make some coffee.

As Sally poured out the grounds and measured the water, she tried to understand. Dad had said that Billy had waked up in the night and seen a man. What did it mean? Sometimes she and Billy would both wake up in the middle of the night and do something crazy like play Monopoly on the hall floor. They'd watch *Chiller Theatre* that came on channel six at two

A.M. Saturday. Or they would talk, spinning dreams in the night. She wanted to get out of Stevensville as much as she'd wanted to get out of all the other little towns where her father taught.

Billy was a pretty bright kid. Surely he wouldn't have agreed to go with some man who came to the house in the middle of the night.

Her brother was also a total innocent when it came to certain things. You could give him an Oreo loaded with tabasco sauce and he'd pop it into his mouth every time. But he wouldn't let himself get kidnapped.

The arrival of the police alerted the neighborhood for the first time to the existence of a possible problem at the Nearys' place. People noticed the green and white car cruising slowly along, watched it as it came to a stop in front of the teacher's unkempt yard. Because they were recent arrivals most of their neighbors did not know the family; some of them didn't even know the name. Mark knew that the appearance of the police car would bring uneasy questions.

He felt queasy, watching the officer come up the walk. A curious distance imposed itself. The policeman approached as if he was a phantom coming up an unreal front walk, beneath a sun as bright as memory. How strange that Billy was not there wanting to see his gun. As he came swiftly across the porch through the door the percolator started rattling. Sally went back to the kitchen.

She went to the percolator, leaned into the steam and inhaled.

"Coffee's ready," she said as she entered the living room. The young policeman smiled.

He asked questions about Billy. His age, his looks, did they have a video to run on television?

Mark was horrified. A video! Television! Billy was gone, really and truly gone. He wasn't in the basement, he wasn't out visiting, he wasn't at the mall.

Mary's impulse was to run somewhere and seek him, shout his name, make more phone calls.

"We don't have a video," Mark said.

"But there are pictures," Mary added. She was sick inside.

64

Just because they had no video didn't mean that Billy was lost forever, but that was how she felt.

"If you get TV they'll run a video a little more than a photo."

Listening to the man, realizing that Billy was truly gone, Mary could have screamed her guts out. But she didn't do that sort of thing, it wasn't her style.

She crossed her legs and leaned forward. She understood nothing about the black storming ocean within her. Life had so far never brought her a suffering such as this. Not even Mother's death compared to it.

She found herself ally to the parents whose children were torn from their arms at Auschwitz, to those who saw their little boys hanged at Tyburn for the theft of a button, to those whose children were raped by the passing Huns or Teutons or Romans, to all who have stood helplessly by while their innocents were caught in the mayhem of the world.

But she sat quietly.

The policeman noted how self-possessed the family seemed. His training had barely touched on missing children. There were certain realities, though, and he was aware of them: Most missing children were found within twenty-four hours; most were runaways. When they were done violence, it was most often at the hand of a parent or another family member. When they were abducted by strangers, they were most often found dead, or never found at all.

There were indications that this child had run away. The bicycle was gone, for one thing. According to the mother there were clothes missing.

"We call in a detective from Wilton in missing child cases. He's had a lot of experience with these cases. I just have to get the preliminaries, so we can put out a bulletin and get the picture over to KKNX. I'm sure they'll want it for the ten o'clock news."

"Billy's been kidnapped." Mary Neary's voice was smooth with terror.

"Well, ma'am, we assume the worst, hope for the best. That's how we do these things. But with his bike gone and the clothes obviously taken, this is very apt to be a runaway. Very apt to be."

"He left his watch behind," Sally said. "He never leaves his watch."

"I don't want to get your hopes up, but we've never lost a runaway here in Stevensville."

At first he thought he was hearing a distant siren. It took a moment of listening for him to understand that the sound was coming out of Mary Neary. Slowly it got louder. He glanced at the husband, who looked perplexed. Then the man's face went pale. As if she was a figure in a dream, the daughter's closed fists slowly came up to her cheeks. Her mother's eyes screwed shut, her arms whipped around her breasts and her whole body seemed to snap.

The sound of her anguish was made more painful to hear by her efforts to stifle it, not opening her mouth, throwing her head back, and all that tortured noise coming from her nose.

Afterward there was a stunned hush.

Sally ran out to the kitchen. She turned, her posture that of a soldier at the edge of the battlefield.

"The coffee's getting cold," she said in a shrill voice. She closed her eyes. In that moment she was wounded as certainly as if somebody had cut her with a whip. For the rest of her life she would be exquisitely sensitive to those sudden hushes that can stop a moment. And she would forever think, when they came, that somebody she loved had just been lost.

8.

At five o'clock in the morning Barton had passed through Des Moines. He had seen only one other vehicle on Interstate 235, a pickup truck going north, its headlights cutting the last of the dark.

He had left the interstate and driven through the streets hunting for a place to get a cup of coffee and a doughnut. Around him the city was drifting toward morning. This was the hour of last dreams, and the quiet was made more true by the dull hum of air conditioners and the slippery sound of an occasional passing car.

The public nakedness of a sleeping city would have thrilled him ordinarily, but this time it only added to his unease. He had expected to be exhilarated by his victory, but he felt an altogether different emotion. He couldn't seem to shake the feeling that something was deeply and terribly wrong, that he had made some mistake so basic he simply could not see it.

Without finding a place to get a doughnut he returned to the highway.

As the van sped westward the sun rose. It first sent the Aerostar's shadow far ahead, then caused it to contract. He thought of the shadow's astonishing cargo. Charming Billy.

What have I done wrong?

From the bed in the back Billy moaned. Barton heard an edge of consciousness in the voice. He would pull into the next rest area and do a heavy needle on the boy, put him out for eighteen hours.

Again there was a sign of consciousness, a thick, muffled word that was probably "Dad."

"Dad'll be here in a minute."

The reply was another moan.

Barton didn't want to stop on the roadside for fear some state trooper might offer help.

Dull thumps emanated from the back of the van. Billy was awake all right. He was struggling against the straps. In the rearview mirror Barton could see the quilt heaving. "It's just a nightmare, Billy!"

"Mmm . . ."

Sleep, little boy, sleep and rest, Father will come to thee soon . . .

"Mmmfff!"

"It's a nightmare!"

"Hh—mmmff!"

Come on, come on, doesn't Iowa believe in rest stops!

The road stretched out straight and empty. Behind him Billy jerked and moaned. Barton gripped the wheel, pressed the gas pedal as far down as he dared.

Five minutes passed, then ten. All the while the boy struggled. Finally, after twenty minutes, a rest stop appeared. *Thank you oh dear God who loves your Barton.* He pulled in toward the picnic tables and outhouses, then past a long line of parked eighteen-wheelers, finally stopping near a little grove of trees at the far end of the picnic grounds.

Quickly he opened the glove compartment and took out the black wallet containing syringes, alcohol and a small bottle of diazepam formulated for injection. He'd chosen the drug after reading medical textbooks. It was safer than a barbiturate and had, in addition to inducing sleep with a sufficient dose, the property of reducing anxiety.

He put some alcohol on a cotton ball and drew two cc's of the drug into one of his syringes. Then he climbed over the seats into the back, pushing past the bicycle and the bag of clothes, to the bed where the boy lay strapped and moaning.

The moaning became a high-pitched wail as he dug beneath the soft quilt and found Billy's arm. Billy's head jerked from side to side. He was trying to push the quilt away from his eyes.

His arm quaked when Barton touched it, but Barton was strong and quick. He swabbed the skin and delivered the drug. But it wouldn't go to work at once and the word coming from behind the gag was now distinct: "Dad! Dad!"

"You're in an ambulance, son!"

"Dad!"

"Dad and Mother are fine. Your sister is fine. There was a fire. Sleep now, son."

There were more sounds as Billy struggled to respond. In a moment he was going to be conscious enough to understand that he was gagged. Barton decided to take the risk of a scream and remove the tape, try to calm the child down. As he pulled it off, Billy smacked and coughed. Then he spoke.

"A—fire?"

"You're going to be fine. Sleep now."

"Did I get burned?"

"No, son, just a little smoke."

"I can't move . . ."

"So you won't fall off the stretcher. You're in an ambulance. You're very sleepy now. Go to sleep."

At last the breathing changed, grew ragged and then long, and Barton closed his own eyes and let his own breath sigh slowly out.

"Ether is a relatively short-duration soporific that was administered in gaseous form as an anesthetic during the early history of anesthesia."

They had been on the road nearly two hours. Barton should have given Billy the diazepam on the other side of Des Moines. To punish himself for his stupidity he slammed the empty needle into his own thigh. Stupidity must always be punished. Everything had to be plan-perfect.

"Ether is a short duration soporific," he said as he yanked the needle out.

To Barton's surprise Billy's hand was dangling. His struggles had been so extreme that he had freed it, something Barton had never seen any boy accomplish before.

Barton threw back the quilt and loosened the strap that bound the child about his midriff. He returned the hand to Billy's side, really touching him for the first time, holding his soft skin and feeling a rush of hurting desire. Despite the abrasions resulting from the child's effort to free it from the strap, it was a lovely hand, pale and silky.

He wanted to kiss it, to somehow meld with its beauty. He looked at the skin, now burnished by a shaft of sunlight. It was so exotic, so perfect down even to the dusting of fine hairs that came down from the wrist and spread along the outer edges toward thumb and little finger. That they would thicken and darken seemed impossible to believe: and yet this perfect being would soon be cast down the cliff of manhood.

Barton bent toward the hand, his lips parted . . . it would be a sign of love, of respect, even of awe . . . his secret . . .

Inwardly, he made demands of himself. 'Don't! It's ugly and perverse and wrong.' But he longed to, he could hardly bear not just once touching his lips to that soft skin. 'It's monstrous! Don't!' He trembled. 'It isn't you, Barton. You're a decent, lonely man trying to recapture something pure, you are not a filthy lecher!'

He gripped the limp hand hard. Then he dropped it. He watched the sleeping form. Billy's slimness made Barton feel like a big, fat lump.

He wanted to give Billy a father's warm kiss, and feel him return it, and then Billy would be bound by the rich and healthy love that flourishes between father and son.

Laughing a little to himself, Barton climbed over into the driver's seat. He backed the van up to the outhouses and dropped the black curtain that hid the rear area from anybody who might look in the windshield. He didn't really need to use the facilities, but he knew better than to pass up a chance. He couldn't risk leaving the van while he was getting gas, and he didn't feel safe in rest stops during the day when they were full of meddling children and watchful parents.

Outside he breathed deeply of the early morning air. He was feeling better and better. This thing was going to work, he could sense it. At first it would be hard, but Billy would find that Barton Royal could show him such love, such attention. It would be quite beyond what he had known before. Their life together would be wonderful.

The outhouse was full of busy flies and had an oily, chemical stench. To Barton's surprise, some little creature screeched as he stepped in. Wriggling beneath his foot was a mouse. Involuntarily Barton jumped back, but the little animal was so damaged it could barely drag itself away. It was horribly injured. Probably it had already been weakened by poison before he stepped on it. Barton's first impulse was to use another outhouse, but then he thought he ought to put the little thing out of its misery.

With the intention of stomping on it he raised his foot. But then a sort of hesitancy entered his mind. He brought his heel down carefully, just pinning the creature. Its screams filled the tiny room. They were surprisingly loud. Bit by bit he increased the weight on its back. He could feel it writhing.

Kill it!

He slid his foot back and forth. The tail twisted and turned in the dust beside his shoe. A delicious warmth filled his body. As the mouse screamed, he hummed.

At last he decided that it was time for the creature to die. By inches he increased the weight on its back, until finally there was a crunch and the screeching stopped. He finished his business and returned to the van.

It was just a mouse, for God's sake.

He rolled down the windows and let the wind flood the van. Cotton clouds rushed up from the south. They were colored pink and gold against the sky. Before him stretched the road to the mountains and the wide western deserts, and finally home, his house tucked into its own very private quarter-acre of the Hollywood Hills.

He was within fifty miles of the Nebraska border when a state trooper suddenly pulled in behind him. For some time he'd been watching the police car coming up on his left. It was no more than two car lengths back when it shifted into his lane.

He checked his speedometer: fifty-eight. Not fast enough to warrant a ticket, not so slow as to be suspicious. The trooper came closer and closer, until he was less than twenty feet away. Inside the car Barton could see a shadowy, expressionless young driver, an older man beside him. He gulped air and tried to think. What could possibly have drawn them to him?

What indeed: he was engaged in an incredibly risky enterprise. For all he knew a neighbor had seen his van at the Nearys', seen him hurry across the lawn with the boy in his arms, seen him wheeling the bike into the back of the van.

He had no reason to feel secure. Safety was an illusion. He was the worst imaginable sort of criminal—a child abductor—

and he was on the run with a drugged twelve-year-old trussed up in his van.

This trooper was about to catch a monster, and maybe that would be best. The authorities would paw him, chain him, put him in prison . . . or worse.

Barton Royal was *not* insane!

He should have used back roads, gotten out of the state that way. It had been stupid to cling to the interstates.

Why did the trooper just stay back there, watching? Why was he playing games? He hadn't had to piss when he was at the rest stop, but he had to do it now, his whole body was tensing, every muscle tightening, every sinew straining against bone and cartilage. His mouth had gone dry, his eyes felt like they would burst out of his head.

"Get it over with, you bastards!"

Wait, he had options. He remembered the scanner. *Turn it on, fool! Turn it on and keep it on!*

He watched out of the corner of his eye as the little red dot raced up and down its face, seeking for some snatch of dialogue.

Silence. The trooper wasn't on the radio. Of course not, not *now*, fool! He's already done that. He's just waiting, watching, hoping for something more than the description, something that'll give him probable cause to enter the van.

He was trying to break Barton's nerve, that was it. If he took off the trooper would chase him down. That would give him his right to search.

God, God, please help your child Barton. You made me, God, now you help me! I'm going through hell here!

The trooper's light bar started flashing.

Oh, God, please don't let it be now. He wanted just a month with Billy, then he would willingly die! Yes, die for thirty happy days!

He sat up straight, became prim. "Pull the van over," he told himself, "be as proper as a schoolgirl in church." The trooper followed him. He tried to calm himself, get some spittle into his dry mouth. 'OK, Barton baby, here he comes. My, what a clean-shaven face that trooper has. I wonder if he needs to shave at all?' He blanked his mind, cranked up a smile. His voice was calm, concerned, perfect as he said, "I don't think I was speeding, officer."

"Driver's license, please." The voice was calm and clear.

"Yeah, I have it, just a second." Barton tried not to tremble as he pulled out his wallet.

"California license, Mr. Royal?"

The voice had dropped an octave. Suspicion.

"Yeah. I have my summer place in Utah."

A long silence. Here it came. They would utter the murderous formula: "We'd like to have a look in the back."

"Your plates are expired."

Oh, no, not stupidity again. Fool, fool fool! But wait. How could that be? On the way to Iowa he'd stopped at the mail drop in Salt Lake, gotten the renewal. He'd put on the sticker.

"No, I don't think so."

"No sticker."

It was on the front plate. Wasn't that what he was supposed to do? "It's on the front."

Please, Oh Lord of heaven, I will do anything, I will serve you body and soul forevermore—

The trooper went around to the front of the car, looked at the plate. He came back to the window. "Mr. Royal, you ought to have stickers on both plates."

"They only sent me one."

"Well, I suggest you get another if you don't want this to keep happening."

"Thank you, officer."

"We're not going to issue a summons this time, Mr. Royal, but you'd better stop at DPS in Salt Lake and get that sticker."

"I sure will, officer."

Billy uttered three short, sharp cries. The trooper leaned farther into the window. At that moment inspiration struck. "I have a capuchin," Barton said.

"A capuchin?"

"The sounds. A monkey. A little monkey in the back."

The officer's face grew tight. He drew back from the van. "All right, Mr. Royal. You can go now."

He put the van into drive and accelerated back onto the

highway. The troopers remained on the roadside, their light bar still flashing.

Barton's face flushed, his temples throbbed. Huge sparks danced in his eyes. Did he need to see a doctor about these intense stress reactions? He was overweight, sure, but this— maybe there was high blood pressure or something.

He imagined himself dead on the road with a boy in the back. Never!

9.

The Nearys had been dropped into hell. Nothing had prepared them for this. Their hell had neither gate nor horizon, and its demons were police officers with sad, suspicious eyes. They tormented not with blows but with questions. And always there was the central question, the one nobody could answer. Hell's characteristic sound was a silent telephone.

Neither Mark nor Mary gave voice to the hope they privately shared, that this awful day would end with Billy's straggling reappearance, home late from some boyhood escapade.

He was such an adventurous little boy!

During the afternoon hope slowly died. It began to fade after the police had left, when they were supposed to be eating lunch.

The ham sandwiches Sally made eventually drew flies. As the afternoon grew old the edges of the bread curled and the lettuce became slack. The day wore through four, then five. The day began to end, and still he did not come.

It was decided to inventory his room once again, to see this time if some clue to his whereabouts could be determined from any toys he might have taken with him. Detective Walter Toddcaster, who had come up from Wilton, insisted on participating in this task. At first they thought his motive was some hidden mistrust. But when they faced the quiet, immensely familiar little room, they understood that it was compassion.

Handling the toys was as hard as it would have been to grab flaring briquettes from a backyard grill. But once picked up, putting something down was even worse, like dropping one's wedding ring down the drain, or giving up one's life, or letting go the hand of God.

So thick were the memories, so great the pain, only Todd-caster could manage anything even approaching a coherent inventory.

Mary and Mark sat in the middle of the floor with the drawers under the bed open before them. They fumbled in a haze of stifled tears.

Mark remembered the voice of his son muttering long fantasies of play, his cars in his hands, his Lego, his Brio trains, the decrepit stuffed Garfield the Cat doll gone anorexic from age and cuddling. "Has he been practicing his guitar?" Mark asked automatically.

Mary was in her own pain. "I've been meaning to gift out this Brio," she said quietly. "He doesn't use it anymore."

From Sally's room came the voices of the Beatles: "Give Peace a Chance." Mark's mind shifted suddenly to his college days. He had sung that song before Billy was even a possibility in the world. Gratefully he let it draw him into other times. Other voices seemed to rise around him: "Let it be . . ." There had been some good times.

When Billy was a newborn Mark had cuddled him inside his robe. He fed him his bottle while reading the morning paper. It was there he had said his first word: "Da."

Mary was clutching a red Brio train engine to her chest. "I remember his first word," she said in a tiny voice. "Ma. Remember that?"

Sally came in. "We're going to find Billy," she said.

Detective Toddcaster added. "This inventory is going to help us."

Suddenly Mark and Mary were clear-eyed again. Mary sat up. "Yes, we are." Then she frowned, looking very like a little girl.

A shadow entered the room. Sally understood first. "The sun just set," she said in a hushed voice.

"I think we're finished here, if nobody can spot any missing toys." The detective got to his feet, a sense of bustle in his movements. "So what we're missing is the street clothes. Shirts, pants, underwear, socks. And his duffel."

"Like he went on an overnight."

"Except for the shoes," Mark said.

Detective Toddcaster glanced around. "The shoes?"

"Look. The black sneakers, the dress loafers. Even his slippers and his flip-flops. They're all here. When he left he was barefoot."

Mary held out her hands as if warding off a blow. She picked up a scuffed shoe. "He's about to go into men's sizes, Mark. Did I tell you that?"

Mark nodded. He could not speak. But he knew as certainly as he knew his own bones that Billy had been taken by that man in the yard. "He wouldn't go out without shoes, especially not on his bike."

"Not even in August, Mr. Neary?"

"My brother never went barefoot. It's not the style anymore," Sally said.

"No, I guess not." Walter Toddcaster was a compact man with a great, bobbing ball of a head. He had come up from Wilton in an olive drab Chevrolet, which was currently parked in the driveway. Now he looked down at Billy's shoes as if they might reveal some secret only a professional could interpret. "My grandson loves British Knights," he said. "Wouldn't be caught dead in anything else." Looking at Billy's tattered sneakers, he blinked as if somebody had just given him a small slap.

Seeing the expression on Mary's face, he reached out a neat hand, startlingly thin in a man so portly, and caressed the air near her shoulder. "I have confidence, Mary. We're gonna find Billy. I'll even tell you where. Walking his bike along some country road, either busted or with a flat tire. And we'll find him soon, because he will have noticed that the sun's going down and he'll have given up waiting or whatever he's been doing and started to walk."

"He wouldn't just take off without telling us. My son is a natural adventurer, but he's also a good boy." She dropped the shoe with a thud. "My son never lies. He is never lied to."

"Momma—" Sally had folded her arms.

She tilted her head as if she was hearing some special music. Her face worked. "My point is that Billy is a smart little boy, but he's also trusting. He could so easily be deceived. That's what worries me!"

Mark was deeply worried by what he saw appearing in her.

Not even in labor had she looked this bad. After fifteen hours trying to have Sally she had grabbed Mark and said, "It's gonna come again and I can't stand it, Markie, I'm gonna scream." "Scream, for God's sake," Dr. Epstein had said. "You're driving me nuts with your strong, silent shtick. Woman, scream!" And again she contracted and her eyes were like glass and she did not scream, could not, she had to be in control and Mark knew that for her it would be a kind of death to scream.

It had taken fifteen hours. She stank, she ran streams of sweat, and finally Sally appeared, her head looking like a little blue banana. She snorted and then wailed like the wind, high and thin.

Billy had been easier, because he was her second. For days afterward he had been placid. Until he was about six months old he had been a docile baby. Since then he had not stopped for a moment.

Toddcaster watched them. He'd seen this stage many times before. They had a runaway but they didn't want to admit it. And why should they? Their child had despised his home so much he'd decided to leave. The fact that he'd done it on a bicycle meant he was almost certain to be found. This case would be closed within twenty-four hours, and that would be that.

In the meantime a little handholding was all that was required. He was bored and he wanted a cigar. But he was embarrassed to ask if they minded. Their house was so clean, the air fresh and faintly scented with some potpourri the woman must have made.

It was time to get this show on the road. "Look, he took shirts, pants, things that he'd need if he was going to stay away for a few days. He went on his bike. I think we should assume that Billy ran away."

From the door their daughter said, "No way."

Something in her voice made Walter Toddcaster jerk around to face her. He knew that kind of conviction. "What makes you say that?" If he was wrong, OK. He wanted to find out the truth and, above all, the boy. "What makes you so sure?"

"He was happy. We have a happy family." The girl looked up at him, a pale, heart-shaped face, blond hair, a real heartbreaker.

"Sometimes things build up—a kid just can't see his way, communications fail—"

Mark Neary went to his feet. "For God's sake, our son's been kidnapped. He even *saw* the kidnapper last night right out in the front yard! We're wasting time debating about it."

His wife looked dully at the floor. "It's easier for you if he's listed as a runaway, isn't it?"

"We want to get your boy back."

Mark wanted to grab his lapels, shake some sense into the man. "Then put out a bulletin!"

"We APB'd his description to every police force in the state this morning. You know that."

"And you haven't heard a word. Not a single cop in the state of Iowa's so much as glimpsed him."

Toddcaster looked at him. Mark looked right back, and was surprised to see in the detective's eyes something that he had not noticed before. It was as unexpected as a cold wind in the middle of the August heat. He did not like it, not in *those* eyes. If the police felt helpless, where did that leave Billy?

"We have to go on the evidence, and the evidence is that Billy left on his bicycle, taking his clothing with him. That's what I have. That's reality."

"Just to be safe, why not report it as a kidnapping?"

Walt Toddcaster wished that he could do just that. His instinct was always to expect the worst, but the fact was that if he put in a report a lot of police organizations were going to crank themselves up. You cared about abducted kids. Cops had families; they knew how much this hurt. The first thing outside investigators would find was that the bike was missing. And that would be very embarrassing.

"Get me some hard evidence."

"The testimony of his family!" Mary's voice was rough. She thought to herself that she wanted to die but she could not, not and leave Billy.

When he was a baby he'd had blond curls. She had cried silently, her back straight and a smile plastered on her face, when Mr. Terry cut them off. Clip, clip, clip, and there went babyhood down to the floor of the barbershop.

The sound of the doorbell ringing shot through every one

of them, even Walt Toddcaster, who had been in this same sort of house with this same sort of people too many times.

Three bedraggled young men stood at the door, their faces sheepish. They had cameras and equipment with them. A blue and gray van lettered KKNX EYEWITNESS NEWS was parked at the curb.

"You have the missing child?"

Mark opened the door wider. The men came in, looking into the corners of the hallway, glancing at the ceilings. "Set up in the living room," one of them said. His voice was pitched to a funereal hush.

"No," Sally said, "in the basement."

"The basement?"

"Oh, Mark, she's right! His stuff is down there. Our son is a computer nut. You ought to put it on TV."

"That'll be a good visual, ma'am."

As the TV crew followed Sally downstairs, Toddcaster pulled Mark and Mary aside. "Listen," he said, "the voice of experience talking. You're very self-contained. You keep your feelings inside. Nothing against that, I do the same. Ulcers instead of tears, less embarrassing. But the more emotion you show on the tube, the more stations'll pick this up and run it. Take it from me. Voice of experience."

"What will you say, Walt?"

"He's going to say what he thinks, Mark. That Billy ran away."

Walt Toddcaster made another half-gesture toward Mary. "I want Billy to get found. I want a win on this. Guarantee I do."

"A runaway means we're bad parents. That we somehow drove him away. And meanwhile, *somebody has our boy.*"

A member of the television crew met them on the stairs. "Is there any other entrance to the basement? It's a great location, but we've gotta bring in some lights. We need a straight stairway."

It took Mark a moment to remember. "There's an old storm door, but we haven't used it since we moved in. I don't know if we can even get it open."

When he pushed at it, though, he found that it opened smoothly. Toddcaster began peering at it as if it had somehow hypnotized him. The thought crossed Mark's mind that maybe he was a little off. 'How good could the cops in these backwater towns be?' he wondered. *God help Billy.*

While the men from the TV station brought in their lights Mark sat at the computer, idly going through its inventory of games and projects. Mary went upstairs and got the photo album. There was last year's birthday party, and a couple of recent shots of him sitting at the computer.

The detective hovered like a ghost near the storm door. Now he was touching the hinges with his handkerchief. His face had acquired the appearance of bad sculpture, at once intense and empty. Finally he stopped, rocked back on his heels and returned to the basement.

The TV crew finished their preparations. Mark and Mary and Sally sat together in front of Billy's Amiga. The crew turned on the lights. Their blue glare shocked, the sense of exposure intensifying Mark's pain. His eyes were wet, but the tears there did not come from the part of him that spoke and thought and acted. They were a signal from the dark, and Mark in that moment knew what it meant to experience the unbearable.

Then the camera was rolling and the director was asking Walt a question. "What happened to Billy Neary, Lieutenant Toddcaster?"

"In these cases we always look for a runaway or kidnapping by a parent living out of the home. But the Nearys are a happy family. This is typical Iowa we have here.

"Abduction by strangers does happen, but it's very rare. At first we thought this was a runaway. It looked like a clear case. The boy's bike was missing, clothes had been taken from his room. In fact, if you hadn't wanted to use that storm door, I'd still be wasting my time on the runaway theory. But this boy was kidnapped all right. I'd bet my badge on it. And the kidnapper's a clever one, taking the bike like that."

Mary and Mark gave way together, like two trees knocked down by the wind. She was silent. Trying to disguise his tears, he made peculiar gobbling noises. Sally took both her parents' hands.

"Can you describe your son, Mrs. Neary?"

She struggled for the words. "Four feet tall. Reddish-blond hair. Will you show his picture? Please?"

Then Sally spoke. "Please, whoever you are, my mom and

dad didn't do anything to hurt you. Please, please give Billy back to us."

The camera lingered a moment and then it was over. Without saying a word, the crew began folding up their equipment. When the lights went out the basement seemed like a kind of tomb.

Dumb with sorrow and surprise, the family followed Walt Toddcaster upstairs. He went straight to the phone. They could hear him talking to the FBI field office in Des Moines. His tone was urgent.

Then he turned to them. "Somebody oiled the hinges of that storm door. And it was recent, probably within the past twenty-four hours."

"Nobody oiled any hinges," Mark said.

"I know *you* didn't. The abductor did it. That's how he got in the house. He had to oil the hinges or the creaking might have waked somebody up."

Mary flew into his arms. "Hey," he said.

"You're a genius!"

He turned away from her, away from them all. He went to the window, stood looking across the front lawn. "I'm a dumb cop. It took me all day to figure out you folks were right. Now I want to get a crime squad in here. Dust for prints, look for clues."

"What clues? We've touched everything, been everywhere. It's too late for clues!"

"I hope you're wrong, Mark. The FBI's in on it now. They're sending a crew up from Des Moines. The drill is, they'll gather evidence and coordinate any national search. We'll do the in-state footwork. They'll be here in an hour. And in the meantime, I have a suggestion. We ought to send somebody out for food. You haven't eaten all day and you're gonna need your strength."

"We could all go out," Sally said.

"No. From now on, this is rule number one: See that phone? You never, ever leave that phone unattended. Never. If none of you can be here, get a neighbor, get a friend. Use it as little as possible. If you want to make calls freely, order in another line."

"We have call waiting."

"That's not good enough. And always answer on the first or second ring. Another thing. We're going to loan you a special recorder. Every time the phone is picked up, it'll start automatically. And if Billy calls, just say one thing. Not 'I love you,' not 'Are you OK?' Just say, 'Where are you?' Remember that, 'Where are you?' Any scrap of information he can give—God willing, maybe it'll help us."

"Do they usually call?"

"Well, look at it this way. Right now your son has one thing on his mind. He wants to go home. He wants you. And if he sees a phone, there's a chance he'll try to use it. But he might not have much time. And it'll be dangerous. So after he says where he is, tells you anything he can, you say to him, 'Hang up.' Do that as fast as you can. I can't impress on you enough, do not stay on the phone with him. Look at it from the kidnapper's viewpoint. He sees the kid on the phone. What does it mean? He's just been made, in all probability. This kid has now worn out his welcome. He offs the kid, and he's outa there."

"He just—he kills Billy—"

"Mary, we have to face it. A man who does this kind of thing is not a Mr. Niceguy. He does not have normal human responses to things. Chances are he's unstable and he's undoubtedly mean."

The phone rang, once again sending shock waves through everybody in the house. Mary answered it, her voice smooth, but hushed by pain and suspense. "Neary residence."

It was the local police. They'd just gotten the FBI bulletin and Chief Lacy was coming over.

"They've been cruising around hunting for Billy all day," Walt said. "Now they'll shift tactics. They'll start going through their files looking at possible perps. A town this size, the likelihood is they won't find any candidates. But we'll be knocking on a few doors in Des Moines and Davenport, you can be sure."

Mark went to the front window. "He stood under that tree. He went up the driveway, along the side of the garage, into the backyard. And then he came in."

"The storm door was never locked, I take it."

"I don't remember." To himself Mark said, *It's my fault.*

Walt came over to him. "I know what you're thinking. If you'd done this, if you'd done that. Forget it. The guy wanted Billy. He was going to get him no matter what."

"Why my son, Walt?" Mary had taken on the hollow expression that warned Walter Toddcaster of an impending explosion.

Despite her deteriorating emotional state, he continued on. He had a job to do, and it was suddenly damn urgent. "There isn't anything in your background—anybody who hates you—either of you?"

Mark shook his head. Mary looked at him. "My husband has strong political ideals."

"What kind of politics?"

"I'm pretty far left," Mark said. "I've lost a couple of jobs because of it."

Walt Toddcaster's only politics was that of the policeman: vote for the guy who protects the police budget and hates crooks. That probably made him conservative. He'd never thought much about it. "What jobs?"

"I'm a history teacher. Most recently I got canned over the flag-burning issue."

"You think people should be allowed to burn flags?"

"Essentially, yes. But does that make my son a target for kidnapping?"

"It might." Mark bowed his head. Walter realized how harsh his statement sounded, but he did not like the kind of causes he suspected this man supported. Neary was the sort of misguided soul who wanted to put the cops behind bars and let the criminals run the streets. "You make a public stink? Get in the papers, maybe?"

"I'm just a high school teacher. Stories about me don't show up in the paper. When I get fired, nobody notices."

"Now, Mark, that's not quite true. The ACLU—"

"Got me reinstated with back pay. And so they changed the master plan and eliminated the position altogether."

"None of this got in the papers?"

"Not a word."

"We don't know why a given perpetrator picks a given kid. There've been studies, but most of them conclude it's just random. He picked a boy he found attractive. Your boy."

Sally, who had been flipping endlessly through the channels on TV, turned back to KKNX and put the set on mute. "I'm going out for Kentucky Fried Chicken," she said. "I'll bring back a bucket."

A moment after she went out the front door Mary leapt up and ran after her. "Sally! Sally, no!" She grabbed her daughter, clung to her. "Don't go out there!"

"We have to eat, Mother! You didn't touch the sandwiches I made."

"They're still here—"

"I threw them out. They got dry. Momma, I'm not gonna have anything happen to me walking two blocks. It's still light out."

Mary strode across the porch. "I'll go," she said as she headed for the garage. "Walt can move his car."

"Mom, there's no need!"

Mary did not answer. Walt hurried out and pulled his car to the front of the house. He watched Mary back down the drive, turn into the street and drive slowly off. She really ought to be using her headlights. If he'd been out on patrol, he would have given her a warning for no lights after sunset.

Mark and Sally were standing together on the porch as Walt returned to the house. He hated this part, watching the family suffer. Some of them disintegrated, others did not. It was largely a matter of luck.

"Maybe they'll get it on the seven o'clock news," Sally said.

They were still watching when Mary returned. Walt and Sally ate.

"Twelve-year-old William Neary, son of popular Stevensville High School teacher Mark Neary, disappeared from his home early this morning. Police are saying that he was abducted by a stranger who entered the house while the family was sleeping. Full details at ten."

Mark felt his face grow hot. He was hardly popular. The kids barely knew him, he was so new here.

The next moment the phone rang. It was Tom Benton, Stevensville principal. "Mark, Jesus Christ—"

What did he say? "He's gone, Tom." It was so hard to talk about it. To say that, to say "He's gone," it was like heaping coals on your own head.

"You take all the time you need, Mark. Forget that makeup class you were going to do. I don't want to see you."

The instant Mark put down the phone it rang again. This time it was one of Billy's friends, Jerry Edwards. Jerry's voice was hushed. The Edwards family had already been questioned both by Mark and by Walt Toddcaster. "Mr. Neary, we just heard it on TV. Billy—"

The boy's father came on. "If there's anything we can do, buddy. Any damn thing."

As Mark put down the phone the doorbell rang. Sally followed him to the door. A man in a camouflage jacket stood there. For a brief, hopeful moment Mark thought, they all thought—

"Look, we never met. I live two doors down. I want you to know, if there's anything I can do to help—"

"Thank you," Mark said. "But the police are doing all they can."

Walt came to the door. "Wait a minute. There's lots your neighbors can do to help." He pushed his way in front of the family. "Come on in, Mr.—"

"Gerrard. Mike Gerrard. I manage the Walmart over at the mall."

"The Nearys are going to have a poster printed with Billy's picture on it. You could put some up where you work. And they need people to cover the phone when they can't do it themselves." He took Mike Gerrard aside. "They need friends, Mr. Gerrard."

"Hell, yes," Gerrard said. He looked to Mark like somebody from another planet, huge and strong, with tiny, quick eyes. And Mark thought, 'What if he's the man who took my boy.' He forced himself to dismiss the thought.

The sudden outburst of concern was making it all so terribly real. Mark felt physically weighted down, as if somebody had loaded his shoulders with chains. He smiled though, gamely trying to keep going. He had to keep going. Billy needed him. He needed Dad's strength and intelligence and bravery, the things he'd always believed in.

Mark felt like a scrap of nothing.

The phone rang again. This time it was one of Mary's friends. "Keep the calls brief," Walt said.

Mark had just hung up when a car stopped out front. Two men got out, young men wearing neat suits. The family knew at once that the FBI had arrived. The men hurried up to the porch, passing through the little knot of neighbors that was gathering on the sidewalk.

The porch was shadowy and Mark turned on the light. The young men introduced themselves. They came into the house. Realizing that his presence was no longer needed, Mike Gerrard went out to the sidewalk and began conferring in an intense undertone with other neighbors who had gathered there.

The two young men were full of crisp confidence. But they wanted to be taken down the same road that Walt had traveled, the painful road through every corner of Billy's young life.

There were forms to fill out and work to be done. A truck appeared, containing a laboratory team from Des Moines. Suddenly the house was full of people, pictures were being made, fingerprints being taken, steps and couches and every inch of Billy's room vacuumed.

One of the FBI agents, a redhead named Franklin Young, showed Sally and Mark a form. "This is the National Crime Information Center Missing Person Report," he said. "We're going to fill it out together, then it's going to be faxed to Washington."

Young filled out part of the form himself. "I'm going to list Billy as believed endangered in the message key. That doesn't mean we know something you don't. It's policy for any stranger abduction of a juvenile. Also, it'll give the case highest priority."

Once again Mary and Mark addressed themselves to the details of their son's life. As she worked Mary felt a kind of fury building in her. She had a brief, bloody fantasy of seeing the kidnapper's head explode.

Under "Miscellaneous Information" they wrote a description of the kidnapping, the fact that Billy had waked Mark up with the story about the man in the front yard, the detail of the oiled storm door, the missing clothing and bike. The agents were careful and patient; they left nothing out.

When the form was finally completed, Franklin Young took it out to his car. As he drove off to fax it to the National Crime Information Center, one of the police lab workers began fingerprinting the Nearys so that any prints left by a stranger in their house could be identified.

To Mary all this activity made it seem as if the world's bindings had come loose. She could not move, could not think anymore, could not fill out forms, talk, explain, thank, hope.

When the phone rang again Mary very carefully took a throw pillow from the couch and pressed it against her face. She screamed, then, and screamed again. She felt Mark's hand touching her arm, clasping it, heard his voice as if from a long, long distance. "Mary! Mary, for God's sake!"

She went on screaming, louder and louder. She did not try to stop, did not even want to. She thought she might scream on forever.

10.

Billy knew he was in bed, which was fine, but there was this humming sound. Then he was a balloon full of warm air, and the humming was making him vibrate. He was a red balloon, sailing through a clear sky, sailing slowly higher and higher—

What *was* that humming, and that jostling? Once in a while, the bed would definitely jostle.

Light flickered behind his eyes. Everything was all warm and soft. But it wasn't nice, not at all. He felt like something very old and very dead had been poured down his throat. Had he come down with the flu during the night? No, the doctor had said—

The doctor?

My house burned down and I'm in the hospital!

He tried to get up but it didn't work, and he remembered why. A long, long time ago he'd waked up, and he'd discovered that he was held down by straps.

So why do they tie you up in the hospital? Only one reason, you're so bad off they don't want you to move.

He decided to take a quick inventory of himself, using Dad's self-examination technique for when you got hurt and there was nobody around. "Your attention is like the beam of a flashlight, Billy, and you can move it through your body. You point it at your left foot, then your right. Left hand, right hand. Legs, arms, torso, head."

He felt like he was in one piece, but there was this fuzziness that was strange, and he was definitely sick. What was that, "something, something and palely loitering," from the Shelley poem—or was it Keats? Kelley and Sheets.

He should have won poetry reading at the Speech Fair. Instead, What's-her-name Pugh had won with "My Last Duchess." His poem was "La Belle Dame Sans Merci." The beautiful lady without mercy. Yeah. Every beautiful lady he knew was like that. Amanda wanted football, not poetry. "La Belle Dame . . ." Alone and palely loitering.

And humming. The humming went on and on, rising and falling, and with it that slight jostling. Off in the distance, somebody was playing opera. The humming twisted and turned, merging with the music.

Why in the world was he strapped to his bed? Surely not even a children's ward did that. Maybe—

"Am I still in the ambulance?"

Distantly a voice: "Yes, son. Go to sleep."

Still in the ambulance . . . but then where was it going? Stevensville Central Hospital was on Route 19, wasn't it? Yes. That wasn't but a few minutes from the house. He wasn't sure how long he'd been in this ambulance, but it was certainly longer than five or ten minutes.

He felt a tiny, cold hand on his cheek. Very tiny, very cold. He shuddered and the feeling left him. No hand. At least, not a real one.

Maybe this was all a great big nightmare.

Billy's voice was so melodic, it made Barton's heart ache just to hear it. But its presence was alarming. He mustn't wake up this soon—especially not in the middle of Denver.

Barton himself had been awake for over twenty hours. Along with the highway, the hours swept away behind him in a quivering, hypnotic line. It was now six-thirty in the evening, and he had been driving for fourteen hours and thirty minutes. He had pushed hard, knowing that a confrontation with the boy was inevitable, and that it was going to happen on the road.

He had it all planned, a tender, painful moment. "Billy," he would say, "I will be more to you than your mother and father ever could be. You need me but you don't know it now. You will come to love me as I love you, with a very special love."

90

The one thing he believed in totally was his love. Nothing so pure, so noble, could be wrong.

Billy would panic and flutter against the straps, and he would cry. Barton would hold him, maybe kiss his cheek, there was nothing inappropriate about that, speak sweetly to him: "We will have a beautiful life together, you will come to love me as I love you . . ." Those words, so incredible, said to his perfect beauty: I love you.

A man before beauty, his head bowed, fighting the urgency to kneel, to adore that which God has made in the image of His faultless self.

"I give you my heart and soul, Billy."

He listened to the hissing of the tires. He whispered, "I give you my soul."

The scanner burped, a trooper calling in position from somewhere in the mountains. It sounded again, a trouble report on the Denver police frequency.

He heard police talking. Then the humming grew and changed, became a whining and got higher. Was that the siren? No, there was no siren. This ambulance didn't have a siren.

A fire . . . there'd been a fire . . . and he was hurt.

The bread maker! It had been responsible for the fire! He knew it, the thing ran so hot! They never should have bought it.

He flew to full wakefulness. "What happened to my mom and dad?"

"Your parents are fine, son! Everybody's just fine. You suffered a little smoke inhalation, that's all."

God help him, he was driving down a crowded freeway in the middle of one of the biggest cities in the United States and Billy was waking up. This was supposed to happen later, back in the mountains where there were plenty of side roads and nothing but the wind to hear his screams. There Barton could reach out to him, could communicate, soothe and offer himself as father, friend and slave.

Here all he could do was clench the steering wheel and hope the child stayed reasonable.

* * *

Billy took experimental breaths, in and out, in and out. There was nothing wrong with his lungs. He felt sick, not hurt. So why in the world had he spent hours in this ambulance? What was going on here?

"Let me go home! I'm fine!" He had to go to the bathroom at once. "I have to use the john. I have to right now!"

Billy was going to realize any second what was happening. Then he would start screaming and struggling, and oh dear God, hadn't he loosened the straps to make sure Billy could breathe? Hadn't he? Yes . . . back in Ogallala . . . loosened the strap around the chest because the child's breathing seemed labored.

He might get free!

Barton began maneuvering through the traffic, taking a few risks. This was getting dreadfully ugly. A few more miles and it would have been different. Even out of the boy's pain Barton could create love, he knew he could. But not now, not under these impossible conditions.

He loathed traffic!

Why didn't the driver say anything except just "go to sleep, go to sleep"? Why didn't he explain? And what about that doctor? Hadn't there been a doctor back here with him, who'd given him a shot . . .

Late last night somebody got him out of his bed, he remembered that. Yes, they put a rag over his face, he thought it was Sally giving him a hard time. Then he got all numb . . . then there was this humming.

Again he tried to get up. It made sense for an ambulance bed to have straps, but not the little ones that held down his wrists and ankles. They weren't just meant to keep him from falling out of bed, not only that. He was *really* strapped in this thing.

"Let me up!"

Still no answer. It would help a lot if he could see something. He took a deep breath and blew, trying to get the cover off his face. Earlier he'd tried it, he remembered. But the effort was vague, like a barely recalled nightmare. Hadn't he struggled and fought and almost gotten out? Maybe, or maybe he'd just dreamed it.

No, his wrist still hurt where he'd pulled it out of the strap. So that part was real.

What were these *straps* all about, anyway?

"Will somebody tell me what's going on here!"

Oh, God. He's fully conscious and he's starting to understand and I am just passing the Arvada exit.

At least the towers of the city were now behind him and the traffic was a little thinner. Could people hear somebody screaming from inside a van? If they drove alongside with their windows open, maybe so. He hadn't counted on this and now he wasn't sure of anything except that he was dog-dead tired and beginning to simply give out just when he needed every bit of what was strongest and best in him.

Maybe he had to take action, and maybe it was going to be not the best thing for Billy. Maybe he had to hit him with a real drug. For an extreme emergency there was some two-percent solution. Not a lot, but enough to send Billy flying for a few hours.

Morphine wasn't like those other drugs; morphine worked. Billy would go as high as a kite.

No. Fathers did not give morphine to their sons.

But there was no time to think about it now.

Billy raised his chest as high as it would go, struggling against the straps. He pushed until he couldn't breathe, and pushed still harder—until at last he stopped, gasping, his head pounding with the first real headache he had ever felt in his life.

"Daddy! Daddy!"

He twisted his arms, tried to break his legs loose. The chest strap had give in it, but the others were totally tight. There was no way out. Finally he lay still and tried to think it out. He'd gone to bed last night, everything normal. He'd had his day, spent time at the mall, played Space Harrier and Afterburner with the guys. Then a queer had played RPM with him and after that he'd taken off. He'd worked on his Amiga. Later he'd gotten the bird to reply to him. They'd talked in the moonlight.

At some point he'd seen a man in the front yard. He told Dad, but there was nothing there when they looked. But no, that couldn't be. This was an ambulance, he was hurt. But he didn't feel hurt, and why these straps?

If this *wasn't* an ambulance, if he *wasn't* hurt, then—

A sudden realization made him slam himself against the straps. He knew who'd been in the front yard. 'It's the weirdo who was at the mall!'

Terror descended.

"Help, oh, help me! Somebody help!" But there was nobody—except *him.* Billy screamed. It was not the fearsome noise he had expected, but the fragile piping of a boy, as shrill as the sound of a mouse being tortured by a cruel child.

The noise was like fire. It radiated absolute human terror. Nobody who heard a sound like that could mistake it for anything other than what it was. They would know for certain that there was a child in this van, and that child was desperate.

The windows were all closed but the traffic had slowed down again and there were cars both to the left and the right.

People must hear it. God, yes! If only he'd put the gag back when he'd knocked Billy out. But he couldn't do that now, there was nowhere to stop.

Then it occurred to him to drown out the screaming with music. A fast hand jammed a new tape into the cassette player and turned the volume up to full. It was Lily Pons, one of his treasures, singing "Un Bel Dí" from *Madama,* oh God, and the moon rode low on the horizon and the traffic moved in clotted anguish on the hard-lit road, and Billy screamed as a soul must scream when death first sunders it from the world.

His head bobbed, his teeth clattered and tore as he gnawed at the quilt that obscured his vision. The thought of that man up there driving made a thick, nasty taste rise in his throat.

Opera was blaring out of the radio and streams of memory poured up from deep within Billy's soul, recalling when last year his dad had taken him all the way to Cleveland to see *Carmen* and he'd loved that trip so much, it had been such a happy, happy time. After the opera they'd bought a ton of

Kentucky Fried Chicken and eaten it all in their motel room.

He touched this memory like a thread in a maze and then it was gone and he was back here strapped to this cot. He lay jerking his head hopelessly, chewing at the quilt that covered his face. Warmth spread around his thighs and legs. At first it scared him, then he realized what it was and felt ferocious delight.

He was glad he had wet the bed, and he realized that he could do much worse. In all of his life he had never shat a bed. But he did it now and it seemed awful and also gloriously savage and effective. The stink of it soon filled the close atmosphere under the quilt, and to his pleasure he found that he could also vomit.

The aria wailing out of the radio seemed to deepen and change, becoming something else: a mother singing as if to her child while he slips into dream.

Barton was trying to deal with his map, looking for some back road, some escape from the steel lights of the freeway. Behind him the boy lurched and twisted, shaking the whole van. A horrible stench filled the air: Billy had defecated. Anger flashed through Barton. This was an unneeded and undeserved complication.

If Barton Royal had made a mistake like that he would have been thoroughly dealt with.

He suddenly heard retching, liquescent heaves. The boy had vomited. The odor was so thick it greased his mouth with its foulness. Lily Pons sang on. "Sempre Libera," from *La Traviata* filled the cab. Then the map got away from him and he swerved and there was a dry thump and another car was honking its horn. He'd hit them, God help him. It was a Taurus, green, full of people. It pulled in front of him, and wouldn't you know there was now a convenient shoulder. He had to stop; they could get his license number, description of the van.

Billy heard a grinding thud, felt the car waver a little. Then it began to slow, finally to stop.

Maybe they'd stopped at a gas station. But no, there'd been that thump. Flat tire? No, Dad had plenty of flats and they

95

caused an unmistakable flapping sound. So OK, it was an accident, but not a bad one.

The man addressed him in his sweet and evil voice. "Please, Billy, I know what you think, that I'm a monster. But I am not a monster. Very far from it! I have such hope for you. Yes, hope! You think you know what's happening, but you don't. Just give me a chance. One chance is all I ask."

Billy heard him leave the van. How do you escape if you're all tied up? Billy thought of Indiana Jones. How would he do it? Break the straps, but they were too strong! What would James Bond do? He had all that high-tech stuff.

Billy had nothing. He told people he was a black belt, but the truth was he couldn't even get out of Jerry's headlocks. A kid couldn't get away from a grown man.

About all a kid could do was scream.

The love in Barton's heart welled up until he was almost weeping. Poor little Billy. It was so natural for him to be afraid. Poor little fella. He felt, though, that he had *really* communicated just now. Surely Billy had heard the warmth and decency in his voice and that was going to calm him down, get them both through this first great crisis.

The people in the other car looked like zombies looming out into the yellow sodium vapor lights. Barton opened his door, carefully leaving his engine running. As he closed the door he checked to be absolutely certain it had remained unlocked.

The driver of the Taurus came around to the back of his car. Barton's heart sank. He could see damage—the taillight was smashed, the bumper was buckled, and there was a gash in the fender. His own fender had only a smear of green paint on it.

"What're you gonna do about it, asshole?" The driver was tremendous, wearing an ancient Doors T-shirt, stinking of cigars and beer.

"I'll pay."

From the van there came a terrible shriek. Barton battled the instinct to run for it. The others turned slowly, perhaps drunkenly, absorbing the impact of the sound.

"My child must be having a nightmare," Barton breathed.

"That sounds weird, man."

Barton returned to the van. *The two-percent solution, the two-percent solution, find it, find it!* He pulled the little bottle out of the glove compartment, opened his needle case—and heard the car door click.

The other driver was there, his yellow eyes glaring. He reached in and took Barton's keys. The van shuddered to silence. "After we work out our problem you get 'em back."

"Help me, I'm being kidnapped! Help me!"

The man paused, looked toward the back of the van.

"Please, he's evil, he's a monster!"

"No, no son," Barton said, speaking gently, insistently. He drew solution into the syringe and crawled into the back of the stench-choked van.

Why didn't the other man listen? He was out there, Billy knew it. So why didn't he *listen?* "Call the police! Help! Help!"

"What's goin' on in there?" At last!

"He's having a nightmare!"

"No! He's a kidnapper! He's killing me!" The sound of his own voice terrified him, and a scream burst out of him. It was involuntary and it confused him; he had not known that instinct had a voice. He surged against the straps like a fish on a line, strong and vital and seeking to be free.

Barton struggled with the needle, trying desperately to evacuate air bubbles, then to find a bit of white skin that was motionless enough to inject. He lifted the quilt and then with his free hand pulled down Billy's pajamas. The skin was like milk, it stopped Barton's heart.

Billy's shrieks were unlike anything Barton had ever heard before. They were so high and yet so amazingly fierce, the screams of a young tiger.

"What's the matter with that kid, man, you gotta give him a shot?"

"Epilepsy! And nightmares!"

A gasp, crackling, shuddering, then a bubbling whisper: "Police!"

"Yeah, son, I'll do that. I'll call the police."

"No! He'll be fine! This shot'll do it, you'll see."

"No, man, let the paramedics give the shots. Stop that, man."

Barton choked back his own gorge, striving to maintain control. Sparks were dancing in his eyes. Deep breaths, one, two, come on, search the pale skin and there, just where the thigh was strapped down, he could hold the leg, prick the shining skin.

Whispering started in Billy's mind. Only he couldn't quite understand the words. Ripples were spreading, dying, the sun was setting inside his mind.

No! You have to scream! "Please. I—am—being—kidnapped! Get the police!"

Suddenly the quilt fell away and Billy could see. He was in the back of a van, and there was a bloated, ugly troll squatting beside him. His eyes were bulging, sweat was streaming down his face, his nose was full of pores. In his white, fat hand there was a syringe.

"He was in the mall! I remember him, he was in the mall!"

"Hey, man, that kid's in real trouble!"

"He's merely upset!"

"I'm gonna call the police."

Billy saw, suddenly, that the troll was wearing a blue shirt, and this seemed extremely important. "Officer, he was wearing a blue polo shirt. And he was crying. Yes, crying. I was crying, too."

Barton drew back, watching Billy's head shake from side to side more and more slowly, watching the tautness go out of the straps, the fists unclench and the eyes roll. Barton backed out of the van, climbed down and stood before the drunk, shaken man from the Taurus.

"See, he's gonna be OK."

"Jesus H. Christ, man, you sure?"

"Oh, yeah. It often happens like this. Then we give him his shot and he's OK."

"Look, man, if it's all right with you, I think we oughta call a cop anyway."

"No. I haven't got time. I want to get my little boy home. He's sick, as you saw."

"You got a doctor, man?"

"Yes! Sure! Dr. Ledbetter. A fine doctor. He's why my son's not in a home. Wonderful doctor!"

"Listen, I got five hundred dollars damage to my car. I know, sounds like a lot but these damn bumpers cost on these cars. Repairs are high. So I think we oughta get a cop. Otherwise, you kiss the insurance goodbye. And somebody oughta take a look at that kid. Besides you, if you get my drift."

"I do and I'm not sure I like it—"

The driver called to one of his companions. "Mikey, get the Highway Patrol on the car phone. This guy's got somethin' funny workin' back here." He turned to Barton. "You stink, and your van stinks. It smells like you got an open sewer in there." He peered into the van. "That's just a little boy."

"He's had an epileptic seizure. He'll be fine. Now if you'll let me—" Barton's tongue scraped the roof of his mouth, making a sound in his head like the scaling of a fish. He drew all his cash out of his pocket.

"Hey, man, that's money."

"Yeah, look, I'll give you the five hundred. That'll cover your damage and what say we just let it go?"

"That kid—"

"My son is fine! I don't want him frightened by the police. He's sleeping now, and if he's not bothered he'll sleep the rest of the night. When he wakes up, he won't even remember this happened."

"You got five hundred there?"

"Are we bargaining? Here." Barton counted out the bills. "You got it."

"That makes me feel better, man. I feel like getting back in my car now."

The traffic, the lights, the noise, all became a dream, frightful, glaring, but a dream and in the dream Barton was released. He moved to the front of the van. The other driver had put his key back, and he turned it.

Music burst forth, Lily Pons so loud she sounded like a banshee.

He jabbed at the button and killed the cassette player. Sudden silence, only the hiss of traffic behind the closed window of the van. He started the engine. As he pulled into the traffic he sang, "Glory, glo-ry," and imagined that an angel had taken him and his beloved burden under a golden wing.

Barton and Billy, alone at last.

11.

The first night in hell: red dreams.

In Mary's dream she was at a party. It was not a fun party, and not a good dream. There was a woman there she was afraid might be her mother even though her mother was dead. No matter what she did, Mary could never get this woman to face her. The woman always had her back turned. She was wearing a green silk dress just like Mother's. She was terrifying.

Mary's dream-self knew these things: that a child's soul is as fragile as dew, and souls can be murdered.

Then, in her dream, it was a day in October, a day as gray as old metal, a day worthy only to be thrown away. It was October 12, 1987. *That* day.

Dad died of heart disease in March of 1976, just a few days before his seventy-fifth birthday. Now Mother had also reached seventy-five, with sunken cheeks and drool and a bobbing head. Her eyes were as if sheened with mineral deposits.

She once had said, "My dear, what's happened to your chest? You're concave." Mary had been bending because of a tennis accident.

"Mother, please. Flat-chested I can handle. But if a woman is concave, she might as well give up."

Mother had stared back as if to say, "So, give up." Instead she said, "Mark is giving up in a way, isn't he?" And yes, it was true, she had seen it. They both knew a secret, that any life—all lives—must be constantly healed by soaking torrents of love. We are as dependent upon such healing as the plants in the fields are upon rain.

A thousand years ago Dad had been very successful, a Chevy dealer in Morristown, New Jersey. *The* Chevy dealer. They'd had a maroon Chevy, a blue Chevy, a tan Chevy. They'd had radio ads. "Give the Morristown Chevy toot." So whenever they saw another Chevy on the road, they dutifully tooted. Mary would reach over and hit the horn with her fist.

The woman in the green dress whispered, "It was your fault, dear. You and that hopeless husband of yours. No burglar alarm. Not even a lock on the door! Now look!"

Two tall men were carrying a little boy through a thick, ugly woods. One carried him by the shoulders. The other went comically along with Billy's legs in his hands like the handles of a wheelbarrow. Billy was naked.

If his abductors did not kill him and he could not escape, he would eventually surrender and start trying to make something of his new life. Kids were like that, they adjusted, made do with the present.

If only she'd explained more to him about the dangers of abduction. But how did you do that and preserve the joy of childhood?

Even if a miracle happened and Billy got back home, his childhood would be shattered.

His voice came in her dream, clear and fast and high: "Momma, will you bathe me tonight?" She had done it until he was seven. It was like a sacred act, so much fun with the rubber ducky song playing and the wonderful toy ferryboat from Germany full of cars and the little frogman who really swam, and they made storms in the tub, and the ferryboat would toss and she would go *cra-a-ack* and *bo-o-om* for the thunder and hit the water with her fist where the lightning struck.

"My dear daughter, you might as well have given that child away. Given him away!"

"We were asleep! We didn't know!"

In her dream the two men stopped. She could smell the night flowers, hear the roaring of the cicadas, see moonlight dappling a glade. In that dappled glade the two men sat speaking in low tones. Billy was before them on the ground, trussed like a pig, not even struggling anymore. They took no notice. She floated above them, and saw that they were eating candy bars.

She saw this with total clarity. One man was eating a Hershey bar with almonds, the other a Clark bar. The sounds of their eating involved crunching and sticky slurps and the crackle of candy wrappers. There were tears on Billy's face and she wanted to wipe them but she could not. Her mother said, "You never can, dear. Not in the end."

Then Mary was wide awake and sitting up.

For a long time Sally had watched the night. She sat on her bed and put her elbows on the windowsill with her chin in her cupped hands. In her memory she heard her brother playing in his room, talking to himself under the covers. What was he saying? If you went anywhere near he got quiet.

At eleven-thirty the sound of taps came faintly on the wind, all the way from Fort Stevens down south of town. In her mind she drifted across the oceanic prairies, and farther south to the rolling hills of Kentucky, drifting in the cloud-choked sky, past clouds of American spirit and American dream, and also her own dreams, when a boy would at last notice her and when she would go hand in hand with him and they would laugh together and he would turn to her and lift her chin with his forefinger and thumb and say, "May I kiss you," and she would open her lips a little.

They played taps at midnight, not eleven-thirty. And she couldn't possibly hear it this far away, no matter how the wind was blowing.

A dog or a coon humped across the front yard.

"Where are you, Billy," she said. "You might be dead, brother. You might know the secret. Do you know it, have you died? And did you go to God, or turn into a star, or are you just rotting there in a culvert where he left you?"

She started to think about how a man would do it with a boy, but then she couldn't.

Mark Neary listened to the night around him, the distant sound of a train heading west, far above a jet full of sleeping people. A car whispered down the street and he found himself tensing to its sound. But it went on past.

Beside him his wife of sixteen years sighed in the bed. His

great anguish had paradoxically intensified his interest in the familiar mystery of her body, as if the weight of his suffering drove him to seek the old refuge of the flesh.

How dare he—his child was being raped, brutalized, tortured. He knew it with the certainty natural to his careful mind. The bright, happy, vital child who had been taken from this house was either dead or being destroyed right this second.

Billy was one of those children who were so perfect that it seemed impossible that tragedy could ever reach them.

He'd been so damn complacent. 'Not to do anything about the man in the yard—may God strike me down!'

He imagined excited hands fumbling against his son's naked skin. Then they were parting Billy's naked legs and his father was cringing in agony.

Then the wind swept up from the south bearing its marvelous freight of prairie smells, the aster and the grass and the mystic perfume of the corn.

His son's body lay glowing in the moonlight.

His son's body lay crumpled beneath a tree.

His son's body floated pale in the slow waters of the Pomander River, surfacing from time to time like an exhausted fish.

His son's body lay beneath the pulsating flesh of a huge human maggot, and his eyes were wrinkled shut and his hands were purple they were tied so tight.

"I am praying now," Mark whispered into the perfumed air. "God help my boy."

He turned over and, as he had a dozen times before, placed his face in his pillow. Then he wept in the breeze, in the moonlight, in the sweet Iowa night. A bird sang alone.

12.

It wasn't like waking up, it was sudden and cruel; this was the first time Billy had ever been pulled to awareness by pain. His body jerked against the straps, an involuntary spasm. Then his eyes opened. Even as it left him, his young mind clung to the blackness. For a last blessed instant he was nowhere, he was nobody.

Then he felt the inevitable humming of the van, the humming and the jostling. The air was sweet, scented with pine. The odor penetrated deep into Billy's soul, bringing dense memories.

The kitchen was gold with afternoon light, and there was his apple and glass of milk on the counter, and the air smells piney because Momma has just mopped the floor.

When he reached for the apple the illusion shattered. He knew where he was and who he was with and so he fought, kicking, jerking his arms, shaking his head as the van bored on, deep into the night.

From the front a woman's voice sang, very high:

> *"You are my sunshine, my only sunshine*
> *You make me happy when skies are gray . . ."*

The voice piped and wavered, never quite on note or key. When it went high Billy went with it up the mountains. Then it broke and down they fell, sailing through black air.

As they fell Billy began to become consciously aware of the pain that had awakened him. Memory and dream slipped away

105

and he was left with only the truth: he was thirsty, and it was a torment beyond belief.

Every part of him, his belly, his arms and legs, even his skin suffered for water. His mouth felt like the dentist had jammed it solid with cotton logs. The humming of the van became the muttering of a brook and he saw water bubbling over stones, saw the thick green depths of the Pomander River, tasted water pouring from the faucet under the oak tree in the front yard.

He had stood there. From there *he* had watched. And now *he* drove the van. Even though Billy's head was no longer buried under covers, he could not see *him*, not more than a glimpse and that only if he arched his neck back as far as possible.

Then *he* was a dark hunched bulk behind the wheel.

"I'm thirsty!"

The singing stopped but the van hummed on. Being ignored made Billy's cheeks burn. He wanted to somehow get to that ugly man and hit him until his head broke open like a cantaloupe. "I'm thirsty," he repeated. He tried to sound angry, but he could barely whisper.

The figure remained hunched over the wheel and the van hummed on. Billy's vision wavered. Tears came.

He gazed through his anguish at the shadowy night, the tops of pine trees hurrying past, the stars. It was as if he was at the bottom of a deep, deep hole and he could just barely see the sky way up there. 'The stars,' he thought, 'we used to count them in those days, lying in the front yard and we would talk about all the people in all the worlds so far away.'

Then he thought, 'This is how I will escape. I will turn the straps into molten leather by making my wrists and ankles hotter and hotter like that guru could do—make himself hotter or colder, it said so in the paper—and then I will get him by the throat.' He concentrated on his wrists, imagining them getting hot, imagining that the leather was crackling, creaking, getting weaker.

Of course nothing happened. But couldn't people bend spoons with their minds, either . . . or was that possible in California? He imagined the straps getting hot and weak, hot and weak.

106

They *were* getting looser, too, at least a little. Hotter and hotter, wrists and ankles, and he could smell it now, the stink of the burning leather. Yes, looser by inches, by degrees, looser and looser . . .

With a soft tearing sound his right ankle became free. A moment later his left wrist was out and he was pulling, fumbling, working until at last he was completely free.

The van still hummed, the stars still followed them, the trees still tumbled past. Billy sat up. He turned his head and there just two feet away was the ghoul, dark and hunched, singing through his nose.

To himself Billy said, 'Your muscles are steel, your blood is molten uranium, your bones are hot iron.' He moved as precisely and quietly as a spider. He put his hands around the thick neck of his tormentor, holding them just an inch from the shaking flesh. Then he throttled the life out of *him.*

Something began to happen. Billy felt it first as a change in the humming. Then came the rattling of gravel as the van left the highway. As it moved along a dirt road the tires rumbled. The slower the van went the faster Billy's heart beat.

Billy realized that he was still strapped to the bed, still trapped, still helpless. He tossed his head from side to side, moaning with disappointment. It had been so real!

The engine went off and the van grew silent. Billy listened, his limbs taut against his bonds, his face tickling with tears.

He groaned aloud, a sound that sank into a sob. "Now, now," came a low voice. It had a rattle in it, and a curious lilt as well. If a man and a woman were both talking at exactly the same time, this was how it would sound.

Billy flew into a wild panic. The tighter the straps held him the harder he struggled.

"Billy, relax, son, take it easy. Nobody's going to hurt you." The voice rose as it might when you were comforting a dog: "It's OK, Fido, it's OK, there, there boy. Easy . . ."

"I hate you! I hate you!" He spat but there was no spit, so all that came was a fluffy rasp.

"Son, I have a nice big thermos of Evian water. Have you ever had Evian water? It's cool and clear and it's just as sweet as a fresh mountain stream."

When the man opened the thermos, Billy could smell the water. He'd never noticed before that water had a smell. "Please," he said. He heard the begging in his own voice and wished he could sound stronger, but it was no use. He couldn't fight, he couldn't get away. He was too little and this man was too big and he was so far from home and he didn't know where he was or anything!

The man put his hand behind Billy's head and lifted it, and brushed the edge of the thermos against his lips. The water stung where it touched his cracked mouth, but it tasted so good, so cool, so rich, a million times better even than it had smelled.

He got two big gulps before it was snatched away. "Go slow, Billy, you don't want it to come back up."

That reminded Billy of what he had done, soiled the sheets. That was all gone now, there was nothing left but the kitchen-floor smell of pine. The man had cleaned him off while he slept. That must be why his pajama bottoms were gone. He shuddered.

The water came back and he drank again. This time he got more and it flowed down his throat, bringing with it waves of relief. His head lay against the man's strong hand and he drank and drank.

As he drank he looked at the man's face. It was pale and soft, with cheeks that were too smooth. He looked like he was made of Silly Putty, like if you touched him you would leave a fingerprint. His eyes darted to the window every time a car went past.

He took the thermos away. Then he smiled and when he did everything changed. Crinkles appeared around his nasty eyes, and they became gay and full of laughter. His lips spread and his teeth appeared, smooth and white.

His smile was so unexpected and so bright that Billy uttered a burst of laughter. "So," the man said in his eerie voice, "we aren't all frowns, are we, Billy?"

"How do you know my name?"

"I know a great deal about you." He reached a hand out, hesitated for a moment, then touched Billy's arm. Despite his determination to hate this man, and his conviction of terrible danger, Billy felt relieved.

He was hungry for orientation. "What time is it?"

"Eleven."

Eleven at night. Billy thought about that. "I have to go to the bathroom."

"Not in the bed, please, Billy." The voice pleaded, and Billy had the curious impression that this man was a sort of servant, almost a slave, or wanted to be. Billy realized that he could get the man to do what he wanted, like Uncle Hank had been when Billy was little, always carrying him on his back, buying him toys and candy . . . at least until he married Kate and had Matt.

Mom had said, "My brother loves kids." She explained that certain people were able to stay a child inside even after they grew up. Uncle Hank was such a person.

The man's hand was massaging Billy's upper arm, and Billy tried to move away. "I won't hurt you," the man said. "I've got to work on your circulation."

"I have to go really bad."

"I'll let you up. But you'll have to go on the roadside. Can you do that?"

"There are cars."

"We'll walk a ways into the woods. We're in a thick forest."

Instantly Billy decided he would run off into the forest.

When his wrists were freed his hands started to tingle. Then the same thing happened to his ankles. The man had to help him sit up, and he felt very dizzy and funny, like the van was tumbling slowly over and over. The man crouched before him, rubbing his feet and his hands, rubbing and slapping.

Billy watched his bald spot. He wished he had a gun embedded between his eyes and he could fire it right into that spot and then the man would collapse like a bunch of rags. Then Billy would get out of the van and stand by the roadside until a car stopped, and he would tell them to take him to the nearest phone. But he had no gun, he had nothing. He thought of kicking the man, but it would do no more than make him mad, and that would obviously be a mistake.

When the man looked up Billy was confused by the expression, which was of an intensity quite beyond his experience. The man moved back until he was sitting on the cot opposite. He smiled again, mischievously, and Billy thought of when he used to babysit Matt and the little boy had done something that he knew Billy would fuss at him about. Suddenly the man reached out. Billy flinched, but then the man's fingers were touching his cheek. They were warm and soft and thick, and Billy became aware that the man was fat. "It's not going to be bad," the man said. "Believe me, Billy, I promise you with all my heart and soul."

"I want to go to the bathroom."

"All right! We'll go right now." The man slid open the side of the van, which was at once flooded with crisp night air. It was startlingly cool, and Billy began to shiver. "I don't have any pants."

"You won't need them, it's dark."

"I can't go outside without pants. And I don't have shoes. I can't walk in the woods without shoes."

"Don't be such a baby!" There was a weird, whining harshness there that made Billy even more scared.

"Don't I have any clothes?"

"Of course you have clothes! Now move!"

The tone made Billy scurry straight out of the van. The man took his wrist and without a word led him in among the trees.

Instantly the world changed. Billy was not often in woods this deep. They belonged to fairy tales, the woods dark and deep . . .

They were darker than Billy had thought possible, so dark that he couldn't see anything except the man's small flashlight, a wavering pool of yellow that occasionally revealed a huge trunk.

He heard the calls of forest birds, soft and scary.

A car passed the van. When it slowed the man stiffened and his hand went more tightly around Billy's arm. "It hurts," Billy said, pulling his shoulder away.

The car went on. "I'm sorry," the man said. He loosened his grip. The ground was covered with pine needles and also very steep and it cut into Billy's bare feet. After another couple of minutes the man stopped. "Here," he said.

Billy's mind had focused to a single idea. He was like a bird being held outside of its cage, waiting for the instant that its owner's mind would stray. "I can't do it if you're here."

"I can disappear just like this." The man turned off his flashlight. Now the darkness was so perfect that it seemed to Billy almost to have a life of its own. A feeling of complete helplessness overcame him. He thought he had stifled the sob of despair that built in his chest, but the man's hand touched his shoulder. "It's OK, Billy," the man said. Then, as if the dark might somehow sanctify his words, he added something incredibly icky. "I love you so darn much, son."

That encouraged Billy to overcome his fear and take a couple of steps away. The man made a small sound in his throat, shuffled. Billy took three giant steps, brushing against a tree. The man's breathing was now noticeably farther off. Billy stepped all the way around the tree.

Behind him the flashlight flickered on, then flashed wildly among the tall trunks, just missing Billy's shoulder. "Christ," the man said.

Billy moved off, trying to remember the locations of the trees he'd glimpsed in the beam of the flashlight.

There was a steep slope, and Billy slid down. Uttering a stifled cry, the man followed him. His body was heavy and he slipped and scraped noisily along. When he was close Billy heard the little sounds he was making, like the way the crows muttered when they landed in the front yard.

Without another thought, throwing his hands out in front of him, Billy hurled himself farther down the slope, fumbling against trees as he went, scrambling around them, going down and down. Behind him the man raised a howl and came plunging after him. His light flickered yellow, a magical eye.

The forest spoke a deep unknown language, murmuring to itself as Billy scrabbled along. He skinned his knee, bruised his shoulder. His hands were before him like a blind man, his feet were stinging from the pine needles. Something flapped away, screaming an angry scream.

Billy became aware of the details of the darkness, its thicker places, the directions where the shadows seemed more open. But the flashlight was far more effective than intuition and night-blind eyes, and the man came very fast. Under his breath he kept making sounds, grunting and furious. They no longer reminded Billy of a crow, but rather of the fearsome noises the tiger had made at the Des Moines Zoo during the class trip: back and forth it had gone in its cage, and its snarls said it wanted you.

Billy had to feel his way, his arms outstretched, his hands spread as if to turn a blow. He went through the whipping trees, grasping, pulling, struggling. They spread their piney sap along his arms, their needles pricked his palms and dug into his feet.

The man plunged down the bank, crashing into trees and gasping when the limbs whipped his face.

Soon Billy could not tell which direction he was going in, whether up or down, falling or climbing. His lungs ached, his nostrils flared, his head pounded. As Billy gained speed the man's clamor was gradually absorbed by another sound, a roar as if of a huge wind. But there wasn't any wind. Closer and closer Billy came to this sound. He no longer dared to look behind him. If the flashlight was right there, he didn't want to know it.

Then the stars filled the sky. Billy stopped, incredulous. Before him was a sky more vast even than that of the prairie night. The stars stood in millions and millions. The roaring filled his ears, and then he understood where he was.

Realizing his predicament he reeled forward, his arms turning round and round. Below him he saw like in a model train layout a cluster of cabins marked by a single light. How far down? A hundred feet, five hundred? All around Billy the loose stony earth was coming alive, whispering and rattling. It tickled beneath his feet as it transported him toward the edge.

Fifty feet to his right a mountain stream threw itself off the cliff. Down and down the water went, pale in the starlight, down into the silent valley. To Billy the stream sounded like the trumpet that calls you to death. Some archangel blows it. Supposedly.

He was falling. The slope was too steep and the soil too loose to hold him. He pressed himself back against the bank. It felt like he was in an elevator, just starting off but speeding up quickly. In another moment he was going to be out in the air, falling to the music of the water. He saw a dog walking lazily across the compound between the cabins.

"Momma," he said. He scrabbled, he grabbed at the loose

dirt, he found that he most desperately did not want to die. He'd had hardly any life yet! He threw back his head and screamed, and the stars wavered in his tears.

As if it was a hook made of cold iron, the man's hand closed around his upper arm. Then his face was there, beside Billy's face. "I love you," he said in a voice loud enough to be heard over the gush of the falls.

How Billy hated to hear that! But the man was strong and he laid himself against the arm and watched the stars disappear as he was dragged back into the cliff-hugging woods.

Roughly, the man pulled Billy up the slope. It took him a long time and a lot of rest stops. He wheezed and cursed under his breath, but never for a second did he release Billy's arm, let alone loosen his grip.

At first Billy was defiant, thinking that he would get away again and this time he would find some tiny path down the face of the cliff, secret since the days of the Indians and the mountain men.

But his shoulder and knee hurt where he had hit them, and his feet were raw and he wanted to be warm again.

The man pulled him along, and at length the dim light in the van's ceiling began to flicker in the trees. "Do you still have to do your business?" the man asked.

"Yes," Billy said.

"Come over here." He pulled him toward the van. "I wasn't planning to use these, but it's your fault." He opened the front door and lifted the passenger seat. Underneath it was a toolbox. Billy sucked in his breath when he saw what looked like a small gun in the man's hand. But it wasn't a gun, it was handcuffs in a leather case. They were neat, just like cops had.

He snapped them on Billy's wrists, clicking them until they were tight. Then he checked them with the flashlight. "OK," he said, "you have three minutes. If you pull anything like that again, you're going to find out that I punish."

Billy tried to walk on his own but could only stagger. His feet hurt so much he had to balance on their sides, bandy-legged. He lifted the front of his pajama shirt and pissed where he stood, watching the stream of urine smoke in the mountain cold.

"Where are we?" he asked as he finished.

"The mountains of the moon, as far as you're concerned. Get in the van."

The man made him lie on the miserable little bed again, and the straps soon replaced the handcuffs. The cot had become so familiar he felt almost like he belonged there.

"This is gonna be tight," the man said, wrapping the thickest of the straps around his chest, "and it's gonna be hell because it is so tight. But I can do worse. I can certainly do worse."

He tightened the strap until Billy was reduced to shallow breaths. "I can't—"

He slapped a strip of wide gray tape over Billy's mouth. "Can't breathe? That's because the chest strap is too tight. You're being punished this way, and it might go on for some little time."

Billy pressed himself as hard against the strap as he could. He couldn't breathe, he was scared to death!

"You'll manage well enough if you relax." The man took his hair in his fist, forced Billy to look at him. "I am going to attend to your feet. I am going to do everything to help you. And you will find that I can be very, very nice. Our life together can be wonderful, Billy. But I want you to understand something."

He brought his face close and it was horrible to see, sweaty, scratched from the pine needles, fat. The eyes were funny, though. You expected really mean eyes. But this guy had the woebegone expression of a big old floppy hound.

"If you keep trying to get away, if you give me a hard time, if you cause me trouble, then I will turn around and go right back to Stevensville, and you know what I will do? I will kill your parents. Did you hear me? I will kill them both and it will be hard and slow. Then I will kill your sister. And you will watch all this. Then I will burn down your house and leave you naked in the middle of nowhere with no parents and no home and no sister. And it will all be *your fault.*"

These words were like fists blasting Billy's face; the shock of them made him as dizzy as real blows would have. He had never dreamed that his mom and dad were in any danger.

He had to be tough, he mustn't cry! 'Now, like the man says, relax. You do things his way, you won't get Mom and Dad and Sally killed. So do things his way, dumbhead!' Now what was

114

it he was going to say to the man? Something, and it had seemed darn important.

The man began working on his feet. He cleaned them with tweezers and cotton as Billy raised his head and looked down his body at the figure with the flashlight and the little blue first-aid kit. There was a smell of alcohol, and then the pain was so great that Billy threw his head back and shrieked behind the gag.

Soon the sting stopped, though. He felt bandages being put on. That was a lot better.

Then he remembered what it was he had to say. Despite the agony, despite his half-suffocated condition and his gag, he started trying to communicate with the man. Again he lifted his head. He made urgent sounds behind the gag. He worked his mouth, stabbed at the tape with his tongue, mustered what little saliva he had to try to float it off.

Finally the man took notice. He crawled up the van and gingerly removed the tape. Billy swallowed, cleared his throat, and met the eyes. The hound-dog expression was gone, replaced by a warm, contented look.

"My mother," Billy murmured. His voice was so thick it sounded like an animal growling. He stopped talking, tried again to get some spit in his mouth. It seemed enormously important that he be understood. "My mother," he repeated with all the clarity he could muster, "always gives me a cup of hot chocolate when I get hurt."

Part Three

THE CUP
OF KINDNESS

13.

The first day she kept wanting to organize yet another search. But they'd already looked everywhere they could, and they had clear evidence of the abduction.

She kept telling herself, 'It really happened. Some total stranger came in here and just took him.' Her basement, her stairs, his bedroom—as the police painstakingly re-created the movements of the intruder these family places came to seem charged with darkness at midday.

On the second day it seemed as if the investigators would never stop poking through her things, lifting chairs, vacuuming, scraping, spreading dirty fingerprint powders. But when they finally did leave she panicked, fearing that they had given up. She had to stifle the impulse to run after them.

On the third day time revealed itself as the true enemy. There remained nothing but the silent phone and the regular tolling of the clock.

Mary told herself to reestablish the routine of the household. She should start by cleaning up the extensive mess left by the fingerprint men. One impulse moved her to throw herself into it, to put on an apron full of pockets and stuff them with Pine Sol and 409 and Windex and start working. She knew how to disappear into housework.

Because it was an escape from worrying about Billy, she feared work as much as she longed for it.

All Monday and most of Tuesday people had come to the house bringing the kind of covered dishes that made Mary think of funerals. Her mother had always taken a casserole over

119

when a friend had died, apparently on the theory that grief whets the appetite but destroys the ability to cook. When Mother herself passed on, her friends brought fleets of casseroles, whole cooploads of roasted chickens, reefs of salad, enough food to feed the mourners for two years.

Now, as evening fell, Mary was coming to recognize what all the activity of the past forty-eight hours concealed. Behind it was complete helplessness.

The last investigator to leave was a forensic surveyor who had made a map of the property and a set of drawings of the interior of the house. Hundreds of pictures were taken, and every means had been used to gather not only fingerprints, but even glove prints and any bit of hair or debris that might be relevant.

Toddcaster had explained that most of this wasn't intended to gain information that would locate Billy, but rather to find evidence that would place the suspect at the scene when he was eventually found.

"What *will* they do to find him?"

"Old-fashioned police work—following up leads, canvassing, trying to pick up the trail."

"It's a big country," Mark said bitterly. He was full of guilt for not being more aggressive when Billy had reported the man in the front yard. Mary worried that his recriminations were sapping his drive.

They had found the exact place under the tree where the man had stood, and even virtually invisible indentations that indicated he'd spent some time lying down. He'd been able to rest, maybe even take a nap, while he waited for the house to get quiet. What kind of a monster could be that cool?

Mary had gone there late last night and stood watching the windows of the house. Shafts of light fell onto the grass. She saw Mark come into their bedroom, saw Sally's dim night-light and Billy's black window. She saw Mark sitting on the side of their bed with his head in his hands.

The most awful part was that her little boy was so vulnerable. He was full of posturing and bluster. He'd pretend to be tough and that would probably do nothing but make his situation worse.

Her son was one of the brightest, most inventive, most cheerful children she had ever known. It was easy to make friends with Billy, all you had to do was smile. He had a temper, but even when he got mad it only took him a couple of minutes to cool down.

He had his limitations, though; she couldn't imagine him escaping from a smart adult.

You knew exactly how Billy felt at all times. He lied with his eyebrows raised and an expression of comic innocence on his face. He might as well be carrying a sign.

The poor little boy was not in any way equipped for this. Oh, he might run away from his kidnapper if he could, but he wouldn't get very far. You taught your children the basics— don't go with strangers, memorize your phone number—but how could you *ever* teach them to deal with the kind of onslaught he must be enduring now?

Beyond the basics he didn't know much about sex, so he would probably be mystified and revolted by the man's advances. That was the most hideous part, to imagine him being . . . handled. When you thought of the brute process of a man having sex with a little boy, it just made you want to wither and die.

In addition to helping the police and watching the FBI methodically dismember her home, she had been compelled to be a hostess. Winnie Lacy, the wife of the police chief, June Edwards, the mother of Billy's best friend, Tom Benton's perky little assistant principal Dougal Frazer—who had been instrumental in getting Mark his new job—had all come to the house. Mark's best friend among the faculty, Jim McLean, had offered himself as general helper until the autumn term started. Sally, bless her soul, had made iced tea and served the food from the covered dishes.

At first the investigators were reassuring. "Most of these cases have a local slant. Most of these guys are repeat offenders, and we'll interview every known molester in the state. Most of the cases are closed within forty-eight hours."

But the magic forty-eight hours passed, and only silence.

The National Center for Missing and Exploited Children had referred the Nearys to a support group. It met in Des Moines, and they were getting together tonight. There were five other families in the group. Two of them had runaway children and three were victims of parental abduction. Nobody had—with certainty—lost a child to a stranger.

Nevertheless Mark and Mary and Sally got into the car and drove two hours to the meeting, held in the basement of a Catholic church in an unfamiliar part of Des Moines. Behind them they left Jim McLean staring at the TV and snacking from the array of dishes still on the coffee table. He would be there if Billy called.

Mary wanted to drive but Mark insisted. She knew why: he also hungered for control over the nightmare. They were both clawing darkness, falling, and she knew that Mark felt it perhaps even more than she did. He had been having severe headaches, something completely new for him. This morning she had massaged his neck and shoulders for half an hour, and he was taking as much Advil as the label allowed. She watched him twisting his neck as the old wagon wheezed south. "I really don't mind driving," she said.

"It relaxes me."

They rode in silence. To the west the sunset slowly bloomed. Soon the last edge of the red disk dropped below the horizon, leaving a bright orange line shimmering beneath a sky that rose from yellow to infinite green. Night swept down out of the heights. A star floated in the emptiness, enormous and of a beauty so great that it made Mary feel as if she was starving for a sustenance she could not name. Both of her kids were amateur astronomers. "What's that star?" she asked Sally.

"Venus. It sets in an hour."

Was Billy seeing it, too? She hoped not. Stargazing would be sure to remind her poor son of home. He was so sensitive, and so devoted to his family. Summer before last he'd gone to camp, only to return after a week with the most spectacular case of homesickness the counselors had ever seen.

Mark had thought it was because he was insecure, that it was an anxiety he could overcome. But Mary understood her son's real problem: the camp was too structured. Billy was an adventurer, a lover of freedom, hungry for independence . . . on his terms.

She wanted to hug him so badly she thought she was going to go mad.

Mark turned on the radio. There was an all-news station in Des Moines, and they listened to that. The stories were muttered incantations. Mary closed her ears, letting it all bleed into nonmeaning. Her mind waited only for two words: William Neary.

For an hour she waited, but the words never came. So quickly Billy had become old news. "Are you listening?" she asked Mark.

"Not really. Just passing the time."

Sally spoke. "Do you remember the time Billy put the fire crackers in the toaster?"

Mark said, "No, I do not."

"But you remember it exploded?"

"I recall throwing it out the kitchen door. Billy did that?"

Sally laughed. Then she started to sing.

> *"The ants go marching one by one,*
> *The little one stops to get his gun—"*

Mary closed her eyes. She recalled all the old songs, "The Ants Go Marching," "Morningtown Ride," "Charming Billy." Oh, "Charming Billy," how that would make her toddler laugh!

> *"The ants go marching two by two,*
> *The little one stops to go to the zoo—"*

'Darling, stop,' she said in her heart. 'I can't bear it, I just can't!'

"Honey, no!"

Mary was relieved that Mark had made the demand.

"But we always do!"

"Not tonight." Mark's voice was soft with pain. He was the one who most loved the kids' songs . . . even though both kids had really outgrown them.

Sally burst into tears. Mary tried to touch her but she pulled away. She threw her head back and wailed. "He's dead!"

Mark pulled the car over. He turned full around in his seat and reached for his daughter. She let him draw her forward, let him grasp her awkwardly across the seat. "Not for us he isn't. Not ever."

Mary reached out to them, touching Mark's cheek with a nervous, unsure hand. Mark made a low, sad sound. Then he took a deep breath and continued. "You see, this is our strength. We believe in Billy. He is alive and we are going to get him back."

"Daddy, he was so scared sometimes at night. He was scared of the dark. He had such a big imagination! We used to play Monopoly together on the hall floor on nights when he couldn't sleep."

Mary had known of those games, had lain in bed listening to her children's quiet voices and the rattle of the dice. She recalled his efforts to bamboozle his sister into giving up. "I have Park Place and Boardwalk. Mathematically, it means you can't win!" "But Billy, dearest, I have the rest of the board!"

There was so much to remember, a great avalanche of words, smells, acts, adventures, right back to the weight of him in her womb. "Remember when he was born, Mark?"

"You had a hell of a time."

"I thought he'd never come out."

"Wasn't I the hard one, Momma?"

"That's right. Billy was pretty quick."

"He was green," Mark said. "A green prune with a banana head."

Sally laughed a little and Mark released her, half-turning back toward the driver's seat. She reached after him and they clasped hands. "Why was he green?" Sally asked.

"Bilirubin," Mary replied. "They put him under the lights."

"Which turned him puce. A puce banana head. I thought, Jeez, this can't be my kid."

"Your father claimed I must have had ancestors from Neptune. But he turned out so handsome." She was silenced then by the pain of her longing.

Mark started the car.

As they drove through the streets of Des Moines, Mary watched the evening life—lighted signs, people moving down sidewalks.

She was beginning to see that tragedy made you an outsider. By the way people walked, held their faces, stood at lights or crossed the street, Mary could tell which of them had suffered and which had not.

Then they turned a corner and the street they entered was empty, just dim street lamps and a few parked cars. St. Peter's was a huge stone church, dark and forbidding in the shadowy middle of the block. It looked closed, even abandoned. Only a hand-lettered sign impaled on the iron spike fence that ran down the side of the old building indicated that they had come to the right place. SEARCH GROUP IN CAFETORIUM, it said.

Mark pulled the car up to a meter. "Now all we have to do is find the cafetorium."

"What's a cafetorium?"

"A combination cafeteria and auditorium, I assume."

Mary and Sally followed Mark down some metal steps to a black door with bars on the dingy glass window in its center. It was locked and Mark rang the bell. The door opened instantly and a flood of light poured out. With it came a dark figure and a smiling voice. "I'm Bob Turpin," the figure said. "I'm pastor here."

"Mark Neary. This is my wife, Mary." Mary extended her hand. Father Turpin's grasp was cold and bony. "Our daughter, Sally." The priest clapped his hands on her shoulders, a gesture apparently contrived to appear casual. "A fine young woman. And how old are we?"

"I'm thirteen, Father. My brother was twelve."

"Was?"

"Is."

"Yes, is. Right this moment, is." He looked from face to face. He was so thin, Mary wondered if he had some sort of disease. "And you are going to find him." He led them down a corridor lined with, of all things, the tombs of his predecessors. "The kids call this the cryptatorium. Eighth-grade talent shows and priestly funerals carried on amid the steam tables. Still, we've been buried down here since the Paulists built the church. I'm a Paulist, incidentally, if the Church means anything to you."

"We're Catholic," Mark said. "Nominally."

"An interesting word, 'nominally.'"

Then they were in the room with the steam tables. A small

group of people was gathered in a circle of folding chairs. There was a quiet tension among them, a permanent expression of shock in their eyes.

As the Nearys advanced toward them Mary found that she was shaking. More even than the moment they had first called the police, this felt final. She had already faced the fact that Billy was gone. This was different, though. He would never come walking up the street pushing a broken bike. He would never appear at the front door in the care of a couple of kindly policemen.

Mary Neary had always helped. Now she realized that by giving her ten dollars to the Bishop's Relief Fund and Peter's Pence she had been comfortably placing herself outside the victims' pain. Looking at them—the bald man with the crooked glasses, the black woman's smiling welcome, the elaborately overdressed social mother—she realized that she bore a prejudice against life's casualties that until this moment had been entirely unconscious. She had been counting the victims as less—less lucky, less intelligent, less competent—than the golden many.

They took their seats and Mary thought, 'Now me.' Then they all pulled out pictures. Small snapshots, folded "Missing Child" posters. A ritual began, the silent passing of these pictures to the Nearys.

"Where's your picture?" a mother asked.

"I have my snapshot in my wallet," Mark said.

"Listen to me," the bald man said. "Here's what I say, 'My name is Harry Vreeland. I am the father of a missing child named Robbie Vreeland. This is his picture. Have you seen this child?' " He held out a poster of a smiling little boy of about seven. "You got to not only have your pictures with you at all times, you got to have them ready."

The overdressed woman regarded Mary with her coal-black eyes. She was smoking, and her fingers and teeth were yellow from the stains. "*Our* boy ran away." She raised her hands, a gesture of defense. "I admit it. There were problems." She looked straight into Mary's eyes. "He decided he wanted to make his own way." Her voice cracked. "He tried, but he was just too young. . . . This country has a dark side, don't ever think it doesn't. On the dark side of America, children get eaten."

The black mother spoke up. "I'm Jennine Gordon," she said in a soft, precise tone of voice. "We all want to tell our stories, but first we want to hear yours."

Mary heard Mark exhale. How exhausted he sounded.

"We'd like to hear a few other stories first," Mary said. "We need perspective." She wanted Jennine to help her, it was like drowning.

"I know," Jennine said. Mary thought, 'She could become my friend for life.' Jennine continued, "First, we have children here that are classed as runaways, but they are really abductions. They run away and then get abducted off the street. Or the perpetrator is clever and makes it look like a runner."

"Ours tried to do that," Sally said.

People nodded.

"I just want to say that the parental abduction is just as painful as the stranger abduction. Maybe it's more painful, because you *know* how bad it is for your baby." Her voice grew heavy and low and Mary thought, 'There is a terrible mystery here.' But she could not even put a word to it. "My Amelia is fourteen. Her daddy died in 1986 and I married again. My new husband loved my daughter." She stopped, jutted out her jaw. "Oh, how he loved her! I was too stupid and too in love to see!" She shook her head, anguished. Mark's hand found Mary's and she was glad to feel his shuddering touch. Now Jennine's voice went very small and high. "I let him adopt her. The very day we signed the papers, my life became hell. He hit my baby! He beat me up when I told him no. Within two months he was spanking her every day. She was walking humped over. At school she would throw up when it was time to come home." Now, a whisper: "He locked them up together in the garage at night."

Her voice became loud. "I didn't stand for it. No way, baby! I divorced the bastard! Damn right, and got custody with no visiting rights and saw the backside of that man! Then, a month later all of a sudden, Amelia is gone. And I feel—I feel—"

Father Turpin said, "We have an excellent recovery rate in the group. In the ten years we've been going, about thirty percent of our kids have been located."

"What do kids do?" Sally asked.

"Get into it with your friends," said a boy a little older than she. "You never know. Kids hear stuff, especially when school starts up. There might even be somebody who knows."

Mark was looking down at his feet. Mary imagined sand in motion, hopes drowning. Maybe, though, she was projecting her own feeling of helplessness onto her husband. Mark spoke. "What is the single most important thing we can do?"

Vreeland spoke. "Publicity, pure and simple."

"You can hunt for your child. The odds are long, but most of us do it," the overdressed woman added.

It seemed so pitifully little!

The group in its pool of dim light now appeared to Mary like survivors in the tireless ocean. Their raft was hope, but the sea is forever.

Father Turpin handed around a booklet of pictures from the Vanished Children's Alliance. Some of them might like to try to get their kids in this publication, he said.

When Mary glanced at it a sentence stopped her. It was like hearing Dr. Kingsley say of her mother, "We're talking about dying." It read, "Stranger abductions as well as nonrelative abductions are proportionately the greatest risk of life-loss of any missing group."

Her mouth went dry, the voices in the room faded. "No!" Mary was astonished at herself. All eyes were on her. She realized that she'd spoken aloud. She smiled, tried to cover. Nobody smiled back. Maybe the Nearys were the worst off. Maybe they had no chance. Maybe Billy had already died a horrible death. The thought made her very soul ache. She threw back an errant curl. "Our boy will come home."

Jennine Gordon nodded. "When I think of what he's doing to my baby, I'd like to put lead between his eyes. Lord Jesus forgive me! When I'm really goin' nuts—when I can hear my baby screamin' for Momma—oh, God—you want just somebody to hold you. But you are alone. And you think, I did this. I married this fool!"

The mystery was there again, a silent force binding them by their torments.

One by one Mary caught their eyes, and one by one they looked away. She respected this because she understood it. They could not meet her eyes because of what they shared—not the hope, but the tragedy.

These people with their nervous smoking, their clenching hands, their tattered pictures and little sheafs of records—they were really not here at all. That was the essence of the mystery that had enveloped them.

When a child was stolen, a part of each parent was also stolen. Without that essential part they would never again be whole; no matter the beauty of the day, they could not see it, nor could they enjoy the touch of love, for it might corrupt their vigil with an instant's transport. They do not hope and they do not laugh. Night and imagination are their curses. Mary saw it all.

"We will get him back," she said. How thin was her voice, how weak! She felt Mark's hand come into hers, and Sally beside her shook like the leaf of the aspen. "You'll see. We will."

Soon thereafter the meeting ended in a flurry of information passing: how to find social workers who care or a psychologist who was good but not too costly; where to get a new device that told you the number from which you were receiving a call.

At the side of the cafetorium a spectacularly aged parish volunteer offered coffee, and there was a box of Hostess doughnuts opened on the table beside her. She smiled when Father Turpin took one.

Mark insisted that Mary drink some coffee. "You'll want it," he said. "It's a long trip home, and we both need your strength. This time you do the driving."

14.

They were sailing across the desert on a clear blue afternoon. In a massive feat of endurance driving Barton had gotten
them past Las Vegas before he had finally left the interstate in
order to sleep. His only stop had been to ditch the bicycle.

Afterward he had at last been able to stretch out on the cot
beside Billy's and close his eyes. The air had been fresh and
desert-cool. The sun was just rising. As its light slowly filled the
van, Barton had taken Billy's hand in his own.

The warmth that filled his heart reassured him that he had
not sinned in taking the child. "Every act on behalf of love is
heroic." Who had said that? Some poet, Barton thought, the
name forgotten since high school and Gen. Lit.

Then he had slept. He had dreamed of a little man following
him in a comical midget car. The dream had awakened him to
high sun and left him with an urge to get rolling again. Now
it was nearly noon and the next thing on the agenda was a
drive-through restaurant and some much needed sustenance.
Too bad you couldn't get decent food from chain outlets,
especially as celebration was presently suggested.

"Good old Route 15," he sang out. "You know what I see?"
He was about to point out the Devil's Playground, but thought
better of it. Once they were home in L.A. he might be able to
prevent Billy from finding out where he was, maybe for a long
time. That was always best.

"Where are we?" asked a breathy voice. It made Barton sit
right up; this didn't sound like Billy. Rather, it recalled Dad on
his deathbed, his lungs full of cancer and emphysema. Why

would Billy sound like that? Then he remembered: he'd punished him by tightening the chest strap. That was a long time ago. Hours and hours—at least twelve hours, probably more.

He pulled the van over. Throwing back the quilt, he saw that the boy's gut was sucked in, his chest distended. There were ridges of paper-white skin pushing up around the thick strap, purple welts bulging through the buckles. A froth of mucus made Billy look like he was exhaling bubble bath. His face was gray. "Oh, son!"

When Barton touched the buckles Billy shook his head from side to side and shrieked. Instinctively Barton glanced out the windows, but they were alone on an empty desert road.

"OK," Barton said. Again he touched the buckles. When Billy started shaking his head again and pulling against his wrist straps, Barton felt something else inside himself. This *something* made him slow and careful.

He laid his hand on the row of three buckles, pressed. Billy grew frantic. He looked down at Billy's naked body and he found that he could not stop pressing on the buckles. His legs were weak with the pleasure of the moment. "I love him," he told himself, "that's why I can't stop touching him even though it hurts him." Billy's eyes searched his face, pleading. "We'll have to do this for some little time," Barton heard himself say.

No, this was vicious! He had to release the child at once. But his hands were heavy. He imagined the struggle to breathe across hours and hours. A hideous struggle. He had experimented with suffocation, and he knew how awful it was. Next to burning, slow suffocation was the worst death.

Billy's screaming stopped. His twisting and turning stopped. His body seemed to sink into itself. He made a fragile, discontented gabbling sound. It was like a baby.

This unexpected surrender shattered the moment. Barton saw himself, saw what he was doing. 'Disgusting creature, *you're* the one who ought to be suffering. Imagine, forgetting for twelve long hours what was supposed to be a fifteen-minute punishment! You fat pig! Fat Royal!'

He remembered the little dove he had found under the honeysuckle hedge, the poor thing scuttling along with its wing broken. He had caught it in his hands and taken it to his room and splinted the wing with drafting tape and a Popsicle stick.

He'd fed that dove with his own hands and nursed it and kept its box warm with a light. In the end the splinting had worked and his mother had put her arm around his shoulder and said, "You have such fine hands, maybe you'll be a surgeon."

He could nurse a dove back to health, but he could not remember to alleviate a magnificent child's suffering. His fingers fumbled with the buckles while Billy shrieked.

"My dove flew away," he shouted over Billy's noise. "I healed it and it flew away."

He had to push the swollen skin through the buckles. It was rubbery and hot and when he finally lifted the strap Billy started taking deep breaths and coughing up great gobs of mucus.

Quickly he unstrapped his ankles, then his hands. "No more," he said. "No more, Billy."

Billy sat up. Barton grabbed the sheet from his own cot and tried to clean Billy's chest. But the boy coughed again, the sound rattling the whole van, and more came up. Then he vomited froth, which Barton swept away in the sheet.

Through even this loathsome ordeal a part of Barton remained calmly objective. It told him he had really done what he had done because it was necessary to break the boy's will.

There was no use pretending that Billy loved or even liked him. It was much too soon. What he had to do was get Billy to quit fighting and accept his new situation. That required strong medicine, yes, but it had to be tempered with gentleness or it would lead to nothing but fear.

"My chest—" Billy put his hands on the marks. They were deep and now the line where the strap had cut into him was turning purple like the skin that had been compressed under the buckles.

Barton pulled his first-aid kit out from under the bed and produced a tube of antiseptic cream. "Lie back," he said. "I'll tend to it."

Billy turned his head. Barton remembered the time Duke had trapped that kitten in the tree. Its face was full of fear and it was so helpless. Barton had climbed the tree with Duke clawing the trunk and moaning. He had gotten the kitten, but then he'd slipped, and Duke—

No. He hadn't slipped. He'd held the kitten squirming in his hand, held it over Duke's head while Duke went mad, leaping and snarling, and the kitten had hissed and writhed and bitten at the hand, until his fingers loosened their grip . . .

Barton shook his head. Those memories, they would come and take him over, he was back there again and he had to be here. What if Billy just walked right out of the van right now? Began running like in the mountains?

Oh, that had been horrible! His heart had practically burst, exerting himself like that. The damned kid—but Barton had turned it into an effective display of dominance and power. On the way back to the van Billy had lain in his arms, surrendered to the greater power of the adult.

He'd read a lot about brainwashing. One of the techniques the Chinese used in Korea was to allow men to escape, only to bring them back with an overwhelming show of power. They would put the men in coffins and pretend to bury them alive, all the while feeding them just enough oxygen to prevent them from losing consciousness. They would go mad in the coffins, dying and yet unable to die. When they were released they would be so surprised and grateful that fine young men from Cincinnati and Bakersfield would crouch like coolies and place their lips against the scuffed boots of sneering Chinese teen-agers.

The key thing was the element of surprise. Barton thought he probably needed some of that now. He could not provide the overwhelming sense of deliverance that was the genius of the coffin torture. But wasn't there something he could do, some little softening that might make Billy revise his opinion of his captor?

He brushed Billy's cheek with a kiss. The boy's eyes flashed, and Barton was disappointed to see that his expression was one of disgust. "I know you hate me," Barton said. "But I love you. I love you more than you have ever been loved before."

"You're a dirty queer."

"The word is 'homosexual,' son. Think of their feelings. Anyway, I am not a homosexual."

"You're not?"

"I want to see you grow into the best of the best. I'm rich. I can give you everything you want. I want to be more a father to you than anybody else could ever be."

"My chest hurts."

He gave Billy a double dose of the children's aspirin he had packed in the first-aid kit.

"My feet hurt too," Billy said. He coughed, long and hard. "They sting."

Barton looked at them. "They seem better than they were," he said hopefully.

"The circulation was cut off. I'm likely to get an infection."

"I used lots of Mycitracin."

"I was in my pajamas. Where are they now?"

"They were a mess. From what you did."

Billy gave him a long, appraising look. "I'd like to have some clothes on."

Barton got the duffel he'd packed in Billy's bedroom. It seemed an alien object, beautiful and enigmatic. Boys' things always appeared that way to Barton, as if they were charged with potent and heartbreaking magic. When he unzipped the bag the clothes he'd pushed in came fluffing out. "That's my stuff," Billy said, his voice cracking. He grabbed the clothes, held them to his face, inhaled their smell as if seeking to recapture whatever element of home he could. He moaned with pleasure. "My Kafka T-Shirt. You got my Kafka T-shirt!"

Barton laughed, delighted that his random choices were such a success.

Billy put down the clothes. His eyes were full of anguish. "Didn't my Garfie get to come?"

"The stuffed toy?"

"Garfield is hardly a stuffed toy." His hand fluttered across his chest. "You really hurt me," he muttered.

Barton wished he'd thought to bring some Benadryl cream to mix into the antibiotic, but he hadn't considered injuries this serious. He'd gotten his other boys much closer to home, and it had been a simple matter to take them to the house.

He hadn't thought ahead about this journey, at least not well enough. Somehow he'd visualized Billy sleeping the whole way. But they'd started out on Sunday night and it was now

Wednesday. If he'd drugged the boy heavily enough to keep him out all this time there might have been brain damage or even death.

As Barton thought, he selected clothes for Billy. Shorts, a T-shirt. No shoes, though—that was one of Barton's smartest rules. Bare feet were no big deal in his time, but they slowed these modern kids down considerably. "We're going to go to some fabulous stores," he said. "You'll be able to dress in absolute fashion."

"My mother buys my clothes."

"But you like style, you like to look your best."

Billy pushed aside the blue T-shirt Barton had given him. "I want to wear my Kafka shirt." Wincing, he raised his arms to drag it over his head.

"Let me help you."

"I can do it!" Then he grabbed the briefs that were in Barton's hand and drew them up his smooth legs. He put on the shorts.

The T-shirt was odd. If Barton had realized what was on it, he wouldn't have brought it. The shirt was light gray, and on the front there was a photograph of a hollow-eyed young man in what appeared to be a cheap suit and striped club tie. Under it was the caption KAFKA LIVES.

Franz Kafka . . . wasn't he some sort of horror novelist? Barton wasn't sure. "I'll have to teach you about Kafka," he said briskly to cover his ignorance. "Would you like to learn?"

"I know about Kafka."

Barton heard the hate in Billy's words. But it was also true that Billy was for the first time responding to him as a human being. This was an initiatory moment: their first genuine conversation.

"I know about Kafka, too, Billy."

"*Wir graben den Schacht von Babel.*"

Barton realized that the words were German. It would be a potentially serious disadvantage if Billy knew a language that he himself could not understand. Billy was watching his reaction.

Barton had first seen the boy playing games in a video arcade. There had been nothing to indicate that he was unusually educated. But then, a lot of schools in his part of the Midwest taught German. The area had been settled by Germans, hadn't it?

"It means, 'We are digging the pit of Babel.' "

"A remarkable sentiment. I've always thought that horror novelists—"

"Let me spell it out. I'm trying to communicate that I don't want to talk to you. If you want to stick me in the butt, do it and get it over with. But don't try to fool with my mind."

The words came as melody; they lilted. The music of Billy's voice made the contempt more plain. Barton bowed his head. "You will never get away from me, Billy."

"Of course I won't. If I do, you kill my parents."

Barton was astonished. "I never said that!"

"You don't even know what you tell people."

Barton had *dreamed* of threatening Billy with that. He'd *contemplated* it. He never had the feeling that he said and did things that he didn't know about. Of course not. Barton Royal was a very special man with very special needs. But he was quite sane. That was his rock. Everything he did, he did for a perfectly sound reason.

"If I said that I didn't mean it."

Billy could not have looked more relieved if he'd been instructed by a director. "Come into the front," Barton said, in a spirit of appeasement.

Billy crawled forward. He hunched into the passenger seat.

"Do you usually sit like that?"

"No."

"I've always believed that a gentleman's inner bearing is reflected in his posture."

Billy raised his T-shirt. Inwardly, Barton chided himself. He had so much on his mind, it was hard to remember the details.

There was, however, a detail that he *did* remember. "I have a suggestion. Let's eat!"

"Not very hungry."

"No? You haven't eaten in two and a half days. You must be famished."

In the silence of the moment that followed, Barton heard a small sound. Billy was clenching and unclenching his left fist against the seat.

Jack had tried to starve himself at first. Little boys never succeeded at this. "I'll get myself a nice cheeseburger," Barton said. "You don't have to eat."

Billy snorted out his contempt for Barton. The anger that rose in Barton made him want to grab those shoulders and shake them *damn hard!*

"Come on, Billy. It isn't going to be bad, living with me. We're going to be friends, you'll see."

"You can't make me."

Barton felt the flush enter his cheeks. He gripped the steering wheel. 'Now, calm down,' he said to himself. 'Take it easy.' He breathed in, breathed out. *The hostile little bastard!*

No, don't let that get out. He doesn't need your anger, he needs your love. He needs understanding and firm, kind support. He's just a boy.

The little shit!

You could just put your hands around his *fucking neck and squeeze!*

That's the way choking works, you squeeze until the windpipe pops. Then you can just sit back and watch. It doesn't happen right away, but they die. They clutch their throats, they run, they might even try to fight back. But then they get all black and the tongue comes out and they start shaking. They lose their bladder and they go down and they die at your feet *like fucking rats!*

He was going to throttle this child, and he was going to do it *right now!*

No!

But his hands were rising from the wheel, going to claws. Stop, take it easy!

The little *shit!*

He grabbed the steering wheel and hung on with all his strength. His fingers kept snaking off, but he fought it, he had to fight it, he had to somehow regain control, he wanted the boy, he did, he could still make it work, he just knew it!

Pop the windpipe! Watch him smother! *Scum, you filthy little scum!*

His feet thudded against the firewall, against the brake and gas pedal. It would just be *so damn satisfying* to break the little bastard's neck!

Then the boy, who was looking on with wide eyes, suddenly reached out a hand and began patting his shoulder. "It's OK, mister," he said. His voice was the softest of whispers.

Barton was so surprised that his anger went spitting out of him. He sank down, breathing hard. "Please don't make me mad like that," he said.

"I won't! Not ever again! I promise!"

When Barton released the steering wheel he saw that his right hand had split the plastic. The torn piece hung off the wheel, its vinyl covering twisted and ripped.

They drove for a time without talking.

Then the boy began to sing:

> *"The ants go marching one by one*
> *The little one stops to get his gun,*
> *And they all go down, around,*
> *Get out of the rain!"*

How delightful! He knew that well, of course, from his job. He knew all sorts of children's songs. Billy was really coming around, this was going to work!

Barton sang the second verse:

> *"The ants go marching two by two,*
> *The little one stops to tie his shoe,*
> *And they all go down, around,*
> *Get out of the rain!"*

Laughing with pleasure, Barton pulled the van onto 15. As he glanced around to check the traffic he saw the face of the child he had been enjoying so much.

It was soaked with tears, the eyes like slits, the nose running, the cheeks bright red. And the lips were pulled back from the teeth in a particularly horrible way that managed to communicate all at once disgust, rage, hate and the blackest, most dreadful fear.

Barton returned his gaze to the highway. He pressed the gas pedal.

They went on.

15.

Billy slumped in the seat, his chest tormented, his lungs rattling when he breathed, his feet still tender from last night's escape attempt. There was blood on his Kafka T-shirt. Could you wash blood out? Mom would know.

The sun was beginning to set and it blasted into his face, making his eyes ache as much as his heart. Then he opened his eyes wide, glaring directly at the sun. 'Maybe if I'm blind,' he thought, 'he'll feel sorry for me.' He shut his eyes tight: he didn't want to be blind, then he'd never be able to get back home!

He stared at the glove compartment, which hung open before him. It was full of tapes. They were mostly the operas which the man was constantly playing. He saw *Madama Butterfly* and *La Gioconda* and *The Flying Dutchman.* He decided he didn't like opera much anymore, even though he'd liked *Carmen.*

There was also a small flashlight there, black, with a long silver scratch on it. That was the light that had bobbed along behind him in the woods. If only it had broken, if only it hadn't even been there, or he had dropped it down the cliff.

Then what? Billy imagined himself falling into the yard of the little cabin beneath the bluff, and they would carry him inside and he would die, and then he would go home. He saw the hearse, a black Cadillac with a flower car behind it, and the St. Stephen's choir was singing "Nearer My God to Thee." The coffin was gray.

He read the inspection sticker on the windshield backward. Utah. Were they going there? What was Utah like? Was this Utah?

He counted the buttons on the radio. It was a real nice one, a Sony. He wanted to ask if it had memory and was there a CD player in the van since it had CD controls on it. It would be neat to hear a CD in a car.

He sat nursing his pains and being hungry. He was so hungry that he kept thinking he smelled a hamburger. The memory reminded him of the Stevensville Burger King, and his gang. A great bunch of guys, even the registered nerds like Jerry Edwards.

Going to the Burger King with the guys, ordering a Whopper with fries and a Coke, and afterward having a fried cherry pie for dessert, and no parents around. Getting on your bikes early in the morning and riding all the way out to the place where the railroad trestle crosses the river, building a fire and roasting hot dogs, waiting for the train to come and flatten the pennies you put on the track. And plus you could lie under the trestle as it went across, a shaking, rumbling cataract of sound that left you feeling like you'd been shaken apart and come back together again. There was also walking the trestle when you heard the first blast of the horn. That was when the train crossed Main Street in Stevensville. It took ten minutes to walk across, and the train made the distance between the town and the trestle in fourteen if it was running exactly on schedule.

Billy had done that a dozen times, always cutting a little more off his start time. He loved it, the jitters in his stomach when he started, the hypnosis of the passing ties, the other guys screaming his times and the train's horn blowing and mourning and then the tracks jumping and seeing its light in the middle of the day glaring like the eye of death, and throwing himself off the trestle at the last minute into the tender grass that grew beside the tracks, and lying there breathing grass and watching the passing Amtrak cars, red and blue and silver, and the flash of a pale face in a window.

He looked at his own hands in his lap and thought, 'He says he loves me. He says I am beautiful. What does he mean?'

The man looked like a fear of the night become real. Billy sat up, forced his pain to the background. His only restraint at the moment was having the seat belt pulled tight across his lap with his arms pinned underneath. It wasn't a very good way to keep somebody captive.

If only he had thirty seconds and a telephone, he knew exactly what he would do. Too bad they were going sixty, he could jump out.

His mind snatched at whatever bits of information it could find. 'We're going west because the sun is setting in my face. This is IH 15 because that's what the signs say, and also he said it. We're in a desert that looks like the surface of Mars. We carry a Utah inspection sticker, which probably means that we're either in Utah or on our way there.'

They passed a filling station and he saw a bank of phones shining in the last sun. The tires hummed. The cassette played. The man sat there driving and pulling at the piece of steering wheel he'd broken. Billy saw that the gas gauge was close to empty.

The man drove, occasionally making a little sound in his throat, like he was secretly talking to himself. He was like a huge queen termite, all smooth and pale and big. Once Billy had dissected a queen termite—fifth-grade science. Eggs poured out of her and he felt sad even though she was really incredibly yucky.

Sal Geller had said, "You could dry the eggs and make them into a cereal." Billy replied, "Eat them damp and they'd be like rice. A whole bowl. Nice and hot." Mrs. Chapman overheard them and sent them both to the office for being nauseating little boys.

He cried silently, telling himself it was for the lady termite. 'Mommy, it's gonna be night and I know you miss me. Dad, I'm here, I'm still alive.' They loved him so much, they must be suffering hell and there was nothing he could do except sit here and get taken farther and farther—

The man moved slightly in his seat. The van began to slow. About half a mile ahead Billy saw a Mobil station. He made his mind blank. Then he closed his eyes, let his head drop to one side. He began breathing rhythmically, pretending to sleep.

The van stopped. There was a click and the engine turned off. A moment later the man's door was opened and closed. Billy looked: the man was out by the gas pumps. This was a self-service station.

Billy pulled his hands out from under the belt and unlatched it. But when he pushed the window button nothing happened. OK. He reached over, turned the key, tried it again. Still nothing. Then he saw a child lock. He flipped it, and this time the window went down. In an instant he was out of the van. There was nobody in the station office. From the garage beside it he heard a machine whining. There was a Toyota being greased. At the far corner of the station he saw the phones. He ran for them. There was almost no time, he knew that. Maybe he was already seen.

He grabbed the receiver, pressed "0." The phone rang once, twice. "Operator."

"My name is William Neary from Stevensville, Iowa. I've been kidnapped by a man in a white Aerostar. We're on Route 15 heading west."

"What's the number of that phone, son?"

"702-995-0091." He couldn't risk another second. He hung up. *Jesus let the operator tell Mom and Dad!*

Billy started to run into the garage, but the click of the gas pump turning off stopped him. There were only seconds left and the attendant was nowhere in sight. The only thing saving Billy was the fact that the man's view of him was blocked by the smoked glass of the van's windows. But the man had to be moving. In another few seconds he would come around the front of the van—

Billy crossed the tarmac at a crouching run, slipped like an eel into the window. The man was no more than five feet away, walking toward the gas station. Billy dropped into his seat, pulled the belt over his hands. As he sat watching the man pay, he cursed his luck with the attendant, who had appeared to take the man's money. If only there'd been another ten seconds, Billy might be free right now. But what if the attendant was as stupid as the people back in Denver had been, letting the van go despite the fact that there was a kid inside screaming he'd been kidnapped? The stupid dumbheads in that Taurus, Billy wished them into the depths of hell. How could they not understand, not care?

The man got in. Billy had leaned his head back against the seat and was again breathing as if he was asleep.

They were accelerating onto the highway when Billy realized

his terrible mistake. He had left his window open, and the man was sure to notice. Then the wind stopped. The man had raised the window with his button. Billy waited, but there were no screamed questions, just the silence of the road.

When he opened his eyes a slit he saw that the man was looking at him. Was it suspicion? Certain knowledge? Or did he just like to look at the bee-you-tiful little boy?

What the hell did it mean that you were beautiful? It meant that there were certain people who wanted to destroy you, that's what it meant.

When the man's voice suddenly started Billy was jolted by a tremendous shock.

"What'd I tell you? A great, big, delicious Roy Rogers! Hamburgers, here we come."

It was all Billy could do not to burst out laughing with relief.

"I'll bet you could sure use some food. I know I could."

Where'd he get that voice? Those voices? One sentence he sounded like a man, the next a sort of half-man. It was like there was a boy in him who had never grown up, and if you listened a woman, too.

But he wasn't gentle, he'd torn apart the steering wheel!

Billy looked at his meaty face, at the hurt eyes. The man was smiling, a big, harsh grin. It was the kind of smile somebody who hates kids makes when they have to be with a kid. Those fat hands concealed iron bones, and they had wanted to grab him around the throat and choke him worse than the straps.

When he was in the straps he'd cried out to the man, he'd promised never ever to try to get away again but the man hadn't seemed to hear him, he'd just sat there driving like he was part of the van itself. Billy had struggled for hours and hours just to get enough breath. He'd slept and dreamed he was at the bottom of the sea and he swam into a giant clam and it closed and it was crushing his chest. He had to breathe and he knew the next breath he took was gonna be water.

Waking up felt like that time Jerry sat on him too long and made him pass out. But that was different, Jerry had paid him two dollars not to tell his dad. Although, of course, he had stolen back one of the dollars later.

Billy remembered how the man had seemed like a bat coming after him through the woods all graceful and fast, his big body maneuvering among the trees. It was ballet to see him run, this swift lump of a man.

"Give us two cheeseburgers with the works, two orders of fries, a water and a large chocolate shake." The man turned a sheened, smiling face toward Billy. "Sound good, old chap?"

"Sure," Billy replied. He tried to sound like a robot.

The man pursed his lips and then his hand just sort of happened to drop onto Billy's leg. Billy looked at it there, at the school ring too worn to read, at the wrinkles along the knuckles, at the white back that was almost but not quite like a woman's. "Now look, Billy, you're going to make it. You're going to be very happy! You should see the house where you're going to live. Wow! It's a big house and I have beautiful furniture. Antiques, even. And you can see for miles, it has a huge view, and you will have everything you ever wanted or dreamed of. You have to pull yourself together. The chest strap was harsh, I admit that, but goodness, in all those hours you didn't utter a word of protest! You poor boy, how you must have suffered!" The hand patted his. "Honest to God I am so sorry. If you'd said one single word I would have loosened it immediately. But you had to be punished, you surely see that. You ran away and that is a no-no. The ultimate no-no! But ten minutes, fifteen. I just got so absorbed in my driving—"

"I asked you and asked you and asked you and you never even turned around! Then you came back and went to sleep."

The man's eyes widened. Then the order came and he was fooling with the white Roy Rogers bags and his wallet and little blue change purse like an old lady's.

In front of them Billy saw a station wagon full of guys his age. They were horsing around and he could hear their faint voices full of laughter. He leaned forward against his shoulder strap, listening, watching and wishing.

It was a Buick wagon, recent model. The kids were wearing hockey outfits. Normally Billy didn't run with the jocks, but right now the interior of that car looked like heaven.

The man tapped his horn a couple of times. He was smiling and nodding into the windshield. "Come on," he said, "please, that's right, step on the gas pedal, dear." He stomped the floor with his left foot, so hard the whole van vibrated with the blow.

Billy tried telepathy. He'd done it with Eric Worden a long time ago. The Wordens had a Ouija board and Mrs. Worden said it worked. 'Help me,' Billy said in his mind, 'help the boy in the van behind you.'

The wagon went to the end of the parking lot and returned to the interstate. Nobody inside even glanced back. The van followed and then they were briefly behind the wagon again. Billy tried to direct pure thought into the head of the driver. 'Help the boy in the van behind you. Help me, help me!' His lips were a determined, silent line.

As the car pulled away for the last time, Billy saw that it had an Arizona license plate. So maybe they were in Arizona. 'The capital of Arizona is Phoenix.' That was what he knew about Arizona. Or maybe Tucson was the capital.

They went down the highway with the food on the console between them. Billy decided not to eat.

If the operator had told the police, they should be here by now. Every second the van was farther away!

"I hope you *like* burgers and shakes," the man said. His hands were tight on the steering wheel, his one visible eye was rolling in Billy's direction.

"Yeah, sure."

"Eat. Don't wait for me. I'll grab my burger when the traffic thins out."

The smell of the food made his mouth start watering. He didn't *want* to eat, though. That man would not get the satisfaction of seeing him eat food his filthy hands had touched.

Normally Billy moved through life from food break to food break. Breakfast at home, lunch at school, snack in the afternoon, then dinner and before bed a final glass of milk. Plus as many cookies and as much candy in between as he could get away with.

He looked at the bent steering wheel, then at the man's tense face. He recalled how slow he'd been taking off the strap, how he'd hesitated with his hand on the buckle and his face red. With a guy this nuts it was best to do what you were told to do and wait for your chance. After all, the more Billy cooperated the more the man would relax. Plus the police were coming. They had to come, he'd *told* that operator!

No hamburger had ever smelled as good as this one did. This Roy Rogers must be special. He could smell every separate thing, the salad dressing, the tomatoes, the lettuce, the meat. It just seemed automatic to lift it to his mouth and take a big bite.

"Not too much at once, honey. It's been a long time since you ate and it'll all come up again."

Honey? Screw you.

As he chewed Billy stared across the hood of the van, watching the oncoming traffic. People were beginning to turn their lights on. The sky ahead was glowing pale orange and green, the land was dark. Ahead of them he saw a truck with about a dozen license plates, he couldn't even tell all the states. California. North Carolina. Arkansas.

A car passed with California plates, then another.

"How's the burger?"

"It's OK."

"That's my boy! You looking forward to the shake? You like a chocolate shake?"

Billy would not give him that. "Not much."

The man played with the steering wheel. "What's your name?" Billy asked. A smile came over the man's face, big and ugly and kind of sad, like when he'd had that hangdog look.

"Well, well, well, I think we're warming up a little at last! I am Barton. And please do not call me Bart. Barton."

"How old are you?"

"Thirty."

"What happened to you?"

"Pardon me?"

"You look a lot older than my dad, and he's over forty."

"Well, never mind. Eat your supper." He began to hum along with the opera he had put on. "You know," the man said, settling back in his seat, "I remember when I was your age, you know what we did? When I was twelve." Billy wondered how he knew so much. His name, now his age. Had the man been studying him, watching him, maybe for weeks? The thought was sickening.

The man was looking at him now, a look that at first seemed warm and friendly. But his eyes were not right. They stared for so long that Billy got worried the van would run off the road.

Of course that would be great, if he survived. The police would come and then it would be all over. Maybe he could try grabbing the steering wheel when the man wasn't looking, and pull it and reach his foot over and jam down the gas.

"Do you know what we did?" the man asked again. Billy knew he had to answer.

"No," he said. He took his last mouthful of hamburger and started on the shake, which was so delicious that he felt a stab of literally physical pleasure when he tasted it.

"Well, we had a great time! There was this lady in our neighborhood who was very old. She used to sit beside her window and listen to the radio. One day we climbed in when she wasn't in the living room and attached wires to the microphone. She came in to listen to the news, and we hid outside and announced the end of the world. It was quite a newscast! And you know what she was doing when we went to see how she had reacted? She was sound asleep." He chuckled. "I guess there's something to be said for getting old."

"You couldn't have attached wires to the microphone because regular radios don't have a microphone."

"Well, I meant the speaker. It's a detail. Do you have any funny stories?"

"Not really."

"You've never done anything funny?"

"I guess not."

"But you've laughed. Tell me something that made you laugh."

The mere thought of laughter brought tears to Billy's eyes. He could hardly talk. But he had to say something, he didn't want to make Barton mad again. "We don't laugh, we aren't allowed to."

"Aren't allowed to? Why not?"

"Religion." He thought fast. "We're Charismatics. We don't laugh, we only speak in the tongues."

There was a period of silence. Billy knew he had been at least partly accurate. He'd heard the Charismatics bellowing away in the basement at St. Stephen's. "Lamma lamma sammi," they would yell, or, "Globbalubbyboof!" They would make long sentences of these words and scream, "Praise God, praise Him!"

That was speaking in the tongues. After the hollering died down they would all say "Amen" and sing a hymn. Any kid who heard this would have to be carried off on a stretcher from laughing so hard. The Charismatics themselves did not laugh at all.

"You're very religious," Barton said. The wariness in his voice delighted Billy, and he thought it wise to expand on the theme.

"We go to Mass and Communion every morning. I confess every Thursday. We all have statues of Jesus and Mary in our rooms, and when I'm not eating or sleeping or doing homework, I pray."

"You must have very few sins, and yet you go to confession every week."

"No, I have plenty of sins. The more strict your religion, the more sins you have. That's why probably all the holiest people are in hell, my dad says."

Barton nodded. "They have the strictest religions and therefore the most sins. Makes sense. But you haven't told me your sins."

Should he say something stupid like he did the once or twice a year he went to real confession, or should he—dared he—try another tack? He wanted to seem tough and dangerous to this man. But would anything be believable? Being near Barton made Billy feel helpless. If he didn't try, though, if he didn't try *everything* he was going to be near Barton forever.

"Well," he said, "you aren't supposed to tell." He glanced at Barton. How would he take this? "But I killed a man."

Barton burst out laughing and Billy hated himself at once for being so stupid. "You shouldn't laugh," he yelled. "I tied him to a bed just like you did me and I connected him to an extension cord. And I plugged it in."

"Who was this? Who did you kill, little boy?"

"A man who tried to kiss me."

Barton sighed. Billy, who had been sucking his shake between sentences, came to the bottom and rattled the straw.

"That isn't nice!"

He did it again, rattling it long and hard.

"Oh, please," Barton sang out, "don't make me punish you.

I find it so embarrassing." But he sounded like he found it fun. Billy stopped.

As night fell and the desert became flecked with the lights of distant towns, Billy felt a loneliness so overwhelming that it seemed almost sacred.

He watched the gathering dark.

16.

Sally lay motionless, staring into the dark. She listened. The silence told her nobody else was awake.

So what had waked her up?

She heard a creak close to her bed. She turned her head, but all she saw was total blackness.

It felt like she was awake and dreaming at the same time. Another creak came, and suddenly there was a hand over her mouth, a slick hand that stank of rubber. She twisted away, intaking breath, trying to scream. The rubber of the glove pulled her skin.

Then her mouth was free and she heard herself bellow. As the scream died into its own reverberations she could hear his brutal grunting. His other arm came under the covers, sought her waist, started dragging her.

"Daddy! Daddy, oh, God, he's back, he's taking me! Daddy!"

The lights came on. Her heart was thrashing, sweat was pouring down her cheeks, she was crouched against the wall behind the bed. Her mother and father were two ghosts bobbing in the warm glow of the overhead light. Daddy rushed up to her and scooped her up in real arms that were warm and strong.

She let herself gc like a rag in his hug and the strength of him filled her. "He was here," she moaned.

"No," Mother said, "no, baby."

Air whistled into her lungs, her heart's motion became stronger and slower, the night wind began to dry the sweat that was soaking her.

She heard herself moaning, "He was here, he was here," and it was like another kid was doing it. Then she was being shaken back and forth, her head lolling, the ceiling fixture swinging before her eyes.

She caught her breath. There was Mom, her face white, her eyes puffy, and Dad with his glasses crooked and that haggard look she wished she could wash off his face.

"No, baby," Dad said. "Nobody was here. You were dreaming."

It seemed unbelievable. "Really?"

He held her tight and she smelled him, a waxy old smell like a grandfather. But she put her arms around him, and Mom held her hands behind his back. "You had a nightmare," Mom said.

"I'm scared at night."

"Why didn't you tell us, Sally?"

She looked into her father's eyes. "Because I didn't want to." She pulled away. "I want coffee."

"I think we could all use coffee," Dad said.

"At four A.M.?" Mom asked. Then she made it a statement: "At four A.M." They wouldn't be getting back to sleep, none of them. Sally put on her robe and followed her parents downstairs. As they moved through the house she turned on every light.

Walter Toddcaster was dragged out of his sleep by the ringing of the telephone. He wasn't surprised; it was part of the job. His wife didn't even stir.

"Yeah?"

"We got a lead in the kid case. He called in."

"Tell me about it."

"An operator took the call from a pay phone at a Mobil station near Estes, Nevada. He's in a white Ford Aerostar, traveling west on IH 15. That's all we got."

"License number? Anything?"

"As a matter of fact there is a little more. The call came in at eight-fifty-one their time last night. The phone company reported it to the state police. They got to the booth at nine-twelve. No Aerostar. But the attendant remembered the van."

"And its driver?"

"A white male aged about forty-five to fifty. Five foot ten, somewhat overweight, wearing a pale blue Izod shirt and black slacks."

"This is good news."

"Not entirely."

"Hit me."

"The attendant also *thinks* he saw a boy—get this—climbing *into* the window of the van. The boy was wearing a white T-shirt with a photo on it and shorts. He thinks the kid might have had a big red spot on his shirt."

"What are you telling me?"

"He thought it looked like blood."

Toddcaster sighed, thanked the duty officer and hung up the phone. The question was now a personal one: did he clam up on this family, or stay emotionally involved? A man has to protect himself. You can break, you get too involved.

To a cop blood usually means death. This particular abductor, at some point, will kill this child.

Taking places around the red Formica table in the kitchen was another of the unspoken family rituals that had given Sally quiet pleasure, and now created distress. Dad set the coffeepot to perking, and it was soon rattling away, a painfully merry sound.

Mom sat with her arms folded before her and her head down, like you used to at naptime in grade school. Sally reached over and touched her hair. So suddenly that there seemed anger in the movement, her mother raised her head. "Did you see him?"

"You said—"

"It was a nightmare, Mary."

"No, Mark—I mean when he took Billy. Did you see him?"

Sally was confused by the question. She hadn't seen him . . . had she?

"The dream, Sally. Maybe it's a buried memory."

"No, I—I don't think so."

Her mother's face changed, the eyes growing narrow, the lips curling into an expression that Sally had never seen before. "If you remember anything, you tell us!"

"Mom, I don't!"

"I think you do!"

"Mary, hey!"

"She doesn't realize how serious this is! She's a child. It's a game." Abruptly she stopped talking.

Sally thought in a dull, helpless way, 'She's angry at me because I'm the one who was left behind.' Slowly, Mom's hands went to her face. "Mom?"

"I'm sorry, honey. I love you, you know I do. I just want Billy back so darned bad!"

The pot rattled and chattered, and the room filled with the smell of fresh-brewed coffee. Sally knew that something was being destroyed in this family, something that was fragile and necessary. Was it a kind of family sentiment, a sort of shared lie—or was it a truth crushed by the savage reality of a world that sees children as objects to be consumed?

She said all she could think to say, "I'm sorry it wasn't me, Mom. I know he was the baby." Mary gave a loud, tragic wail and reached toward her daughter. They twined hands across the table. "I don't think I ever saw him or heard him, but I'm so afraid he'll come back I almost can't stand it. I don't want to die like—"

"He's not dead! *He is not dead!*"

"I know—I'm sorry, Mom, I—"

Sally watched as her mother seized the coffeepot and filled the mugs. Her hands, which had been clenched and trembling, became deft and efficient when she performed the familiar chore. Sally saw something about her mother that she had never seen before, and knew that it was the bravery of continuing on even when you wanted to roll up into a little ball and die.

Mary's voice rang clear and suddenly very strong. "We cannot have a defeatist attitude, because this family is all he has. If we don't get out there and do our own investigation and find our boy, he's gone."

"Mary, the police—"

"What did they do? They came here, they ruined my house with their filthy tests and then they went back to their other damned cases, the ones they have some chance of solving.

Nobody's looking for Billy. Canvassing every known pederast in the state! That's their idea of working this case. Billy's not in Iowa. He probably hasn't been in Iowa since Sunday morning. He could be anywhere! And we are going to have to find him. Nobody else will. Nobody else gives a tinker's damn." Noisily she sipped her scalding coffee. Sally watched her, full of admiration.

"It's one thing to do publicity, but we can't possibly mount an investigation on our own. Where would we start?"

"Somewhere!"

As Toddcaster dressed he thought of the next steps to be taken. They had to put out a request for incident reports on white Aerostars up and down IH 15. They had to follow up anything they might get. And the family had to participate. They needed to take their poster to every truck stop and filling station on the west side of that highway. It was a big job, but not impossible. He could find out the approximate range of the Aerostar, and they could concentrate their postering in areas where it was most likely to have stopped for gas.

He was going to tell them that Billy was alive, and they were going to emote all over him.

The part about the blood he would leave out. And he wouldn't explain why the boy had gone back to the van, although he understood. The blood told him: Billy Neary was being tortured. Kidnappers did it to brainwash their victims, literally to intimidate them into obedience. They did it out of fear, out of anger. Mostly, though, they did it for fun.

Maybe there would come a time when Billy wouldn't make a phone call even if he could. That happened, he'd seen that. There was an unholy love that entered these relationships. Sometimes they kissed the hand that would, in the end, kill them.

Sally considered how many crannies there were in the world, and how small her brother was.

The familiar, dull hopelessness began to reassert itself. Noble sentiments aside, they were just like the other families of the Searchers group with their pictures and their desperate strategies.

Mother had become a woman possessed. "We'll get him back. We'll find a way."

"We could canvass the neighborhood," Mark ventured.

"Do you know that the police *did not do that!* Did you notice? They didn't so much as knock on a single door in this neighborhood! If *we* get our picture into the right hands and somebody says, 'Hey, I've seen this kid,' then they'll have something to go on. Otherwise, it's just basically waiting for something to turn up."

"That's not exactly a fair characterization, Mary. They're doing a lot more than that."

"I don't want to be fair! I want Billy!" With a glare like the enraged Medusa in Sally's ancient-history book, her mother reared back and hurled her mug against the wall. Coffee went everywhere and the little framed cross-stitch she had made, "Bless my kitchen, Lord, and all that come herein," was shattered and fell to the floor amid the showering bits of the mug.

Silence followed the outburst. Dad seemed frozen in his chair, like Sally too astonished to make a sound.

Scuttling like a coolie, Mother hurried to pick up the pieces. "Don't anybody else move, you'll get glass in your feet!"

"What about your feet, Mom," Sally said. She went down to help. Together they picked up the larger pieces of glass while Mark sopped up coffee and slivers with paper towels.

Sally watched as her father finished, then came over and enfolded his wife in his arms right there in the kitchen. They seemed so small, and so much older than Sally had ever before noticed. She got up, slowly backing away from them. She wished they wouldn't keep revealing themselves as little and helpless—but they *were,* just look at them.

"We can work as a team," she said, trying to interject a hopefulness she did not feel. Her parents seemed hardly to hear her. They were on their feet now, Mom sobbing, Dad holding her in painful silence. "We can work as a team," Sally repeated, this time a bit more loudly.

Dad was so haggard; right now he looked like a total stranger.

To cover her disquiet Sally kept talking, her voice fast and thin. "We can, if we organize. We'll buy a book, learn how to be detectives. We'll become a family of detectives."

Mom blinked, and suddenly her face softened. Sally and Mom had many long talks. At the best moments, they were sisters. But usually Mom was on her case. "This isn't one of those young adult mystery novels."

"I don't read that junk anymore, as you well know. I just think we can accomplish something—realistically. I do."

"Maybe I don't! Maybe that's why I threw the mug! I'm so damn frustrated, I could just tear my hair out!"

"We can try your idea, Mary," Dad said. Sally watched her father as he continued to awkwardly caress her mother. Then they went together in a kiss. Usually they were casually affectionate but never extremely intimate in front of her and Billy. She didn't know what to do, lower her eyes or what. She was delighted.

Just then they all heard a sound outside the open kitchen window. All looked. The moon had set, and the window was black. Instinctively they drew closer together. Sally's eyes went to the rack of knives.

There was a knock at the door. It was more as if a branch was tapping against the frame. There was none of the firmness of the human hand.

Dad went to the door. "Who is it?" Sally stepped closer to the knives—and as she did it, she discovered a truth about herself. Neither of her parents had so much as thought about getting a weapon. And why should they? Neither of them would dream of using one.

Sally could do it.

Then Dad swung the door open and there stood Detective Toddcaster blinking in the sudden light. Sally must have gasped, because he turned toward her, his expression full of apology. "I saw the lights on," he said. He stepped heavily into the kitchen, dominating it with his large, clumsy body, his stale-cigar reek and his wrinkled, intense face.

"You've been here—how long?"

"I just came over. I drove by. I guess maybe I'm glad I saw lights. I have news. Billy is alive. He called the operator from a pay phone in Estes, Nevada, at eight-fifty-one their time last night."

Sally felt a shock go through her body as if somebody had slapped her across the face. Mother cried out. Dad went to the detective and grabbed his shoulders. "Is he OK?"

"He's alive."

Her mother was shaking, twisting her hands together, moaning, "He's alive, he's alive."

Sally saw that all along she hadn't believed it. Hidden behind her brave words had been a secret certainty: Billy was dead. And Sally knew that she had thought so, too. She had thought her brother was dead. But he wasn't, he was somewhere, he was alive right now, breathing and hoping and wanting to be home. Sally just could not bear that thought, it hurt so terribly, it was like fire raging in every soft place of her soul. She went the two steps to her mother, her arms out, seeking embrace. They fell together and then Dad was on them both.

Not until Toddcaster cleared his throat did Sally remember that he was there. He stood squinting at them, as if their bodies gave off light. "We have a description of the vehicle he was in and the man driving it."

Sally listened to his rough, sullen voice. She had never before met a man so tough-sounding.

"Thank you," Mom said. "We were just—despairing—I mean, we don't know *what* to do—"

"The Searchers—"

"Oh, God, they're as bad off as we are."

"It was a pretty grim scene," Dad added.

"You have work to do now."

"Tell us," Mark said.

Toddcaster's expression changed. Was there a hardening around the eyes, a twinge of pain or even anger? Sally wasn't sure. "Do you want coffee?" she asked, breaking away from her mother's taut grasp.

"If I don't have to lick it off the wall."

Mary laughed. "One of my discoveries this week is that I have a temper. If Mary Neary ever gets near this guy, you are going to see what a real mad woman can do to a real bad man."

Sally poured him a mug of coffee.

"So tell us!" Her mother's voice teased like it always did when she wanted something, but now there was also a high, scary note of terror.

Toddcaster pulled back a chair, sank into it. His chin on his chest, his mug crouching in his big hands, he looked like a man who had suffered some catastrophe of the skeleton. "What you need to do is canvas IH 15 from the point of the sighting all the way to L.A. Take your posters."

Dad put his hand on his cheek, caressing it as if the skin had become hypersensitive. "That's thousands of miles!"

"Start at Las Vegas and work west."

Sally did not like the guarded sound in his voice. Wasn't this all incredibly good news?

He had pulled out a cigar and was alternately sipping the coffee and gumming it, in what Sally thought must be a rhythm that he found comforting. "Lemme tell you about these cases. They are hell to solve, unless you get a break. Well, we have something of a break. No question. But your man is also very clever. I will tell you a little bit about your man. Clever man. This is not knowledge, you understand. We don't *know* these things. This is experience. Voice of experience. You have basically four kinds of people who do stranger abduction. First, they kidnap for ransom. Rare. This is not that, not the son of a teacher. Then there's the political kidnapping. You're a controversial guy, Mark. But let's face it, the controversy is not a large one. Then there is the sexual kidnapping. Pederast. Usually, though, these are impulse crimes. A kid goes out to the convenience store and never comes back. Also, usually younger kids than Billy. These are people who can't confront their own sexuality. They want kids who are too young to understand. Fourth type, the complex abductor. Maybe he is searching for his own lost childhood. Maybe he is deeply angry. Mentally ill. Certainly a psychopath. Could be a sadist. Any damn thing. This guy will be a loner, a bachelor. For whatever reason he needs a child."

"So he steals one."

"For him this is acting out a fantasy. He hardly troubles himself about issues like kidnapping, is it wrong? He just *acts*. All of a sudden, he's doing his thing. Shrinks talk about motivation. The hell. The horrible truth about being human is that we can't put our real motivations into words. We don't know why people do what they do. We don't even know what the hell we are, any of us. We're just here.

"But remember, this man is psychopathic, and there's very special meaning attached to that word. It means that he has trouble understanding the consequences of his own actions. Time has no meaning for him. It's all now. Yesterday is gone forever. Tomorrow—who ever thinks about that?"

It was so hard to listen. The guy could do anything, that's what Toddcaster was really saying. *Anything!*

As if he was himself caught in a relentless wave, Toddcaster continued. "Odds on this guy is a complex abductor. He thought about it. He planned it. Then he executed the plan.

"Tell you what's gonna happen. You get out there with your posters. Keep me informed as to your whereabouts, and any information you come up with. We'll follow up by requesting incident reports on a white Aerostar all along their probable route of march. Did he get a ticket, have a fender bender? Maybe we'll get lucky. But it ain't a perfect world. Cops don't necessarily *file* incident reports. The hell, you'd be filling out forms until you died."

He took a long pull of coffee. "That beats the hot acid they dispense at Donnie Doughnut. Look, I'm gonna go home and console my wife for a couple of hours. At last report she'd given me up for dead." With a long, groaning sigh he launched himself from the chair. "Gravity," he said, "not my friend."

Sally followed him to the back door, watched as he went down the flagstone walk into the dark. Moths were fluttering around the dim light, their shadows dancing on the tiny concrete porch.

Far in the west she could see a glow, all that was left of the moon. Her mind returned to her nightmare. In it she'd seen, just for an instant, a face as pale as the moon.

Billy had probably had just such a nightmare. Only in his case, it turned out to be real.

"Brother," she whispered. It was an unaccustomed word. She hadn't called him that; she hadn't even used it much. But now it was precious. It was all she had left of him.

She watched the fading sky. "Brother?"

17.

Barton had driven until four A.M., then slept once again in the back with Billy. It was now Thursday and they were both riding up front. Billy's seat belt was clasped over his arms, which were cuffed together. They were not far from home.

Billy hadn't had a good night. Barton could see that he was fading. His cheeks were sunken, his hair stringy. He sat crouched forward, silent. He wasn't beautiful now. Barton had been thinking that maybe he couldn't handle this child.

The other boys had never really tried to escape. They'd been possible to tame, at least to a degree; fundamentally this was because they were very unhappy children to begin with. Their ambivalence about their home lives made them somewhat compliant.

Billy's midnight dash through that forest had been daring and courageous. Facts had to be faced: Billy was probably a mistake of a new and different kind. Because he was a well-loved and cared-for child, he was much more desirable. But that also meant he was far less cooperative.

Barton also saw that he should have stayed in California. He could have gone up the coast north of San Fran. There were lots of perfect small towns up that way. Then he would have been closer to home, and gotten his boy back with a lot less wear and tear, not to mention the reduced risk. The long hours in the van were what had turned Billy into the stringy, sullen thing that sat beside him now.

Too fucking bad!

* * *

161

Barton caught Billy's attention when he sucked his breath in hard. He watched him grip the steering wheel until it twisted. He was so strong that it was weird.

His temples were covered with beads of sweat, his eyeballs were popping out. Obviously he was furious, but why? Not a word had been said for hours.

Billy didn't like this at all. Barton acted mad and disappointed. 'I'm not good enough,' Billy thought—and suddenly there appeared the miraculous possibility that he might be freed.

"If you want to let me go," he said, "you don't have to take me back to Stevensville. I'll be OK."

Slowly Barton's head turned until he was facing Billy full, not looking at the road at all. "No," he said. Then he jerked back, quickly returning his attention to the highway. In his voice there was a menacing sweetness which Billy did not want to hear.

But he did hear, and he was pretty sure he understood.

Barton's mind whispered its secrets. 'You really shouldn't think about the black room. No, you should not.' It was so awful and stuffy in there. The kids didn't like it.

He remembered such moments there . . . 'So *I* go, "You don't come out of the black room." And *he* goes, "What if I have to take a piss?" Timmy, the big genius.'

In the black room, Barton could take his time. They weren't coming out, there was no hurry. You had to know anatomy. You had to understand the nervous system. There was no way they could escape, there was no way anybody would hear.

There was a corner of heaven under Barton Royal's house, called the black room. In that place and in that place alone he was fully himself.

They were getting into heavier and heavier traffic when Barton suddenly pulled the van onto the shoulder. His face, which had been dark and empty while he was driving, was altered by a smile. "You gotta go in the back. I'm really sorry, but you must understand."

"Yeah, sure," Billy said aloud. 'Don't cross him,' his mind warned. He had to be very, very careful.

162

"I'm sorry, son, but we're coming into a city. Get on the cot."
Not that! "Oh, come on, Barton. I won't try to run away
anymore. I promise."

Barton's smile got even wider. "Get on the cot." His low,
sullen tone made the smile seem all the more eerie.

"Barton, look, I don't think I can stand the straps anymore.
I'm sorry, Barton, but please, you have the handcuffs, and I
could just sit back here with them on—"

"Get on that cot, you *fucking little scum!*"

Billy had never been yelled at like that before, never even
heard anybody yell like that except maybe in a movie. He
hopped right up and put his hands rigidly to his sides, waiting
for the straps. He tried to fight the sobs but he couldn't, he was
just too tired. As Barton strapped him in he was wracked by
waves of blackest despair.

As Barton tightened the straps down he tried to be pleasant,
even affable. No need to panic the little creep. He would have
him in the black room within the hour, then he could let it *all*
out.

The little shit was going to have a hell of a time in the black
room. It was eleven. Given traffic, they'd be home by twelve—
twelve-fifteen. Then he'd have to call in, God knew, maybe he
didn't even have a job left, it'd been a week since he was due
back from Hawaii. More than a week.

No, Gina might be mad, but she'd never get rid of Uncle
Squiggly. Tiny Tales needed him.

'Gina Roman, you bitch, you better not fire me. I had the flu!
It wasn't my fault it happened on Maui.'

He'd make it up to her, do a show every Saturday without fail
from now on. They had forty kids a week last month, at five
dollars a head. That left her one hundred fifty dollars a week
clear, you take out his fifty. Uncle Squiggly would get that
Squiggle Box cranked up until all the little boys and girls would
be laughing and laughing and laughing, the *little pieces of shit!*

The van continued along the highway for about twenty minutes, then it slowed and Billy knew they were taking an exit.
This time there was no question of screaming. Not only was he
strapped down, his mouth was taped up tight. He tried to pray.

163

'Hail Mary,' he thought, 'womb of Jesus—' He was too scared to remember the words.

The van was moving up and down hills, Billy could tell that. Up a long hill, curving this way and that, then down and then a sharp turn. Even though it was useless, Billy struggled.

If only.

If only he could just get out of this van, he could run fast enough to beat fat Barton.

If only!

Familiar old L.A.: a sea of convenience stores punctuated by an occasional mass of houses. He made his way down Santa Monica, turned right at Hugo's, scene of many a breakfast of omelet, fresh-squeezed o.j. and that great coffee of theirs.

L.A., West Hollywood, the Hills. This was his town and he loved it dearly. Just for fun he turned on Fountain so he would pass Tiny Tales. The store was open, Gina was in the window putting out the display for that new *Pat the Bunny* reissue. So the point-of-sale stuff that had been promised last month had finally come. She was doing Barton's work for him—and let her. Let her wonder. For what she paid she didn't *deserve* employees who were reliable.

"I had the flu. My mother had the flu. The whole fucking *world* had the flu, Gina!"

Mrs. Worden said people could go out of their bodies. Maybe if he got out he could fly home and tell Mom and Dad where he was. But how do you do it? She sat on the floor and went "Ommmmm" and said she'd been to the Pleiades. What is the female word for dork?

If only that phone operator had told somebody! Probably she thought, 'Just a kid playing another prank.' They were all so dumb!

He couldn't bear the straps another second. Every sinew strained against them, strained and could not stop straining. Behind the gag he was screaming. His head was bobbing.

For a time he was lost in his terror and in the choking claustrophobia of the little cot that was his prison.

Then something happened. He did not know what it was,

could not have known the power of the reserves that lie within us, that by grace and need may be briefly tapped.

Souls can fly from bodies, withered legs can carry us again, empty eyes can recover sight, the dead can rise in silence—but not often, not often at all.

What Billy found in the well of miracles was clarity.

'You have to charm him,' his inner voice said. 'Win him over. Make him love you.'

How? Adults were incredibly good at telling if you lied. Plus he didn't know how to be an actor.

He'd better learn.

They reached Sunset, passed the lovely St. James Club with its wonderful suites Barton could never possibly afford, then the Mondrian where he sometimes had supper when he was feeling flush.

When he turned onto King's Road and began going up into the Hollywood Hills themselves he was oppressed by a sense of looming menace, as if the whole escarpment was going to slide down into Sunset and bury him. The tranquillity of King's Road replaced Sunset's zipping traffic.

He wanted to stop at the video store and rent *Cabaret* for later. He also needed to go to the liquor store and get a bottle of that '84 Mouton-Cadet if it was still on sale. Sally Bowles and fine claret were a ritual after the black room.

Billy noticed that the van was going slower. There was no traffic anymore. They were climbing a hill that was steeper and longer than the others. Hill, Los Angeles: didn't they have a place called Beverly Hills? He must be in Beverly Hills, California!

'God,' his heart said, 'give me the strength I need. Please, God.' But, did he really believe in God? He'd had his doubts. But not right now. Right now, he decided, he believed totally. 'And God, if I've been asking too many questions, please don't mind. It wasn't a big deal, I'm just a kid with a lot of questions. Still, the business about the loaves and the fishes—if you calculate the size of the crowd and the amount a single man could eat, you had to create loaves and fishes at the rate of about a hundred and sixty of each per minute, which is amazing. And also, why do you have *fishes*, God, when we have just plain fish? Were yours something special, like maybe a bunch of minnows?'

No, Billy, shut up! 'God, I believe all the miracles! Really! I love Jesus, and that is *really* true! I'll put up His statue in my room, pray every day. I'll be an altar boy like Dad was. Oh, God save me!'

It was surprisingly cool for an August day in L.A., sunny and hardly more than seventy. This was the kind of weather that had drawn the millions to this place.

By four the smog would be almost unbearable, but Barton would be safely sealed up where no smog could penetrate. He shuddered deliciously, thinking that he'd be *doing it* at four. By then they'd be a couple of hours into it. He'd be sweaty and possibly even a tad bored. The *fucking thing* that was eating his heart right out of his body would at last be getting quiet. Billy would be almost unrecognizable.

Tonight would be a blessed night. Wine, the stars, and *Cabaret*. Sally Bowles, his love.

When the engine went quiet Billy really started squirming. There was a short silence, then the rumble of a garage door closing. It got dark.

"We're ho-o-me," Barton sang out. "Welcome to my world, Billy boy!"

Barton rolled the side door of the van open. Despite everything Billy was eager to see the mansion. He loved big houses. If he'd been in control of things, Dad would have made more money and they would live in a huge house with columns. Instead of the old wagon they would have something incredible, like maybe a bright red Bentley Turbo, zero to sixty in six and a half seconds, top end a hundred and sixty, the fastest production sedan in the world.

"I'm just going to take in our stuff," Barton said. "Then I'll be back for you."

When the smell of the strange garage came into his nose, Billy's fevered thoughts went quiet. He felt sad. Unexpectedly,

166

he remembered the way he'd dropped his bike on top of Sally's the last time he'd come home.

The last time!

"OK, my boy, now for the big moment." Barton crawled up into the van and unstrapped him. Immediately Billy pulled off the gag. Barton cocked his head, smiled. "Now, did I tell you to do that?"

Billy began at once to carry out his plan of good behavior. "I'm sorry, Barton."

Barton tousled his hair. "No problem. C'mon, let's take a look around."

There was a second car in the garage, but it was no Mercedes. Billy saw an old tan Celica with a taped-up window on the passenger side.

They went into a tiny, filthy kitchen. It stank in here! Barton was whistling. "Here is where I prepare meals fit for royalty. All I have to do is dig down and start cooking!" He chuckled.

This was no mansion. Barton had lied, he was poor. The only new thing he had was that van.

Barton realized that he'd left rather a mess. He'd been eager to get away after doing Timmy. He'd wanted another child so bad he could hardly stand it!

This place did not smell too good. Timmy had taken a lot more out of him than he'd admitted at the time. They'd been together for two months. Jack had lasted even longer, almost half a year.

Billy was going to be a record in the opposite direction. It was really very sad to get a new boy only to do him right away. But God, the black room was thrilling.

Barton bustled around all happy. He kept looking at Billy, though, and his eyes said he was completely and totally crazy. But of course he was crazy, look at what he had done and how he lived! He probably didn't even know this wasn't a mansion.

The kitchen opened onto a small living-dining room. Barton hadn't misled about one thing, the view was pretty neat. They were at the top of a high canyon. Below them there was a long gully full of brush and exposed sewer pipes. Billy could see a glimpse of a road, and beyond that the vast Los Angeles basin.

"Do you know where you are?"

Billy didn't think he ought to admit it, but it was so obvious that they were overlooking L.A. "I—I'm not sure."

"You know damn well, don't you?"

Billy nodded.

"Sure you do. Now you're going to have to get undressed."

Billy didn't like this. Why would he want him naked, except to do something bad?

"Can't I wait until bedtime?"

Barton laughed, deep and rich. When Billy started to laugh too, Barton grabbed his shirt and pulled him almost off the floor. "You'd better learn right now to obey me, Billy. You don't get second chances around here!"

Billy did as he was told, until he was down to his briefs. "That's fine," Barton said. Billy stood waiting, miserable and afraid.

He still had creamy smooth skin, and the chest was healing with surprising speed. Well, never mind, the black room awaited. He would get Billy completely trussed up and then tell him what he was going to do to him.

That part of it was incredible. Timmy hadn't believed. Even when he was in the black room he hadn't believed. Then Barton started, and finally he believed.

Billy would believe right away.

Mom would say it over the dinner table: "I'm going to punish you after supper, Barton." He would have to eat every morsel and laugh if somebody told a joke and speak when he was spoken to, and then Mom would take him by the hand into the living room and his father wouldn't even glance up from the paper while she did it, even when it went on and on.

Then they would play cards, and he would have to play, too, even though it was excruciating to sit down.

He carried them down to the black room after he told them. Billy would believe and he would be as rigid as a child made of wood, his skin cool and dry, and would either be silent or whimpering.

"You know, Barton," Billy said in a shaking voice, "I guess I really am kind of glad to be here."

168

Barton had not expected this. It was obvious that Billy hated him. This boy was a failure.

"I had a rough time at home," Billy continued. "My dad beat me. You won't, will you, Barton?"

Was this for real?

Billy's mind was rushing from idea to idea. He had a very bad feeling about the way things were developing. There was something Barton was getting ready to do, and must not do.

"Your dad beat you?"

"Yeah. With a real whip."

Barton snorted with obvious disbelief.

"No, he kept it on a shelf in his closet. He beat me if I was late. And my mom drank and Barton, I'm really glad to be here."

Barton folded his arms. "That's not true."

"I'm homesick as hell, I admit that, but I know you want a boy and you're going to be nicer."

Barton went to the big picture window.

Saying what he said made Billy sick inside, but it was probably his only chance. If he didn't betray Mom and Dad he was never going to see them again.

"I hate them," he yelled. His voice sounded flat and insincere. Barton shook his head, said nothing. Billy tried to get some more feeling into it. "I hate them!"

Barton went to a built-in bookcase on the wall beside the couch. He opened it and took out a big, thick rope.

"Come here, Billy."

18.

Father Turpin sat awkwardly in the Nearys' living room. Mark had given him coffee, and now watched him busy himself with cup, sugar and milk. Mark had not expected him. After Toddcaster left they had all gone back to bed. Despite everything Mary and Sally had gotten to sleep; Mark hadn't been so lucky.

Having a priest in the house brought back childhood habits of awkward and excessive courtesy. "Yes, Father, no, Father . . ."

Mark's eyes went to the priest's black briefcase, then up to his face. Father Turpin sat on the edge of his chair, his saucer held in his left hand. With his right he raised the cup to his lips. His eyes, looking back at Mark's, seemed at first genial, surrounded as they were by wrinkles that might be laugh lines. When he smiled, though, seeing that Mark was regarding him, something baleful appeared. Mark was struck by how predatory he seemed, and how that appearance must hamper his work.

"I was hoping Mary and Sally would be able to join us."

"I'd wake them—"

"No, no." He leaned forward. "Detective Toddcaster called me." He fell silent, as if this statement had enormous importance. His expression became sly. "You're going hunting."

"This afternoon I fly to Las Vegas. I'll poster westward toward L.A."

The priest put down his cup. All geniality had left his face. "I've come to tell you that there's a little money for folks with major breaks. The Searchers cut a check for five hundred dollars."

170

Mark stared astonished at the check that was being offered him. "The Searchers are with you. I'm with you. The Lord is with you—at least, nominally."

"Father—"

"Bob. I'm Bob." He cleared his throat, put the check into Mark's hand. He opened his briefcase. "Now, I gather you're at the point of realizing just how little you know about conducting an investigation, and how important self-help is going to be."

"There isn't anybody else!"

"That isn't quite true. The police do a great deal, but you and Mary and Sally represent Billy's best chance of coming home." He glanced around the room. "I presume you can't afford a private detective."

"I'm a high school teacher."

"Well, there's a man in Des Moines. Richard Jones. He's a detective, and a good one."

"I cannot even begin to afford that sort of thing—in spite of this check. I've got a two-thirty flight and I'm exhausted and I have a hell of a lot of work to do before I leave."

Turpin held up his hands, as if defending himself. "Mr. Jones does this for free. No actual searching, mind you. But advice. You need it, especially now, before you hit the road."

Suddenly here was another thread in Mark's hand. "When can I see him?"

"We'd better leave as soon as possible if you're going to make a two-thirty flight." He withdrew a thick green book from the case. "You can borrow it."

Mark took the book. *Techniques of Investigation.*

"It's a basic text on police science. The chapters on missing persons will be quite useful. You can use them to make certain the police are doing all they can, and that your own investigation is sensibly organized."

An image of Father Turpin's bleak cavern of a church rose in Mark's mind. How did it feel, week after week, to say Mass for twenty or thirty people in a nave meant to accommodate four hundred? That was this man's truth—and yet there was absolutely no sense of despair. None at all.

"I've gotta get packed. Give me ten minutes."

"I'm not the one in a hurry, Mark."

Mark went upstairs and threw some clothes into the ancient Samsonite two-suiter he took to teachers' conventions. Then he topped off the pile with a box of five hundred of their brand-new missing child posters. He woke up Mary and told her he was going with Turpin.

"He's here?"

"He brought this." He handed her the check. Without another word she got up and went downstairs.

"We need this so bad, Bob. We've only got a couple of thousand dollars to our names." There were tears forming in the corners of her eyes.

Turpin stroked her head, a clumsy gesture. In his eyes there was a sort of desperation. Sally came down behind her mother, like her wearing a robe over her nightgown. They stood on the front porch as Mark and the priest left. Sally waved a small wave. "I'll call tonight," Mark said.

Turpin's car was old, an enormous Chrysler from the mid seventies. "I share this tank with the Sacred Heart Convent," he said as he started it. "Five aged nuns who seem to have little to do but clean the damn thing with Q-tips."

"It looks like it just came off the assembly line."

"Embarrassing, but I live with it. Wheels are wheels."

"It's sweet that they do it for you."

"I'm their confessor."

"Elderly nuns?"

"You'd be surprised. I've been hearing confessions for over forty years, and those sisters are about the only ones left who can still surprise me."

As soon as they were out on the highway, Mark began wondering. Had Billy been taken this way? Did he see these signs, this long, flat view, smell this air while he was in the hands of his abductor?

Mark closed his eyes. He tried to blank his mind, but his mind wouldn't stop. Had he been tied, gagged? Had he been trussed up on the floor of that white Aerostar, or simply sitting there too scared to move? Mark's thoughts left the realm of words, and he began to see his son, a bright shadow in a dark space. When shadow Billy said "Dad!" Mark started awake. They were halfway there; an amazing thirty minutes had passed. "Want some music?" Father Turpin said.

"Yeah." Mark started to look through his cassettes.

"I'm afraid they're all pretty schmaltzy. I'm a sentimental guy."

"Where from?"

"I'm a Mick from Queens. Irish heaven. And I've got the drinking scars to prove it. As well as the Clancy Brothers tapes."

Mark abandoned the cassettes.

"Want to talk?"

"About?"

"Whatever it is that's been making you moan in your sleep like that."

"Billy."

Turpin took an exit and moved through the center of town, stopping at last in front of a small office building. Mark followed the priest into a pink granite lobby.

It was all very modern and bland. There should have been an elevator with a rattling brass accordion door and an elderly operator with the name "Pete" embroidered on the pocket of his threadbare uniform.

As it was, Richard Jones's office was on the street floor. Father Turpin's fist had hit the door of the office once when it was pulled open. A gust of cold air poured out.

Jones was a tall man, heavyset, with a surprised expression on his face. It took Mark a moment to realize that this expression was permanent. He smiled at Father Turpin, then gave Mark a long look. "Sorry about your boy, Mark. Can I call you Mark?"

"Yeah, of course."

"I guess you've been given a lot of advice already." He stepped back into his pin-neat office and indicated a chair. "Make yourself comfortable. I know you have a time problem, so I'll keep this to an hour."

Jones dropped down behind his desk. "So you've talked to Toddcaster, the Searchers. Now me. You're hitting all the stations on the missing children underground. Next you'll be onto the foundations. First off, I will do things for you that you cannot do for yourself. I am a licensed private investigator, which means that I can find out certain things in the pursuit of my trade. Give me a license plate and I can make it for you.

Give me a name and I can get you an address—maybe. *If* you know the right state.

"Now let's talk brass tacks. You are the victim of a rare and terrible crime. Stranger abduction. Your son's been missing less than a week, yet you already have a major lead. This is very good news. But it might not go anywhere. Most leads peter out. Your genuine stranger abduction is a very hard crime to solve. It is often fatal. Face that." His lips became a hard line. "Be damned careful following up your lead. I'll be frank with you. There are satanist cults out there stealing kids for very nasty reasons. Why? Because they're jerks. Satan does not answer prayers. In this respect he is as bad as God. There are kiddie porn rings and kiddie prostitution rings. Your son could be sold to a pederast. You know what that is?"

"Yes, of course."

"Everybody has their pet theories. Toddcaster tell you about the 'complex abductor'?"

"He did."

"That's his pet theory. That, plus the fact that motivations can't be understood. Maybe not, except that sex and money and fear are all very understandable motivations, aren't they? Toddcaster thinks they're too complex to understand. I don't agree. People are motivated by the raw emotions—greed, anger, fear. Even love—at times." He smiled a rueful little smile. "I urge you, mister, don't settle on any one theory. Keep your mind open. Toddcaster may be right. But he may also be wrong, remember this. And another thing: the police have limited scope. They can only think locally, statewide. Their impact diminishes the farther you get from Iowa. *You* have to think nationally, even internationally if the clues lead that way."

"I'm leaving this afternoon."

"You want to make sure you stay *behind* your man. You don't want him to see the posters coming up ahead of him. This might be your boy's death warrant. *Comprende?*"

"I understand."

"Make sure the police are keeping up their end of the bargain. But you've got to do the work. *You* get the leads. *You* take them to the cops. *You* make sure they are doing their job right because *you* are on top of them. This is your boy, Mark."

"For the love of God, I know that!" The moment he heard the rage in his own voice Mark regretted his tone. Jones apparently didn't notice. Mark looked at Father Turpin, who was sitting silently, his fingers held in a tent.

Jones had what soon became a torrent of advice, so much that Mark found himself dashing off notes on a yellow legal pad. How to interpret clues, how to generate, follow up and network leads, where to put his posters, which foundations would help spread the word, which were active and which were wastes of time.

At the end of one hour almost to the second the meeting was over. Jones leaned across the desk. "It's a hell of a lot of work, investigating one of these cases. I just have one piece of advice: don't give up hope. And if you do, call Turpin."

Jones and Turpin gave one another a silent look. Mark thought that they must have gone through a great deal together.

On the way to the airport Mark Neary closed his eyes. Father Turpin saw the yellow pad clutched tightly in the man's hand. 'Lord,' Bob Turpin said, 'please give him back his kid. If you don't do it for him, do it for me, Lord. If I still have any pull with you, of course, in view of my empty pews.'

Part Four

HER IN THE DARK

19.

They'd been talking for what seemed like fifty hours and the rope was lying on the coffee table.

Billy was bargaining not to be tied up with it. He watched the afternoon light playing across the fat twist of its strands.

Then Barton started in again. "I'll be a good dad!" Why did he have to keep saying it, like he didn't believe it. Billy wanted him to be a good dad, he was all he had right now.

"Great," Billy said for the hundredth time.

"I'm going to show you the town. L.A. is incredible! You know how far it is from one end to the other? Nearly a hundred miles."

"Wow!"

"You're getting to like me, I can tell!" He shifted eagerly around in his seat.

Billy fought himself. By sheer will, he created a smile on his face. "You're cooler than my dad."

"I *am* your dad!"

Why did he smile like that when he talked? It wasn't a good smile. Billy could not help it, he still thought he was going to get killed. But he kept on anyway, gamely trying to project something like enthusiasm.

"I mean—you know. Than Mark." When he had to betray Dad it was terrifying. Dad always knew his thoughts. What if this was hurting Dad's feelings? Then would he never come?

Finally Barton stood. He now bustled around, cleaning up and chattering about himself. Billy listened. Billy felt the cool bite of the handcuffs around his wrists. He managed to get his shorts back on. When Barton saw this, he silently opened the handcuffs so that Billy could finish dressing. Then he closed them and returned to his cleaning. While Barton talked, Billy stared at the rope.

"I think I must have been too good—oh, look at this *shirt*, it's got—yuk—anyway, I was always highly obedient. My mother used corporal punishment. Slightly. It's not right, really. I mean, why do they do it? Punishing embarrasses me. It demeans you both. I mean, God, don't they realize that punishment simply *creates* punishers? It's obvious if people would just think, but they don't think. My parents were sweet."

He gathered up an armful of newspapers that Billy thought might have been used as toilet paper because they stank. "Oh, my, maybe you're thirsty! Are you thirsty?"

"I could live through a Coke."

"But you like Dr Peppers better. I looked in your fridge! Sure! I wanted to know just what you liked the most! I saw the squash in the crisper. You like squash?"

This guy *would* notice that stuff. "It's OK."

"I'm kidding. I know you hate it. All boys hate it. We were clean-platers at my house. You had to have a clean plate or you couldn't get up from the table. My folks were very loving. I also know you like Butterfingers. You see, I remember those things!" He came over to Billy. "Just look how smooth your skin is, son. May I call you son?"

"OK."

"You must be at least half Irish."

"I am. And my mother's Scottish."

"The Celts! The most beautiful people on earth. Such complexions, like you have. But I'll bet you don't *feel* smooth and pale, do you? You feel like a boy. Strong."

"In a manner of speaking."

"In a manner of speaking! Out of the mouths of babes! I love your command of English."

He started pulling at Billy's shoulders, trying to get him to stand up. Billy pressed himself down into the couch.

"Oh, come on, son." Barton began mincing backward, pulling Billy up. Billy was wary. He wanted to stay right here. "You have a bedroom, you know. It's nice, come and see!"

Slowly he stood up. Barton took hold of the chain between

180

his handcuffs and drew him across the living-dining room toward a pale green door that stood open a crack. Billy didn't like that door, didn't like the darkness of the room beyond.

Closer they went to the door, and closer yet.

As they passed the kitchen Billy heard water dripping and smelled a smell of old grease. He could see dishes piled up on the counter, even on the floor. There was what looked like a pair of fireplace tongs stuck into a pot of water in the sink. The water was gray and had dark chunks floating in it.

"I'm going to go get you some Dr Peppers and us some supper, then I'll be back."

"I'll clean up the kitchen while you're gone," Billy ventured.

Barton's curls bounced as he shook his head with the vehemence of a toddler saying "No!"

Then he kicked the door open and thrust Billy in. Billy whirled, trying to get his foot in the jamb but the door was slammed almost instantly. "It's not a prison, son! I swear it's only your bedroom."

The deadbolt lock clicked. Billy almost panicked; he wanted to rush at that door, to kick it, to break it down! But he had to keep playing the game. If he didn't play the game, Barton would get mad and tie him up with that rope. Then Barton would—

"It's such a nice room, look at the walls."

There was wallpaper with fat little airplanes on it, like something from a nursery. "Yeah," Billy said, forcing lightness into his voice. The airplanes had faces, and all the little faces were smiling. The paper was yellowed, and in places there were rips. "It's real nice, Barton."

"Keen?"

"Really."

The door creaked, Billy heard breathing. Barton must be leaning against it. "Really, really?"

"It's a nice room!" Billy looked at the mattress on the floor, at the ugly black bars on the inside of the window, at the door with the screwheads showing from the deadbolt on the other side. "I'm gonna just love it!"

"Oh, I'm so glad! If you like it—that's very important to me. Son."

"Yeah."

There was another creak, then the sound of departing footsteps. Pulling nervously at his handcuffs, Billy went to the window. Behind the bars were closed blinds. Even pressing his fingers between the tightly spaced bars, he could barely manage to touch them. He couldn't raise them.

His skin crawled, a clammy feeling came over him. Then he noticed that there was another door, this one with a handle. He rushed to it, found that it opened.

It was a small closet. There was a pole, and on the pole were some coat hangers. One of them had a plastic cleaner's bag hanging on it, and another bore a white jacket that looked to be about Billy's size.

Moving his cuffed hands together, he took the jacket down and examined it. In one pocket was a crushed cigarette pack that had obviously been through the wash a few times. The other pocket was empty. Sewn into the collar was a name tag, "Timothy Weathers."

Billy sank to the floor, the jacket in his hands. He could barely breathe, he was so shocked by what he was seeing.

William Neary was not the first: Barton had done this before. And where was Timothy Weathers now? Billy listened, as if he could somehow drag the sound of another boy's presence out of the silence of the house.

He heard something, a sort of rapid, undulating buzz. Was it a wasp, or a pipe buzzing in the wall? It took him a moment to realize that it was a voice.

Was Timothy Weathers still here after all?

Dropping the jacket to the floor, he listened. When he stepped away from the closet, he didn't hear it anymore. But if he went inside, it was louder. He pressed his ear against the wooden planks that formed the back wall.

It wasn't another kid, it was Barton. He was talking in a wheedling, pleading voice. "I'm sorry, Gina, I swear it, it was just the most devastating sickness I have ever endured. I think it was the plane." There was a silence. Billy realized that he was hearing Barton talking on the phone. Then he started again. This time his voice was edged with desperation. "Don't say that! Don't say those words! No. Come on, Gina. You know they love Uncle Squiggly. It's a big draw, you can't tell me it isn't. Look I *know* you can get along without me, but what am

I going to do, I've got to keep body and soul together! Please, Gina, I'm begging you, if you've already got another shop assistant OK, just let me do Uncle Squiggly. That's all I need! OK, look, I'll do it for half the money! Yes, *half!* Just don't fire me, Gina, I beg you!"

There was a long silence, punctuated by bursts of sugar-coated crap from Barton. He was really laying it on.

He'd obviously left work to go out and get Billy. He hadn't thought about the consequences and now he was pleading for his job.

Billy allowed himself to hope that Timothy Weathers had gotten away. Maybe even now he was leading the police back to this place.

No. If that was true they would already be here.

The wheedling voice started up again. "Oh, thank you Gina, thank you and thank God! I'll be in right away. Fifteen minutes! OK, thanks baby! Thanks from the bottom of my heart."

The receiver clicked and Barton's voice came through much louder. *"Fucking shitty cunt-face bitch!"* When he stopped shouting Billy could still hear his breath, long, raging, ragged gasps.

Billy drew back from the wall. The way the guy shouted went right through him every time.

For fear that Barton would burst in and find him listening, he backed out of the closet and closed the door.

By the creak of his footsteps Billy tracked Barton's movements. He came out of his room, down the hall, paused before this door. Billy literally flinched at the click of the lock. But the door didn't open. He must have just tested the lock as he went past.

Then there came the distinct sound of the garage door rolling open. A car ground to life. It took a long time to get it started. That meant the Celica.

Again Billy went to his window. He pushed his fingers through the bars, but couldn't quite reach the blinds. He needed something—like a coat hanger. An instant later he was in the closet, then back with one in his hands. He could push up the blinds just a crack, but it was enough to see Barton's Celica disappear down the steep street. When it was gone silence settled on the house.

For the first time since this awful, awful thing had happened

Billy felt a little bit safe. Tears sprang into his eyes. Then waves of sheer relief poured over him. He sank down bawling loudly.

Billy was young and full of vitality. He wanted to have his life!

The truth that he had not expressed consciously before now rushed forth: 'This afternoon I fought for my life.' He didn't know how to do that! Kids shouldn't have to!

He jumped up, lifted the blind again, peered hungrily through the crack. The sky was a glaring, bronzed blue, the light very hard and white. But there was a neighborhood out there! Houses meant people, and maybe somebody would hear him, maybe somebody would finally come!

"HEY HEY HEY HEY!"

The neighborhood was totally still and quiet. From this point he could see two other houses, one of them very modern, the other older and lower, like this one. Both had flowering trees in their yards. The modern one had a blue Mercedes in the driveway.

As he watched, a cat came along the street, sniffing at things in the gutters. Leaves moved on trees, but he couldn't hear a breeze. He tapped the thick glass with the end of the coat hanger. You couldn't make much noise like this. His throat began to ache for the freedom that conceals itself everywhere, and when lost proves to be as essential as air.

For a moment he felt calm, then all of a sudden he had to try the door. He kicked it, then kicked it again. Then he stopped, feeling it more carefully.

It was made of steel. "You dirty bastard!" He threw himself against it, kicking and screaming until he was hoarse. Finally he dropped down on the mattress, which stank faintly of urine and the sweet-nasty smell of unwashed sheets like Jerry sometimes had when his mother was on strike and refused to go in his room until it was—as she put it—"scraped."

Jerry! He hadn't thought of Jerry since the disaster. With all his might he wished Jerry was here right now. He could see him, could hear him cursing over Space Harrier, "Shit, it ate my quarter. *Shit!*" "It's not the game's fault, Jer. Your problem is, you're totally sucky."

You love people in a lot of different ways. You couldn't hug friends like Jer, so you kicked each other around instead. The more you fought, the tighter you got. "I'm in a hell of a lot of trouble, buddy." His own voice reminded him of the way Dad sounded when he talked. He was growing up; he was a lot like Dad, too.

All at once something he had been hiding even from himself burst into consciousness. He felt awful, vomiting anger, and he shouted it all for all the world and the bars to hear: "Dad, why don't you find me! Dad, where are you!"

His voice died.

He whispered, "Where are you?"

Despite his desire to never be asleep when Barton could sneak up on him, the silence and the dimness of the room were beginning to have an effect. He was alone for the first time since Barton, and his body began to sink of its own accord into the softness of the mattress. "Daddy," he repeated, but this time his voice was thick and slow.

Abruptly, he slept—and as abruptly awoke. He had no watch, he couldn't tell if he'd been asleep for a second or an hour. If he strained, he could hear the water dripping into the pot where the tongs soaked. What were they used for, barbecue or something? Who cooked with things like that?

Light was coming out from under the closet door, blue and baleful. The light was not normal. It seemed almost like a living thing, as if the brightness itself was full of feeling and need. It poured out into the bedroom. Billy watched, amazed. It was as if the whole moon had been stuffed into the closet.

A voice was singing,

"Where have you been, Billy boy, Billy boy,
Where have you been, charming Billy . . ."

Momma's song that she sang when he was a baby! It was so good to hear, and it hurt so darn much!

Then there was a boy in the room all covered with light. He had Timothy Weathers's white jacket slung over his shoulder. His hair was as blond as the light that surrounded him.

Billy was deathly afraid of this boy and his chalk-blue eyes. He sat up in bed, horrified beyond words, as the boy's face worked.

185

He thought, 'I'm awake but I'm still dreaming.' He was screaming, the boy, screaming as if in great agony. It was terrible to see, more terrible still not to hear. The boy was suffering, he was suffering horribly! Billy tried to talk but all that came out was a breathy whisper. The boy began twisting in the light, his face melting, his eyes melting and oozing down his cheeks. He was being dissolved by the sheer light, he was dying horribly and Billy could not even scream with him.

Then the closet door flew open. The light was coming out of the floor. It was open like a trapdoor. The other boy turned, still screaming, and went down.

This time Billy was really awake. He was staring at the ceiling, confused at first about where he was and what had just happened. But when he tried to touch an itch on his nose his handcuffs reminded him of everything.

He leapt up from the bed, rushed straight to the closet. He was heartbroken: his dream was wrong, there was no trapdoor. Again he went to the window. The shadows were long across the street, the cat and the Mercedes were gone. But there was a person out there. A boy! He was walking his bike up the hill, he was coming this way! The boy had black, straight hair. His bike was blue, and new. When he reached the top of the hill he wasn't fifty feet away.

Billy screamed with all his breath and it would have been a word but it was too loud, too shrill, it was just the scraped-raw sound of his pain.

Totally oblivious, the boy turned the bike around and as Billy jabbed the coat hanger into the window glass again and again—making only the slightest tapping sound—he mounted the bike and disappeared down the hill.

Away he sailed in freedom.

The glass was not only thick, it had dewdrops inside, meaning that it was double-pane as well. Billy threw down the coat hanger in bitter disgust. There was a neighborhood out there, and kids and cats and bikes and laughter and evenings in the backyard, and he was in here in this stinking prison pretending under pain of death to love a human maggot more than he did his own precious dad and mom.

He wanted to scrunch down inside himself forever, to just

twist and turn until he was nothing but a little, tiny black knot of flesh that didn't have any brain or any memories or even any eyes.

He rushed to the door. He was so frantic that sweat was breaking out all over his body. The tiny room seemed to be getting smaller by the second. The walls, the ceiling were curving in toward him; all the air was being sucked out. He couldn't breathe, he couldn't move, he was being crushed to death.

Somebody on another planet was screaming. It was kind of funny, so high-pitched. Babies cry, they don't scream. But if a baby screamed, it would sound like this. Only when Billy really listened to the funny screaming did he realize it was him.

The walls weren't closing in, the ceiling was still where it belonged. And there was somebody singing in the living room:

> *"You are my sunshine,*
> *my only sunshine,*
> *you make me happy*
> *when skies are gray."*

That was a woman's voice! Billy rushed to the door. He smashed his ear against it, listened with all the concentration he could manage.

> *"You will never know, dear,*
> *how much I love you.*
> *Please don't take my sunshine away."*

It stopped, cleared its throat. This was a real woman, not the stereo. Gina, maybe it was Gina! *Oh, God, please, please, please!*

He listened, dangling as if from a thread of absolute need, as the woman moved around in the room.

Then the lock clicked, the handle of the door gleamed as it was turned.

The door came open.

A figure appeared backed by a halo of light from the setting sun. Billy stepped away, gasping, unable to speak, so glad, so glad—

"He-e-y," Barton said. He moved out of the halo of sunlight.

"It's been pretty loud in here. And here I thought you liked me." There were tears forming in the bottoms of his eyes. "I really did." He folded his arms.

Billy looked beyond him, but there was nobody else there. The woman's voice must have been just his imagination.

Barton stood with his head bowed, apparently overcome with emotion. Slowly his hands came up, covered his face. The moan that emerged from behind them was heartrending.

So Barton wanted love. That was totally disgusting. It was also sad, though, because he was so ugly and so mean and nobody could ever possibly love him even for one single second.

Billy reached out his clanking, cuffed hands.

20.

He ought to press a nice hot iron against those pretty, grasping little hands!

Then Billy moved forward into the light and Barton was struck silent by wonder.

At sunset the light shone across the living room and into this bedroom. When he came into this light Billy's beauty was such that Barton was instantly swept by a wave of regret for his anger. Billy had the softest, finest face he had ever seen. The light made his exhaustion disappear.

He'd been in there screaming, though. Like Timmy, like Jack he had been trying to make himself heard by the little Holcombe boy.

It had hurt when the others did it, but when Billy did it Barton felt betrayed to his very essence. It was as if the best part of his own soul was traitor to him.

He'd slapped Jack right across the room, and that devil Timmy, he'd had some really thorough attention paid to him, I should say!

The sunlight made Billy's skin go pink and pale white, made his hair glow as if it was precious metal, shone in his eyes like the very light of heaven.

"Billy," he said in a breaking tone. "Please, I want it to work so bad."

He lowered his eyes, unable to bear the boy's gaze. There was mischief in that face, and lies and fear and all the dark things that formed a boy. But there was also something he had never seen before. It awed him.

"Don't get steamed now, Barton, OK?"

God help him, though, the anger kept rushing into his blood, flushing him with its thrill. The rituals associated with it had enormous sexual potency. No matter Billy's beauty, he could fall victim.

The black room—

Don't even think about it!

But he wanted to think about it. Even though Billy was so beautiful and so awesome, he wanted to take him there.

Tear him apart!

Oh, yeah. People didn't realize what they were really saying when they spoke of the "pornography of evil." They thought they were expressing loathing, but those same people would gladly go to a hanging.

This peculiar pleasure was part of the ordinary state of man. The few that didn't enjoy the actual suffering of the condemned were secretly relieved by the death. To live on past the death of another was to taste the arrogance of the immortal. It was in such moments that death and sex would embrace.

During the Nazi years whores used to work the crack expresses that ran between Berlin and Warsaw. As the trains passed the fuming crematoria of Oświęcim every whore would be humping a customer.

Similarly, boys used to present their painted cheeks to the crowds as they left the Colosseum at Rome. Barton had walked those long arches, imagining the waspish cries of the boys, the distinguished grunts of their customers, the whoosh of togas stinking of semen and fuller's earth, the clink of small coins in small hands.

Those days, when he'd gone to Italy . . . 1972. He was so young then, so afraid. He'd wandered the Roman back streets, listening to the voices, longing to join the lovely Roman gutter world. But he'd held back: his heart ached for ancient days, when Rome had been a more grand and brutal place. To shuffle through the Forum Trajani in the crowded morning, to hear the savage bellows of the crowds drifting down to the Circus Maximus or the Colosseum, to smell the sharply seasoned foods cooking in the stalls, to kiss Roman skin and feel the brute pressure of Roman love . . . he'd wandered past coffee bars and restaurants and fruit sellers in an anguish of desire.

He'd always ended up in those days by finding a woman. He loved the sodden smells of the body—waste and sweat and rancid, unwashed skin. It was delicious to kiss an ashen mouth, to be attached by its sucking passion, all the while quivering inside with delectable loathing.

Billy stood now with a subtle pout on his face. Since they had not been grasped as he had hoped, his cuffed hands had been lowered. Barton just could not believe that a human being could be this exquisite. It wasn't possible for him to resist this magnificent boy. He'd been tempted—it was too horrible to imagine.

"Billy!" He threw himself at the boy, scooped him up in his arms, suddenly, helplessly showering him with kisses. He shouldn't, it wasn't right, but he just couldn't help it.

"Oh," Billy said, leaning back away from the embrace. Just "Oh," a little surprise, no more. In the holy body Barton thought he detected a relaxation that suggested acceptance, even—dare he hope—enjoyment. There had been that first second of surprised resistance, but now he was relaxing into the hug. Billy *liked* to be held.

Barton came looming down on him, a bloated, black shadow swooping out of the sunlit living room. Roughly he grabbed, pawed. Then he kissed and when his lips touched Billy's cheek it was like wet, horrible fire. 'This is it,' Billy thought, and he felt a sudden burst of rage against his father: *Why don't you find me, Dad, what's the matter with you!*

Inside himself Barton said, slow, slow, careful, careful. He did not like the stirring within him, it wasn't moral, it wasn't healthy, above all it was not normal.

He was normal! For God's sake, loneliness was a normal emotion. He had misplaced his own childhood. . . . From his diary when he was nine: "My hated woman parent sent me upstairs . . . my hated male parent decides tonight if I am to go to boarding school. . . ." Like dying, like dying, the gleam of crossed guns on your collar tabs, the stink of Brasso, his dreadful uniform, the white duck trousers and sky-blue jacket, and combing the ruff of your helmet just so . . .

Oh, he was *holding* dear little Billy and Billy was not resisting, no sir, he was just leaning up against his new dad.

They say that the child is condemned to repeat the mistakes of the parents . . . and to some extent that was true.

As far as Barton Royal was concerned, though, the mistakes had just stopped. Here and now, this instant! "I'll *never* lay a hand on you, Billy." He held him back to arm's length, held him by the shoulder, and the tinkle of the chain between his handcuffs sounded as loud as a shattering window. "You know, I've been thinking. I wonder if you would like to call yourself Billy Royal? William Royal." He cocked his head, winked. "Don't you think it's grand?"

Billy had forced himself to relax into the iron embrace, to feel the rattle of the heart and the quaking of the hands as they swept his back. His single concern was that Barton not fly into a rage because of his attempt to attract attention. He'd thought Barton was still gone. The man was by habit extremely quiet.

Over Barton's shoulder he could see the thick rope lying on the coffee table. Afternoon light bathed it in a kind of unholy glory. It was like a sleeping snake . . . or maybe not sleeping.

Plans raced through Barton's mind. "Look, we need to unpack you. We haven't even done that yet. And then your dad has a beautiful dinner for you. I'm going to cook it myself. I went to the store and got some very nice things. Very nice. Oh!" He broke away, swept out to the kitchen, opened and closed the refrigerator, returned with a huge Butterfinger in his hand.

"As luck would have it, there's free extra candy," he said. "That's why it's so big." He held it out. Would Billy like it? Would he take it? This part was a little like taming an animal. Oh, nonsense, what a thought! This boy was angelic!

Billy held out his hands. Barton was surprised at how hard his own heart was beating. It sounded positively mechanical. When it crossed his mind that men his age did in fact have heart attacks a complex welter of thoughts and feelings tried to surface. He didn't want to die, except sometimes when he couldn't sleep at night and he had to face the fact that his needs were

192

sick and ugly, and so unique that there would probably never be a cure.

Billy was holding the candy in his two hands. "Do you want me to eat this?"

"Do I want—oh, please! I don't *want.* What I want is, if you *would like* to eat it. OK?"

He tried to tear the wrapper. "I can't—" The candy was too big, his hands too close together. He couldn't open it without breaking the bar in half.

The handcuffs were certainly an aesthetic disaster. They intruded into even the tenderest moments, and it was an ugly intrusion.

Would he try to escape? Barton thought about it, but only for a moment: he decided that he didn't want to find out. No matter how tame, you must not be tempted to bring an unclipped bird out of its cage. Los Angeles was full of parrots and parakeets that people had thought were tame.

"Here, I'll open it for you." He took the fat candy bar and tore away some of the paper. When he gave it back, Billy took a big bite. As he chewed he smiled up at Barton.

"May I?" Barton asked. Billy handed him the candy and he bit some off himself—not much! Where Billy had bitten he saw that the chocolate surface was slick with spittle. To take that into his mouth was like communing with Lord Jesus himself. He did it with reverence.

He was careful to bite just with his teeth; he assumed that Billy would be offended if he left any of his own spittle on the bar.

The taste of a Butterfinger, the smell of it, brought back so much home that Billy wanted more than anything to wither up and disappear. Two summers ago he'd been homesick at camp, but it was nothing compared to this. That had been a rich, poignant feeling made almost beautiful by sunset and the singing of the kids. "Yes, sir, that's my baby. No, sir, I don't mean maybe." And, "Mah dear old Swanee . . ." from Mr. Lockyear, which was so funny they all practically died. The sun set across Lake Williams and the campfire flared . . . they had toasted marshmallows and drunk bug juice which was really just cherry

Kool-Aid, and Mom and Dad and Sally had moved like ghosts through his mind.

In the simple, ordinary flavor of the candy he tasted home. He wanted Mom to be saying, "I hate junk food," and Sally to be complaining that he'd stolen hers as well as eaten his own when all the time the thief was really Dad.

The last time he'd eaten a Butterfinger was the night Barton came. He'd been working on his birdsong.

Billy chewed with great deliberation. He had to swallow this and keep it down. C'mon, guy, give him a *big* smile!

Billy was enjoying it, he was relishing it! Barton was an excellent judge of character, all the mommies said so after Uncle Squiggly shows. This little boy was being won over, he was sure of it. He was being seduced. Yes, and wasn't that a beautiful thing?

Barton had dreams, and he loved smooth skin, but he would never—oh, absolutely not! No. Who was it who had claimed that there can be no crime in the mind? "That which remains within is sanctified by the silence that contains it." Walter Pater? No, too modern for him. R. D. Laing, perhaps. He suspected that a lot of fathers, seeing the glorious beauty of their sons and their sons' friends ached to make the leap of Plato's *Symposium*.

You didn't, though. In Plato's time a man who loved a boy risked only the outrage of the father. And with good reason—it was ugly, it was vile, it was just plain wrong.

Because the poor boy, if he liked it, then for the rest of his life would never be sure of his own sexuality. He would be cursed with desires he could not accept. Sex would be permanently out of focus.

Barton knew all too well.

It's a big, dark shadow and it's moving fast—it's Dad! His embrace was so soft, so insistent . . . and his touch—his *touch*—

It never happened! Never! Never!

He was only worried about it a little, that was all. Dad was a fine man, so gentle that Mom had to do all the punishing.

"Aren't we going to have supper soon?"

Barton had been a thousand miles away. "What?"

"If we are, I don't want to finish the candy."

"Oh, yes! Sweets before supper are a no-no. I remember that Timmy—"

"Timmy?"

The question had an edge to it. For a disquieting instant Barton thought that Billy might know something about Timmy. But no, that was just his natural suspicion. He'd even been a suspicious child. Mother had always commented on it.

"He's my nephew. When he stays with me he waits until supper's cooking, then he comes out and inventories the contents of the pots and pans. If he doesn't like what's being prepared, he'll go to his room and load up on Hershey's Kisses. I have to virtually smell them out if I want to get rid of them. He even hid some in the light fixture, once."

"He stays with you?"

"Occasionally."

"How old is he?"

"He's about your age."

Billy was keeping him talking partly because he hated the idea of any more hugging. But there was also another reason. Barton had mentioned unpacking him and he did not want to face all the reminders of home.

He could not allow Barton to see what was really going on in his mind.

With careful intention he turned his mind away from unpacking and toward Timmy Weathers. There might be something to be learned here. He watched Barton for some sign.

If he could learn the fate of Timmy Weathers, he would probably know his own.

Like hell Timmy was Barton's nephew. Barton was such a fabulous liar, it was awesome. But you could still read him, kind of.

He remembered the face of the Timmy Weathers in his dream. It wasn't true that he didn't know what Barton had done to Timmy. He knew exactly what Barton had done.

Barton really had to organize himself; he just wasn't getting things together for his boy. Boys need their fathers to be reliable so that they'll grow up confident, and take a good example with them into adulthood.

He had to get Billy's things, which were still in the Aerostar. He didn't want the boy to see the inside of the van again, but he also didn't want to leave him alone in the house. Neither did he wish to lock Billy in his room just for the three minutes it would take. That would imply such an utter lack of trust. Of course, there *was* an utter lack of trust—but Barton kept hoping that it was only temporary.

The will to escape could be broken. Barton could enact the beautiful life he had originally envisioned. He would introduce Billy to the finer things, would teach him literature and indulge his nascent appreciation of good music and the arts. He would cause this brilliant creature to blossom as never before. As that happened Billy would gradually lose interest in escape. In the end he would come to value his new father.

'I'll be loved,' Barton thought. What an odd notion.

He solved the problem of the bags as best he could. "Come on, Billy, we've got to get your things." They went together to the garage. As he expected, Billy became silent when he saw the van. Barton stood him in the doorway of the garage, beside the Celica. He crossed the concrete floor with its cracks and oil spots, and slid open the van door.

It smelled of bodies and excrement and fear. He'd have to wash it soon, which was inconvenient because it would have to be taken into the driveway. He considered it dangerous to show the Aerostar too soon after a hit.

Barton knew all about incident reports, and there had been at least one and possibly two incidents on the road. The first had been the matter of the missing plate renewal sticker. Then there was the confrontation in Denver. That could easily have led to a delayed police report. For God's sake, Billy's screams would have kept any normal human being awake nights. When they sobered up, those people might well have called the cops.

The likelihood was small in either case that a description of the Aerostar had ended up in police files, but you could not be too careful.

He gathered up the heap of clothes that had come out of the duffel and stuffed them back.

"Now we'll organize your closet and dresser. You'll be all moved in."

Billy accompanied him like a robot, his movements stiff and controlled. He did not speak.

Somehow Billy had to keep going. Just glimpsing his clothes as Barton put them in his duffel had been hard. Now he would have to sort through them.

Dad!

They left the dim, stuffy garage and moved through the gray little house to Billy's dismal room. Didn't Barton realize how incredibly dingy and depressing this place was? Maybe he really believed it was a mansion. He could, he was that nutso.

Billy stood beside him as he dropped the duffel onto the mattress. The room was furnished with a pine dresser that Billy already knew was empty, that and the closet with Timmy's jacket in it.

Barton opened the closet door. If he saw Timmy's jacket on the floor he showed no interest.

They went through Billy's things together. "Oh, this is cute," Barton announced as he pulled out a red hockey shirt with white sleeves. "I think you're kind of fashionable after all."

On the road Barton had said the opposite. He was going to furnish Billy with a whole new wardrobe. But, of course, he was totally too poor. So now Billy's clothes became "fashionable."

Two hockey pullovers, three knits and Billy's one dress shirt comprised all the shirts Barton had brought. Then there were shorts and jeans. Also the shorts he was wearing and his now filthy Kafka T-shirt.

There were no shoes, and Billy decided that this had been intentional. If he made a run for it, Barton naturally wanted him to be as slow as possible.

He was surprised that thinking about his clothes made him more homesick than handling them. He put them away, then sat down on the mattress.

"I'll fix supper," Barton said. "It's going to be quite pleasant, I think!" He left the room, locking the door behind him.

Billy saw at once that Timmy's jacket was gone. This was very curious, since Barton's hands had been empty when he left.

Barton set about the preparation of a lovely meal. Mother had let him have some of the "Blue Towers" china and he set the table with it. Every single dish he'd been given was chipped, but a little boy wouldn't notice that.

When the setting was complete it looked more than a little impressive: the handsome plates, two long-stemmed wine-glasses, all of it over a nice piece of linen that you could hardly tell was a bed sheet.

Barton took out his groceries and set about their preparation. He'd cheated a bit, but Billy was probably too hungry to notice. Everything could be microwaved, even the cherry pie.

"Whistle while you work," he sang. He didn't know the rest of the words, so he simply repeated the phrase again and again, in an undertone as rapid as his movements. "Whistle while you work! Whistle while you work!"

The meal was coming together nicely.

Billy had been examining the closet for some moments. There had to be an explanation for the disappearance of the jacket. The ceiling was intact, just ordinary Sheetrock. Besides, Barton wasn't tall enough to get anything up that high, even if there had been a hatch into an attic.

Now he turned his attention to the floor. He'd always loved secret passages. There was a period when he wanted to be a professional secret passage designer when he grew up.

"William Neary, Ph.D. Secret Passages Designed and Constructed." Despite his excellent plans, nothing could ever induce Dad to install his designs in any of the houses they'd lived in. "I don't need anything that turns the shower stall into an elevator." That had been his final word on the last one.

The back of the floor was built up and slanted forward. A one-by-one strip along its middle indicated that it was intended to hold shoes. The strip would hook the heels. Their house in New Jersey had a similar arrangement in the master bedroom. Billy had once tied string to all of Mother's and Dad's shoes, and run it through a small hole drilled into the attic, and down to a similar hole in his own bedroom. When his parents were peacefully reading in bed he pulled the string and all of their shoes suddenly shot out of the closet.

Dad had theorized about what he called a "microquake." Later he'd heard his father at a party: "One night all of our shoes came jumping out of the closet." In the silence that followed this remark, he had laughed nervously. "It was a mini-earthquake," he'd added lamely. He'd never brought the matter up again.

Billy tapped the floor. Hollow. He pressed against it in various places, trying to see if there was any give. Then he noticed that the line between the board that held the shoes and the one on which it rested was slightly irregular. This gave him an idea. Sure enough, when he pushed, the board lifted easily. But he did not find a small storage space with a jacket in it. Instead, there was blackness and depth. A musty, greasy stench came from the opening.

He peered down into what could be darkness without end. He thought to himself: *It's hell.*

21.

Even setting, the sun of the West was brutal. As Mark drove it beat him in the face; it was a harder sun than he had ever known back East.

He was traveling his son's path down Interstate 15 in the little Plymouth he'd rented for twenty-five dollars a day after landing at McCarran Airport in Las Vegas. His plane had landed at seven, two hours late. It was already eight-fifteen. He was trying to get to Estes where Billy had made the call by eight-thirty.

He wanted to be there when his son had been there, to see what he'd seen, to hear the sounds of the place, to walk and think and breathe there. Above all, he wanted to ask questions there, and at that time. No doubt this wasn't a professional investigative technique, but it seemed sensible to him.

He knew he was chasing a shadow. Billy was gone. The time of day didn't matter anymore.

When the road rose to the summit of one of the long hills it was crossing, he could see an ocean of lights in the rearview mirror. Soon though, they were swallowed in the dark eastern sky.

That had been Las Vegas. Billy's plight seemed so enormous to him it was difficult to believe that the lights were not dimmed and the voices of laughter subdued. A child was being carried to destruction, but only one soul trailed along behind.

The road spun endlessly past, and his mind went over and over his small resources. He had little money. It had cost him the fantastic sum of four hundred and eighty-three dollars to fly to Las Vegas. That would take care of most of the Searchers' check right there.

You couldn't make two thousand dollars go very far. And people spent hundreds of thousands on their searches, offered rewards in the six figures, expended years, created foundations, hired publicists.

Xerox Express in Stevensville had made up their five hundred posters for the cost of the paper. On the road he would eat one meal a day and sleep in the car. His present salary was twenty-two thousand dollars a year, and there was nothing in the budget for an extended leave of absence.

If he didn't find Billy soon, he was going to have to bear the pain of standing in front of classrooms full of kids who knew him, lecturing on the Battle of Chickamauga and the Teapot Dome Scandal. He could hardly conceive of anything more excruciating.

He drove toward his destination with one critical resource: he loved his lost son with the passion of the damned. This pallid, staring, gaunt man just wasn't going to stop.

Driving along in his shabby slacks and shirt, a plastic shield protecting his pocket from his pens, he was alert to possibilities. Billy was alive. A few hours ago he'd been right here, looking at this very sunset at this very hour.

Mark had sat in the plane listening to the whoosh of the engines, drinking the coffee they gave him, eating the breadsticks and processed cheese while reading *Techniques of Investigation.*

He felt comfortable with the methods suggested by the book. Crime and history were strikingly similar, and so were the techniques of discovery. You had to be relentless and logical. Both the historical event and the crime were generally brutal and stupid, and both obscured by shabby camouflage.

Suddenly he realized that he was passing a small town. A water tower stood black against the orange horizon, a McDonald's flooded the highway with curiously pure light. A couple of gas stations stood at the roadside, then there was a big truck stop, its lot choked with eighteen-wheelers. He noted all of these places for tomorrow's postering effort.

He was supposed to go straight to the sheriff's office when

he reached Estes, but because of the time he had changed his plan and headed for the Mobil station instead.

Now that the sun had set the highway had become a black strip disappearing into the purple distance.

God help my son.

It was still ten miles away when he saw the first, faint indication of the station. About here the abductor must have glanced at his gas gauge, seen it was standing on empty. As he drew closer the familiar Mobil logo came into clearer focus.

The station itself was a pool of light in the large darkness of the desert. There were two cars at the pumps when Mark pulled up, a Pontiac and an elderly BMW with its sun roof open. Around the side of the station there was a dun Plymouth Duster, probably the attendant's transportation.

Mark saw him standing behind the register, taking money from a customer. He was wearing a coverall uniform. His face was long and solemn, and he wore a pair of aluminum-framed glasses. He was an old man.

Just beyond the station was a bank of telephones. They stood a little apart, and the light around them was dim.

With exaggerated care Mark pulled his car to a stop beside the Duster. Would the attendant be helpful? Cold? How did he explain himself? What did he say? He got out and started toward the station. There was a customer there, and Mark was too polite to interrupt. He used the time to examine the telephones. One after another he read the numbers on the dials.

It was the third one from the end. He had held this exact telephone in his hand, had pressed that "0," had spoken into this mouthpiece. Mark held the phone, too. He put it to his ear, listening to the wavering dial tone. The phone was covered with a faint film of graphite dust in which numerous fingerprints could be seen. Mark could have wept; the police were still working the case.

Until this moment he hadn't realized that coming here would be painful in the same way that visiting a grave is painful. He could smell and taste his son, could hear his voice, could almost see him standing here. He looked down and was appalled to observe the clear print of naked toes in the dust. Billy had been taken from the house without shoes.

Mark bent down. They were small enough to be a boy's prints. He could be looking at a mark left by his own son. He wondered if the police had noticed these prints. And then he thought, so what? They already knew Billy had been at this phone. The footprints were a poignant hint, nothing more.

"I figure you for the father."

The voice startled Mark. He looked up into the face of the attendant. Mark got to his feet. "Yeah. I don't want to disturb you while you're working—"

"Oh, come on. Come up to the station, I'll tell you everything I can."

Walking beside the man, Mark felt a sense of reassurance. "You have kids?"

"Four kids and eight grandkids."

"Wow."

The man chuckled. They entered the station. "I just sit in here makin' change mostly. Welcome a little talk. Especially if it can do some good."

"First, let me put up one of my posters."

"I'll do it. 'Course, I don't know company policy. Only the owner knows that and he's not around here except on Tuesdays. He'll take it down, for all I know."

Feeling enormously reassured, Mark went back to the car and got three posters.

"Gimme 'em," the man said. "Hm. Same picture the sheriff has. I just got a glimpse, but I saw your boy. William Neary. That your name, too?"

"No, excuse me, I should have introduced myself. I'm Mark Neary."

The attendant, whose coverall said "George," opened the battered steel desk that held the cash register and took out a big felt-tipped pen. "I think this'll be a good idea, Mark," he said. On the poster he wrote, "Seen at this station getting in a white Ford Aerostar at 8:40 P.M., August 17, 1989." He underlined the first four words a number of times. Then he looked up at Mark. Quite suddenly, he smiled. "I'm George Yost." He took the poster and Scotch-taped it into the window. "You want the whole story, I guess."

"If you can, I sure would like it."

"I told the sheriff and the state police."

"Still—"

"You don't have to explain." He put a hard hand down on Mark's shoulder. There was nothing Mark could do but lower his eyes. His emotions were in an uproar. It seemed the greatest blessing in the world that this man was being kind. "I was out working on a lube job we'd got in that afternoon. Lube and oil change and check the brakes." He paused, picked up a coffee mug captioned "Maximum Leader," gestured with it.

"No thanks."

"I know, eats your stomach lining. Well, it's my poison of choice since I stopped smoking." He poured a mugful from a deadly looking pot that sat on an automatic hotplate at the edge of the desk. "So I came out of the lube hole and there was this Aerostar sitting there. Big deal, guy's filling up. He's on the far side and I can't see him. Hell, I don't but glance at the van. Why look at it? The state police brought an Aerostar in here and took measurements and figured out that the man is no taller than five foot ten. Based on I couldn't see the top of his head across the roof of the van." He blinked, seemingly amazed at this deduction. "So then all of a sudden I notice this boy. He is going back to the van from the phones. He's noticeable, first because he's hunched, like, and running like he was scared half to death. Second, I can just see the front of his shirt and it seems to me that it's covered with blood." At those words the world receded to a bright dot at the end of a long tunnel. To cover his shock, Mark went for the coffee. His hands shook so much he had to concentrate on every detail of getting a mug, grasping the pot, pouring. "You told the police this?"

George nodded. He must have perceived that Mark was hearing it for the first time, because his voice became very soft. "I thought to myself, how does that guy feel—meanin' you— when the cops told me you were on your way. I just wish to God I could say somethin' more about your boy."

Mark gulped down hot coffee and poured himself more. His overwhelming urge was to jump in his car and give chase. For an insane moment he contemplated trying to catch the Aerostar.

"I noticed one other thing. When they were pulling out, I got that it was a Utah plate. Normally I never see a plate. But that boy, runnin' like that, and the blood—you know. Don't ask about numbers. I don't remember, except a '3.' "

He took a deep breath, let it out slowly. "I've tried to remember more. There's only one thing I wonder about: Why didn't Billy just come in here? Why didn't he come to me? I woulda helped him."

Mark had heard stories of children being won over by their abductors, or terrified into compliance. But if that had happened, he obviously wouldn't even have made the phone call. "I suspect that the abductor was armed. If my boy had gone to you for help, he risked getting you killed. Knowing Billy, he wouldn't have taken a risk like that with somebody else's life."

"A little boy who thinks like that?"

"Admittedly I might be crediting him with too much insight. You want to believe your kid can handle himself. But Billy *is* very bright."

"My youngest is at Stanford. Full scholarship. First Yost to go to college in a long time. My great-granddad went, so they say."

"Stanford's a fine school."

"Gonna go for a law degree. That's the way to make money these days. Them lawyers . . . you see the Mercedes, the Jag, the big Lincoln—odds on, you're lookin' at a lawyer's car. And if there's a chauffeur, then you're plumb certain."

"Did you see the man who had Billy?"

"Glimpsed. A long glimpse, though. I'd recognize him by his profile. He had a sort of blunt face. The police are going to do an IdentiKit job Saturday morning. They're takin' me up to Las Vegas for it. What they do is, get a guy to put together the profile from my description, then they use a computer to turn it into a front view. Hell of a thing."

Mark wanted to ask if the man had looked cruel or crazy, but he didn't know how to phrase the question. "Did he seem—"

"He was just normal. Dark, curly hair."

"Like me?"

"Nah. *Really* curly. He had a pug nose, and I remember his skin seemed really smooth. It was kind of sickly looking, too. 'Course people all look like Count Dracula under these sodium lights they got here."

Mark feared that he was finally getting at the truth. "Is that how he looked—like a vampire? A monster?" Inside himself he asked the real question: 'Was he the kind of man who would not only wound but kill? Please, tell me.' *Tell me why my boy was covered with blood!*

"He was just a guy in a car. Like I say, I wouldn't have noticed, it hadn't been for that blood on your little fella's chest."

Walter Toddcaster was not waiting for calls. He never waited for calls. What he was doing when the call came was reading a follow report on a young man who was almost certainly dealing crack behind the Studer Theatre. They were about ready to make him and send him to boarding school for a couple of years.

He picked up his phone on the second ring. "Yeah?"

"Detective Toddcaster?" A young male voice, with the pasteurized tone that said trooper.

"This is Officer Torrence of the State Police. I'm calling in reference to your inquiry about incident reports on a white Ford Aerostar."

"Yes?"

"We had one stopped and warned last Monday at eleven-fifteen A.M. on IH 80 outside of Neola. Failure to display the proper renewal sticker on a license plate. The license number was Utah 1-C32A. It was registered to a Utah resident named Barton Samuel Royal. The town of registration is Salt Lake. We have an address."

"Jesus."

"Problem is, the address is a mail drop. The driver was carrying a California license, no notations and no record kept."

"This is gold, Officer Torrence."

"Yes, sir."

When Torrence hung up Walter just sat there for a moment. Neola was about forty miles from Council Bluffs. Billy's abductor could have easily made it that far on Monday morning. They had a possible make working here.

He went into the ready room and pulled down a tattered Rand McNally Road Atlas. A few measurements with a ruler told him that the position was time-consistent with the later sighting in Nevada as well.

Walt picked up the phone and called the California Department of Motor Vehicles. They wanted his request on letterhead, but would respond immediately if he faxed it to them.

Half an hour later he was looking at the driving record of Barton Royal. The man had an address in Sacramento. There was only one problem. According to the report, Royal had deceased on October 12, 1985. The bastard had managed to pull himself out of the records.

There were moments when a man wanted to kill. Walter Toddcaster had one of those moments.

Estes was profoundly rural: Las Vegas very definitely did not extend this far west. Mark had come forty-five miles and he was in a place of an entirely different order. The moment he turned off the interstate he was in America's past, a world of dusty pickups and feed stores.

The sheriff's office was constructed of tan brick. It was a small building on the main street, newer than most. "Amon County Sheriff's Department, Estes Substation." Mark went in. He knew who he was supposed to meet: Deputy Richards. As it turned out, the only person present was Deputy Richards, who could not have been more than twenty-five. As Mark entered, he unfolded from his chair.

"I'm Mark Neary. I've just been out to the Mobil station."

"George is a good guy. He's been pumpin' gas in this town ever since I can remember. I don't know why he does it. He owns three stations. He could afford to drive a Cadillac, I guess."

"He said he was just the attendant."

"That's George. He tell you what you want to know?"

"No, he didn't tell me where my boy was." But he had taken three posters, Mark remembered. And now he knew why: he owned three stations.

"That's the sixty-four-dollar question. We've got the idea that the guy was going to California. This isn't exactly a deduction. Fifteen is the road to L.A. We've made inquiries at all the gas stations from here to the border, and we sent a request to the California State Police that they do the same. But that's a hell of a lot of stations. They'll get it done, though. They'll take your kid's picture with them."

They were trying, and they were trying hard. The trouble was the damned statistics. Kids just don't make it out of the kind of predicament Billy was in.

Barton Royal. Toddcaster wished it rang some sort of bell. He looked at the driver's license photograph, distorted as it was by the fax. Was this the same man who'd been driving the Aerostar?

That he could find out. He would ask California to send a better print to Nevada where they had that witness. The guy was scheduled to do an IdentiKit on Saturday morning, so he must have gotten a pretty good look at the man.

Then he made another call, this time to the Nevada State Police Division of Investigation. As he talked with Lieutenant Davis he faxed the California report through. They would both call Sacramento and get sharper pictures.

Toddcaster knew exactly what he was going to do with his: he'd have it shown to Billy's friends, then walked to every place the child had been on Saturday. If the face was Barton Royal's, and Barton Royal was the man carrying the license, they would get a positive from somebody.

His guess was that little Jerry Edwards would make the identification. It was highly likely that the man who had played RPM with Billy was Royal.

Deceased October 12, 1985.

It might just be possible to convince the state you were dead, if you knew what you were doing. He thought about it. You'd have to stop using your own name. And yet Royal had pulled out this license.

So he'd killed himself off and now had another identity. He'd have been scared to death when he was stopped by the Iowa State Police. So he used the Royal license, knowing that it would lead to this dead end.

The man was smart. In more ways than one, that was bad news. The smarter the crazy, the meaner. Toddcaster's Law.

At eleven P.M. Mark's phone rang, drawing him out of heavy, exhausted sleep. It was Toddcaster.

"How'd you find me?"

"I'm a detective. Listen, we might have made the abductor. He might be a man named Barton Royal, carrying a California driver's license, driving an Aerostar with a Utah plate that we have also made. There are a few details to clear up. But we have a picture. I want you to look at it."

"You want me to come back?"

"Nah, the Nevada State Police have a copy. You be at that IdentiKit session tomorrow morning. You look at the picture."

"But I never saw the guy."

"You don't know that. Just look at the picture. We're gonna have every kid Billy was with that day look at it. We're gonna shop it at random around the mall and at the Burger King and see if we can't hit paydirt."

"What about Mary?"

"I haven't told her yet. I was saving that for you."

To save money Mark and Mary had decided to limit their communications except in emergencies.

She answered on the first ring, her voice singing with tension. When Mark gave her the news she cried silently. "I wish we could hold each other."

"Me too, darling."

"I have hope, Mark. Is that a mistake? I'm so afraid it is."

How could he answer? There was no reason to remind her of the statistics. She knew the statistics. "It's never a mistake to hope," he said. It sounded lame. He longed to tell her about the blood, but he forced himself to keep silent.

A moment later they had said goodbye. He was alone again. He wanted desperately to sleep, but there was no way he was going to wait until morning to look at the picture. He was going into Las Vegas right now. What if he *had* seen the man, what if his identification was critical?

Mark got back into his car and drove off. Now he would see the glaring lights, the city of electric pleasure. But he wouldn't participate, not the exhausted man in the gray car, looking for State Police Headquarters.

They'd told him it would be easy to find: no neon.

22.

Because things were getting a little bit normal Billy wanted to curl up into a ball and disappear.

Barton was dancing around the kitchen as he prepared supper, with Billy standing in the door watching. He swept across the small space and kissed him on the top of the head. "How about giving a helping hand, son? We're both going to enjoy it, after all."

Billy did what he was told. At home he could conceivably enjoy helping. He had learned to cook steak like his dad did, and his dad was an expert. The only kitchen stuff that disgusted him at home were chewed gristle on the edge of plates and sinks full of goopy water.

Even though it was slightly cleaner than it had been at first, this whole kitchen totally disgusted him. At least the big pot with the tongs and the floating bits was gone, and the dirty dishes had been put in the dishwasher.

"You'll be amazed at what I can do with chicken nuggets," Barton announced, pulling a box out of his grocery bag. "Incredible things, my boy."

Billy still hoped, however forlornly, for the police to show up in response to his call to the operator. That had been so scary and so hard. He was pretty sure, though, that they were never coming.

Damn them! Why didn't anybody want to help him, anyway? The police were just as dumb as the people in the car when they had the wreck. Nobody cared.

He told God that he would gladly go to hell if only he didn't have to stay here.

"What you have to do, dearest, is just take this knife like this and—see?" With a butter knife he pried one of the chicken nuggets out of the frozen lump.

Clumsily, Billy took the knife with his cuffed hands.

"If you weren't such an escape artist we wouldn't have to use those things." Barton spoke in the happy-scoldy singsong Billy's math teacher used when the class was loud.

"I'm sorry." As he worked separating the nuggets with the dull knife he decided that the only hope he had left was to somehow call home. Fat chance he'd ever get into Barton's bedroom on his own.

Barton ruffled his hair. "Very nicely done," he said, collecting the pile of chicken. He was happy with Billy now, but what about the way he'd smiled when he held that rope? Barton enjoyed the bad stuff, too.

Just as the jacket had disappeared from the floor of the closet, the rope had disappeared from the coffee table. But they both still existed, and Billy knew exactly where they were: under the house, in the blackness he'd glimpsed when he opened the trap in the closet.

"This is going to be delish! I'm telling you Billy boy, when your dad gets into a kitchen, wonderful things happen!"

What kind of a fool goes to all this trouble with frozen chicken nuggets? All you had to do was heat them in the microwave, it said so right on the box.

Barton tossed the nuggets into an ancient food processor with chopped celery, a can of mushrooms and a can of pearl onions. Then he turned it on, using Half & Half to liquefy the mess. The nuggets danced and rattled. Soon the whole thing was a sort of gray-green slop.

What did he think he was doing? He opened the food processor and tasted the unbelievably gukky ik inside with a wooden spoon. "Mmm!"

"Smells really good, Barton."

"Taste?"

Billy lifted his lips, showed his teeth. Did it look like a smile? He hoped it did. He tried to sound all happy: "I want to wait till after it's cooked. I want to be surprised!"

Barton thrust the spoon into his face. It took iron discipline for Billy to touch his lips to the stuff. It didn't actually taste horrible. It was kind of bland. But it sure did look like upchuck. "Good," he mumbled.

He watched Barton's back as he poured the slops into a skillet full of hot olive oil. There was a lot of steam. Barton giggled as it wreathed his face. Billy thought he'd better laugh, too. The snicker he managed was sharp and ugly, and Barton half-turned, a question in his face. When he saw Billy's smile, though, he relaxed and went back to his cooking.

The knife was still in Billy's hands. He could easily plunge it into Barton's back—if only it wasn't a butter knife. The most he would manage was to make Barton mad again.

Even though it wasn't cold he started to shiver. The air touching his skin had a deadness in it, the deadness of Barton. Barton was drinking wine from a huge glass as he sailed around in the stinking smoke from the stove. When he kissed his forehead again Billy smelled a gust of his breath, which was so strong it overpowered even the smell of the cooking. Nothing in his experience had ever smelled like that. It might have been an exhalation from the grave. Billy had to suck in his gut to overcome the flutters in his stomach. Mom always said rotting teeth gave you bad breath. But Barton smelled like he was drinking acetone nail polish remover like you used to clean off instant-bonding glue.

"Do you know how to use a grater?"

"Sure."

"You were a real helper at home, weren't you?"

Billy saw a chance to help himself. "I am at home, Barton."

Barton's smile was so big it was painful to see. "Yes," he said, "yes, indeed." He held out some carrots. "Can you grate these, please, son?"

"Sure." He ought to say "dad" but it was too much, he couldn't do it.

Carrot salad. Sally always claimed the raisins in it looked like roaches. With this guy they would probably *be* roaches.

As Billy grated he thought about how to find out more from Barton. If he was going to call home, he had to be able to tell them where he was. He didn't even know the address, except that it was Beverly Hills. Or rather, probably Beverly Hills. That was the only "Hills" he knew about in Los Angeles.

He did not know how to question people, especially not people who didn't want to answer the questions. Presumably you did it like the cops on TV, or like the Gestapo with a big light in their face.

"What's your favorite movie, Barton?"

Barton became suddenly very still. *"Cabaret,"* he said in a suspicious voice.

"I didn't see it. Where'd you go to college?"

"I was too free a spirit for that, I'm afraid. I spent a year in Europe. Mostly I lived in Rome. I love Rome."

"The Vatican is in Rome."

"I lived in a little *pensione* behind the Pantheon. I used to go inside it all the time, just to walk those floors, smell the air, enjoy the magnificence."

"I know the names of all twelve Caesars. Dad and Mom have the *Satyricon.*"

"God, I *loved* the *Satyricon!*"

"Which translation did you read?"

"It's a movie, son. Brilliant!"

"So you went from Rome to Beverly Hills?"

"The Hollywood Hills, please."

Oh, wow, this was neat! This was really *very* neat! What a wild technique! It was like spies would really do and he'd thought it up all by himself.

"Now, my dear, *we eat!*"

Billy tried to pretend that munchkins were inside his stomach lining it with steel. It didn't work very well. If he vomited, Barton was sure to get crazy. But the flutters had turned to nausea. He sweated, struggling to contain himself.

"You look worried. Are you a finicky eater? I wanted to be one, but that just was not allowed in the Royal household. If you don't eat what's on your plate, you can *just starve!* No, just kidding. I'll go out and get you a pizza if this doesn't do it for you. There's a lovely pizza place down on Sunset, it's quite pleasant. Do you like pizza?"

So they were near a street called Sunset. Duly noted. "I can eat it." Dealing with Barton was like walking on spring ice. If you kept your balance, OK. But if you fell you broke through and that was that.

" 'I can eat it.' That's what I call *enthusiasm!* What's the matter, do I have BO? You keep pulling back when I get near you. Do you realize that?" He gave an annoyed sigh. "I want us to *like* each other. And I think we can. Yes, in time. Now sit down and we'll eat. This is called skillet chicken, it's an old family favorite of the Royals."

The fried slops looked like a giant scab and smelled like a cigar butt.

The carrot salad was just carrots and mayonnaise. He'd forgotten the raisins completely and the mayo was sour.

To drink there was something called Valpolicella, a wine in a bottle with a basket around it. Billy had never tasted wine and didn't particularly want to start. Like Barton's, though, his wineglass was huge. Where had he gotten these bathtubs—from a clown supply store?

Billy watched miserably as Barton cut off a slice of the chicken scab and slid it onto his plate. It was followed by a gob of carrot salad delivered via ice-cream scoop. Then came the wine, sluicing into the glass with sickening gurgles.

The meal proceeded. Barton "oohed" and "ahhed" with every bite, closing his eyes to concentrate on the incredible deliciousness of the flavors. Billy found that the fried slops turned to mush in his mouth. He put them as far back on his tongue as he could and swallowed each bite hard. The only way to cut the flavor was with the wine, which tasted like turpentine. Billy decided that he would rather lick the floor of the latrine at camp than eat this meal.

Thinking about licking latrine floors would do nothing to lessen his nausea. He was not a master upchucker like Joey Mox who could projectile-vomit on demand, but he was capable of making himself pretty sick when he wanted to. Only he didn't want to! He had to cut this out. No latrines. Instead he thought of a beautiful ham sandwich with fresh lettuce and mayonnaise and French's mustard, which he dearly loved. He would have his with a Dr Pepper and then go totally brain-dead watching *Duck Tales* on TV.

Dad and Mom did not allow much ordinary television. They watched *Masterpiece Theatre,* which was fine during the occasional nanosecond that it wasn't totally boring. He and Sally would sometimes sneak down late at night and watch Dario Argento horror movies on *Chiller Theatre*. That and Fu Manchu, Sally loved the old Fu Manchu movies. Billy preferred the Peter Sellers version where the British agent Dr. Neyland Smith pushed a lawnmower at all times.

All of a sudden he was about to cry because Peter Sellers was dead.

He couldn't do that, not when Barton was so happy. He imagined that there was an iron rod going straight up through his body, and it was connected to the strongest place in the world. He blew his nose on his napkin in order to cover the tears.

"I'd like to propose a toast!" Barton got to his feet. He was in his glory, face flushed, gleaming with sweat. His smile was ear-to-ear and so fixed it looked painted on.

He looked at Billy with melting eyes. "To the very finest young man I have ever had the privilege of knowing. To you, Billy." He held out his glass.

Billy's glass felt like it weighed at least ten pounds. Carefully, so that his chained hands would not drop it, he lifted it from the tabletop.

Barton clinked glasses. Billy stayed still.

23.

Walter and Mary were sitting in her kitchen.

"We've got a tough problem with this guy, Mary. We know his name, we know what he's driving, we even know the fact that his car is registered in Utah and he travels on a California license. But we can't find him, although we strongly suspect he's in L.A. because of the route he took."

Walter's way of telling you something made you wait. Mary hated that. She knew that there was nothing she could do but keep listening and hope he'd land on the point soon.

"As far as California is concerned, the bastard is dead. What this means is, he's living publicly under another name. When he's in danger he pulls out his real ID, which makes as a deceased. It's a damned clever wrinkle."

Absently, she twisted a piece of Kleenex she had in her hand until it was reduced to little, rolled-up bits. She wanted to scream, to throw things, to hit. But she was wiser now in the ways of her rage.

"Have you told Mark?" It was so hard to have him out doing things while she just sat. The nights were long, the days were long, and she and Sally were getting on each other's nerves. The poor girl was scared it would happen to her, too—and in a curious way ashamed that it hadn't.

"That gets me to the good news. And it's very good."

"Why didn't you tell me right away!"

"I—"

"No, I'm sorry. Forgive me. I'm just on edge."

He pulled a piece of paper out of his briefcase. "This is the man that kidnapped Billy."

Mary took the picture in her hands. Before her was a pudgy man with wide-set eyes and thick, sensuous lips. The nose was broad, the brows were light and curved in such a way that the eyes looked back with startling innocence. It was not an adult countenance. Barton Royal looked like a very sad little boy who had weathered.

"The IdentiKit done by the Nevada witness fit this picture very closely. So did the one done by the trooper who stopped him out in Neola."

"But here's the kicker." He dropped an acetate sheet over the photograph, and suddenly Barton Royal was wearing dark glasses. "Jerry Edwards says this is definitely the guy who played RPM with Billy."

"Is this implying—did Billy *know*—"

"He was just a guy in the arcade. Billy showed no evidence of knowing him."

"But they played—why?"

"The guy asked Billy for a game."

She looked at the picture, trying to imagine this man with her son. She thought of him stalking Billy, of him coming through these very rooms that night, of him standing right here in the living room. This man, with his sensuous lips and his big, baby eyes, had been here. He had carried Billy out of the house in his arms.

"Barton Royal, present age forty-four."

"We can have this picture?"

Walter handed it to her. "It's yours. We're going to use it, too. The FBI's put Royal on their 'most wanted' list, which changes everything. Now that they have a name, an identity, things are going to get much hotter for your man. This poster will go up at every 'wanted' location in the U.S. We're also going to put Billy's picture on the poster."

Hope flowered in her heart, followed at once by questing impatience. She was so emotionally fragile that any news— good or bad—brought tears. Carefully, she regarded her lap, smoothed her dress. She wished to display only the calm, efficient exterior that she liked and trusted. The gushing, mercurial Mary Neary she had found inside herself was not reliable.

"What can I do? I'm having a really rough time just sitting here, Walter."

"I think you might have another shot with the media. If we have a little luck here and there, we're going to get this man. You can't hide behind a false ID forever. He left a trail somewhere. We'll find that trail. You could help a lot if you could get another round of TV."

This was one of those awful decisions that made her come wide awake in the middle of the night. "What if Barton Royal sees his face on TV?"

Walter raised his eyebrows.

"I know he's already hurt Billy. Mark told me."

"Publicity—"

"If he realizes that he's got problems—I don't see Billy living through that!"

Walter did not reply.

"You don't have an answer."

"No. It's obviously a possibility."

"Anyway, the publicity—we won't get on TV in a big place like L.A. They wouldn't give us ten seconds. We'll get Des Moines. A lot of good it does, anyway. People bring you those damned covered dishes and then they tune you out. They don't *care*, Walter."

"We care."

"The police care professionally."

"I want to close the case. But I also want to help that little boy, Mary, and you know it! There are cops eating their hearts out over this case. Believe it!"

It was true that people cared.

Jim McLean had been an angel. The whole school board had helped, the police chief, teachers, kids, parents, the neighborhood. She knew that she had to make just one or two calls and the new poster with Barton Royal's face on it would be up in store windows from here to Des Moines before tomorrow noon.

"My instincts tell me to hunt for him. We're just dead broke, but I could get out to L.A. on plastic."

"It's an impulse lots of parents follow. You might even get lucky."

Again she felt the wild flush of hope, then the familiar dead sensation that followed it. She shook her head, trying literally to shake off the chains that bound her to her agony. "The thing is, if he's never found I'll feel like this for the rest of my life."

He reached out to her with the familiar half-gesture that never completed itself. But this time things changed: she took the grasping hand. "You always do this. You reach for me. Then you stop."

He was looking gravely at her. Had there been sexual content in his expression she would have withdrawn. Clumsily because she was sitting down, she let herself go toward him. They stood up as politely as if he had asked her to dance. Then he was holding her. Under his suit Walter Toddcaster was massive and unyielding. This was not a fat man, but a strong one. She could feel his gun tucked in its holster. He smelled of cigars and Paco Rabanne.

She was so tired now, so afraid. She was not a physically intimate person, except with Mark. But he was a long way away and Walter had the gruff softness of her dad.

She leaned over and pressed her cheek against his shoulder. He stopped dead still. Then he began stroking her hair with quick, nervous gestures.

They were silent. 'This is like time of war,' she thought, 'when people cease to believe in their own futures.'

"It's OK," Walter said. "It's OK."

She lifted her head. It was shocking to realize how little it would take for her to go to bed with this man. Through her sixteen married years she had touched no man but Mark. Such subtle ruptures as these are among the most destructive of the many undocumented side effects of violence.

She drew away from him. "Mary," he said, his voice low and harsh. She knew that tone well: it was the voice of desire.

"Walt—I'm sorry."

He nodded, as if to say that he understood what he must now do. He lowered his head, his lips became a tight line and a distant expression replaced the softness that had filled his eyes. She saw the truth of his life—a barren old marriage long worn out, two people like ghosts in one another's lives.

Victims were Walter's family, stolen kids his children. When he sorrowed for them, he sorrowed also for himself, and when he fought for them it was really the soul of Walter Toddcaster he sought to redeem.

I'm going to drive down to Des Moines to get some of the official posters," he said. "They'll be printed by noon, and I'll bring them up. We'll start by giving them to schools, to the Y, places like that."

"I'll call Father Turpin's poster committee, and Jim McLean. We'll get them out as soon as you get them to us."

Quite suddenly and without another word he left the house. The kitchen door slammed behind him. Even though she had seen it swinging closed, Mary jumped. The sound wasn't what had startled her. She hated being alone.

She was as if bound to her chair, her kitchen, its silence. This morning she'd tracked a smell to the cookie jar. It was full of moldy Oreos. Cleaning it reminded her of the old ritual of the washing of the body.

"Lots to do," she said. First she would alert Jim McLean. Then she would phone Sally, get her back from Donna's. She was beginning to spend all her days in that dark, air-conditioned house with its purple drapes and its big-screen television. Sprawled together on the Antonios' cream-colored couch, Sally and Donna watched soaps and sitcoms. They ate Twinkies and drank Cokes and sometimes, Donna had said, Sally would just cry.

When Mark left, Sally went silent. Her dream of the family becoming a detective team had been the foundation of her hopes. But teams cost money. Sally's solution was to anesthetize her mind. Mary didn't like it, but she also couldn't blame her daughter. Again she considered just going after Mark and the hell with the money. In addition to what cash they still had, there was some credit on their MasterCard. Perhaps another thousand dollars. She didn't want to think about it. She was afraid that she might have to go and not be able to afford it. What would she do then—beg?

Damn right she would. She'd call Father Turpin, ask for more money. She would ask some of the rich families like the Edwardses for a loan.

She phoned Jim, who wanted to come right away to see the picture. He could get the picture into the local paper, maybe also the Des Moines *Register*.

Then she called Sally. Every time her daughter left her immediate presence, Mary became uneasy. The phone rang once, then a second time. On the third ring her hands were sweating. On the fourth her throat was getting tight.

When the phone was answered she closed her eyes, let out her breath. "This is Mary."

"Just a second."

Sally came on.

"Do you know it's nearly eleven? Why don't you come home."

"Sorry, Mom."

"Sally, we've had a break. We know what Barton Royal looks like."

"Are we gonna get him?"

"Sally—" She had to stop. The choking tears hit her. Since Mark had left they'd been coming on like this, suddenly and without warning.

"Mommy?"

She managed to croak the words, "Come home."

When she was here alone she had taken to visiting Billy's room. Earlier this evening she had embraced his pillow, inhaled the fading odor of him that was still in the sheets. She had cried until her throat started closing and she was afraid she would gag. There had been murmurs in the hall, muffled footsteps. For a time she had been afraid to leave the room.

Last night Billy had called her name. She'd heard his voice so clearly it had woken her right up. She'd gone into his room then, too. The night made it seem somehow dangerous, as if the shadow of Barton Royal waited there.

A bird had been singing on the wire outside his window. She'd leaned on his windowsill, and listened to it for a long time. Now she took Barton Royal's picture in her hands. "Barton," she said. She tasted the name. "Barton Barton Barton." If she could, she was going to get this man. When she got him she was going to kill him.

She had believed that crime was a psychosocial illness, evil a medieval concept invented to frighten the serfs into compliance. But life was turning out to be more mysterious than either of those notions would allow. Evil had most assuredly walked the floors of this house. And Barton Royal was also a sick, sick man.

"I will kill you, Barton Royal," she said as she stared at the picture. Then she laughed. For Mary Neary this kind of laughter—so bleak, so bitter—was something very new. She understood little about grief, except that it always has a concrete origin: somebody is lost.

As if his life depended on it she raced up to Billy's room. Once there she did nothing but stand in the doorway. She was as still as a resting moth.

How could it hurt this bad? She didn't know anything could hurt this bad. Moonlight was just appearing in the window where last night she had listened to that bird. It must be the one he'd been trying so hard to imitate. Imagine wanting to talk to a bird! She could almost hear his voice singing in the wind, see him on the faraway. Where he was it was dark, except she knew he was dancing. "Billy," she said, and the name touched her lips like balm.

A voice screamed deep and long, and then there was silence. The sound might have sliced her heart in half, a child in jeopardy. But she knew it was only some toddler chasing lightning bugs. That child was up too late!

Somewhere Billy was dancing. She imagined a ballroom full of painted men and their prisoner boys.

Then came the bird, singing as the moon rose. As if by a cunning hypnosis she was drawn again to its voice. It was just a little thing standing on a wire, but its song was so very free, so very wild. Part of Billy was there.

There was something there deeper than the freedom, the wildness. There, she heard it. Yes, then it was gone again. It was so mysterious, as if her very grief had secretly possessed the heart of the bird. Or no, it was not grief. In the bird's song she heard something more primal: encased as in an amber of sound was the first savage screaming of the beast.

It was to that music her son's ghost danced.

24.

At first Billy did not understand what was happening to Barton. He left the table and went across to the living room, taking the wine bottle and his glass with him. "What's your taste in music?" he asked. "My collection is eclectic." His voice was high and weird. It was getting scarier and scarier around here.

This wasn't because Barton was getting mad again. It was for the opposite reason. He was totally overfriendly. For once he didn't sound like he was going to get mad again any second. Billy watched him as he flipped through his pile of old record albums. "I suppose you like rock."

"Sure."

"I despise rock. It's mean-spirited. What else?"

Billy knew one good way to make people like you was to let them get their way. "I like all kinds of stuff. *You* decide."

"I have the sound track from *Cabaret.* I have the divine Kiri singing *Songs of the Auvergne.* I have the sound track to *The Singing Detective.* Did you see that on TV?"

He remembered it, a public television special about a writer with all his skin flaking off, which was pretty neat. "My folks wouldn't let us watch much of it."

"Well, the sound track is marvelous." He drank down his glass of wine and put on a record. Billy was fascinated with the ancient hi-fi. It looked like something you saw in old black-and-white movies, huge and made of wood with an "RCA" emblem in the middle of the speaker. It only had the one big speaker, so it couldn't even be a stereo. Barton must be worse than poor, he must be on his way to living out of a bag.

The record came on and a song rose up out of an ocean of scratches. It was frowzy music from very long ago, the kind that was popular when dancing meant hugging each other and sliding along the floor.

The first song he played started out, "You always hurt the one you love." Barton said, "Don't be bashful, come over here with me." He poured himself more of the wine.

As Billy went toward him he suddenly spit out a word. "Dance!" His voice had changed, and now he didn't look friendly anymore. He advanced on Billy. "Dance!"

Billy had no idea what to do. He had hardly ever danced in his life. He knew there were special steps to the old dances, but what were they? He stood there.

Barton folded his arms, gave him an appraising look. "You can't dance?"

"I don't know how."

"Fox-trot, rumba, swing, jitterbug. Any of those words mean anything to you?"

Billy shook his head.

"You always hurt the one you love," the singer crooned, "the one you shouldn't hurt at all . . ."

"OK," Barton said. Billy saw something in his hand, then all of a sudden he was unlocking one of his handcuffs. As quickly as it had appeared, the key went back into his pocket.

"You always take the sweetest rose, and crush it till the petals fall . . ."

"I'll teach you," Barton said. But he didn't say it pleasantly. There was menace in it, sneering and hard. He yanked Billy to him. "I'll teach you to fox-trot first, that's the easiest."

Being close to Barton was seriously creepy.

"Come and trip it as you go, on the light fantastic toe. Do you know that?"

"No."

Barton slipped his arm around Billy's waist. "Now you put your right hand on my shoulder. No, don't grab it, you're not drowning. Lightly, delicately. That's it. Better, anyway. It's Milton, incidentally. You've read Milton, surely?"

Billy was trying not to cry but it was hard. This was a hateful thing Barton was making him do. Nevertheless he stood with his hand poised on Barton's shoulder. If he let himself cry it might be all over. He could not allow Barton to know how awful he really felt.

"Milton—surely you have. You're so *fucking smart!*"

There was that tone again, from the car. No more friendliness. Barton was getting like he'd been when he tore up the steering wheel. Only now Billy was leaning against his moist shirt, and the record was spinning and Barton was full of wine.

Barton swung Billy through the air, tightening his grip around his waist. Billy closed his eyes and went limp.

"If I broke your heart last night," Barton sang, "it's because I love you most of all . . ." His singing voice was thin. He sounded like a boy littler than Billy, or a woman.

Billy pretended he was in his own room. It was night, and the summer wind was billowing the curtains across his bed and he was looking up at the moon.

They swept around the room and the windows passed and the doors, and out the back door there was an ocean of lights.

The song stopped but Barton just slowed down. Now he hung heavily on Billy's shoulders, weighing him down so much he thought he might collapse. "Now we clasp our left hands— intertwine our fingers—yes, that's the way. This is how you are when you really dance." He pulled Billy yet closer. Another song started.

"I get along without you very well," the voice sang. Barton slid and sidled along. "Of course I do, except when soft rain falls . . ."

Barton was leaning over, burying his face in Billy's hair. Then Billy heard him crying and all of a sudden he couldn't help himself any longer and he was crying too.

". . . but I should never think of spring, for that would surely break my heart in two."

Because of his crying Barton gradually lost the rhythm of the dance. Billy bore his weight as best he could. Now they just shuffled, ignoring the music. "Do I worry when the iceman calls . . . do I worry if Niagara falls . . ."

"Am I furious 'bout your little white lies . . ." Barton sang along with the record, his voice sunken to a weepy whisper.

His hand in Billy's was ice cold and soaking wet. His other

hand was like a claw around Billy's waist, each finger pressing tightly against his skin. Round and round they went, slow-dancing, Barton doing a rough box step while Billy stumbled along with his bruised and bare feet, trying not to connect with Barton's shoes.

Barton was now kissing his hair. The feeling of lips tickling against his scalp was almost unbearable. Then there was some-thing else, a wet, squeezing something. When Billy realized that it was Barton's tongue, he quite involuntarily cried out and pulled back.

Barton flung his arms wide, as if Billy's body had suddenly become awful to hold. Without skipping a breath, he said, "'Therefore never send to know for whom the bell tolls; it tolls for thee,' *Billy!* Author, quick!"

"Hemingway!"

"And I thought you were supposed to be so *fucking smart!* The author is John Donne. Hemingway used the line for a title." He threw himself down on the couch, spreading his arms out along the back. Then he patted a place beside him. "C'mere."

He put his arm around Billy's shoulders, absently massaging his chest. "Do you ever think about death?" His voice was very gentle.

"No. Well, hardly ever."

"'Never, never, never say a big big "D."' Well, hardly ever.' That's from *HMS Pinafore.* Do you know Gilbert and Sullivan?"

"I'm not sure."

"Well, hardly ever. Let me see your palm."

Billy held his hand out as flat and straight as a soldier might.

"No, come on, relax. I can't see the lines that way." He took Billy's hand. "I've forgotten you felt like I should," the record sang, "of course I have . . ." Barton traced the line in Billy's hand with a fat finger. "I was a boy once. I was! They called me Fat Royal. I've never told that to a living soul. Oh, look, this is your lifeline—do you know palmistry?"

"No. I don't believe in it."

"OK, OK, we're just doing this my way, OK? Your lifeline is this one here. See it?"

Billy looked into his palm. "I'll get along without you very well," Barton sang with the record.

Billy's very soul yearned for home. He could smell breakfast cooking, could see the east light pouring in his door, could hear Sally singing in her shower.

"Dear child, your lifeline is *so short!*" Barton took another long drink of wine, refilled his glass with the last of the second bottle. "Well, the good die young, I guess." He raised his eyebrows. "Let me ask you a question. Have you ever been whipped?"

"I don't know."

Barton chuckled. "You lied to me. Your father never whipped anybody. Let me tell you, the first couple of licks, you think you're going to make it. Strong, silent type. Then the third time, maybe the fourth, you let out some sound, just can't help it. By then it's hurting so bad you think it can't get worse." He paused. He was choking as he talked, slurring his words. "Have you ever wanted to kill anybody?"

"No."

"You're a liar! You'd like to kill me!"

"No, Barton! I like you! Really!"

"This isn't a game, you little asshole. This is the real thing. Do you understand?"

Billy was too scared to talk. Barton turned over his hand. "I see blood vessels." He traced the blue shadow along the back of Billy's hand. "Do you ever wonder what you look like inside. Like, inside your hand?"

Billy nodded. "Yeah, I wondered that." He'd once gotten into an awful lot of trouble for operating on a live frog.

"The stomach is protected by first a layer of skin, then fatty tissue, then there are muscles that look like beef jerky, but light pink. Under that there's the viscera, which is hard and stringy when you pull it apart. Then there are the organs. Have you wondered, ever, what it's like to look inside a living body? How it would feel to touch a heart while it was still beating?"

"No, I never wondered that."

"But you have a science class at your school, don't you?"

"We dissected shrimp," Billy said miserably.

"Shrimp, really! You dissect shrimp at the dinner table. The thing about L.A. is, it's practically always summer. So you can always barbecue if you feel like it. But they have strict laws. No emissions! The air is terrible here. Have you ever barbecued shrimp?"

"Yeah. Dad makes Shrimp Wilder. He likes to barbecue."

"Oh, Shrimp *Wilder*. That's a very elegant dish. The sauce is green, as I recall."

"Yeah, it is."

"Do you like me holding your hand?"

"I don't care."

He laughed silently, throwing his head back. "You care." Then he took Billy's open hand to his mouth and licked it with his fat tongue. "Do you like that?"

It made Billy start shaking again. His heart was hammering so hard he almost couldn't hear. "I don't care," he stammered again.

Barton stopped. "I disgust you."

"No, you don't, Barton. Really, it's OK."

"No, it isn't." He drew Billy closer. "Put your head on my shoulder. That's it."

It was like Mom would do, especially when she was feeling sad about something. She liked to lean her head on Dad's shoulder.

Barton was getting more tense by the second. His muscles were hard. There was deep trembling, slowly getting stronger and stronger.

"We all have to die," Barton said. " 'After the first death there is no other.' How about that line? Do you know that?"

"No."

" 'A Refusal to Mourn the Death, by Fire, of a Child in London.' Do you know Dylan Thomas?"

" 'Never until the mankind's making bird, beast and flower'—I know that."

"Well, you know a little Dylan Thomas. The death of a child by fire—it's an incredibly sad thought. When death is quick, it's best. But it's usually a slow thing. The body struggles. Everything alive wants to keep living. We have a very sick attitude toward death in our society. A writer named Henry James called it 'the distinguished thing.' I think that's quite beautiful. 'The distinguished thing.' "

Billy wished Barton would stop talking about death. But he did not stop.

His voice grew mellow, like he was remembering things from a long time ago. "I guess the worst death is to be told in detail how it's going to be done, and then have it done." He stretched out his legs, wriggled in his seat, sighed. "That's the worst, all right. There is no worse death."

Billy was devastated. He knew, now, that there was no hope and there had never been any hope. He was here for one purpose and one purpose only: to be killed.

His chest seemed to burst open and a great roar of pain poured up his throat and just stuck there. Barton held his head, stroking it. "I'm goin' to Jesus," Billy said. It was so strange, so very mysterious!

Barton seemed more like a force of nature now. "You go ahead and cry, darling. It's best to have a good cry when you first realize. Then you'll get it together and it'll become like a kind of project we do together."

Billy looked at him in amazed horror. Had he heard that right? Barton's eyes were twinkling. He took a long pull on the wine bottle. His glass lay on the floor.

"Barton, please let me be your son."

"That's just a game, Billy. The game is over."

"I'm a good boy, Daddy!"

"No, that game's over." His voice bubbled. "New rules." Now he sounded more serious. "I think you have to get philosophical about it. It's going to happen, Billy. I didn't want it to. When I got you, I wanted you to be a real son to me. I thought we'd work it out."

"We still can, Barton, honest. Honest!"

"But you turned out to be nothing but a *fucking little actor!*"

"I'm not, I'm not!"

"You are an actor and a liar!"

Billy jumped up and ran straight toward the big glass door that opened out onto the backyard. Beyond that was the canyon, and beyond the canyon Los Angeles itself. If he could just make it down that hill, then he would be safe, he would be free!

He threw open the door. Barton, slowed by drink, was not quite fast enough to stop the desperate, racing child. He did not try particularly hard, however. Had Billy seen the slight smile on his face, he might not have run so fast, or been filled with such wild hope.

But all he knew was that he was free. Free! He had the use of his hands and the lights of the city to guide him.

At the end of the yard he ran hard into a fence, but it was low and only stopped him for a moment. He climbed the few dry logs easily and hopped into the rougher ground beyond. His feet were still healing, and they were too sensitive for him to run really fast on the tumble of stones that formed the bottom of the canyon.

"Jesus, help me," he breathed. "Jesus help me," a gasping litany. He pumped along making stifled little screams because of the pain caused by the sharp stones.

After what seemed to him a long time he stopped and turned around. He could see into the house. The living room was empty. But there was no flashlight bobbing along behind him.

Stones or not he flew down that canyon. The ground got steeper. Down he went toward the lights. He could even hear cars now, the great whisper of the city. A helicopter chugged across the night sky. Billy waved as he ran—he never knew, they might see him.

Then, quite suddenly, the ground was flat and smooth. Surprised, he stopped. He reached down, felt warmth and hardness. The road, he'd reached the road! "Thank you, Jesus," he said. "Thank you, Jesus." He was trotting now, moving easily downhill. Then he saw car lights ahead. They glowed, faded, glowed brighter as the car came around one bend and then another.

It was over. He'd won, he was safe. Tears sprang to his eyes. He shook them away as the car came around the last bend. Taking no chances, he went right out into the middle of the road and waved both arms.

The car stopped, the lights boring into him. "I got kidnapped and I got away," he said. He talked loud, between gasping breaths. "Please take me to the nearest police."

As he ran around to the side of the car his heart almost stopped: it was a brown Celica. But it was being driven by a woman, he was still OK!

He got in the car. "That was a dangerous stunt," she said.

"I had to stop you, a man got me and took me to his house—"

"A man?"

She sounded so happy, why did she sound happy? She started the car. "Take me to the police station," he said.

"Oh, that's ten miles away. Why don't I take you to my house? We'll call 911 from there."

As the car began to move, he again realized he was free. That meant he was going to live, he was going to see Mom and Dad again! He hugged himself, moaning with delight and relief.

They went round and round on the curving road. "Where do you live?" he asked.

"Not far."

She was a thick, mean-looking woman with lots of blond hair. Her dress was loose and her hands were pudgy. Billy could smell liquor on her breath.

They kept going round and round, one street after another. He thought to himself, 'I'd better catch the names.' "Is it much farther?"

"Be quiet and let me drive!"

"OK, sorry."

They were on Mount Crest, then Ridgeway. Then they went around two other corners, up and down steep hills, around another corner where there were houses on stilts. One of them had a number, 314. 'Where am I?' he wondered. The drunk woman was taking him on a dizzying journey into total confusion. The tires squealed, the gears clicked as she shifted up and down the range.

Suddenly the car whipped into a driveway so fast the wheels must have left the pavement. They came to a screeching stop inside a garage. "We're ho-o-me," the woman shrilled. She pushed a button on a remote control clipped to the visor and the garage door rumbled down, leaving them in total darkness. For a moment the only sound was the woman's furious breathing. Then her door clicked and opened, and dim light filled the car. Barton's Aerostar was parked in the other bay. Seeing it, Billy simply screamed.

The woman threw back her head and laughed a high, shrieking laugh. "Come on," she said, "I think you've finally earned some serious punishment, *you fucking little creep!*"

Part Five

THE GOD DAMNED

25.

It was the most delicious, special feeling, like invading the soul of your mother and making her do evil deeds. "All right," he said and it was *her* voice, oh, it was her! And how the little boy scurried. Look at his eyes, as big as plates, look at his pale face in the hard garage light. "Barton is so-o nice, isn't he, my boy? Well, I am not nice! Get in that house this instant!"

Off he ran. "Barton, Barton," he cried. He didn't know, he really *didn't know!* This was lovely. Never before had it been like this. The others had seen right through the layers of makeup to the man beneath, but this child was much more innocent. The idea of cross-dressing had probably never occurred to Billy.

Barton marched into the house, went down the narrow hallway to the guest room and stood in the doorway, folded his arms. "Barton won't be answering you tonight, my boy. He's being punished too, for letting you escape again. The very idea!"

"Who—who—"

"I am Death."

When he saw the absolute horror on that face he couldn't contain himself a moment longer. He slammed the door and gave himself over to silent, agonizing mirth. Then he marched down the hall and into his room. He pushed back the rug and opened the hatch.

He'd only had time for the wig and the dress and a load of powder. For this occasion he was going to make himself up perfectly, using all the magnificent array of toys he possessed:

the jars of foundation, the lovely powders and rouges, the eye shadows with their glorious names, Aziza, Revlon, Charles of the Ritz. He adored that last one, the way it clicked like a spike heel upon a marble step. The Ritz, *Ritz*, RITZ!

He went directly to his makeup table and turned it on. The lights were merciless, revealing the face in the mirror just as it really appeared. He was drunk, yes, but he could still see the great ape of a man behind the sloppy powdering he'd given himself. He poured some water from the pitcher and splashed in it until his face was clean. Then he covered his beard with Nair and went to work adjusting the wig. First he took it off and slicked his hair with oil so that it would take the fit perfectly. He daubed spirit gum around his forehead and sideburns and along the back of his neck.

Now he put the wig on properly. Once he'd pulled a few ringlets down here and there it was perfect, impossible to distinguish except at closest range. It should be perfect, he'd shoplifted it from an exclusive Rodeo Drive boutique. Indeed, all of his lovely collection was stolen either from the best boutiques or from dear Gina's extensive collection of goodies. It was soon time to take off the depilatory, which he did with a bladeless razor. Now his face was as lovely and smooth as his hands.

What Barton did was not transvestism, it was disguise. He had nothing against gays, but he himself was totally heterosexual. He would never allow himself to be one of those vile, disgusting lechers that touched boys—

Men like that ought to be killed.

'You have to understand,' he would tell himself, 'that what you do is ritual magic.' For example, the dress was a disguise intended to evoke one of the unconscious selves hidden within him, as indeed the powerful mother of childhood is hidden within all men. The difference between him and ordinary people was that he expressed the unconscious and they didn't. They were scared, he was not.

When they saw him in his ritual clothing more than one of those other kids had screamed with laughter. But only at first. Then they had just screamed.

Barton went to work on his face, applying foundation, then

powder, blush, rouge, then finishing around the lips and eyes. He painted on his lovely Summer Rose lip blush with quick, snapping movements, then applied Mystic Sea eye shadow, a beautiful, metallic turquoise.

The effect was simply magical.

He was always raptured by her. If only he could kiss her, swoon at her feet, give himself to her!

A blonde with vivid lips and exotic, pouting eyes stared out at him from the mirror. The eye shadow, however, had drawn the pain in those eyes to the surface. The sadness of his expression was his least fortunate feature. He corrected it with a little adjustment. Alter the line of the mascara, build up the lashes a bit—like magic, sad was sexy.

All the while Billy was waiting and worrying. He had reason to worry, too! He was about to get just exactly what he needed, and get it good and proper. The fun was over, the game was ended. Now the serious part had begun. Watching that little fucking scum acting his heart out, that had made Barton incredibly mad. Did he really think his inept hamming had convinced?

They'd tried the canyon before. You just drove around to where it opened onto Monarch and waited. The walls were too steep to climb, so there was no chance at all you would miss them.

It had happened so consistently with the other boys that Barton now looked forward to the canyon run. It was fun.

Dear little Billy was going to leap to the least snap of fingers from now on. He would worship the very ground Barton Royal walked upon; he would learn it was a privilege to obey a truly awesome human being to the letter.

He went down into the black room and selected the leather strap. He turned out the light, closed the trapdoor and covered it with the rug. Now he had to pause and prepare himself. This took consummate strength, perfect acting. He had to feel her, enter her, be her in all her glorious femininity and sternness. And she was *so* stern. Once she had set her will to it, there was absolutely nothing that would stop her. You could plead—and they had, God knew—but it made no difference. You could even lie, if you dared. Nothing stopped her.

With exaggerated care he hefted the strap with his right hand, holding the end of it loosely in his left. He walked down the hall, making sure his feet creaked the boards so Billy would hear. He paused outside the door to put an edge on the boy's fear.

The sobbing that started within the room was a deep music, marvelously stirring. His whole body began to tingle, and the more Billy sobbed the more delightful the sensation became. When finally he felt ready to intensify his delight, he unlocked the door and threw it open. Billy gasped as he stepped into the room. His eyes were fixed on the strap. His mouth dropped open. Then, no doubt imagining the pain, he squirmed where he sat.

"You're getting ten," Barton said in his best voice.

"Ten what, ma'am?"

He slapped the strap against his hand, and nodded his head.

"Please," Billy said, "I don't think I can stand it, ma'am. I've never had it done to me before."

"Most of them can't talk at this moment. You are quite a brave boy. For your bravery, I'll add three more."

Billy rushed to the closet. What was he going to do—try to hide?

Barton grabbed the handcuff still dangling from the child's wrist and dragged him back to the center of the room. "It's a slow thing, I'm afraid," he said. "Thirteen blows with this thing will basically take you apart."

He pushed Billy face down onto the bed. "Drop your pants. Can you manage?" When the child fumbled Barton yanked them roughly down around his knees. Billy put his hands to his head. His face was buried in the sheets. He was clutching his hair, pulling convulsively. Barton had never seen this before: the boy appeared to be tearing out his hair.

Fat Royal snapped the strap against his palm again. Billy gave a little kick. "Please, lady," he said, "I just wanted to look at the stars."

Barton's response was the first blow. It was smart and nicely delivered across both buttocks. There was a single, solid *crack*.

Billy bounced. He made a sound of surprise. No doubt it had hurt more than he had imagined possible.

238

The second blow was placed just above the red stripe made
by the first. It was so hard that the strap whistled on its way to
contact, and the moment of connection caused a spattering
sound. Immediately the skin turned white and puckered. Then
the blush started.

Billy cried out.

If this had been the black room Barton would have done a
really thorough job. Given the soundproof window you could
have some screaming up here, but he had to take care.

The third blow would be placed below the first, which was
now a well-raised, fiery red stripe exactly across the center of
both buttocks. He raised his arm until he felt the strap lightly
touching his own back. A tide of anger flowed in him, directed
at this willful, arrogant child.

The third blow landed with the sound of a pistol shot. Billy
threw back his head. Some garbled words came out, "Jesus" or
"Sorry," or something. There was no way to tell, and what's
more, Barton didn't care.

This had always been what it was about. He didn't want a son
to love, he wanted the sweetness of this. People did not understand that. They did not understand that a soul could reach
beyond good and evil, to regions where suffering and pleasure
were the same.

"Billy?"

"Yes ma'am!"

"How do you feel?"

There was no reply.

"Now listen to me, I'm waiting for the welts to come up
properly. Then I'm going to do the ten and it's going to drive
you mad with pain. Have you ever been mad with pain?"

Billy made a high noise, a sort of keening.

A moment later the welts were properly livid. Barton delivered a quick, vicious series to the center of the buttocks. Billy
shrieked more with each strike. Then he began to squirm away,
twisting from side to side, using his hands to ward off the
blows. His will to appease with compliance had broken down.
He was on his way to becoming a squirming, squalling animal.

The fury came upon Barton then, velvet and fire in his head.
He attained a rhythm, up and down, up and down, until flecks

of blood and skin began to fly up, forming a sort of haze around the leaping flesh.

At last Billy lost everything. His back arched, his eyes became teary, wrinkled lines, his screams pealed. Now, if they were in the black room, Barton would have let go completely, would have transported himself by the torment he was inflicting into heaven itself.

There was a last flash of rage and a final, brutal slash of the strap, and he was finished.

It was as if he had just awakened from hypnosis. The velvet in his mind was gone, the extraordinary calm that had formed its base was changed to sorrow and disgust.

What was he doing in these ridiculous clothes, hurting this poor child? My God, look at him, look at what had happened to Billy!

Throwing down the strap as if it was crusted with filth, he turned and rushed from the room. He closed the door. Maybe he should also have cuffed the poor creature and locked the lock, but what was the point? Barton knew from experience that Billy would be unable to move when he returned to consciousness. Sometime in the night the child would wake up in severe pain, and cry himself to sleep. Tomorrow morning there would emerge a quiet, compliant boy, walking stiff-legged. In his eyes there would be something of the rat.

Walking into his own bedroom, Barton glimpsed himself in the floor-length mirror that hung on the back of his closet door. Instantly he looked away, but it was too late. He knew what happened when he did this, and yet he did it every time.

"No," he said, trying to force himself not to look again. But he did look, he could not help looking.

There stood a fat, middle-aged man loaded with lurid makeup. His underarms were soaked, his spike heels wobbling absurdly. By the time he'd lurched into the bathroom he was sobbing.

This mirror was worse, the fluorescent light made him look like a ghoul.

The lips were fat, the eyes glaring, mad. He was so incredibly, totally screwed up. He was worse than that, he was completely psychotic.

He had just maimed another human being and would almost certainly end by visiting him with a horrible death.

You cannot stop, you cannot prevent yourself!

All his justifications were lies. Nothing explained him, not even his hard childhood. He did what he did because he got pleasure from it.

That makes you evil.

Evil, he was evil! He was an ugly, vicious, *evil* swine!

A huge roach crawled slowly out from his dress and up his face. He could feel the tickle of its claws, the faint, frantic scratching as it made a trench in his makeup.

When he clapped his hands to his face the makeup came off like sodden clay. He wiped at it, making little screams in his throat, his whole body twisting with the loathing he felt for himself. There was no roach under his hand. He ripped off the dress and stood naked, a sweated lump who stank of his ugly labor.

He fell to his knees, he crouched down, drove his fists into his eye sockets until he saw bursts of red and yellow. His mouth opened, he gagged, he felt something awful and black within him slither to the surface.

A snake was flipping on the floor, slick and wet as if it had been coiled in his gut. He fell down moaning and as black sorrow closed upon him he wished with all his heart that he would be free.

Billy was a dot of light in the middle of the forever dark. He'd been killed, he thought, whipped to death. "Momma," he said. "Momma?" It was so still, so very silent.

The whipping was a red memory.

"I don't want to be dead!"

Such a great agony assailed him when he moved that he flew into panicked thrashing. His screams were broken and soft, pitched to the tone of small wind. He was completely unfamiliar with great physical pain, but nevertheless he finally managed to calm himself down.

The overhead light was still on, filling the room with its hard, yellow glow. Billy was lying in a wet spot on the bed. Slowly, he slid to the side. With trembling fingers he felt his buttocks.

The skin was lumpy and covered with something sticky. When he looked at it, he saw that it was blood.

The sound of his own moaning made him feel so sad that he forced himself to stop. Nobody could ever be bad enough to deserve what he'd just been given. It wasn't possible to be that bad.

Billy was a good person, with a natural desire to find good in his fellow man. His innocence, which had so disadvantaged him until now, came to his rescue by preventing him from understanding the hopelessness of his situation. Beneath his suffering there was fresh water flowing, the very water of life. It bubbled up in him no matter how hard his fortune, and would not run dry.

This deep strength, which had not been so vividly present in the other children Barton had abducted, enabled Billy to continue his struggle. Although it hurt terribly, he fought his way to his feet.

"Mommy," Billy said. He wanted her so badly, she made it not hurt anymore! "Oh, Mommy!" He was sinking back through the layers of his young personality, back to the days when she carried him on her hip. "Carry me, Mommy, I is tired now." When he moved the pain clutched at him. "I sorry, I sorry . . ."

A part of him reminded himself, 'You aren't a baby, you can make it, you must try to get out of this.' It was just so hard—he had been whipped so terribly. His legs were like two posts, almost impossible to move. When he did, fire raced up and down his back, making him flail his arms and grit his bared teeth.

Like any normal child, Billy's sorrow would have extended to the hand that had hurt him if he felt he was dependent upon it for his survival. He would have accepted help even from the blond woman. When she was gentle to him he would have reacted with gratitude.

This is why children cleave so tenaciously even to hard parents. It takes repeated beatings, long periods of brutal treatment, considered and relentless injustice to break hope. As spectacular as Barton's assault had been, Billy had nevertheless survived like a little coal in the ashes; he was still struggling and would not stop. The pity of the abused child is that he does not cease to hope, not until the last beam of his life has faded.

So he wobbled across the floor, raised his arm to the knob on the door and tried. Every movement caused agony; the buttocks relate to so many other important muscles. To shuffle, to stand still, to raise his arm, to tighten his fingers on the silver doorknob—all of it hurt.

Under his breath he was uttering a new litany. Gone was "Jesus," gone was "God." He was down deeper now than those words, which come to have meaning in a child's vocabulary only at the age of four or five. "Ma," he said with each step. "Ma-ma-ma" as he crept along.

He did not exult to find himself in the hall, nor did he even think of where he was going or what he needed to do. He simply kept sliding one foot after the other, and so made it into Barton's bedroom. He had never seen it before, but he did not notice the beautiful canopied bed, the lovely silken sheets, the lace curtains or the perfume in the air.

He did see Barton, a shadowy heap on the bathroom floor. As far as he was concerned, though, this was not Barton. The blond hair told him that it was the woman who had whipped him. He went over, concern for her rising in him. But then he saw she was sleeping, her dress drawn over her like a coverlet. He returned to the task at hand.

He had come to call Mama. When you got hurt and nobody else would help, that was what you did, you called Mama. He looked around him. On a small, ornate desk was a telephone. "Mama," he said. He put his hand on the phone, picked it up, heard the dial tone in his ear.

Although his danger was now extreme, he was beyond caring about whether or not he was caught.

He began to press the numbers on the phone.

26.

The skin was being savagely scourged from her back when the ringing of the telephone woke Mary. For an instant the agony of the whip mingled with the noise of the phone. She came to consciousness in blood and rage, flailing frantically for the receiver, composing herself. Try not to sound sleepy, be calm, it might be the end.

"Ma-ma."

Some baby was up early and playing with the phone. "You put the phone down, honey, you aren't supposed to be calling people at this hour."

"Ma-ma!"

In an instant she couldn't think, couldn't remember even how to speak. Frantically she swallowed, fighting to respond. "Billy!"

"Mommy."

An instinctive impulse to grab him almost made her hurl the phone away from her. But she held it hard to her ear. 'OK, settle down now, take it easy, remember the instructions, get information.' One deep intake of breath was all she allowed herself. Calmly, distinctly, she asked: "Where are you, Billy?"

"Hollywood Hills."

When his voice stopped the silence in the phone was tremendous.

"What street?"

"Near Ridgeway . . ."

"Do you know the name?"

"No. The people next door have a blue Mercedes. Barton has an Aerostar."

"We know about the Aerostar. We know he's called Barton Royal. Anything else?"

"He has a brown Celica. He hid the Aerostar."

"What does the house look like?"

"Garage in front . . . dead-end street—" His voice dropped to a whisper, then she heard weeping like she had never heard before in her life. It burned into the depths of her soul, as if a hot knife was plunging into her. She gritted her teeth.

"Anything else." She managed to sound quite calm.

"We're the last house. Top of the hill—"

"Number on the house?"

"Ma-ma, I got spanked, I got bad, bad—"

She bit her knuckle. The skin crunched in her teeth, she tasted the blood. The pain seemed to belong to a distant, fraudulent life. Think, woman! "Is he nearby?"

"She in the bafroom."

My God, he sounds like he's a toddler! He's regressing, he's hurt, he's being tortured to death, oh God in heaven help me I am not strong—

"Hang up."

"Mama wait!"

"Say goodbye."

"Goodbye Ma-ma."

The silence continued on the line. He was frozen, he couldn't put the phone down!

"Goodbye. Hang up now."

He began weeping, a sound like little rain.

She jerked her head away from that pitiful baby's voice as if it was a bellow of agony. Her beautiful, brilliant child—all the labor and the love—was being ruined! He was suffering, oh, terribly, yes, there was no question that it was terrible, terrible—

At that instant a door opened in her and she came to the part of her that was as strong as stone. Here Mary Neary was objective and effective. When she spoke again her voice radiated sure confidence. "Now put the phone down and get away from it. Don't try to call Mommy again. The police will be there as soon as they can." She stopped, and when she did the big silence assaulted her again.

"Mommy—"

Again she writhed. A huge sob came up into her throat. She

threw her head back, sucked air into her open mouth, spoke again. "You have to hang up now, honey."

But he didn't hang up. He was unable to break his connection to her. So powerful was her desire to radiate strength, to fill him with her own health and courage and her very blood she literally snapped to attention beside the bed. "Put that phone down," she barked. "I want to hear the dial tone this instant!"

"Mommy help. Mommy help."

"Hang up right this instant."

"Ma-ma, Billy wants—"

"I know, darling, I know. But you have to hang up. Right now. Do it, Billy!" The silence replied. Her free hand was a fist against her chest. She was shaking so hard she could barely see. *"This is an order, young man! Obey me instantly!"*

Click. Then at last the dial tone. She sank to her knees, crouched with the phone hugged against her chest. *Oh let it be that he was not seen. God, please.* Aloud she whispered into the silent room, "I love you, honey, Momma loves you."

With exaggerated care she put the receiver back on its cradle, and then stared at the phone as if it contained a living spirit. Something happened to her that was beyond tears. When she thought of him out there somewhere suffering that much—my God, some vicious *thing* had beaten him, had reduced him to a gibbering jelly, tortured him—her mind swarmed with images, each one more hideous than the last. She sank to the floor, twisted this way and that. Her hands twined in her hair.

She couldn't help herself, she started pulling and pulling. Her body burned with the agony of her son's voice and she knew then the deepest, truest meaning of motherhood, that it has to do with the very spirit become blood and bone. She had borne him and held his naked body in her arms, and he was of her, and was her own self transformed.

Her hands dug into her hair, her body seemed to sputter flames, she felt rising on her buttocks the welts her son had received, the heartless whipping splashing into flesh that had never been struck, and shattering not only the body of the boy but his little soul's light.

"Momma!"

Sally had come into the room. She wore her summer shorty pajamas. Her face was stricken. Mary realized that the poor thing must think she was dying.

She got to her feet, drew herself up. "I just got a call from Billy and we have work to do."

"Momma, what's wrong with you!"

"I'm upset. But that doesn't matter—"

"You're bleeding, Momma, you're bleeding all over your face!"

Mary withdrew her hands from the tangle of her hair. Her scalp was tender; there was wet all down her forehead. She hurried into the bathroom. She had literally been pulling her hair out at the roots. Sally turned on the water, got a washcloth wet and began daubing her mother's face. "Momma, is he—"

"Oh, Sally, he sounded like hell." To hear herself saying those words made her congeal inside. Again she began to tremble.

"Did he say where he is?"

She all but threw herself out of the bathroom, grabbed the phone again, jabbed in Toddcaster's home number. "Walter, he called—"

With a muttered "I'm coming," he slammed up the phone. Mary took the precious tape out of the recorder, put in a new one.

Five minutes later the phone and the doorbell rang at the same time. The phone was the FBI in Des Moines. Walter had already called them. "He said he's in the Hollywood Hills at the end of a dead-end street near a street called Ridgeway, but it isn't Ridgeway. They're at the top of a hill. The man drives a brown Celica. There's a blue Mercedes parked next door."

Walter joined her and in a moment the tape was being replayed so that he and the FBI officer on the phone could both listen. While it played Sally cradled her mother in her arms, cleaning her face with a damp washcloth.

Walt finished with the tape. "That's a hell of a stress reaction you got going there," he said, touching her bloody face. "It's called sweating blood when you do that, hon."

He stepped into the hall, motioned Sally to follow him. But

Walter Toddcaster was not a man who could readily whisper. "She's about had it," he said in a low voice. "They start pulling their hair out, they're losing it."

Sally's reply was an inarticulate whisper.

"We gotta help her, keep her going, because this thing will play through real quick."

"Play through?"

"It means we're going to find your brother real soon." Walter went back to Mary, glanced into her watchful eyes. "You heard me, didn't you? Which I guess I wanted. You gotta get some Valium or something, hon. You can't take this pressure. Nobody can."

"The hell I can't, Walter Toddcaster. No way am I going to dull my mind with pills at a time like this."

"Hey. Just trying to assist. I think you did good on that phone call. Real, real good."

Sally suddenly went for the phone. Mary's first impulse was to pull her off it in case there was another call.

"What time is it in Nevada?" Sally said. Mary realized that she was calling Mark. 'Oh, Mark, I forgot you, I called Walter first!'

"Dad, it's me. He called. We know approximately where he is."

Mary grabbed the phone. "I talked to him, Mark. I talked to him!"

"Where?"

"The Hollywood Hills."

"Address?"

She told him what they knew.

"I'm going to fly to L.A. as soon as I can. I'll call the police when I get in."

"The FBI's already done that. Maybe they'll have him by the time you get there."

"Maybe. Look, I love you, and I'm outa here."

Mary put down the phone. Sally grabbed it again. In moments she was talking to American Airlines, ordering tickets for the two of them.

Toddcaster stood in the doorway to the living room, looking as if his presence here had become tentative, uncertain. "Walter?"

"The case is outa my hands. It's up to the FBI and the Los Angeles police now. All we can do from here is offer support as needed."

"I'm going."

"Of course. But be careful, Mary. There are don'ts in this thing, major don'ts. Don't try to find him on your own. When you get to LAX report to the police. They have a missing persons unit. By then they will know your name, they will be on the case. *Do not* go to Hollywood by yourself."

Sally put down the phone. "If we can make the seven-twenty flight to Albuquerque, we can be in L.A. by nine-thirty their time."

By the time Mary was grabbing her clothes out of the dresser Walter Toddcaster had faded into the background of her life. She didn't even see him leave the room.

By the time she was snapping her bra he was already a memory. In ten minutes she was dressed; she even had an overnight bag with some things stuffed into it. As they ran to the car Sally was still pulling her curlers out, throwing them on the dew-fresh grass. Toddcaster watched from the front porch. "I'll man the phone," he said.

Mary glimpsed him once, a shadow on the porch. She heard a shout, big and powerful, cutting the silence of the morning. "Drive carefully," he yelled.

Mary hardly heard him. In moments she was doing seventy down Lincoln. She had exactly thirty-five minutes to get to the airport. Even given the sparse early morning traffic, the trip would take forty.

"Momma, you'd better let me do the driving."

"You've never driven a car before in your life."

"Momma, I take the car at night when you and Dad are asleep. I've been doing it ever since I was tall enough."

"Sally, you're kidding!"

"I'm a good driver, Mom. And if you don't slow down we're going to get a ticket and miss the plane!"

"With you behind the wheel we'd be worse off—you don't even have a license, you're thirteen."

"I do a lot of things you don't know about."

As much as she could bear, Mary slowed down. They must not miss that plane. Her boy needed his mother desperately.

If he was found, she had to be there. This was probably the single most essential thing she would ever do.

Until they reached the interstate she took Sally's advice and kept to the speed limit. Then she pushed it. Otherwise there was no chance. The old wagon shuddered at ninety, then seemed to get a second wind as it passed through a hundred. At a hundred and ten it felt like it was floating. The engine made a sound like a herd of cattle.

They were still thirty miles from Des Moines when a light bar started flashing behind them. "Fuck," Mary said, causing her daughter to stare in amazement at her. She pulled over. The black-and-white came up beside her. One of the two policemen in the front seat leaned out.

"You're Mary Neary?"

"Yes."

"We're here to give you an escort. Let's go."

They made the plane with three minutes to spare.

It was not until they were in the eventless void of the flight that her mind began to open the doors to the dark. He was badly hurt, he was with a desperate man, he was so darned *out of it!*

If he'd turned into a baby again, he was at the end of his strength. When that man asked him, "Billy, did you make a phone call," he'd probably say yes.

She remembered him when he was a toddler, guileless and so absurdly serious that Mark had nicknamed him "the Judge." God help him, he'd *regressed!*

Mary felt her daughter's warm, light fingers placing gentle pressure on her own. Since Billy's disappearance she had not had much room inside herself for Sally, and she regretted that. But Billy's plight was so terrible and her own suffering so great that she simply could not invest her daughter's needs with the importance she knew they deserved.

The Good Mother was being broken by the strain of the tragedy. If she lost Billy, then what would be left for the girl? Or worse, if he came back ruined, requiring years of therapy, what then?

"Mother?"

She turned, appalled by the interruption of Sally's voice.

"She wants to know if you want breakfast?"

To Mary's surprise the flight attendant was there with her trolley. "A Coke," she said automatically.

"No, Momma, we need food."

"It's a cheese omelette," said the flight attendant.

Mary ate her omelette and drank coffee, and watched beneath as her familiar world slid slowly away.

She had a question, asked to the sky, to the hazy prairie below: were they really going to get Billy back, or was it too late for that?

27.

When Barton came to he was still on the floor of the bath-room. The sour taste of last night's wine filled his mouth, and he was teetering on the brink of nausea. His tongue felt rough, his thirst was extraordinary. His skin felt tight and withered, his face was desert-dry from the caked, peeling makeup. The white dress, now filthy, covered him like a sheet. When he threw it off he smelled his own stink. As soon as he sat up his head began pounding so hard he thought he was going to faint from the pain. Blood rumbled in his temples and dark waves obscured his field of vision. The room rocked like a very nasty little boat in very big seas.

He'd drunk himself silly last night. It was the first time that had happened in ages.

This was Sunday. God, he was doing a show—two shows. What a miserable way to start his first day back at work.

Damn that Billy. You loved him, but you knew damn well *he* was faking it. It just hurt like hell was the problem. You wanted to make him love you, and when he just went on faking it you wanted to hurt him.

You destroy everything but oh, it felt so good! The relief when it was over and he was sitting on the couch, watching *Cabaret* and sipping a truly fabulous wine, was so very great.

For a couple of hours afterward he would be all right. It was like it never happened, never could happen. It was so completely over that the idea of doing it again was utterly absurd.

He pulled himself up by the edge of the sink and drank three glasses of water. He took a handful of Advils.

The remains of the makeup, the wig hanging by a few bits of spirit gum, the dress—the sight made him turn away from his mirror.

But why? Why did he persist in these feelings about himself? It was a *disguise,* for God's sake, and that's all it was.

He forced another look into the mirror. His was an interesting face. People thought it looked sad; he'd be going along perfectly happy and all of a sudden somebody would say, "Are you OK?"

I'm just fine, thank you. No I'm not. It didn't help to pray, it didn't help to read books about psychiatric abnormalities. Worse, he was smarter than any shrink he'd ever encountered. As a result he didn't know why he was like this and he couldn't find out and he couldn't stop. The only way he had found to deal with it was to accept that he was just a very unusual man.

He tried a little smile. *Look at you!* He cocked his head, turned aside and glanced at himself in three-quarter profile. This way he didn't look sad, he looked mad.

No, mean. Kind of funny and kind of mean. A mean munchkin. He wiggled his eyebrows. "Fuck you," he said.

Nobody loves me but me. Nobody ever will.

To just be loved, what a thing. It was commonplace!

I am terrible.

He turned away from the mirror.

Wrapping a towel around his middle, he went into his bedroom and threw back the scatter rug that concealed the door to the basement. He tossed the wig and dress down.

Then he flipped on his tiny bedroom TV, but it was Sunday and there was no *Good Morning America,* only some spectacularly banal cartoon about turtles. American television considers American children *drek.* That's why it feeds them garbage. He *tsked,* jabbing the power button. The set died, leaving a single white star in the middle of the black screen.

It would be nice if this headache would start to abate. Maybe he could use another handful of Advil. Couldn't you OD on that stuff? Didn't it kill the liver or something? He didn't want to take any of that codeine, it always made him nauseous.

As he prepared his shower a dream came back to him. It was vague at first, but it held his interest because it was something about Billy. What had he seen about Billy in the landscape of this dream?

Billows of steam rose, the water drummed against the tin shower stall. When Barton stepped in his whole body was grateful. His skin sucked up the moisture, the ancient makeup was swept off his face; the sins of the night went down the drain forever.

He took a deep breath of the steam gusting up around him, then let it slowly flow out as life and feeling poured back into him.

"Ma-ma," Billy had said in the dream. He'd been thrilling to see, tall and imposing. Barton shuddered, shaking his head, stepping back from the stream. It made him extremely uneasy to imagine Billy standing over him.

Ma-ma?

Billy opened his eyes. He was on the floor of his bedroom; his bed stank too badly of pee to use. Even so he'd pulled part of the filthy sheet over him in his sleep. Now he pushed it away.

He sat up. His bottom hurt terribly; he could barely move. That woman had really walloped him. He'd seen her lying on the floor of Barton's bathroom, when he'd been calling Momma on the phone.

He'd called Momma! The memory of her voice made him open his eyes wide. Then he was filled with such deep sadness that he just couldn't even sit up and fell right over on his side. His knees came up to his chin and he wanted his Garfie but it wasn't there anywhere so he put his thumb in his mouth instead and closed his eyes.

He stayed like that, dreaming about how she sounded.

He'd *told* her, yes he had!

It was so quiet in here.

Momma said the police would come. "Police," he whispered around his thumb. "Police, come!"

The silence seemed to close more tightly around him. He did not like this kind of quiet. Very softly, he sang against it.

> *"The ants go marching six by six,*
> *the little one stops to pick up sticks,*

and they all go marching down, around,
get out of the rain!"

Being all scrunched up hurt his bottom *and* his chest. The only place it didn't hurt was his feet, which were almost completely healed anyway. And so was his chest, except for one long scab that he knew he shouldn't pick.

Sometime after the beating he must have drawn up his shorts, because he was dressed.

Moving with the exaggerated care that would have been more appropriate in a man of eighty, he unwound himself. Slowly, propping himself against the side of the bed, he came to his feet. "Police," he said. "Momma said. Momma told me."

He began a journey toward the bedroom door. "Police. Police."

Barton finished his shower and dried himself with his big, coarse towel. As he shaved he kept listening to that word "ma-ma" repeated in his mind. How strange that it was associated with the image of Billy as hero rather than as helpless child.

It was impossible to erase the image of Billy looking down on him, his head backed by the soft glow of the night sky.

Oh, Billy. I love you, really and truly. And so you are dangerous to me, really and truly.

When Billy heard the hiss of clothing in the hall he wobbled back away from the door. He'd almost had his hand on the knob. Now he moved more quickly, going toward his bathroom, attempting escape from her.

The door swung open and there stood Barton. He was wearing a white shirt with a wide green necktie. On the tie were written in yellow the words, "Uncle Squiggly."

"Good morning, Billy boy."

" 'Morning."

"Come here to me."

Billy gave him a wary glance. He seemed happy, though, and that was reassuring.

"Come on."

Slowly Billy walked over. Barton hugged him to himself. "Hmpf! You need a bath, young man."

"I wet my bed after she whipped me."

"It smells like an animal lives in here!" He folded his arms. "What 'she'? What are you talking about?"

"The lady. After I ran away she came and got me. She brought me back and whipped me."

"That was just a little spanking, a little way of letting you know you'd been bad."

Billy hung his head and was silent.

"Now take your shower. I want you all clean before I go to work. I have to be at the bookstore by ten and it's already nearly nine."

Billy gingerly touched his buttocks.

"Still smarts, eh? Well, you'll survive." Then he smiled that terrifying smile of his and Billy backed toward the bathroom door.

Barton brushed past him, pulling all the sheets off his bed. "When you come out there'll be fresh sheets. You're to make this bed up perfectly. If *she* sees it's not done right, she's capable of dishing out another just like the last one."

Holding the dirty sheets at arm's length, he left the room.

These sheets were really filthy. They'd been on the bed at least since Timmy. For an instant a door within him was cracked open, and he glimpsed something so bizarre that he was made momentarily dizzy.

Well, that certainly wasn't real! Lord, what a mind you have! There had been Timmy and there had been Jack, end of story.

He stuffed the sheets in the washer and poured in lots of bleach and detergent. With an angry snap of his wrist he turned the machine on, immediately returning to Billy's room. The shower was running. When Barton entered the bathroom and pulled back the shower curtain Billy turned away. Barton's eyes widened: the child wasn't kidding about the whipping.

His buttocks were deeply bruised, with open cuts and long, raised welts. Barton stared in amazement. He did not remember delivering such a beating as this. A few smart blows wouldn't do this. It must be that delicate skin, he told himself. Skin like that showed every little mark. He reached his hand out, touched the contusions. Billy flinched away.

All of Barton's reserve of tenderness emerged. The little guy was really suffering. But when Billy squirmed away from his probing, a delightful shiver went through him. *No! I don't want that!*

Oh, yes you do.

Billy was cringing away like a wild creature at the far edge of a cage, and it was simply awful. His heart seemed to close on itself.

"It hurts," Billy said in a small voice.

"Nonsense! It's barely visible."

"Really?"

"The pain is all in your head." He helped the boy out of the shower. "Billy," he said.

"Yes?"

"Hold out your hands."

"Please, no. I won't try to run away, I promise."

"I ought to cuff you behind your back, but I'm going to be gone all day and I don't want you pissing on yourself again."

After his first punishment Timmy had made breakfast and served Barton like a butler. He'd remained on his best behavior until the very end. Even on the table, he was polite.

He must not think about the black room! The mistake was taking them down there. The black room was only a fantasy.

Most people—even people who'd had shitty parents—weren't like Barton. Most of them were fine. So why him? Why did he have to bear these driving, uncontrollable passions? What was the answer? It was part of the secret everyday world, where there was no place for him. All he could do was reach in and steal the children.

It was secret only from him, that was what was so sad. Everybody else *lived* there, *the fucking scum!*

Barton was all over him, pawing him, muttering. He smelled like after-shave, and what did that name on his tie mean? Billy bit his lips to keep from crying out when Barton touched his bottom.

"Who's Uncle Squiggly?" Billy asked breathlessly, trying to cover the fact that he kept pulling away.

"It has to do with my work."

The shower made it easier to move, but he still hurt bad.

"Who is she?"

"Uncle Squiggly is a character I play at the bookstore where I work."

"No, I mean the lady."

"You'll find out more about her later." For a moment he went out of the bedroom.

Billy stared after him, his heart flooding with amazement and hope. He'd left the door wide open! Billy could see right into the kitchen, and even see the tangled shrubbery beyond the kitchen door. He could make a dash—

No, he couldn't. It hurt too much.

Barton came back in with folded sheets in his arms, closing the door and locking it. With a glance at his watch he sat down on the foot of the bed. He had a little, fascinated smile on his face. He crossed his legs. "How many times have you tried to escape, Billy?"

Billy hadn't dried very well, and he was cold. His hair was dripping wet, and before he replied he blew some water off the end of his nose. "Three times."

"And each time you've failed. What does that tell you?"

Billy thought of his call to Momma. "I didn't!"

"Didn't what?"

He looked from wall to wall, frantic for an answer. He mustn't tell about the phone call, he mustn't do that!

"I didn't escape." Surely Barton saw how afraid he was.

"And you never will. I'm a lot stronger and a lot smarter than you are, Billy." He gave him a frank look. "You know that I've had other boys living here, of course."

Billy nodded. "I thought so."

"Where are they now, do you think?"

The police had to hurry up!

"Can't you answer?"

Billy shook his head.

When Barton smiled again Billy clapped his hands to his face, his cuffs clanking.

* * *

The child was in extremis, there was just no other word for it. Barton patted the bed beside him. "Come on, sit down, we'll talk."

"I don't want to!"

"I don't have much time, I've got to get to work!" He pulled the boy down beside him, put an arm around his shoulders. He could not resist pressing down, feeling the squirming as the child smarted.

He remembered how he had screamed, how the pain had swept him in fiery waves, how little his protests had mattered. "I love you," he'd said, again and again until all he could do was scream. After it was over he would be expected to thank her.

He lifted Billy's cuffed hands to his lips and kissed them. The boy glanced up at him, his eyes wary and calculating. Barton knew his thought: 'If he kisses me, maybe he loves me.'

Pitiful little creature.

There was hope again. Barton was being nice now. When Billy had risked a glance at him he'd seen a nice smile on his face. He did not dare look up again, he didn't want Barton to get mad at him. If you looked him in the eye, he always got furious.

"Billy, when I get home tonight, I'm going to complete my work with you."

Could it be true? Would he—"I can go home?"

"To your long home. Do you know what that is?"

"My home isn't long. It's just normal. You've seen it."

"The long home is a phrase from the Bible. It's in Ecclesiastes. Can you quote your Bible?"

"Not much."

" 'Also when they shall be afraid of that which is high, and fears shall be in the way, and the almond tree shall flourish, and the grasshopper shall be a burden, and desire shall fail: because man goeth to his long home, and the mourners go about the streets.' Do you know that?"

"No." Coldest fear was coming into Billy's heart.

"What is the long home, son? Can you understand?"

Billy's mouth was dry. Looking to the door, to the barred window back to the door, he was like a fragile sentinel. Barton removed his arm from Billy's shoulders and put it around his waist. Billy could not help it, he was so scared and so alone: he leaned against the grown-up shoulder.

" 'Or ever the silver cord be loosed, or the golden bowl be broken, or the pitcher be broken at the fountain, or the wheel broken at the cistern, then shall the dust return to the earth as it was: and the spirit shall return unto God who gave it.' "

Billy hardly even heard the droning words.

"Do you know what it means?"

Hot tears came welling up in Billy's eyes.

Barton stroked his head. "I love you from the depth of my soul," he said. His voice was rough with emotion.

For a time they were silent together.

"Did you make a phone call last night?"

"No!"

"You little bastard, you *fucking well did!*"

"No, I didn't, no!"

"Ma-ma! Remember that? When did I hear you say it?"

"N-never. I never did!"

Barton grabbed his shoulders and twisted him and glared into his face. "You're a fucking liar!"

Billy could not speak in reply to the roaring, furious energy of that voice. He shook his head as hard as he could.

"Yes. You got out of here somehow and you made a call! Confess!"

Billy began to cry. There was nothing else he could do now.

Barton grabbed him, pulled him close. "Oh, please forgive. Forgive poor Barton! I am so afraid!"

"It's OK," Billy said in a clumsy, halting tone. "OK, Barton, OK."

Barton sighed elaborately. "This house is full of mirrors," he whispered. "Well, I have to go to work." Again he hugged Billy, kissing him on the cheek for a long moment. "I'll speak to her. I'll give her hell for whipping you so hard."

The instant the lock clicked Billy began to have trouble breathing. He sucked in air but it didn't seem to help. He was seized by kinetic terror, and began lurching around the room, helpless to stop himself.

BILLY

He heard himself making sounds as he moved, "Ah, ah, ah," pacing like that big monkey they kept all alone in a separate cage in the Des Moines Zoo, going down one wall to the corner, turning, going down the next wall—go down the wall with the door, *slam* his hand flat against it, then past the bathroom and back again.

Again he made the circuit, and again. He thought, 'I'll never stop.'

Barton leaned against the door, listening.

He stepped back from the door, made a conscious effort to relax. Take a deep breath, let it out slowly. Drop your shoulders. Let the tension slide off and sink into the floor.

The child hadn't gotten out. "Ma-ma" was a dream.

In the black room all imbalances were corrected.

But now there was something urgent awaiting: real life, a sunny morning, work to be done!

He went into the bathroom and got his makeup kit. For the next few hours he was going to be Uncle Squiggly. Oh, he might sneak away to check on Billy from time to time, but basically he would be in character all day. Afterward he would buy the wine and rent *Cabaret*.

Parting was such sweet sorrow.

28.

Quite unexpectedly she saw him. At first she wasn't sure—
she hadn't been certain that he would be at the airport when
they landed. He looked so old, so dusty, so exhausted, she
could hardly believe it was Mark. His hair was frazzled and
seemed to have gotten gray virtually overnight. He moved with
the clumsy roll of a stiff old man. She could not imagine him
jogging beside her down Lincoln Avenue, or climbing on the
roof with a bundle of shingles on his back.

She raised her head and squared her shoulders. "Mark," she
called. Her eyes caught his. "Oh, Mark!"

Then they were holding each other, such relief! Then she
opened her right arm and drew Sally into the hug.

"How did you find us, Daddy?"

"Toddcaster told me the flight you'd be on. I've only been
here for an hour myself."

"Mark, where do we go? What do we do?"

"The police—it's huge here, honey. You have no idea. They
have a special squad that specializes just in hostage situations."

"He's not a hostage."

"They use them to free anybody who's being unlawfully
held. I think they'll assault the house when they find it."

Within herself she thought that Billy would be killed. Aloud,
she said: "Mark, how close are they?"

"I haven't talked to them personally. This is all coming from
Toddcaster. Until they find the house, this is being handled by
the missing persons unit. Then the hostage team gets it. The
FBI is acting in an advisory capacity, but they'll participate in
the arrest."

262

But Billy—what about Billy? What if Royal saw the police coming? He would kill Billy then. Or if they were clumsy and he had more advance notice, he would run and take Billy with him. If that happened her instinct told her they would never see their son again, alive or dead.

She did not give voice to these fears until they were in their rented car. "We're at the Crown Motel on Hollywood Boulevard," Mark said. "It's seventy-five dollars a night and not far from the Hollywood Hills. Above all, they take MasterCard."

Even transmitting simple information there was a graveside hush in his voice. He also feared that Billy would be destroyed by the efforts of the people who were trying to save him.

They were going down a long, long street with low buildings on either side. The sky was white, and everything was flooded with early sun. The air smelled faintly of exhaust fumes and flowers.

Sally had taken control of the map and was enthusiastically navigating.

"The police know where we'll be staying?" Mary asked.

"I told Toddcaster where we'd be. But he advised me to call in anyway. My impression is we're supposed to just wait. They'll bring Billy to us."

"I want to be there."

"It'll be dangerous—"

"Most of all for my son!"

"Our son."

"It's almost worse when you're close."

Sally's hand came over the backseat, caressing Mary's cheek. She leaned against her daughter's touch. "You're the greatest, sweetheart."

They drove for what seemed a very long time. Small shopping centers passed one another in an endless, incredibly dreary parade. How many video stores, cleaners, doughnut shops, convenience markets could there be?

Mark must have been having the same thoughts, because he finally asked Sally, "Do I turn anytime soon?"

"La Cienega ends in Santa Monica. We take a jog there and go up to Hollywood Boulevard. It's really your basic grid pattern with a few wrinkles."

"And a lot of miles."

"I feel so out of control," Mary said. "I nearly lost my mind on the plane."

"My flight was only an hour. So when I almost went nuts was waiting for you in the airport. You don't want to be out of communication."

The traffic got worse, and finally they were creeping. Mary kept picturing a certain house surrounded by police in flak jackets, and her little boy inside with Barton Royal. "Is there an all-news station?" she finally asked.

"Probably two or three of them in a place as big as this."

She turned on the radio, twisted the dial until she heard an announcer. But he was talking about *Lucia di Lammermoor.* "That's FM, Momma. Try AM."

She found the little switch and shifted to the AM band. Soon there was more talk. "If baby alligators *are* growing in our sewers—" She turned the dial again, forcing herself to control the panicky rush that kept threatening to seize her.

"Hurry the fuck up," Mark suddenly screamed, leaning on his horn. "People in this town drive like the living dead!"

"Want me to take over?"

"Mary—"

"I'll be glad to."

"You're crazy behind the wheel. We'll be up on sidewalks."

"She got a police escort on the way to the airport," Sally said. "She was incredible. We went a hundred and ten!"

He pulled out of the stream of traffic and turned the wheel over to Mary.

"First, Sally, give me a course that's off the main roads."

"This map isn't exactly perfect. There are a lot more streets than it shows."

"Do it, Sally!" Mary cried.

"Take a right whenever you can. When you hit Crescent Heights go left."

They were soon on Crescent Heights, where the traffic was less. From time to time Mary managed to open the little car up. She managed fifty, even sixty for short periods. The car was sluggish, hard to steer, noisy. She made a mental note never to buy one, whatever it was.

They reached Hollywood Boulevard, and were soon moving

east. She was only dimly aware that they were passing corners famous in the history of American popular culture.

"What is it somebody called this place—a bunch of shacks at the end of the rainbow?"

"That's what it looks like."

"I think that's an actual quote. Raymond Chandler or John Ford or somebody said it. 'Hollywood is a bunch of shacks at the end of the rainbow.'"

"Except that it's beautiful," Sally said.

"You've suffered a clear collapse of aesthetic sense," Mark replied.

"Daddy, it's beautiful because it's where Billy is."

To their left rose the Hollywood Hills. Even in the sunlight they seemed dark to Mary. This was an ugly, forbidding place. As they waited at a light a family of six in identical Hawaiian shirts crossed the street. The children all carried baby ducks. Mary leaned her head on the steering wheel. Billy was probably within ten minutes of this very spot.

Sally rustled her map. Mark said, "The light changed!" Mary was surprised at how rough he sounded. Mark was the mildest of creatures.

She realized that the anger that was in them all was coming to the surface. Sally spoke with trembling fervor. "If I got this guy, I would stab him in the heart."

"I'd make it slow," Mary announced with gusto.

"The Crown Motel!"

"Beautiful job, ladies!"

They piled out of the car and entered the lobby of the motel, which was grimly surfaced in linoleum and Formica. The picture window, however, rose out of a planter bursting with flowers.

"Reservation?" asked the woman behind the counter.

"Neary. Party of three."

"Lemme just take an imprint. You've got 207, drive around the side, you can park right at the door."

A few minutes later they were established in a room with a green shag carpet that smelled of stale cigarette smoke. Mark headed straight for the phone, tossing his overnight case onto the bed as he went.

Mary hovered close to him; Sally began to try to turn on the huge old Chrysler air conditioner that jutted from the wall opposite the dresser.

"This is Mark Neary. May I speak to Lieutenant Jameson?" Silence. "Robert F. Jameson." More silence. "Is this Missing Persons? It's about my son, William Neary. We received a call from him. He was abducted, and he told his mother he was in a house in the Hollywood Hills. We just got here. From Iowa." Yet more silence. Mark's face flushed. "Look, the FBI is in on this, the Iowa State Police, the Stevensville, Iowa, police, half a dozen missing children groups! I don't need to come in and give you a description! Lieutenant Jameson is supposed to know all about it! I am not yelling at you!" Silence, the receiver clutched. "You must know about it! You should have been working on it for hours! What about the FBI, aren't they involved? They were *very* involved in Des Moines, believe me." Silence, during which Mark shook his head angrily. "I am not being rude," he snapped. Then he stared at the receiver in amazement. "The bastard just hung up on me!" Mark hammered the receiver against the table.

"Don't break that phone," Mary screamed, grabbing the instrument.

"I can't believe this! 'Lieutenant Jameson is out on a case.' You would not believe the fucking, officious, arrogant *prig* I just talked to—Jesus and God!"

"Try the FBI, Mark."

"I don't have a name there."

"Then Toddcaster. I'll call Toddcaster." She looked at her watch. Three o'clock in Des Moines. He'd be at his office. He picked up on the second ring. "Toddcaster."

"Hi, it's me."

"Hi, me. Do you have a name?"

"Mary. Mary Neary."

"Oh, Christ, excuse me, baby. Have you got him yet?"

"We're in a motel here."

"Right. The Crown Motel on Hollywood Boulevard."

"My husband called the Los Angeles police and they acted like they didn't even know about the case. They wouldn't help us at all."

"OK, I got it. I'll make a couple of calls."

"And call us back?"

"Give me ten minutes."

She hung up and threw herself back on the squeaky bed. "He'll call us back," she said. Sally was watching CNN on TV. Mary tried the radio in the room, but it didn't work. "Of course not," she muttered.

Mark lay down beside her. "CNN won't have anything," he told his daughter. "We're nobody, as far as they're concerned. You don't get on national news unless you're Donald Trump and your kid got a bloody nose in the schoolyard. We're just ordinary trash, suffering like hell. We're not interesting. Oh, *Christ!*"

The frustration in his voice gave stark emphasis to their helplessness. "I hate all the publicity anyway," Mary said. "The only person who's gonna see your kid is the person who has him. I'll bet they haunt the postering places."

"I feel so damn useless. That's what I hate. I mean, he's probably no more than a couple of miles from here!"

"Maybe we could find him ourselves," Sally said.

There were a lot of things a child couldn't understand, even a bright little girl of thirteen.

"We could poster," Mark said. "I've got two hundred right in my suitcase."

"I just think it's dangerous."

He leapt up off the bed. "Well, if I do nothing but sit here and wait like this I am going to go completely crazy, Mary dear!"

She reached out to him, hesitated.

"Maybe they have a street directory for sale in the lobby," Sally said. "I'll bet they do if salesmen stay here."

"Fine, go see if you can get a street directory. Your mother and I'll wait for that old fatty in Des Moines to get around to calling us back."

"He's not fat. He's corpulent."

"You're talking about synonyms."

"I define 'corpulent' as marginally more dignified. Anyway, we owe him a lot."

"And we owe Turpin, and Richard Jones, who is a hell of a nice guy by the way, and the Searchers. Thank you, thank you, thank you one and all! Where in hell is my son!"

Sally rushed out of the room.

"Mark, I want you to tone it down! It can't help her to see you like this."

"Us, baby. You're not exactly peaches to be with. You ought to look at yourself in a mirror. Your face looks like an advertisement for dead skin."

"I almost pulled my hair out at the roots when Billy called."

He rushed to her, grabbed her into his arms. "Baby, baby, I'm sorry. My poor baby." When he stroked her sore temple, she closed her eyes.

After a moment he broke away, shaking his head and laughing bitterly. "That was about the most spectacularly unfeeling, high-handed bastard I have ever encountered. And I have dealt with school boards, for Chrissake!"

The phone rang. "Walter!" Mary grabbed the receiver.

"To make a long story short, Lieutenant Jameson runs the whole show. My guess is, he's never gonna be in. They do have a team of officers working on Billy. It's a big, active case, never fear about that. The problem they're up against is that unless they're very sure they have the right house they can't get a warrant to enter. The California judges aren't that easy to deal with, apparently."

She'd expected half the police department to be combing the Hollywood Hills, looking in every attic and basement for her little boy. But Walter was talking about search warrants and judges and things that all added up to the same central fact: Billy was not getting found.

"So what do they need? What would get them moving?"

"They've got all their black-and-whites in the area trying to spot the Aerostar—"

"He's hiding the Aerostar! Billy said that! Don't they understand?"

"Whoa, just let me finish. Or the brown Celica. If they see a man fitting Barton's description driving either car, they'll follow him home, then go to the judge."

"But why did they give Mark the runaround? It was incredibly cruel, to pretend like they didn't even *know.*"

"They're aware of your address. But they're wary. They want you out of the way when they make their move."

"We love him, he's our child!"

"Men like Barton are dangerous in the extreme, Mary. The L.A. police know this just as well as we do, and probably better. Barton Royal will kill Billy if he realizes that the cops are on top of him. They want to make it as easy for themselves as they can. And not letting the frantic parents get in their hair must be high on their list of priorities."

Her voice was barely a whisper when she thanked him. Mark slammed his fist against the bathroom door. "They don't want us around in case Billy gets killed because they're afraid of misconduct charges, or a goddamn lawsuit."

It was at that moment Sally appeared with something called *The Thomas Guide.* "The ultimate street directory," she said. "It's so radical!"

Mary took it in her hands. The thing wasn't a map, it was a thick book. She thumbed through it.

"Where are the Hollywood Hills, kid?" Mark had grabbed the book.

"Grids thirty-three and thirty-four. They may also be covered in twenty-three and twenty-four."

"Ridgeway," Mark said. "Right here."

They all looked at it.

"It's such a small area," Mary said. "We could cover every single street that dead-ends off Ridgeway inside of an hour."

"He said *near* Ridgeway, Momma, not off Ridgeway."

"But he can see Los Angeles from the house, which means it faces south. That ought to narrow it down."

"No good, Momma. At night this place must be a sea of lights. All that really tells us is that the house is high. But all the houses are high up there!"

"So it's really a huge area we have to cover." Mark threw himself back down on the bed.

"No," Sally said. " 'Near Ridgeway.' If we're lucky that might be enough."

Three minutes later they were in the car. Mary drove, Sally navigated.

"Just keep on Hollywood. When it crosses Laurel Canyon it changes to another kind of street."

It did. Mary had never seen anything quite like this crazy

labyrinth of little streets, with every intersection hidden around another curve. The car didn't much like the hills, either.

"King's Road," Sally said. "Go slow, Ridgeway's the next one to the right."

"This is Queen's Road."

"Take a right anyway."

Mary saw it. Ridgeway. Billy was probably within a mile of this precise spot. She turned onto the street almost on two wheels, slammed the gearbox into first and gunned the motor to climb the steep hill.

"Next street's a dead end," Sally said. Her voice was tense. She was so involved in the map she practically never even looked out. "Take a right," she said quickly.

"I can feel him," Mary said.

"There," Mark said. "That's a house that fits."

Mary was so stunned she didn't downshift as the incline steepened, and killed the engine. The car lurched along on the starter until she threw it into neutral. By then it was flooded and they had to wait.

The house was just where it should be, at the end of the street. There was a garage to one side, then a wall beneath what was probably a bathroom window. Next came the front door, and beside it a larger window completely blocked by a shade Beyond that was a wing that must contain a bedroom.

Most telling, there was a small brown car parked in front. "Is that a Celica?" Mary asked.

"Toyota, certainly," Mark replied.

"It's a Mazda 626, Daddy."

Mary looked at the house, imagining her son just behind the windows. "He's there," she said.

She compelled herself to be very calm now, very methodical. Again she tried the car. This time it started. She drove up to the house.

Mark looked at her. She looked back. Sally asked the question that remained unspoken between them. "What do we do?"

"We've got to get in there, obviously."

"I knew we'd end up in this situation." Mark's tone expressed his uncertainty most eloquently.

Mary brushed it off, anger in her voice. "Obviously he doesn't know what we look like. We invent a pretext."

"That isn't obvious at all, Mother. He was in the house. For all we know, he took good looks at all three of us."

"We break in, then," Mark said.

Mary demurred. "If he hears us or sees us, Billy's dead. Maybe all of us are dead."

"Look, you two, I think it should be completely simple. *I* go up to the house. I say my bike broke down, I need to use the phone. Then I'm in."

She was a brave child and that was an absolutely horrifying idea. "That gets us nowhere, except then he'll have both our kids."

"I can take care of myself, Mom!"

"Trained police go into houses like that in flak jackets."

"Billy's in there, we all know it!"

"If we did this—and that is an *if*, honey—the way we go about it is, you get evidence. That's all you do. Anything in the house that looks suspicious—if you see anything you know belongs to Billy, or if you hear him—"

"Mark, she must not go in that house! Never!"

"What if I see him?"

"You ignore him."

"No, I know that. I mean, what about his reaction?"

"That's a problem, all right."

"But Daddy, he's in that house. I know it!"

"I'll do it," Mary announced. She got out of the car and started up the front walk. She would say they'd broken down and needed to use the phone. Given the heap they were in, it was perfectly believable.

The morning sun bore down on her. Overhead the sky had turned deep blue. The beauty of the day was painful to see.

She was almost in a trance of fear when she rang the doorbell. Instantly a small dog began barking, a sound as raucous as a Cuisinart cutting up block Parmesan.

The door swept open. A truly ancient woman stood there, her face very sweet and very wrinkled.

"May I help you?"

"I—we—the car—"

"Yes?"

"We've broken down. I need to call a garage."

The woman fixed her with faded green eyes. Mary tried to smile. Realizing that she was twisting her fingers together, she put her hands down to her sides, then to cover the suddenness of the motion pretended to brush off her skirt.

"I can let you use the phone," the woman said, opening the door more widely. "It's no problem."

Mary stepped into the foyer. The interior of the house was dim, and she knew at once that they'd been wrong. There was a living room, but the view was of a brushy canyon and other houses on the hillside beyond.

Also, Billy surely wouldn't have forgotten to mention the ridiculous Pekinese that came squabbling and snuffling up to her, its whole body wagging.

"It's in the kitchen, dear," the woman said. She smiled. "I was making Bundt for my daughter."

"It smells wonderful," Mary said, but her voice broke and she could say no more. Without another sound she rushed out of the house and returned to the car, leaving the woman standing perplexed in her doorway.

"It's the wrong house."

"How do you know?"

"It's the wrong house, Mark! We're going."

She started the car. Back in the doorway the elderly woman muttered, "It fixed itself." Smiling, she returned to her baking.

The little car moved away down the sunny street.

29.

Barton burst into Tiny Tales and threw his arms around Gina. "Oh baby, baby, I'm so damn sorry!"

"Richie, stop it."

She was standing near the register in that blue and white checked dress of hers. It was far too young for Gina. It stated in clearest terms that her youth was at the bottom of a closet. Her dark hair was swept up around her skillfully porcelainized face.

"You look so utterly, utterly extraordinary, Gina dear."

"Richie, *where were you?*"

"I told you, I got sick on Maui. It was simply the most horrible thing. You know that *kahuna* I was supposed to meet?"

"He called me about you. You never showed up. You never even called."

"I was just wrapped up in blankets in the motel room the entire time. I absolutely could not move, could not think. I've never been so sick in my life!"

Gina folded her arms. "You disappear all the time, Richie. I told you in June—"

"That was a death in the family, you can't hold me responsible!" He adopted an elaborate pout.

The slightest of smiles played across Gina's lips, and Barton knew he would win yet again.

"OK, Richie, you always come back with some lame excuse. For a week I can't even get your answering machine and it turns out you were putting your mother in a nursing home in Anaheim. And that room of yours in Los Feliz—God, every time you disappear I think you've been mugged to death."

Barton put on the saddest, silliest most hangdog expression he could muster. "That room is what I can afford." He batted his eyes. "This is an expensive town and Richie is not a wealthy man, despite his name." He did his imitation of Stan Laurel in trouble with Ollie.

It took a full minute, but the flicker finally broadened into a real smile. "I do have some rather good news."

He clapped his hands, gave a little jump.

"You might earn enough money today to move to West Hollywood because we have a hundred and fifty-three reservations!"

This *was* good news. A hundred and fifty-three kids at five dollars a head—that was a good day's money, no two ways about it.

"Uncle Squiggly is becoming a hit, Richard dear."

Gina's tone told him that apologies and acceptances were over. Barton could drop the act. "He sure as hell is."

"Stephanie Strauss is bringing her little boy, and that means more heavy-duty Hollywood mommies are just behind."

"This is extremely exciting."

"Here's the icing on the cake. L.A. *Style* is doing a write-up on the store. And you are the featured subject."

He felt the blood slowly drain out of his face. He'd wanted Uncle Squiggly to be a success, but he had not counted on something like this. L.A. *Style* went in for lots of big, glossy pictures.

But that was OK. He'd be in his Uncle Squiggly makeup.

Then he thought: the reporter would certainly check his record. L.A. *Style* often did wrecking jobs. They'd love to print a story about how West Hollywood's favorite children's entertainer was a mystery man living under an alias.

"Richie Williams" was at best thinly constructed. The ID would never hold up under professional scrutiny. He was little more than a Social Security number and a couple of lousy credit cards.

Barton started back to the stockroom to put on his face.

"What about the store," Gina called after him. "Don't you think the store's lovely?"

There were new displays of books everywhere, ranging from

Bill Peet's delightful stories for tots to Judy Blume and John Bellairs for the older children. There were tables stacked with books, shelves of books, reading nooks in various themes: the Dinosaur Nook, the Fire Truck Nook, Home Sweet Nook, Uncle Squiggly's Squigglenook, all appropriately decorated.

"Really great, Gina. Really!"

The stockroom was dark and hidden away behind a door covered with bookshelves.

Barton liked it best with the lights out.

The moment he heard Barton's car start, Billy had raised the corner of the blinds. He watched the Celica back down the driveway, pull out and leave. For a long time, he observed the neighborhood. Nothing much happened, but he didn't stop, couldn't; he was hypnotized by his own longing.

He was also waiting for somebody.

Momma had said they would come. Momma *told* him.

The blue Mercedes sat in its driveway. Nobody came or went in the other houses. The street remained empty.

"Momma," he said aloud. The sound of his own anger brought him a little strength. "Where are they," he shouted. "Momma, you *said!* Where are they!"

Then he thought: 'That woman! What if that woman's in here listening? She'll hear me yell, she'll be in here with the whip!'

No. If she had heard him, she would have come in instantly. He'd be getting it right now.

Still, he crept to his door and listened. There was nothing except water dripping in the kitchen. That reminded him he was hungry. Barton had been mean not to give him any breakfast. He might not get any food all day.

Or ever again—he might not get any food ever again!

He had to get out of here and he couldn't!

Oh, wait a second. Of course he could! He made a rush toward the closet. It still hurt to move, though, and he quickly slowed down. He put his hand on the cool glass doorknob, slowly turned it, opened the door. He stepped inside, bent painfully, then opened the hidden entrance to the basement.

The darkness within was absolute.

* * *

"Now is there anybody here who's at least sixty-teen
y-e-e-ears old!"

They roared as one: "NO!"

"What, nobody's sixty-teen years old?" He looked at the
mothers, mock horror on his face. "Why did you bring me all
these little teenie tiny tinsie tootsie cutesies?" And he thought,
'They paid five bucks for this,' and laughed within. "They
aren't even sixty-teen yet!"

"I'm sixty-teen," one little girl announced.

"Uh-ho," Barton crowed, sweeping her up into his arms.
"What is your name, Miss Sixty-Teen?"

"Sukie."

"Sukie Tawdry," he muttered to himself. Her blond ringlets
bobbed. She looked very, very serious. "You know what we do
to bad little girls, don't you, Sukie?"

She wriggled and giggled and stared at the Squiggle Box,
which was the whole point of the show.

Nobody knew what went on inside it. This was a comedy
suspense routine for the Mairsie Doats set. Children adore
suspense.

Would Sukie be the first ever to get put in the Squiggle Box?

Barton looked around the room. "We'll take a vote! Is Sukie
really sixty-teen years old? Who says—NO-O-O!" They
roared, they went wild, the ones who'd been up in the past
yelled with eager delight.

"Sukie, do you know what this means?" Barton said. He was
very serious now.

Sukie was giggling so much she couldn't talk. Barton took
her over to the big box covered with red wrapping paper. Now
Sukie was laughing, but Barton knew to be careful. The wee
people were very sensitive.

Barton pushed the yellow frownie-faced button on the
Squiggle Box. It emitted an enormous roar and all the kids
screamed.

"Do you want to go in, Miss Sixty-Teen-Year-Old Sukie?"

"YES!" all the kids shouted.

Sukie shook her head very, very hard.

Barton looked around in confusion. "But Sukie says
NO-O-O!" He whispered to her, "I won't put you in."

276

"I know, Uncle Squiggly," she said, and kissed him.

Her kiss was moist, and her skin had a lovely, milky smell.

Billy peered into the dark, damp-smelling hole. How far down was it? If he jumped in he might fall forever and ever and ever. Or he might fall ten feet and not be able to get back out. He was afflicted by what was truly an agony of uncertainty. He'd called Momma hours and hours ago. Nobody ever came for him! Nobody!

But that wasn't true, Momma cared about him! She sure sounded like it even when she got mad because he didn't want to quit talking to her.

Maybe if he could get into the basement this way, he could get out by another door, and then he could call Momma and talk as long as he wanted. They could even trace the call, like they did in detective movies.

He sat on the edge, his legs dangling into the darkness.

He hated the dark.

"Now let's see, maybe if *I* put *my* hand in the Squiggle Box—" He nudged the button and got another big roar from inside. The kids fell silent. As often as some of them had seen this, the doubt always captured them. "Uh-oh," Barton said in reaction to the roar. He yanked his hand back as if it had been burned. "Sukie," he said plaintively, "would you just put your *pinkie* in the Squiggle Box?" He pressed the button again.

"Why does the Squiggle only roar when you push the button?" a voice called from the crowd.

Now, that was smart. "Who-o-o said tha-at?" Barton cried. He saw a delightful little boy with a sly smile on his face. "It was you, wasn't it?" In a few years this boy would stop the heart, such would be his beauty.

"Yeth!" He was one of the oldest, perhaps six or seven.

"What's your name?"

"Christopher!"

Barton said to Sukie, "Will you go and get Christopher and bring him up here? I think we need a little *haaalp!*"

The boy said, "Uh-ho."

"Y'know," Barton said to the crowd as Sukie very importantly strutted down and got Christopher, "sometimes a boy

Chris's size comes *out* of the Squiggle Box in one piece! But it's a very, *very*, VERY small piece!" As he spoke he measured with his hands, making them come closer and closer together until his ten fingers were all crunched up and he was peering at a microscopic crumb between them.

They were screaming with laughter. It was amazing how much enjoyment they could derive from a simple cardboard box and a little suspense. This was a lovely group.

Sukie and Chris arrived hand in hand, their faces beaming up at him. While he was at it, he thought he might as well get Chris's last name.

Billy hit hard and pitched forward, falling against a rough concrete floor. The pain made him shriek and roll, and that hurt even more. It took him a long time, but he finally recovered himself. He stood beneath the thin light from above, trying to see the rest of the room he was in.

The first thing he noticed was Timothy's jacket, which lay on the floor a few feet away. Just as he had thought, Barton had shoved it in here to get it out of sight.

Billy picked up the jacket. "I wonder if you were like me," he said. "Timothy Weathers." He held it close to him. "You're dead." The silence was total. "Timothy Weathers, tell me what it's like to be dead."

"Now, since Sukie won't put her hand in the Squiggle Box, and Christopher won't put *his* hand in the Squiggle Box, somebody's gotta do it!" He punched the button with his elbow. The roar this time was a little off-key. Before the afternoon show he'd have to replace the batteries in the cassette. Gina had faulted him for having cheap props before, and he didn't care to give her more ammunition. God, but this group was getting excited. They were *too damn loud!*

"Now, I'm gonna sing a song, and if I get every word right, then you're *all* gonna have to put your hands in the Squiggle Box together. But if I get even one word wrong, then *I'm* gonna have to do it! OK?"

They shouted agreement.

"Sing a song of sixpence, rockets full of pie—" The crowd

bellowed. He went doggedly on, leaning into the shrieks, "Four and twenty blackbirds baked in a pie!" He smiled and said, "I got it right, so let's go—get your hands in that Squiggle Box!"

The response was happy pandemonium.

The ceiling was solid. There were no stairs. There weren't even any windows to the outside. He'd hardly allowed himself to dream that he might get out while Barton was gone.

As he fumbled along he wished that he had a flashlight or some matches. It wasn't long before he understood why it was so dark: most of the basement was behind a cinder-block wall. The only way out was a narrow steel door in the middle of that wall.

Billy went to the door. It clanked when he tapped it; it was the kind of door you would use on a prison.

He put his ear to it. At first he heard nothing, but then he wasn't so sure.

Slowly, carefully, he drew back.

Then—behind him! He whirled around. But there was nothing there—just blackness and the dim shaft of light from the closet.

He stood still, afraid to go back, afraid to go forward. He started to pray, but stopped. It hadn't helped before now, why would that change?

God probably couldn't even hear him. Maybe there was no God. Probably not. Probably there was just the devil.

This had been a big mistake, and he had to get out of here! He rushed over to the shaft of light, tried to jump. It was no good. He was way too far down.

The only other exit was the steel door.

He began to cry.

Nearly done, all that was left was snack and chitchat with parents. Wonderful show, and every single one of them had paid the two bucks for the "Uncle Squiggly" balloons that had poured out of the Squiggle Box at the end.

"Is it a Squiggle in there?" Chris Mohler's tiny face peered up at him.

"No."

"Then why's it called a Squiggle Box?"

"Because it makes little boys like you squiggle!" He reached down as he talked, tickling him.

The children were mobbing him. He could not help being gladdened by their delight, and for a brief moment it was as if the steel door that sealed his heart was opened a crack.

"Have you worked with children long, Mr. Williams?"

The voice was thin and strident. It belonged to a young woman who looked like she was made of string. Her eyes were close together, her hair was disastrous. What had happened to her—was that rusty steel wool on her head, or the result of an extremely unfortunate home permanent?

"You must be from L.A. *Style,*" Barton yelled over the noise of the kids. "We'll be done in ten minutes, I'll talk to you then."

He kept smiling hard, lest she come to know that he was deathly afraid.

'There aren't any monsters,' Billy told himself, 'not like what you're afraid of.' But what was that breathing, then, behind the door? He'd heard it, it was there.

He couldn't get out of here, and now he was worse off than he'd been upstairs! His choices had all run out: shaking like the terrified little boy that he was, he dragged himself slowly back to the door.

He put his hand on the knob.

Then he thought: 'The woman. Maybe this is where she hides during the day.' This made him pull his hand away as if the knob was red hot. Images of her were burned into his mind—her bright blond hair, her flowing dress, her fat, wet lips. He remembered her voice, high and nasal and full of fury. Above all he remembered that big, black strap.

What she had done to him was branded into the very core and essence of the boy. Remembering, he bent as if cringing away from blows. He sucked in his breath until his lungs were ready to burst. But there was no other way out. Either he opened the door or he waited here until Barton came home.

He stood, his fists clenched, his head bowed down, a small creature in a very dark place.

* * *

Gina was obviously delighted, but Barton found the reporter horrible. Her photographer had taken close-up pictures while he was doing snack, and each time the flashbulb popped he would wince.

"Can we have one shot out of costume?"

Have a care, here. "Oh, I don't think so. I'd rather just be Uncle Squiggly."

"Then can you give me a little of your background? You seem to have a really intuitive thing with the kids. Where does that come from?"

"A happy home life. My parents were Quakers, and we just had a very peaceful, very sweet upbringing."

"Sort of a modern-day *Friendly Persuasion?*"

"Well, hardly that. But it was a loving family. Unfortunately my mother and dad have passed away."

"Do you have any children of your own?"

He answered politely in the negative, pretending to be rueful about it. As he spoke Billy's face drifted up out of the dark.

Her next question concerned his previous experience.

"No, no previous experience with children. Of course, I *was* one once, ha ha ha. Just an out-of-work actor who happens to like kids."

The questions droned on and on. He answered until he started to get hoarse. As they talked he kept smiling, waving to departing customers.

"I've just got another couple of questions. You've never said exactly where you're from, Mr. Williams."

He returned his smiling attention to his inquisitor, *the stupid fucking bitch!*

Billy hunted with the fervor of a distraught puppy for some way out other than that door.

Again and again he tried to jump up and grab the edge of the opening through which he'd dropped. Each leap caused agony, but a corner kept brushing the tips of his fingers.

He was hampered not only by the pain but also by his handcuffs. Twisting, pulling, he tried to squeeze out.

His mind raced with excuses. "Barton I fell in, Barton the

trapdoor was just opened, Barton it was an accident, Barton
please don't do anything to me, Barton, don't tell *her!*"

Finally he had to stop. He was out of breath and his buttocks
just plain hurt too much.

Again he approached the steel door. "God, if you're real
remember I got born, I'm alive, I'm down here—"

Tears were blinding him. When he tried to brush them away
the salt of his sweat stung his eyes.

He gritted his teeth so hard his jaws cracked, but he put his
two hands on the knob. This time he turned it.

The door moved smoothly, opening away from a thickly
padded jamb. Billy had the impression that the door was extremely heavy, more like something that belonged on a safe
than in a basement.

Inside was like a starless night.

What was this place, and what was that *smell?*

Barton wanted time to take a quick run up to the house. His
little escape *artiste* was a caution and a worry. Timmy was rough
trade, but at least he could be counted on to be there when you
got back. Rough trade and rather stupid—coarse, to be frank—
but still, the heart misses that which is familiar.

He was due to start the next show in less than an hour. Damn
the reporter, damn them all! "We just *love* Uncle Squiggly!"
Gush, gush, gush.

"Richie, look at this!" Gina opened the register. She was
speaking in a whisper because the store was still jammed.

Barton stared dully into the cash register. It was packed with
money. "Nice," he said. "Look, I want to take a run over to my
apartment." He had been careful to really rent the dump in Los
Feliz. But he never went there. The point was, nobody must
know about his house. The secret-life aspect of things was
usually part of the fun, but it could get wearing at times.

"You can't go now, you'll be late for the next show!"

"No, I—"

Gina held up her watch. Barton was appalled. He'd been
stuck with the reporter longer than he realized, and the enormous joke watch he wore as Uncle Squiggly kept lousy time.

"Gina, I have to!"

"You can't!"

"Gina, I think I left the oven on!"

"Ovens can stay on all day, otherwise how would we cook turkeys, Richie dear? You stay here. I cannot imagine what I'd do with a crowd of preschoolers who were all keyed up for you. They'd tear the place apart!"

He glared at her. She glared right back.

The dim light from the trapdoor barely penetrated this far. Billy was cringing, waiting for *her* to come leaping out of the blackness.

But he didn't hear any breathing now. Maybe he'd been the only one breathing. That had to be it, because there wasn't anybody in here now.

Except there was something on the floor. It glowed white, but it didn't move. He went down on all fours, began crawling toward it. The thing was all twisty, like a piece of cloth would be, but it was also lumpy. It looked almost solid.

Finally he could touch it. He reached out, felt it with quick fingers. It wasn't solid, it was stringy. He picked it up, felt it.

It was hair. He fingered it more carefully. Inside there was stiff netting, and it smelled like glue. Hair you glue on is a wig, like that purple wig Sally wore Halloween before last when she went as a punk.

The wig was yucky and he dropped it into the gloom. There was still white stuff over there. He looked at the pale mass. Was it a sheet?

The moment he touched the fabric he knew that it was her white silk dress. He looked up. Above this part of the basement must be Barton's bedroom.

So this dress and this wig—he thought of her pudgy hands, her stocky form stuffed into the flimsy dress, her hard eyes.

"Oh, no," he whispered. "Please, no."

Being trapped like this was hideous. He *hated* these people, but there was no escape, he simply could not get away. When he got back to the house he was going to march that kid straight down and strap him to the table. Then you just close the door and forget it. No more worries.

"Oh, is this your *dolly* you're holding out to me?"

"She wants Miffie to go in the Squiggle Box," the mother said, all laughter and twinkling eyes.

"Oh, poor Miffie, she'd be so scared!"

"She's only a dolly. She's made out of plastic. My brother chewed her foot and she didn't mind."

He tried to retreat around the counter, but now there was a little boy there, trying to reach the intentionally tempting display of gourmet lollipops Gina had set up. "They cost me twenty-eight cents apiece, dahling. And look at the tags." You could get coconut, vanilla bean, root beer, cola—for a dollar fifty apiece.

"Want one," the child announced.

"We're going now," his mother replied, picking him up.

"Uncle Squiggly, give me one."

The hell. Gina'd take the buck fifty right out of his share.

"Your mommy says it's time to go." Smile, smile, smile. He pictured Billy digging at the edges of the window, picking the lock, pulling out the grating that covered the vent in the bathroom ceiling.

Get me the hell out of here!

Another kid: "I want an autograph!"

OK, sure, sure, sure.

"I want to kiss you, Uncle Squiggly!"

My made-up cheek?

"But I *need* a lollipop, Uncle Squiggly!"

"Your mommy says no!" Why don't you just take him out the door, you foolish bitch. Smile, smile, smile.

"But I won't eat it, I'll just *hold* it!" Screws up face, takes deep breath, screams like he was being tortured with hot pincers.

Finally the mother retreats, her shrieking creature in her arms.

Yet more children came crowding around him. And the reporter was back, hovering at the edge of the crowd, obviously being just simply *tormented* by one last question.

He hated them all, in general and in detail. They were his captors, the evil, stinking swine.

But he smiled from ear to ear, clapped his hands and uttered a high, piercing laugh to get attention. "Bye bye," he shrilled. "Bye bye everybody!"

Came a chorus of tiny voices: "Bye, Uncle Squiggly!"

At last they began leaving in earnest. The reporter still hovered at the edge of the retreating crowd, but she was going to be dismissed with a claim of laryngitis.

He could escape.

But yet another diminutive grinning face was thrust at him. "Oh-h-h, what a big boy! You must be at least fifty-teen!" Smile, smile, smile.

Another couple of kids behind him, another couple of minutes. Then he was making his run, no matter what.

If he was late for the next show, so be it. This was about survival, he could smell it. You better be damn careful, Billy, you *vicious little scumbag!*

If there was a light in here the only way Billy was going to find it was by feeling along the wall. He swept the rough cinderblock surface with his cuffed hands, moving step by step deeper into the room. The doorway was now a faint gray outline in the black.

Billy's hands brushed something, which swung back and forth, making a grating sound against the wall. He touched it again, gingerly, feeling a substantial handle. His fingers felt along, and soon came to metal. Yes, and a very particular type of toothed blade. He realized that this was a saw. Something tough and dry adhered to some of the teeth. He rolled bits of it off in his fingers, but could not identify it.

Was this a tool room? Surely a tool room would have a light. All along the wall he found other tools: there was something with a metal tip and a long cord that he thought might be an old-fashioned soldering iron. He felt also something he recognized from upstairs: the pincers that had been soaking in the kitchen sink. They were smooth and clean now.

Then he found an object he could not at first identify by feel. He touched the weave of its handle, following this down to a clutch of leather strips. Something stabbed his left index finger and he snatched his hand back. He sucked his finger, tasted the salt of his own blood.

As lightly as he could, he touched the spot again. There was a small metallic object tied to the end of the thong. It had an almost familiar feel to it. It was a curved hook with a tooth on it.

All of the thongs ended with a fish hook.

When Billy realized that this was a whip he leapt back—and slammed into a piece of furniture that dominated the center of the room.

He turned around, feeling frantically. This was a wooden bed—no, too high. It was a table. The instant he felt the straps he knew what this place was for.

"Momma, it's a dungeon!"

For all its problems, Los Angeles was a lovely city. The way it shone at night like an ocean of stars, and the way it was now, kissed by that tart Pacific breeze, wreathed in flowers, the hills shining, water running down the gutters along Ridgeway—for all its problems, Los Angeles enjoyed a special connection to heaven.

As the Celica labored up the hills, Barton watched the peaceful day life of the neighborhood. There a Mexican gardener was lovingly tending a trellis of climbing roses, and there an ancient lady was walking her silly little dog. The big floppy hat and old-fashioned cake makeup marked her as old Hollywood. Probably a founding member of the Extras Union.

He had triumphed this morning—or Uncle Squiggly had. It had been a fine show, and this afternoon's would be even better. He was going to gain some minor celebrity, too, with the article in L.A. *Style.* They wouldn't be cruel, and he felt more confident that the reporter wasn't going to check into Richie Williams's background too closely. Why bother? As far as Gina and the rest of the world were concerned, he was just another out-of-work actor. Richie held a card in the Extras Union.

He turned the last corner, pressed the gas pedal and began to ascend the last hill.

As Billy leaned over the table, feeling the straps, understanding exactly what it was, he felt something gently touch the top of his head. It went swinging away, then came back again. He grabbed the edge of a light fixture, felt the socket, the bulb. And here was the switch.

A moment later the room was flooded with a white glare that made Billy squint.

Here was the saw, here the soldering iron with a caked, black tip, the pincers polished and clean, the whip. A big knife lay on the table with some brown-stained paper towels partly covering its blade.

Then Billy saw that there was another, smaller room to one side. A bead curtain hung in front of its door. Behind the curtain there was a stack of at least a dozen black plastic lawn and leaf bags, all of them elaborately sealed with duct tape.

They gleamed in the harsh light, and when he approached them he smelled a musty odor, like the time he found that dead rat under the furnace.

The room was deeper than he thought, and stuffed with the bags. There were more than a dozen. He touched one of them, finding it to be much more sturdy than a lawn and leaf bag. He pulled at the plastic, but it was far too thick to tear.

Billy took the knife and slit the nearest of the bags.

The odor that came out was completely unexpected in its revolting intensity. Billy had never smelled anything so totally dead. More than just a smell, it was an actual gas, thick and moist, pouring deep into his sinuses.

A nut-colored fist dropped down from the hole. Within the bag Billy saw the hollow shadow of a face.

At that moment a shaft of light poured down on him, overpowering even the wildly swinging fixture. Billy looked up in terror and in awe. For one vivid second he thought maybe it was the light of God.

Barton said: "You're already down there. Good!"

He descended the ladder from his bedroom with startling speed, sweeping down like an angel from the radiance above.

30.

Sometimes Mark Neary felt that all of his adult life he had been watching things die. He was now deep in the era that his radical youth had called the future.

But even as his hopes for the social body had faded, he had witnessed a glorious and secret increase. This was the growth of his children.

Before they were born, he'd had no notion of the true importance and scale of human souls. Nor had he known about helpless love, that cannot deny and cannot end. This kind of love persisted forever, and so did the relationships that emerged from it. Thus even if the child was lost, he persisted in the heart of the parent, frozen in the beauty of his life.

The neighborhood they searched was choked by dry and highly flammable brush and jammed with flimsy houses. It was so insanely appropriate that this place existed in the most geologically unstable place in North America. He could imagine the stilts snapping and the great houses tumbling over and over into the gullies and canyons, and then everything bursting into flames.

And yet children played, expensive cars whispered past, and the faces behind the windshields were bland.

He drove on, obedient to his daughter's crisp voice. Mary sat in the back, her eyes closed, exhausted by the ordeal of her own time behind the wheel.

"Take a left, then go up the hill."

"Heads up, Mary. We're about to rise to another possibility."

The house was maddeningly similar to many of the others they'd seen. The blank garage door faced the street, there was a dry patch of lawn.

Mary gasped.

"What?"

"A blue Mercedes."

It stood in the driveway of a multitiered, modern house on their left. For a moment Mark watched the shimmer of heat rising from its body. Then he looked back to the much smaller house at the end of the street.

All the windows on the front were closed by blinds. The garage door did not have a window in it at all.

"I'm going to have a closer look," Mark said.

"Be careful, honey."

Hardly aware of her voice, he got out of the car. Surveying the scene, he was fairly sure that Billy wasn't here. The empty street, the silent house—there was a sense of dry rot in the air, as if the place was home to the dead.

Mark stepped quickly up the stub end of the hill, pausing when he reached the driveway. He walked to his right, heading for the corner of the garage, which was bordered by a magnificent oleander tree covered by pink flowers so fragrant that they were in a curious way horrible. Even knowing how foolish this was, Mark went on, compelled by instincts he was unaware of and could not even begin to control.

He maneuvered quickly through the tree into a very different space behind it. The oleander concealed a tangle of brush, twisting vines and rose creepers dense with thorns. Mark picked his way ahead in the sun-dappled dimness. There was a smell here of something dead.

He found two windows, but both were carefully painted on the inside with black paint. Mark examined them minutely. More than the location of the house or even the presence of the blue Mercedes next door, these painted windows raised his suspicions. Who would do this unless they were hiding something?

He ran his fingers along the edges of one of the window frames. It was aluminum and flimsy enough, but he couldn't risk the noise breaking it would make.

Mark was about twenty feet from the back of the garage. Beyond the edge of the wall he could see a flagstone walk which undoubtedly led to the back door.

In the distance a dog's voice rose. The animal was barking furiously. This made him draw back for a moment. But the dog was far away and its barking faded with the slightest shift of air. Mark began moving down the wall. The shade grew deep, caused by a tree that was choked in vines.

From behind the foliage there came music and gentle splashing. A neighbor was enjoying a quiet swim. Tiny birds flittered in the dry leaves that matted the ground.

He could see from the signs of long-ago trimming that the ugly, grasping brush around him had once been a verdant hedge faced by a strip of rosebushes and shaded by what was now the twisted ruin of a jacaranda tree.

He reached the end of the garage wall. Ahead a quarter-acre of unkempt lawn fell away into a deep canyon. The view was tremendous, a sweltering plain lost in haze. He found it difficult to comprehend that such magnitude could be the outcome of human activity.

It made a sound, too, a continuous murmur that seemed to blend with the silence, intensifying Mark's sense of vulnerability.

He was unarmed, and without a weapon he knew that his odds of overpowering somebody were not good. How could a soft and untrained man possibly prevail against the resources of the abductor?

In the distance a helicopter thuttered. The sound died away, rose, died, then got suddenly louder. The machine boomed directly overhead, circling. As it wheeled he saw the police uniform on the pilot, was dazzled by sunlight struck from his aviator glasses.

Then the helicopter departed, disappearing into the haze.

Mark was astonished and angered by this futile and dangerous display of official presence. His guess was that they didn't know whether or not this was the house, and were searching at random. But what would Barton Royal think if he saw a police helicopter two hundred feet overhead? He would assume that he'd been discovered. Billy would bear the consequences.

The dwindling of the helicopter left him with a powerful sense of his own isolation and the incompetence of the authorities. That arrogant, cruel phone call—he'd never forget it.

He had to get to his boy before the police bungled things further.

As hesitant as an edgy kitten, he leaned around the wall that was concealing him. What he saw was a wood-framed screen door leading into a small kitchen. The atmosphere of emptiness and abandonment remained, and was so seductive that he stepped out into the open.

There came the thought that maybe the man had sensed trouble and gone, taking Billy . . . or leaving him behind.

Suddenly Mark recalled his son with perfect and startling clarity. He saw the broad, light smile, the rounded nose, the pure, proud look in his eyes. In the memory of his boy Mark saw the man that had been emerging, and that stabbed him deep.

He stood in full view of the door, agog and unmoving, his legs spread apart, his fists clenched against the pain of his vision.

There was a noise, very faint, that at first seemed like the moan of deteriorated plumbing. Mark was confused and did not clearly understand its meaning: few people have heard the unique sound of great agony.

It stopped, then started again. He listened. Once more he risked a movement into the backyard.

Presently he could discern that the sound did not come from inside the house. His glance went to the concrete foundation. A narrow basement window had been blocked by bricks and rough mortar.

The sound rose again, so thin it might have been the wind, so high it seemed to penetrate to the very center of his head. But the emotions behind it—ferocity, despair—were unmistakable. That was no loose pipe, no straining motor. That was a human sound, a cry. It was coming from the bricked-up basement.

Farther back Billy went, back in among the bags full of other boys. Had he been older and quicker to understand the possibilities of self-defense the room offered, he would have taken the knife.

The thought had not crossed his mind.

As Barton tried to reach him, he screamed. Barton's eyes were shut tight, his teeth bared like the teeth of the dead boy Billy had seen.

For an instant Barton's fingers clutched his ankle. Shouting every curse in his limited vocabulary, Billy yanked away and pushed another bag down.

Again Barton almost reached him and now he was all the way against the back wall.

Then Barton spoke in a low, growling voice. "Don't—make—me—touch—them."

Billy dug down, pushing at the heavy, sodden bags. Inside some there was sloshing, but others were dry and clattered like they were full of lumber.

There were so many!

Barton was dancing at the entrance to the little room, trying to get to Billy without coming into contact with the bags. Billy buried himself in the remains of his predecessors.

When Barton realized that he couldn't get Billy without dragging the bags out of the room, he really started screaming. He paced the floor of the other room. "I didn't," he shouted. "Mother, I did not!" He pounded his forehead against the wall. "There were just the two! Oh, yes, it was unfortunate!" He started crying then, arching his back, his head shaking so much his shoulders and arms shook too and it looked like some huge invisible dog was shaking the life out of him. The sound he made was so terrible to hear that Billy screamed too.

Then Barton went silent. An instant later he started hitting something, harder and harder, the sound of the blows rising in fury. As he lashed out he squealed, a sound high enough to vibrate Billy's teeth, and the blows went on and on. *It's me in his mind, it's me he's hitting!*

That realization made Billy scream again, and their voices melded as those of two singers might, singing a song of love.

Hit him again! Hit him again! Hit him again! Use the hooked whip, use it!

There had been two little mistakes, that was all. Just Jack, just Timmy.

This one is a *fucking big mistake!*

Where the hell did all these bags come from?

—*My, what a fine-looking young man! We must be at least—let me guess—forty-teen!*

—*I'm gonna squiggle you so hard!*

And why not? This was his room, his perfect place, an   1ere he could do anything.

Let's see, here, while I've got him on his stomach . . .

He hefted the whip.

The boy on the table watched with evil, flickering eyes. Of course, he'd always understood this child's filthy secret: there was an ancient evil lurking in him. He brought the hooked whip down with all the strength in him, the muscles pulsing in his back, his arms working like pistons and the stinking little *monster* was howling and it was all coming out now, all of it like black fire out of him at last and he was free!

Except that the table was empty.

Of course it was: to get Billy he was going to have to touch *them!* He would have to pull down the bags and feel *them* in there, and face that they are bones and black liquid and the damp powder that the lime pellets leave.

I didn't do it, I couldn't have!

"Billy for God's sake, come out of there. Come out of there and I'll—I'll—Billy, oh, remember what I have! Yes! I'll get one of those giant Butterfingers for you if you come out!"

He rushed up the ladder, heading for the kitchen. He'd put them in the fridge.

Mark had now been out of Mary's sight for more than seven minutes. She watched the spot where he had disappeared. Why in the world had he gone around behind the garage? What an incredibly foolish thing to do!

"Where the hell is he," she muttered.

"We better go get him, Momma."

That was her immediate impulse, too. But she saw the risks. If he'd been taken hostage himself, they could all end up in the hands of Barton Royal. Or maybe Mark was dead. She could see her poor husband getting himself killed.

The clock in the dashboard ticked busily away. Why had she agreed to wait here, anyway? She was the more resourceful of the two of them; she should have been the one to get out.

"Listen!"

Mary heard nothing. "What?"

Another helicopter had come. This one was black and much quieter. It flew in high, then stopped, hovering over the house. The sound of its rotors dwindled to nothing.

"They know," Sally said. "The police know!" She groaned. "Oh, Daddy, get back here!"

"I'll go get him."

"Momma, be careful!"

"I will, baby. But if I don't come back in five minutes, get out of the car and go next door. Tell them everything, tell them it's an emergency and to call the police."

"Billy's there, Momma."

"Oh, yes, he's there."

Billy heard Barton rush up the ladder and then the loud thud of the trapdoor. Once his mind would have leapt to the possibilities, but he had decided that he liked it back here. The dark was nice, and he enjoyed being with the other kids. He hadn't been with other kids in a long time.

Also, these kids were special: they were his brothers.

If he wanted to, he could hear them talking to him, but it wasn't very interesting, what they had to say. "Get up, Billy, run, grab the knife, turn off the light, break the bulb." But he couldn't do that. Then he would be a bad boy and get another licking.

Instead he scrunched himself down even farther in among the bags. He closed his eyes. This was where he belonged. It was his new room. This was where he was going to stay forever and ever. There was going to be just a little hard time and then he could come back and get to be in his own bag like his brothers. He loved his brothers so much.

"Hey, Timmy, are you gonna grow up and get old?"

(I don't think I'm gonna do that, Billy.)

"You have a really boss jacket, Timmy."

He stopped talking to his brothers and tried to pray again. "Dear God, send the angel Gabriel with his sword of fire. I need that at least. Maybe even the archangel Michael with *his* sword of fire, too. OK?"

He waited but they didn't show up. OK, he'd try the Blessed Virgin. "Hail Mary full of grace—" Nah, no teenage girl in a blue nightgown is gonna be able to handle this.

"Come out, my dear, I have a lovely, huge Butterfinger and it's nice and cold and completely scrumpy!"

"Hey, guys, looks like I ran outa time." As a lover with the body of his love, he ran his hands along the creases and folds of the nearest bag. "See you around."

Barton could not imagine how this had happened. He vaguely remembered a boy named Danny, but that was—oh goodness—years ago. This appalling horror was completely impossible! No, no way at all was he responsible for these piles and piles of bags!

Nobody else came down here, except him and his boys.

Then a face appeared in the gloom of black plastic, a sinister, glaring nymph.

"Who are you?" Barton asked. He was completely mystified by this unexpected presence.

"I'm me!" The boy came crawling out. He tumbled onto the floor. "Hi, Barton."

Barton held out the candy, a trembling sacrifice. Light was pouring from the child, as if the sun itself had entered him. The hand that took the Butterfinger was colder than the frozen candy.

With great solemnity the boy unwrapped the candy. He did not simply tear back the paper, but took the whole bar out and dropped the paper to the floor. Barton picked it up and put it in his pocket.

"I love them cold like this, Father, because you can eat the chocolate off first," Billy said. "Do you like to eat the chocolate off first?"

Barton was beyond words. The voice was gold in his heart, as if all love had entered there. He rocked back on his heels, clutching himself.

Glory poured from Billy's eyes. "Is this your hobby?" he

asked. He looked around the room, his eyebrows raised expectantly. "Is it?" Then he nipped the candy bar, taking off a large slab of chocolate, exposing the brown interior. "You have to be careful doing it this way, because if you eat off *all* the chocolate, then the inside's not as good." He took a bite of the crunchy center of the bar. "So is it your hobby? Killing kids?"

Barton was silent. Words were not a fatal weapon.

"How many of us are there?" Billy asked. He chewed the candy, a frown on his face. "Enough to make a pretty big club, I'll bet. The kids at my school have clubs, but I'm not gonna get in any. I guess that's why I obsess over Kafka. You gotta have something that makes you special." A smile came into his face, and as suddenly disappeared.

Barton found himself moving toward Billy with the precision of a dancer. Gentle, invisible hands were guiding him. He felt a vast presence coming close around him, and had the sense that it was somebody he had always known and always forgotten. Yes, taking his hand, guiding it toward the boy's arm, and curling his fingers around the arm.

Billy threw back his head and cried the most sorrowful cry that Barton had ever heard.

Exquisite.

Mark had seen him, he'd seen Barton Royal! He'd come scuttling right into the kitchen like some prehistoric crab, opened the refrigerator, gotten something and slammed it again.

He had his proof, he was a witness and would swear that Barton Royal was definitely in this house. He wasn't going to take any more crap from the cops, his boy was here!

Be careful, for God's sake, man! If you are heard, if you fucking well make a sound, Billy is dead.

He shrank back, farther into the gloom beside the garage. The prudent thing was obviously to go for the cops. But as he turned he heard a new sound, one so terrible that even his dulled instincts told him that it was a desperate, terminal cry.

More than that, he recognized this voice: it was Billy.

He stepped out of concealment, marched up to the door of the house. From the inside he smelled an odor of coolness and old food. It wasn't a clean house. In fact, it looked filthy. He tried the door. It was locked.

The scream came again, so faint and yet so very, very dark. It made him quail back, made him want to cover his ears, to run. But it also made him take out his keys and tear a hole in the screen.

Sticking his hand in, he felt for a deadbolt, encountered only another keyhole. The door locked on both sides. But how stupid, he simply tore out the whole screen and walked right in.

Barton Royal certainly wasn't expecting trouble.

Or was he? What about motion detectors?

Then the scream came again, a little louder now that he was inside the house. He clapped his hands to his ears, it was terrible to hear! *Billy, oh God help my boy, God help him!*

Where was he? The sound was so faint—muffled. Then he recalled the bricked-up window. Of course, they were in the basement.

Heedless of the dangers, Mark plunged off into the house.

"Shut up!"

Billy knew he was supposed to be quiet but it was just very hard because he saw those straps. If he didn't see the straps it would be easier, but every time he saw them the screams just came out by themselves.

"Sorry, Father!"

"Get up there, Son, go on!"

"Father, please—"

"Do it!"

He tried, but his body would not climb up onto the table. He belonged with his brothers, he knew that, and the only way to join them was to get up on the table. The trouble was, his arms and legs wouldn't do what his head told them. He just stood there.

So Father had to pick him up and lift him onto the table. There, that was much better. Now all he had to do was lie down. Father would take care of the rest.

But when Father leaned over him to grab the buckle of the chest strap Billy was astonished to find himself striking like a snake. The flesh beneath Father's chin crunched and tore and he reared back screaming. Blood spurted.

'I guess I did that,' Billy thought.

Then Father had a great big knife in his hands, and the blade was pale gray.

Mark heard that! Did he ever hear it! That wasn't Billy, that was a grown man and he was in pain. The sound was right underfoot! There was nothing but a throw rug on the floor of this bedroom. Mark turned it back and saw the trapdoor, its ring handle recessed into the floor.

He pulled the door open.

Billy was right there, lying on a table beneath a dim bulb. Beside the table stood the crablike man. In his hand was a machete.

Barton looked up, his eyes squinting against the sudden increase of light.

"Billy!"

Billy smiled a tiny, distant smile, and cocked his head in a gesture almost of apology.

Barton Royal raised the blade.

Mark did not know what in the name of God to do.

Imagining his real dad's voice brought Billy much comfort, even if it was only a dream.

Then all of a sudden a man jumped down out of the light. He was all sweaty and crazy-looking and he had brown fluffy hair and bent-up glasses. Was it Jesus? Surely they didn't send Jesus for every dead kid, so it must be an angel. Maybe God *did* send an angel! That would be really neat!

Father—no, *Barton*—made a funny noise, like he was pretending to be a lion or something. He swung the knife at the man. It went *sst!*

The impossible had happened. And so suddenly, so completely unexpectedly. It was the father! Simply fantastic! Somehow he had been tracking them, he must have moved heaven and earth, he must be more cunning than he looked.

God, this kid was such a huge mistake.

No, it was all right. This wasn't the end. He just had to off this guy and get out of here, and then he would be safe. He had his absolute emergency escape route all planned. Two hours from now he could be in Tijuana, and from there down to Bogotá, and back into the rain forest to hide until better days.

Again Barton swung the machete. The man cried out and jumped ineptly away, slamming into the wall behind him. Billy lay like a life-sized doll on the table.

"Why?" the man said. His face was twisted, his eyes bulging. "Why!"

"It was Billy! He wanted to come—and he was the first! I didn't hurt him. I've wanted a son all my life. I was good to him! There was just your Billy." He could not look at those anguished eyes, and turned his face away.

"You crazy, vicious bastard!"

Even though he was yelling Dad had tears in his voice. Billy did not like that. Dad was in big trouble!

There was an awful whistling sound and a snap and Dad was down. Then Barton was on top of him, snarling, and all of a sudden there was a terrible *thud* and Dad turned into something that looked like a pile of rags.

"Dad!"

There was no response.

He'd been smart, but Billy's father was no fighter. Now he'd finish off the child and be done with it.

But the whole closet was full of bodies!

Somebody else did that.

He chose his weapon. This would be simple, plain, quick: the butcher knife.

As he hefted it he became aware that there was something moving in the basement beyond the steel door.

Oh, God, it was opening! A huge, masked shadow loomed into the room. Another dropped down the ladder. Their plastic eyes were glistening, their guns dark blue in the light. "Freeze! Police!"

Then the blade to the heart.

Part Six

THE BAND
OF BROTHERS

31.

Mark Neary takes a breath, it doesn't work, he takes another, it doesn't work, he feels dizzy, his head hurts, he is in deep trouble, he knows it. "Gotta catch my breath—call my wife—get my breath—call my wife—gotta get my breath!"

"Two cc's, get it in there, OK, you have brain tissue exposed, doctor. Bleeding in the wound."

I'm lying down Billy needs me I'm spinning.

Headache!

There were men on the other side of Barton's room. They had guns and they stood by the far wall. They blocked the door.

His heart was fluttering like it was made of paper. Even when he was very still it did not stop.

He was peace, he was the dove. *I am the white dove, the dove that spreads wing over the cathedral of sacred shit.*

"There are too many tubes in my damn face!"

Then he saw movement, somebody coming through the line of uniformed men.

A woman, moving like a great, wary walking stick. Mother was so gray, so thin!

Her jaw was trembling. "I'm glad they got you."

You and me both!

Her arm came up, the flat of the palm, he turned his head away. "Fourteen, Barton, for God's sake fourteen innocent children!"

"Don't you hit him, lady!" The policemen crowded forward. "Just take it easy, ma'am."

303

"Fourteen!"

Stars exploded in his head. His face burned. The tubes came out and snaked around his face. *I'm sorry, Mother!*

"Get her arms! Quick!"

They dragged her to the far side of the room.

My heart has fire in it.

Fire!

"The case was solved by a massive nationwide FBI-coordinated police investigation. The house was stormed on an emergency basis by tactical police force officers when it was learned that the boy's father had made an unauthorized entry."

'Momma they filled the bathtub up with blood, don't go splash in it, don't go boom! Momma I don't want no storm, it's blood! Open the drain it gonna go over my head! Momma don't go boom! Momma don't put my ferryboat in here! Momma I gotta die now, Barton says to!'

(Your brothers will help you.)

"In a related development all three are in serious condition at Cedars-Sinai Medical Center. Despite a self-inflicted stab wound to his heart, doctors are fighting to save Royal so that he can stand trial."

A woman is weeping. Her name is Mary Neary. She sits on a plastic chair in a waiting room with a gray linoleum floor and pale green walls. There are marks on the ceiling tiles from a long-ago leak. She clears her throat, takes a sip from a Styrofoam cup she is cradling in her hands.

Her daughter, Sally, is playing a word game with Dr. Richard Klass, a child psychiatrist on staff at the hospital.

The thing was, his heart didn't actually beat. It just sort of shook in his chest. If he so much as lifted his head, he began to lose consciousness.

He put out his hand, but Mother did not take it. "I've just been remembering," he said. "We sure had a great time in the old days, didn't we?"

"Son, why did you do it? *Why?*"

He watched a fly circling the ceiling light.

"Mother, you should have seen one of my Uncle Squiggly shows."

As if she was suddenly cold, she wrapped her arms around herself. Again she left.

"I bubble when I breathe, doctor."

The cardiologist smiled and nodded. He was thirty-six, he had five children, he was from Calcutta. He did not feel that his patient would live. For the press he remained guarded, but not blatantly pessimistic.

'Oh you opened the drain I am going down please Momma get me, get Billy, I gotta get outa here Momma, I gonna go down! I slipping, my head is in Momma, I gonna go down, my body is in, the blood is taking me Momma, I am in the drain, I am going down. Momma the devil gonna get Billy! He got claws they is long they gonna go all over me!'

(We are your brothers. We are here.)

"Mr. Neary?"

"Yes?"

"Can you feel this?"

"Needle in my foot!"

"This?"

"Tickles."

"Very good. Now, relax your neck, please. Good. Any pain?"

"Jesus!"

There appears to be no lasting neurological insult to this patient, but the wound continues to heal slowly.

'Oh God why is he like this, he's like plastic, doctor, I can't get through to him, he just stares! Billy! Billy! Remember our lullaby? "Billy boy, Billy boy, where are you going, charming Billy." Sure you do, God in heaven help my poor baby!'

Barton peered into the blackness that had surrounded his bed. Had the room gotten dark, or was it him?

A boy walked out of the shadows. He was an angry boy, a

familiar boy. Barton knew exactly why he was here. "You'll never get me, *never!*"

Things were moving in the boy's eyes. How strange that looked. Barton tried to raise himself, to discern just what that was.

Worms!

Danny was this boy's name. He had long, long arms, and they opened for Barton.

No!

The boy embraced him. Oh, and it was almost like love! (Why did you do it? Only the truth, please.)

"It was fun!"

Impaled baby.

Danny drew back and raised his hands and Barton got heavy, too heavy! His heart began rattling. Something was happening to gravity.

"This is an examination of William Neary, age twelve years and nine months, a traumatized child. The characteristic state of tonus called waxy flexibility is fully evident. The patient can be manipulated and holds postures. Mutism, stupor, apparent absence of will are all present. I do not believe, however, that this child is catatonic. I feel that this is a stress response so extreme that it mimics catastrophic psychosis. The prognosis is nevertheless doubtful."

'I gotta get outa here Momma, it dark, big spider man got his arms all around me, I do-do on myself, I goin' down the hole Momma!'

He sees his brothers for the first time. There is no recognition.

(We will help you.)

"Help him! You've got to help him! I know he's suffering terribly, you can see it in his eyes, Dr. Klass, please!" The doctor feels he should embrace the patient's mother in order to effect some transference of anxiety.

When Barton woke up again there were more boys in the room. They came closer and closer, their hair trailing behind them, their fingernails scraping the linoleum, their faces as pure as purest light.

"Mother!"

(She went home.)

"She went home?"

"When can I see Billy?"

"In a couple more days, honey."

"Christ, Mary, I'm fine. They've got me walking up and down the ward, you saw me!"

"In a few days!"

"Mary, what's the matter?"

"Mark, please—"

"He's not dead! Don't you dare tell me he's dead!"

"Sally, just hold my head for a while. I've been up—"

"Twenty hours, Momma. We can go back to the motel if you need some sleep."

"But it's helping! As long as I hold him, he seems to be better. Just let me get a thirty-second nap, just close my eyes . . ."

A sunken, wobbly remnant, she sinks elaborately to the couch.

"Doctor, she's out."

"Your mother is suffering from complete exhaustion. I think we should just let her sleep right here."

They get a gray blanket from the ward closet and tuck it around her. The life of the waiting room goes on, people arrive, sit and depart, lives are won and lost, tragedy strikes, joy descends, Mary sleeps through an entire day.

"Sir, what are you doing in here with an IV tree?"

"What room is William Neary in?"

"You can't come on the children's pavilion, you're an in-patient!"

"I'm his dad!"

"Psychiatric wing, room 2102."

Mark hurries along, pulling his tree of intravenous lines, his mind racing: psychiatric, psychiatric, psychiatric—he maneuvers himself down the corridor. Its long, waxed floors are treacherous, it makes him dizzy to walk too fast. 'Forty-eight stitches I'm surprised my head wasn't cut in two where does this hall end Jesus.'

He is so tiny! Oh, just look, look how small he's gotten! He is so quiet! "Billy?" Why doesn't he react, his eyes are wide open. "Billy!"

What's the matter here?

The spider opens up its mouth and this man comes out wearing robe of Jesus and he got a coat tree in his hand that's funny and where'd you get those dumb-dumb glasses Daddy?

Mark Neary cannot bear the sight of his broken child. His heart is sick with woe and suddenly he is very, very tired. Like a leaf he slips to the floor, barely noticing the IV tubes ripping from his arms. The lights dim. Then there are nurses. Then he is watching ceiling fixtures go past overhead.

It will be two days before he can leave his bed again.

Barton wanted to hear a Mozart symphony. He wanted to eat a blood orange.

Danny had a green Sohio truck with lights that really turned on. When he went with Uncle Barton he made sure to bring his truck.

(You laid us on the table!)

I didn't do that.

(Our screams made you sweat with pleasure!)

Every act of life is etched forever in the flesh of the soul.

Mary is slumped by Billy's bedside with her head in her hands. She has cuddled him, she has talked to him, she has sung a thousand songs, she has poured her very soul into his empty gaze, and now the woman is spent.

Sally is stroking her brother's head. In a hoarse voice, she sings:

> *"Where have you been, Billy boy, Billy boy,*
> *Where have you been, charming Billy?"*

It is clear to her that Mother cannot go on. It is also clear that she must. "Come on, Momma, let's do it together."

Listlessly Mary joins in, barely lifting her voice, placing her hand on her son's chest.

"Where have you been, Billy boy—"

He mocks them with his emptiness. "Oh, what's the use," Mary wails, "he doesn't hear a thing!"

"Momma, we have to! We have to try! Now come on!"

Again they start.

> *"Where have you been, charming Billy?*
> *I have been to see my wife*—Momma, come
> *on—*
> *She's a young thing and cannot leave her mother!"*

"Oh, Momma, look!" An expression has replaced the emptiness. He stares up at them with the astonished eyes of a newborn baby.

"Let's *go*, Momma! He is looking at us, he sees us!"

Mary sings furiously now. "Where have you been, Billy boy, Billy boy—"

"Hey in there, I see you, yes I do, little brother dear, I see you!"

They are calling him, a chant: "Billy, Billy, Billy, Billy."

Sally chokes, clears her throat. She stops.

"I gotta have a Coke, I'm dying. You want a Coke, Momma?" She jabs at the nurse's button.

Mary remembers that he had such soft hair when he was a baby, like a blond cloud sitting on top of his head.

"I ww—mm!"

"Momma, Momma listen!"

"Mmm! Uhh!"

His voice, the lips hardly moving, but his voice!

"Billy! Billy! Billy!"

"Mmm! I—ww—"

Mary couldn't understand, she wanted to understand, she

bore down on him, pressing her face into his narrow, sour little face. "What, Billy, Mommy is here, Mommy hears you!"

"I want a Dr Pepper!"

Barton took his new plane out of the blue box. Oh, so beautiful! Attach the wheels! Attach the wings! Hook up the propeller to the rubber band! Put on the tail!

"No Barton, oh, no!"

"Oh, Barton, that *hurts!*"

Instruction number fifteen: "Wind propeller one hundred and sixty turns to achieve maximum flight."

He ran up the tall hill. There were clouds piled in the west and sun blazing in the east. The breeze went right through him, it was so pure and he was so good!

"It's hot, Barton, it's so hot!"

"Doctor," Barton said carefully, "it hurts."

"Yes," the doctor replied, smiling, "it will, for a time."

"I want a Whopper with a large fries and a chocolate shake and a fried cherry pie for dessert."

"He still likes that yuck."

"We're gonna get him *just* what he likes, right, Billy?"

"Right, Mommy!"

While he waited for them to come back he read to his brothers. He read *The Lost World,* about finding the land of dinosaurs and the jungle drums beating out the warning, "We will kill you if we can, we will kill you if we can." He said to his brothers, "If only for one second we could go back to the Jurassic and see a real *Tyrannosaurus rex.*" Then he asked, "I wonder if dinosaurs got gas?" Maybe going back to the Jurassic wasn't such a hot idea.

Seeing the Burger King bag reminded Billy of home, and for the first time he thought of Jerry and Amanda and all the kids and hanging out together trying to out-cool each other. He also recalled the fact that he was dead-bone broke. Since he obviously wasn't going to win the American Legion Short Story Contest, maybe he should become a pickpocket.

Then they opened the bags and he bit into the Whopper and it was like being home and all of a sudden he was really very glad.

After he was finished Sally produced a small white box of her own. "You try making this on a motel hotplate!"

"Divinity!"

She folded her arms. "Eat some. Go ahead, I dare you."

The wind was taking his plane higher and higher. At first he was glad, but when it became a tiny black dot he grew worried, then angry. "Come back," he cried, "come back!"

They belong to the wind, they can't come back.

He jumped, he waved his arms.

He heard the voices of the women they would never love, the wailing of their unborn children.

His head fell to one side. The light of other fires invaded his eyes. He was so terribly heavy!

The sky opened like the skin of a rotten fruit, and there came forth the furious legions.

32.

Mom and Dad came into Billy's room with Dr. Klass. Billy watched them walk right through his brothers like they weren't there. He didn't like it when they ignored his brothers. But he would not stand for it when they told him his brothers didn't exist. How dare they, the liars!

But he'd made a concession. He no longer talked to his brothers when the grown-ups were around. Only he and Sally could talk to them. Since they were his brothers, they were hers, too. They were brothers to all kids.

Dad still looked really weird with his huge bandage and the one eye made gigantic by the big lens they had to put in his glasses. Barton had cut a hole in his head. Billy wished he could see in the hole, but he didn't have the nerve to ask.

Right now his dad looked scared. He looked to his mother. She was scared, too.

Dr. Klass took him by the hand. It was OK, but it still made him feel creepy-crawly when they touched him. When the nurse bathed him he had to shut his eyes and sing real loud.

"Billy, we want you to know that Barton Royal died last night just after midnight."

That was OK. No it wasn't. He busted out crying, he just couldn't help it.

Dad rolled his goofy eye at Mom. She pushed past Dr. Klass and put her arms around Billy. Mom smelled so good, Billy liked her so much.

"This is good," Dr. Klass said, "he's unloading some stuff here."

"I missed the funeral!"

As Mommy hugged him he pulled his face away so he wouldn't touch her skin. He sure loved her, but she had skin like a salamander.

"The funeral is at two-thirty," Dr. Klass said, "but we have more important things to do than go to an old funeral. You and I are gonna write another play about Barton today."

"I'm gonna go to the funeral!"

"No, Billy."

"Yes I am, Mom! I have to!"

Dad talked, his voice low. "Billy, you're in the hospital. You aren't even near well yet. You have bandages all over your bottom and you—"

His brothers were all yelling and screaming. He had to go!

"I can go in my bandages. Don't you want me *ever* to get well?"

That shut them right up, as he had figured it would. Sally, who was sitting over by the window working a puzzle and not saying anything, gave him a wink. *She* knew all about why he had to go to the funeral.

"We'll have our own funeral, Billy," Dr. Klass said. He was a nice guy, but he could dork out at a moment's notice. He had just dorked out.

Billy knew how to shut him up. "Gee, I'll make the gravestone and we can use a real coffin," he said like he was all excited about it. "I know they have coffins in hospitals for when people die."

"Ah—"

He looked up at Mom and Dad. "I've gotta go. It's real important to me."

His father bowed his head, then came down on the bed with him and Mom. They held each other's hands.

"I'll navigate," Sally said.

It was a long drive to Anaheim, and they had to start out right away. Mom drove, Dad sat beside her. Billy lay with his head in Sally's lap. Although she claimed she was finding lice and cooties and stuff, he knew she was just rubbing his head.

Billy had never been to a graveyard before. When they got there all kinds of reporters came thundering up yelling questions. Ever since he had seen himself on TV in just his underpants Billy didn't like those jerks.

It wasn't a very good graveyard, he decided. The headstones were mostly small. Here and there somebody had left a few withered flowers in a bottle. When the wind blew, sand swept the stones like dry rain.

Barton's grave site was the only active spot in the whole enormous place. There were three folding chairs, a couple of men in white T-shirts with shovels in their hands, another man in a frayed black suit.

There was also a woman, as Billy had hoped there would be. His brothers had been worried she wouldn't come. He could feel their relief.

The woman sat very still on one of the folding chairs, her brows knitted in the merciless sun. All the time as Billy and his family were coming closer, she watched them.

By the time they had arrived she was staring down at her own feet. She stood. "Make it quick, please, Reverend," she said. Her voice sounded so much like Barton's it made Billy want to vomit.

The man opened a paperback of the Bible and read in a nervous voice: "In the day when the keepers of the house shall tremble, and the strong men shall bow themselves—"

"Two verses after," the woman snapped. She blinked her eyes. "Where I marked."

The Reverend cleared his throat. "Also when they shall be afraid of that which is high, and fears shall be in the way, and the almond tree shall flourish . . ."

Billy heard his brothers repeating in the air, "and the grasshoppers shall be a burden, and desire shall fail . . ." He joined his living voice to their dead ones: "because man goeth to his long home . . ." which was all he remembered.

Barton's mother clutched her hands together, looking straight at him. She looked sad, but also scared.

Dad raised his head. Billy saw the pride that had come into his face, and was glad. "Or ever the silver cord be loosed," Dad and Mom said together, "or the golden bowl be broken—"

They stopped, silenced by the power of the same deep feelings that had compelled Billy to bring them here in the first place.

Barton's mother spoke in tiny words. "Then shall the dust—the dust—" Her composure was broken by the most desperate grief.

She covered her face and shook.

The coffin was lowered by a machine with an angry, screaming whine. Billy watched it drop into the dark hole and with it his life with Barton, and the dim life before. He had come here seeking an ending. He asked his heart, 'Do I hate Barton?' and heard a silence that let him raise his eyes from the grave.

Barton's mother recovered herself enough to throw a clod of soil into the hole. Billy heard it rattle on the coffin.

Now it was time to perform his mission. His brothers gathered around him. They were excited. He had taken them on a big adventure. He dug in his pocket and pulled out the fourteen construction paper notes. On each he had written a name. One by one he dropped them into the grave. Sally, who had helped him make them, said his brothers' names with him.

"Chuck."

"Danny."

"Jack."

"Timmy."

"Andy."

Dad added his voice.

"Ezra."

Mom did, too. Their chant was ragged because only he and Sally knew the names by heart.

"Liam."

"Unknown Child Number One."

"Unknown Child Number Two."

The sweating preacher and the two workers joined their voices.

"Unknown Child Number Three."

"Unknown Child Number Four."

"Unknown Child Number Five."

Mrs. Royal started to do it, too.

"No," Billy said. "Not you."

She nodded her head. She whispered, "No."

"Unknown Child Number Six."

"Unknown Child Number Seven."

Billy stopped. He looked to Barton's mother. He had a last note, which he handed to her.

When she saw what it said she gasped as if stabbed.

"Read it aloud," he told her.

She shook her head. Her eyes were closed tight.

"Read it," one of the workers said.

She muttered something. Then she cleared her throat. "Billy."

"OK." Billy nodded at the grave.

"I want to keep it," she said in a quavering voice.

"Throw it in!"

Billy watched it flutter down, twirling round and round and round, until it hit the side of the coffin and slid into the dark.

A crow rose from a tree, wheeled screaming over the party, and strove for the sky on its black wings. Billy looked from the cheap, gray coffin in its hole up to the raucous, flapping creature in the sky.

"I'm ready to go," he said to his parents.

His father took his hand. In the rough coolness of his fingers Billy felt the future, he and Sally growing up, Mom and Dad getting old and dying. The thought did not upset him. On the contrary, it filled him with a joy that seemed deeper than his own soul, as if it entered him not only from his father's trembling hand, but from the whole contents of the world.

When they got into the car together, Billy was fascinated by details for the first time since his passion. He noticed the way the radio worked and the fact that it had no cassette player. He noticed that there was a climate control as well as a cruise control. He noticed the hole where the cigarette lighter was supposed to be—and wondered what would happen if he put his finger in.

As they pulled away from the curb Billy looked back. Mrs. Royal remained at the grave. She stood watching them leave, her body as narrow as a stake. One hand came up, hesitating, tentative, as if to wave. But she did not wave. Instead her fingers touched her cheek, trembled against the empty skin.

He closed his eyes, listening to the kind old hum of the tires. By the time they turned onto the highway the day had reached its moment of high sun. Everywhere the shadows were in retreat.

Sally started to sing:

> *"The ants go marching two by two,*
> *The little one stops to go to the zoo—"*

"Those aren't the right words."

"You're supposed to make up the words, Billy."

"Are not."

"Are!"

"Are absolutely not no way uh-uh."

"Well, I do!"

Billy sang, "The little one stops to do some doo!"

"Billy Neary, that's gross!"

The journey back had begun.

Author's Note

The theft of a child is perhaps the cruelest of all crimes, unique for its spectacular inhumanity and corrosive potency. Fortunately it is not an everyday crime; neither, however, should it be ignored. The numbers do not matter; the spectre of this crime diminishes as does no other the joy of parenthood and the innocence of the young. Childhood is not immortal; childhood could die. If it does, this will have been among its harshest poisons.

Readers wishing more information about how to help missing and exploited children can write:

The National Center for
Missing and Exploited Children
Publications Department
2101 Wilson Boulevard
Arlington, VA 22201

—Whitley Strieber